"From now on there'll be no more, 'Welcome to Tailburger, the burger of choice for the downtrodden, disabled and incarcerated.' Way too wordy. From here on out, we keep it simple. 'Order, asshole.'"

—Frank Fanoflincoln,
President and Founder of Tailburger

STARBUCK O'DWYER

Red Meat Cures Cancer

Starbuck O'Dwyer is a graduate of Princeton, Oxford, and Cornell. Originally from Rochester, New York, he currently makes his home in the Washington, D.C. area.

Visit his Web site at www.starbuckodwyer.com.

Red Meat Cures Cancer

Red Meat Cures Cancer

A NOVEL

STARBUCK O'DWYER

VINTAGE CONTEMPORARIES
Vintage Books
A Division of Random House, Inc.
New York

FIRST VINTAGE CONTEMPORARIES EDITION, FEBRUARY 2004

Library of Congress Cataloging-in-Publication Data
O'Dwyer, Starbuck.
Red meat cures cancer : a novel / Starbuck O'Dwyer.
p.   cm.
ISBN: 1-4000-3481-7 (trade paper)
1. Meat industry and trade—Fiction.   I. Title.
PS3615.D88R43   2004
813'.6—dc21
2003053823

Book design by Mia Risberg

www.vintagebooks.com

This book is dedicated to my parents,
Alice and Duncan,
and to my sister, Pam,
with infinite love and gratitude.

Contents

Red Meat Cures Cancer

1

The Link

"Good morning! I'd like to welcome all of you to the annual meeting of the corporate shareholders of Tailburger. For those of you who don't know me, and there can't be many of you, I'm Frank Fanoflincoln, founder and president of Tailburger. I gotta tell you folks, I'm tickled as a twenty-dollar whore to be here."

Frank Fanoflincoln, my boss, is a fat man. I'm not talking circus fat or freakish fat or the huge, if I eat three more pints of Ben and Jerry's they'll need to move a wall to get me out of my house, kind of fat. But he's working on it. He also happens to be the most ill-mannered person I've ever met. The day I interviewed with him nearly twenty years ago is one I vividly recall. We went to a Chinese restaurant called the House of Poon, where Fanoflincoln, or the Link as I refer to him, spent most of the time with his left hand firmly entrenched inside his boxer shorts. After ordering moo goo gai pan and a Pepsi, he leaned back in his chair, submarined his overly pudgy mitt below the beltline and left it there. If there exists a single better reason not to take a job, I haven't heard of it, which makes my own presence at today's shareholder meeting, not to mention my continued employment at Tailburger, a source of incredible self-loathing.

"When I started this company in 1962, I never dreamed we'd become a heavyweight in the fast-food industry. And you know what . . . ? We haven't. But we do have the best fried hamburger on the market, and we've carved out a niche for ourselves as the burger of choice for the fringe element. Take a poll at any correctional facility in this country and the inmates will speak volumes. In Texas alone this year, our Tailburger Deluxe was the final meal of choice for no less than eight death-row inmates. What can I say? At Tailburger, we're talkin' proud."

The Link liked to wear bright-colored sweatsuits, preferably ones with comfort-guard waistbands made of industrial-strength elastic. Although he usually had food in his mouth, or at least in his teeth, he was a strangely effective public speaker, and as usual, his opening remarks were met with enthusiastic applause from the audience. A Civil War buff, the Link legally changed his name in his early twenties to Fanoflincoln out of his fondness for our sixteenth president. His weekends were spent standing in cow pastures with other out-of-shape fanatics, reenacting the battle of Vicksburg or Fredericksburg or Pittsburgh for all I knew. Too large for any of the uniforms available, the Link was an easy target in his vibrant athletic gear and had lately been asked to play a campground tent. Undeterred by this apparent demotion, he likened the competitive world of burgers to the epic struggle between the Union and the Confederacy.

"Don't think for a minute that I'm satisfied with our progress. 'Cause I'm not. Far from it! This war is in its infancy and we will fight many battles before we reach our Appomattox! So I ask you, as the great Abraham Lincoln once asked Congress, 'Can we do better? The dogmas of the quiet past are inadequate to the stormy present. The occasion is piled high with difficulty, and we must rise to the occasion. As our case is new, so we must think anew, and act anew!' You're damn right we do!"

The Link shouted at a bewildered crowd. His word-for-word recitation of Lincoln's 1862 exhortation was undoubtedly impressive, at least the first time you heard it. Once you realized it was the only quote from the Great Emancipator that he knew and you'd heard it countless times at various events, it lost a bit of its impact. For half the crowd in attendance, I'm sure it was inspirational.

"Now ordinarily we'd start this meeting by having some stiffs from finance come out here and tell you about the company's performance this past fiscal year. And we will do that later once we've finished cutting those bloodsuckers out of cardboard. But we're gonna start a little differently today. I'm just so damn excited about our new advertising campaign, I've asked Schuyler Thorne, our chief operating officer and senior vice president in charge of marketing, to speak with you first. Sky has been with the company since 1983, and he's a big reason why your dividend checks will soon be fatter than a welfare mother's ass. Get up here, Sky!"

The eyes of the stockholders were upon me as I made my way from the conference room's front row to the podium and shook hands with the Link. Three weeks before, he called me on the carpet and demanded a new marketing direction for our company and for the flagship sandwich of the franchise, known as the Tailpipe. Following our critically acclaimed, but commercially disastrous, "Get Away from My Tailpipe" campaign featuring various gay activists happily chomping on the product, the Link had assured me that I had better not "fuck the company in the ass" this time. Fortunately for me, I functioned well in a hostile work environment.

The Link wanted advertising that was high-concept, a campaign that would "boil the ocean," in his words. He picked up this phrase from a men's lifestyle magazine aimed at disenfranchised twenty-somethings, and though he didn't know what it meant, he sure as hell thought it sounded good. After tremendous growth in the late '80s and '90s, Tailburger was experiencing a bit of a downturn and the Link was getting panicky. Though it hadn't hit our share price on Wall Street yet, internally we all knew that society's curbing of excesses and insidious return to Subarus and sensibility was a killing trend for our company. No fat, low fat, reduced fat, artificial fat—each was anathema to us. When your main product consists of four batter-dipped, deep-fried patties of red meat and a bun, held together by five generous dollops of Cajun-style mayonnaise, you rely on the weakness of men and women. My job was to exploit that weakness. With per capita beef consumption at an all-time low and sales of Mercedes, liquor and guns down, we were looking at a bear market for Tailburger.

Once a lowly marketing executive, I had morphed into the Link's number one lackey, for want of a better term. My advancement to the top of the company had less to do with my business acumen and more to do with my ability to avoid getting fired. The Link shit-canned so many people left and right over the years eventually I was the only one he recognized in the hallways at our headquarters in Mendon, a small town on the southeast side of Rochester. Now he relied on me for everything from marketing campaigns to sales reports to advising him on our casual day policy. If all this wasn't enough for someone making $187,500, my new duty was to stem the tide of simple living. I was instructed by the Link to lead the middle (and especially the lower middle) class back to an era of crass commercialism, basement pot farming and if possible, the Hustle dance craze. "Bring it back, Thorne!" the Link insisted. "Bring it all back. I don't care how you do it." Like a robotic misanthrope, I accepted my tasking without question. Now I faced my first test: the shareholders. Time to spew self-righteous platitudes at the masses.

"Thank you, Frank. It's a real honor for me to have the opportunity to address our shareholders and owner-operators as a group today. You folks are the real reason for the success of Tailburger. This past year we opened up eighty-four new franchises across the U.S., and we remain extremely optimistic about our future growth potential. As Mr. Fanoflincoln said, and as you are aware, we have succeeded at Tailburger by attacking the fringe. Market surveys indicate that our penetration is deepest with groups ranging from alcoholics to deadbeat dads to skate punks with multiple body piercings. We're also big with people who believe exercise is an absolute evil. These folks have been loyal to us for years!"

I took a sip of water and surveyed the crowd. Our shareholders, "mostly trailer trash and former XFL football players," according to the Link, were paying rapt attention. Just my luck.

"So, like I said, these groups are our core customers and we need to cater to them, NOT to families. I fear we've gotten away from that. Some of you even approached me this year about adding a playground to the front of our stores. Now that seems like a harmless enough idea on its surface. I agree. But stop and think about it for a minute. If someone's *out*side using the slide, they're not *in*side eating a Tailburger. And that's no good."

Another sip. Nobody dozing off yet.

"Most disturbing of all, however, I was approached about adding something healthy to our Tailburger menu. Do you know what this tells me? Do you? This tells me that the propaganda machine in America is alive and well. Everyone, from the American Heart Association to Dr. Koop to Richard Simmons, is telling you all you can eat are sprouts and lentils. They say fat is bad and aerobic exercise is good. They say beef kills you. (Pause) Now does anybody here know someone who died from eating a delicious Tailburger? Of course not. These fascists won't be happy until every last one of us is wearing a Lycra bodysuit and jumping around in our living rooms to the worst prepackaged dance music from the eighties you've ever heard. The whole thing is outrageous! We've got to push back against this health craze. And we will!"

Another sip. First sleeping shareholder spotted. I was ready to ramble now—ready to preach the gospel according to Tailburger.

"Who are they to tell us what to do with our bodies? I don't know about you, but I'm sick and tired of it. We get bombarded by one shoddy scientific report after another. It's just not right, I tell you! At Tailburger, we're going to play up our image as fast-food outlaws. We'll continue to be a shining light amidst the darkness. The brand everyone loves to hate. And today, you lucky people will be the first to hear our new national slogan. Mike, will you get the curtain?"

Mike, the hotel's audiovisual guru, took his cue, pressed some button and revealed my marketing greatness on an enormous screen.

TAILBURGER
WHY JUST *ABUSE* YOUR BODY
WHEN YOU CAN *TORTURE* IT?

"That's right. We're going back to our rebellious roots. We will laugh in the faces of the health nuts. All the way to our graves if we have to."

The audience seemed a bit perplexed.

"Okay. All right. I can tell by your confused faces that you need the concept fleshed out. You're going to be seeing a full comple- ment of print, radio, television and Internet spots. We're going to saturate the domestic market with a new theme song by alternarockers Blatherskite called "Torture Me." We're going to have a beverage tie-in with Scuz Cola to continue the theme of self- abuse and we have a tentative agreement with Jelloteous Junder- stack, NBA superstar and major Tailburger fan, to endorse our product line. This is going to be the biggest marketing launch in the history of Tailburger and an emphatic statement about our company's rightful place in the twenty-first century!"

My rousing finish didn't exactly start a riot in the aisles, and the lukewarm response from our shareholders caused the Link's face to convulse as if he were receiving an enema. Though initially enthusiastic about the Torture idea, he met me with a forced smile as I left the podium. I was accustomed to his capriciousness, how- ever, and I remained unfazed. Late for a plane to Washington,

D.C., I didn't have time to worry, and I left for the airport temporarily indifferent to the experience. Not surprisingly, lobbying had somehow found its way into my job description, and a federal bill, calling for increased amounts of food labeling, more frequent safety inspections and stricter meat handling requirements, had been introduced in the Agriculture Committee. This bill needed to be stopped.

How I'd come to this point in my life was more of a disappointment than a mystery. I was six feet tall when I started with Tailburger right out of business school. I was now closer to five eleven, an angry inch of compressed spine the price I'd paid for bearing the weight of the burger world on my shoulders for two decades. My blondish hair had thinned considerably from its blow-dried heyday in the 1970s, my brow was a bit creased and the flesh under my chin was starting to show the not inconsiderable effects of gravity. Still, despite my physical deterioration, something ageless continued to churn inside of me. For as long as I could remember, I'd talked about breaking off on my own and doing something I would enjoy, maybe even love. No more answering to anybody. No more rat race. Sure it was hokey, this hairball of a notion I'd coughed up while reading a library full of self-help books written by the world's leading mind-fuck gurus. But I wanted it, whatever "it" was. Herman Melville said that within every man there exists an insular Tahiti full of peace and joy, something that lies at our very center just waiting to be discovered. Where was my insular Tahiti? Not only couldn't I find it; I wasn't sure where to look. While I saw others reaching this paradise in their own lives, content with their families and careers, I somehow remained stuck on one of the one thousand uninhabited islands in the St. Lawrence Seaway. My existence was tolerable, but hardly paradise. So, unsurprisingly, a certain sadness overcame me every December when the year would end without a change as my mortgage and an unending series of expenses piled up, and small raises and stock options kept me satisfied enough to stay the course—never any closer to that which allegedly lay at my core.

Though I blamed myself primarily (at least on most days), there was also the small matter of my do-nothing older brother, King, a man-child who had managed to go a lifetime without an identifiable job, let alone a career. His résumé, had he ever bothered to put one together, would have read like the perfect reply to the classified section of a Club Med resort circular. Part-time herbalist. Part-time Pilates instructor. Amateur nutritionist. From Amnesty International to Royal Caribbean, King had worked for every major activist organization as well as every major cruise line, but had lasted nowhere for more than three months. He said he had a problem with authority, but whatever the reason, so long as he stayed outside the confines of corporate America, I was under some kind of intangible psychic pressure to stay securely within them. A family could only have one fuckup, and we had King. It had always been that way, from the time we were young until now. The seminal event in my mind was King's decision to skip senior year of high school to work ski patrol at Stowe. Many similar choices, evoking a mixture of sympathy and bewilderment from me, followed. As the years passed, however, my pity for him evolved into envy as I considered all the free time he had at his disposal. Nevertheless, every time I had thought about quitting my own job, I couldn't bring myself to do it. One fuckup is tolerable, but at two fuckups, you unfairly sentence your parents to a lifetime of shunning social events for fear of having to report what their children are doing. I decided long ago that my father would die a horribly painful death the day he had to tell his buddies I was a washroom attendant, or worse, a personal trainer at Gold's Gym.

Until now, it had all been academic really. My financial commitments, the same things that keep everybody at the grindstone, rendered the idea of quitting Tailburger useless. Some time back, having realized this, I accepted my fate as a salaryman, put my head down and began the final drive to retirement: a full thirty-year trek. But now, with only one year to go until I'd have twenty years vested with the company and could opt out early for a reduced Tailburger pension, and with my parents having both recently passed away, I saw my last best hope for a trip to Tahiti.

2

S.W.O.T.

SOMEWHERE OVER PENNSYLVANIA

Flight 789 to Reagan National reached cruising altitude and I turned on my Palm Pilot to do some strategic planning. Strengths * Weaknesses * Opportunities * Threats. This mode of business analysis could easily be applied to my personal life.

Strengths: I'd never killed anyone. I took a certain pride in that. I'd given blood twice; once willingly. I'd seen *The Graduate* forty-eight times. The Rolling Stones a dozen. I loved my two children, even if I didn't always want to be around them.

Weaknesses: My cigarette habit (unfiltered Commodores) was up to three packs a day (you have to die from something). God was no longer a regular visitor to my world. Somewhere along the way, I'd let the big guy slip away without so much as a good-bye. More and more, I felt lonesome. And while we're piling on here, lately I'd become obsessed with the amount of hair I saw in the tub after I showered. When my plumber put me on to a product called the Hair Snare to prevent clogging of the drain, he had no idea how much concern it would cause me.

Opportunities: Despite my preternaturally shitty luck and lapsed faith, I still believed there existed some kind of perverse happiness in my future or perhaps a close facsimile I could settle for while retaining a shred of self-respect. I also believed in redemption and second chances. Scratch that—third chances.

Threats: Trip Baden, a painful reminder of my biggest loss—my late ex-wife, Jess—and a man whose eyes were set squarely on a piece of my Tailburger pension. This requires some explanation.

Jess and I met in college and quickly fell in love. She was this wonderfully refreshing combination of sophistication and innocence, and the only woman I ever met whom I thought I could marry. So I did. And we were happy for ten years until, stupidly, I got immersed in my career climb and she fell into the arms of the golf pro at Wedgewood, a country club for middle management that I went into debt to join. By then she'd given birth to our children, Ethan and Sophia, forever tying our fates together. And though we'd both made mistakes, and were equally at fault for our marital problems, I refused to forgive her for what she'd done. Instead of being understanding, I was self-righteous and hard. Instead of going to counseling, I demanded a divorce.

Then one day, I woke up and I wanted her back. But by the time my anger faded and I realized I'd let go of the greatest part of my life, she was gone—married to Trip Baden, a claims adjuster whose greatest thrill in life was denying insurance coverage to people seriously injured in auto accidents. At least, that's how I liked to think of him. Everybody else called him a software tycoon. Whatever he was, there was no mystery, as far as I was concerned, as to how he'd bamboozled *my* wife. Baden caught Jess when she was down. He said all the right things, manipulating her mind and ego like some wayward EST instructor. On good days, I told myself he brainwashed her. On bad days, I was certain she loved him.

No matter the truth, I couldn't take it at the time. Suddenly this horrible claims adjuster/software tycoon was living with my wife and raising my kids in a thirty-room mansion on the shores of Lake Ontario, and I needed an appointment just to see my family. So started a period of extreme bitterness for me as I grew more and more resentful and learned to despise everything about this guy, right down to his name. I mean, Trip Baden? What kind of a name is that? Like a bad third-string quarterback, he entered my life in the middle of the game and starting calling plays.

Fortunately, Ethan and Sophia never took to Trip, who, according to them, heaped his attention and riches on Butte and Missoula, his two daughters by his first marriage. With their presence merely tolerated by Baden, my kids continually helped me from the inside by probing for cracks in their mother's second union and providing me with constant updates. They knew how much I loved their mom and together, the three of us never gave up on the idea of a reconciliation. At least not until September 8, 1994, when U.S. Airways flight 427 from Chicago to Pittsburgh crashed with Jess aboard. On that day, the flame I'd kept burning for years dimmed but did not go out. And though it was likely just a gesture to make me feel better, the kids insisted that Jess, in quieter, confessional moments, had openly spoken of coming back to me. It may have been a fantasy, but it kept me going in my darkest hours after her death. Since that time, I'd put love at the bottom of my to-do list, preferring to stay uninvolved and unhurt.

So why was Trip Baden still a threat after all these years? It turned out that Mr. Softy had financial problems. Oracle had come along with a product that made his company's technology and stock nearly worthless. Now Trip, magnanimous at the funeral ten years ago (he said he didn't want anything from me back then), had returned to claim his stake in Jess's estate. Since she died without a will, 50 percent of her property, including the portion of my pension that she was entitled to when I retired, was, in theory, his.

Of late, my bad luck in love was matched only by my misfortune in business. Not only were our sales down, but Tailburger was facing unprecedented scrutiny from the media and the government on food safety issues. We were used to fighting back against the fitness freaks, but according to the new breed of activists, beef was unhealthy and dangerous. There was no defense against a tearful mother on television testifying in front of Congress that her five-year-old Petey went out for a Jolly Meal and never came home—the latest victim of the E. coli 0157:H7 bacteria. At the rate of 12.3 dead Peteys per year, we were losing the press battle. So now, every time a burger from Jack in the Box offed someone or a bill was proposed that would raise our cost of doing business, the Link called Rush Limbaugh and sent me down to D.C. to explain our food safety methods and to bitch about overregulation to anyone who'd listen. Bringing the center of every patty up to 159 degrees Fahrenheit, in order to kill bacteria, already cost us millions each year in energy and manpower, and had an ill effect on the taste of your average Tailburger. All in all, I was pretty fucking tired of our representational democracy. HR 214, which promised consumers more detailed product labeling and increased meat inspection standards, could not make its way out of the Agriculture Committee.

My major contact on Capitol Hill was Burton Roxby, a classmate of mine from high school, who'd spent seven years at the Food and Drug Administration before running for Congress. I held him personally responsible for the dual annoyances of Saint-John's-wort and Ginkgo biloba. Representative Roxby, from the 28th Congressional District of New York, which encompassed Rochester, was now the third-ranking Republican on the Agriculture Committee and, by necessity more than anything else, a good friend to Tailburger.

Wholly nonaltruistic, Roxby's pleas on behalf of the farmers and corporations of western New York were about nothing more than keeping his campaign coffers fat. We flagrantly bought his vote on all bills related to food inspection, sanitation and handling, among others, and made enormous contributions to his biannual race for office. Though I couldn't pin it on him, I knew he was misappropriating a portion of his campaign funds to put up a mistress at the Watergate apartment complex. It was common knowledge that when Roxby wasn't home kissing constituent ass, he was sport-fucking his beltway bimbo into oblivion.

I hated Roxby. I thought he was scum, and I was sick of seeing his smirking face on the reelection campaign requests for money that arrived at my house every fifth day. I had it on good authority that he put a portion of Tailburger's donations (read legislative bribe) toward his alma mater, Princeton, to make himself look like a major donor and increase his odds of getting an honorary degree. This was important to him, since he'd never actually graduated.

The Link hated Roxby, too. Tailburger needed him though, so he tolerated the Congressman's continuous stream of bullshit. "Roxby's a prick," the Link would often say. "But he's a beef-lovin' prick!" Every dollar we threw at the beef industry these days seemed to end up in Roxby's pocket. Tailburger gave thousands to the National Cattlemen's Meat Stampede, the largest cattle farmer's association, and the Corral Foundation, the Meat Stampede's right-wing, red-meat think tank, a body that advocated the repeal of most if not all laws related to our main product. In turn, these organizations spent our money supporting Roxby's campaigns. The whole scenario was maddening.

I met Roxby at the Cosmos Club, a Doric-columned work of classical architecture located along Mass. Ave.'s Embassy Row, not far from the White House. This womb of exclusivity had the antiquated ambiance of a private establishment for men and now, after forcible litigation, for women. I was allowed in only because of the reciprocal relationship between the Cosmos Club and Crooked Creek, a club in Rochester that I belonged to, my father belonged to and his father before that belonged to. My membership in Crooked Creek was a mistake of fate as far as I was concerned, but membership had its perks, one of which was the undeniable feeling, within its four walls, that you were better than other people. Although this Darwinian delusion lasted for only the hour or so while you ate lunch, you really got a healthy charge out of it before you were cast back out into the faceless hoi polloi. Another plus, Crooked Creek *was* one of the few things I had that the Link wanted and had been denied. Whenever he asked me to sponsor him, I told him there was an extremely long waiting list. This was a lie.

Inside the Cosmos, imposing hand-carved mahogany walls and deep green marble floors kept conversations hushed, and a newly installed metal detector made sure you didn't steal the silverware. Like all bastions of money and melba toast, the Cosmos Club had taken it on the chin when the tax laws changed and made only 50 percent of business meals and drinks deductible. Membership and usage dwindled, and the drapes now looked like set pieces from *The Shining*.

Entering the foyer, I saw my alleged ally from afar. Like all politicians, Roxby wanted everybody to be his friend. He'd mastered the art of telling you what you wanted to hear. To see a grown man participate in one lifelong popularity contest, so desperately desirous of the love and approval of acquaintances and strangers alike, was peculiarly disheartening. From my experience, politicians were the most insecure people I'd ever met. I didn't know where it came from. Maybe their mommies didn't let them suckle at the tit long enough, or maybe their daddies didn't tell them they were good enough, but whatever the sad condition, Burton Roxby had it bad.

"Schuyler Thorne, how are you? My God, you look great. Are you lifting?"

"Burt, you're a bigger liar than I remember."

"Get out of here. Let me guess. Nautilus circuit, right? Three, maybe four days a week? It's showing. God, it's really great to see you, Sky. C'mon, I've already got a table."

Buried in the back of the main dining room, we ordered iced tea and embarked on more obligatory small talk. As he prattled on about his collection of pre-Colombian art, I tuned his words out and took a look at what Mother Nature and time had done to him. Roxby was a smallish but fit man, about five feet five inches tall, who clearly grappled with a Napoleon complex on a daily basis. Completely bald, having shaved his head two years after his comb-over became a joke, he craved political power and was deathly afraid of losing it. His dark eyes, set a bit too close together, and his large ears, both bent outward by the birthing canal, gave his face an unfortunate Mr. Potato Head quality.

"I don't think Tailburger has anything to worry about. The provisions of HR 214 are not as burdensome as you think."

"C'mon, Burt. I've read it. We'll end up baby-sitting every burger if that thing passes. Listen, the Link doesn't want to leave this to chance. To be blunt, 214 is going to kick our ass financially if it comes out of committee and gets signed. We need to know what it's going to take to kill it."

"Sky, you know this is a very sensitive subject. My loyalties are, of course, first and foremost, to the people of the 28th Congressional District. I have held bills up in the past, but only to give them my full scrutiny for the sake of my constituency. As you know, I've got an election coming up and I think this bill may be in the best interests of the people. Of course, I always give every piece of legislation my fullest. . . ."

"Cut the shit, Burt. I'm not wearing a wire. I need to know what it's going to take to bury this fucker."

"Quite frankly, Sky, you've got much bigger problems than 214."

"What the hell are you talking about?"

"I'm talking about SERMON."

"Oh, Christ. What now?"

SERMON, a.k.a. Stop Eating Red Meat Now, was a sworn enemy of Tailburger and every other organization in the beef business. These tofu-munchers, headed by a zealot named Muffet Meaney, had been spewing their vegan bile in our direction for years. I couldn't remember a time when I hadn't been battling the one propaganda machine more shameless than our own. The look on Roxby's face told me he was either serious or severely constipated.

"Sky, they're going to bring a class action lawsuit against you guys that will make the tobacco settlement dollars look like chump change. As we sit here, SERMON's leadership is strongarming NAAG and every rep on the hill to support one collective movement toward carnegeddon."

"Nag?"

"The National Association of Attorneys General."

"Carnegeddon? What the hell are they suing us for?"

"They're talking about trying to nail you guys for consumer fraud and racketeering. They want to make this a RICO suit."

"Consumer fraud? About what?"

"About the danger of eating beef, of course. For concealing it."

"We never concealed anything. Eating beef is not dangerous."

"I'm with you, Sky, but some very powerful people say it is risky."

"What do they expect to get out of this?"

"You name it, they want it. Funds for every child affected by tainted meat. Antibeef education dollars. Grant money for studies on irradiation. Stepped-up inspection requirements. And the mother of them all: recouped Medicare and Medicaid money for the government's cost of treating heart disease and stroke."

"What about the farmers? And the beef lobby?"

"They've been losing strength for years now. You know that, Sky. Oprah beat the shit out of them in Texas and it's been all downhill from there."

"Goddamn it all to hell! These maggots are trying to drive us out of business and you're just gonna sit by and watch!"

"That's not true. I'll do whatever I can to help."

"Yeah, all right. Whatever. Look, for now, just keep 214 in committee. And keep me informed about this SERMON suit!" My anger was evident.

"Okay, okay, let's keep this civilized," Roxby said as he looked around the dining room to make sure nobody was observing my agitation.

"I'm counting on you, Burt. Do you understand?"

"Yes."

"I'll call you next week."

When the Link heard about the SERMON lawsuit, he would react the way he always does to bad news. After slowly lumbering over to his office gun case, he would remove his favorite Civil War rifle, stroke it twice, tap his finger on the bayonet, and ask me if homicide was still a felony. Once informed that it was, he would tell me to fix the suit by any means necessary like some kind of Malcolm X of meat patties. This meant giving more money to Roxby and made our new marketing push critical. If our Torture campaign was to succeed, I had to get a signed contract with Jelloteous Junderstack, the one man who could save the franchise.

3

Friend of the Devil

Jelloteous Junderstack, a native of Belgium and the starting center for the Los Angeles Lakers, was known to eat twelve Tailburgers at a sitting. "You've got big-ass boogers," Jelloteous told me over the phone the first time we spoke, convincing me right then he wanted to endorse our product. Unlike some other less principled companies that shall go unnamed (Quaker State, Vagisil, Fibercon), we insisted our pitchpersons be Tailburger fans.

Only weeks before, Jelloteous looked like the perfect spokesman for our Torture campaign. Night after night, he maligned opposing defenses with his media-proclaimed "Close to Felonious, Highly Melodious, Last Name Junderstack, First Name Jelloteous, Jam," an Earth-shattering, rim-rocking slam dunk delivered with unnerving ferocity. At eight feet two inches tall, Jello had an unblockable shot and a Q-rating off the Richter scale.

Unfortunately, in a recent game against New Jersey, our titan fell to the floor suddenly and without explanation, only to be trampled by Dikembe Mutombo. The unprovoked tumble raised suspicion about the strength of his heart, a common concern for those of enormous size. Sure enough, tests revealed an irregular heartbeat and a thickening of the heart wall, a genetic condition that was potentially fatal and thus career-ending.

Despite his heart trouble, Jello remained the hottest commodity in the NBA, and Tailburger would treat him as such until he bit the big Belgian waffle. The Link, unimpressed with the "quacks" at Cedars-Sinai, flew in a holistic doctor from Guatemala to give a fourth opinion that, unsurprisingly, ran counter to the previous three. When this tribal witch doctor, whose card read "Ancestral Holy Man," pulled a pebble from a bag of dirt and concluded that Jello could continue to play with little or no risk, it was good enough for us. Until Jello's disease was publicly connected to his impressive intake of our fried food, we were on him like spandex on a streetwalker.

I found Jelloteous on the floor of the Staples Center shooting free throws.

"Jelloteous! Schuyler Thorne from Tailburger. We spoke last week. How are you?"

"Mr. Sky. Helloo!"

We shook hands and my fingers disappeared inside his enormous hamfist.

"Listen, I brought a copy of your revised contract."

"Berry goood."

"And I want to set up a photo shoot for you and Blatherskite next week."

Blatherskite was part of the California punk metal revival, so I was told by Calvin, one of the branding consultants at my disposal.

"Berry goood. I like za Blatherskites."

"Do you remember the song 'I'm in Severe Pain'?"

"Not so sure," Jelloteous said, giving me a confused look.

"Well, the guys in the band are big fans of your felonious, melodious jam. And you're going to have a cameo in the video for their new song, 'Torture Me,' which is the theme of our new campaign. Making sense? (Pause) Trust me. This is going to be one big love-fest."

"Yes, big love-fest," Jelloteous repeated.

By now my neck hurt. Looking up at this big Belgian goober was hard work. I told Jello I'd see him up in the executive offices, where we were scheduled to meet with his agent, Manny "Satan" Manchow. The nickname started as a joke in the industry, but now Manny got off on it. Manchow was part vermin, part vacuum cleaner bag, and bilked every client for 15 instead of the standard 4 percent. He got away with it by negotiating the biggest deals and commanding client loyalty with the provision of hookers, drugs and anything else their spoiled asses desired. Father Flanagan he wasn't.

In a small conference room overlooking the empty arena, I reluctantly gave a copy of the new contract to Manny. Nervous about Jelloteous's heart condition, the Link ordered me to insert a clause calling for automatic termination of the agreement upon death. That way, if Jello blew a gasket during a game, Tailburger's financial commitment would immediately end. Given that the contract paid Junderstack $1.5 million a year while he was living, things seemed generally fair to me. Manny, who read through the agreement and began scowling at me, seemed to have a different opinion.

"What are you trying to do here, Sky? Fuck Jello?"

"No, we're not trying to fuck Jello."

"Yeah, you are. You're trying to fuck Jello big-time."

"Manny, listen . . ."

"Satan. I prefer Satan."

"Very well, Satan. We have no desire to fuck Jello. We believe the contract is fair in light of the situation with Jello's heart."

"And his wife and children? What about them? What about their situation? If he dies on a road trip to Portland and the money stops, what are they going to survive on? ESPY awards and food stamps?"

"Satan, Jello's single with no family."

I looked over to Jelloteous to confirm this fact but he just sat there with a glazed look in his eyes.

"That's irrelevant, Sky. My client and the people of the Belgian Republic deserve and demand better than this piece of shit."

Satan threw the contract back down on the conference table.

"The Belgian Republic? I thought it was a monarchy."

"I don't give a damn if it's a military dictatorship. Jello is the biggest thing to come out of that wasteland since Jean-Claude Van Damme. He's got an obligation to his fellow Belgilonians. They're counting on him."

"Counting on him for what?"

"For landing the best contract he can. He wants to go back and build shelters there for the homeless."

"Do they have homeless people there?"

"I don't know. Does it matter?"

"Oh for Chrissakes, Satan. When was the last time he even went back to Belgium? No offense, Jello."

"It's been a few years."

"How many?"

"Around ten, but what's the difference? He sends money to his village."

"I thought his father was an industrialist who owned four companies. I read all about it in *Sports Illustrated* last week."

"Yes, but they're small companies. By the way, he wants a fully outfitted Hummer."

"Excuse me?"

"A Hummer. One of those military vehicles, but with leather and a CD player, all the bells and whistles. He saw Schwarzenegger's on *Accent Hollywood*."

After agreeing to insure against Jello's possible demise, adding a Hummer, a health club membership and a lifetime supply of Tailpipe Burgers, I left the negotiations with Satan feeling lucky to have retained the bulk of the contract's terms for my employer. I got stuck doing this piece of Tailburger's business because the Link hated paying legal fees and had no intention of hiring outside counsel to do something he felt could be handled internally. Usually things worked out all right, but sometimes we got royally screwed. If Jello dropped dead anytime soon, this had the potential to be such a time.

I flew home from L.A. full of more regret than usual about my decision to stay on the Tailburger treadmill. At forty-eight, I knew my health was for shit, my personal relationships were worse, and I was losing whatever fire I'd once brought to the mission of the company: putting a deep-fried piece of beef into the mouth of every malcontent in the U.S. Now it was me who was cooked. I reminded myself that soon I'd have twenty years in and could take a reduced pension, but even the prospect of that failed to brighten my spirits. A call from my brother, King, who reached me on my cell phone in the Rochester air terminal, only served as a reminder of another way to live.

"Sky, it's King."

"King, where are you?"

I habitually asked my brother where he was whenever he called, then held my breath and waited for the answer. My fear, culled from experience, was that he'd say, "jail," and I'd be forced to go bail him out. Fortunately, this wasn't such an occasion, but it was close.

"I'm in Caqueta."

"Where the hell's that?"

"Colombia. I joined FARC."

"FARC?"

"The Revolutionary Armed Forces of Colombia. Don't you read the papers? We're fighting a war down here."

"Yes, I read the papers. What in God's name are you doing down there?"

"Well, this week I'm getting my automatic weapon training."

FARC, a Marxist guerrilla organization that had fought against the conservative Colombian government and its armed forces for fifty years, had evolved from a legitimate movement of political insurrection to little more than a protection service for drug kingpins.

"You've got to get *out* of there!"

"Not a chance. I'm here to help the oppressed people of this country."

"King, I don't think FARC's updated its recruiting pamphlet. The people of Colombia are fleeing out of fear. You're not going to be helping them. You're going to be conducting kidnappings and making sure the coca and poppy plants are safe for the drug cartels. Do you understand? You'll be working to help drug dealers. Is that what you want to be doing?"

"Well, no. But the guy who hired me didn't say anything about that."

"Are you sure?"

"To be honest, he was talking awfully fast and you know my Spanish isn't that great, so maybe. Have you heard of El Jefe? That's my boss."

"El Heffay? The guy who has all the Bogota journalists and judges executed? Have you gone completely out of your mind?"

"Those are just rumors. He seems like a great guy. Really personable. Look, I need the money, Sky. What can I do?"

"How about trying a different line of work? Maybe a job with a nice 401(k) plan; one that doesn't require a bulletproof vest."

"This pays better than anything I can get up in the States. No health or dental, but lots of cash. Plus, I'm not violating any laws."

"Since when was drug-running legal?"

"I don't run drugs.

"Then what is it that you do?"

"I drive El Jefe around. You know, from one hideout to another. He's always worried about assassination attempts, so he sleeps in a different place every night. It's kind of exciting. And let me tell you, this guy knows how to live. I haven't seen this much leg since that winter I spent as a water aerobics instructor for Carnival out of Miami."

"Why don't you come up to Rochester for a visit? I'd love to see you." With grave danger imminent, lying was necessary.

"Oh, I don't know, Sky. I'd really like to get there. Believe me, I would. It's just hard to make plans that far in advance."

"What are you talking about? You can come anytime you like."

"Yeah, I know, but with El Jefe, every day is a lifetime."

"I can imagine," I said, my concern growing. "You really should come up. I can get some tickets for the Red Wings or something. Would you like that?"

Watching the Rochester Red Wings, the city's AAA baseball team and affiliate to the Minnesota Twins, was as tempting a brother-to-brother outing as I could use to entice King. We'd grown up in the upper decks of Silver Stadium rooting against the likes of the Toledo Mudhens and the Tidewater Tides, urging our Wings on to the Governor's Cup, the greatest heights one can reach at the Triple-A level.

"I'd love it. I haven't been to a Wings game in years."

"They've got a beautiful new stadium. It's called Frontier Field."

"If I come, should I bring El Jefe?"

"Do *not* bring El Jefe!"

"I'm kidding. God, you're tense. You've got to stop working so hard."

The irony of my brother's words escaped him.

"Be careful down there, okay?"

"I'll call you soon."

Closing up my Motorola, I decided that it was the name King that had caused my brother's problems. It must have created a certain sense of entitlement in his youth as he walked around with this royal appellation. He was allowed to get away with anything he wanted. Kings don't have to do much in this world to get by, and when they screw up, they are forgiven, if for no other reason than who they are by birth. This was how it worked with King in our family, something I could never understand and had finally stopped trying to figure out.

On reflection, it occurred to me that I was fortunate in one regard, because you often heard about characters like King, but rarely met them or had one in your own family. Most people's siblings led the same mundane lives they did, working as lawyers or accountants or salesmen with a house in the suburbs, a wife, a few kids and a dog. They didn't come close to living life without the proverbial net, but were perpetually fascinated by those who did. People like King, who flitted from one thing to the next, moving entirely outside the conventional and often suffocating expectations of themselves and others. People whom we pitied one moment and admired the next. People whose lives we'd like to step into, if only for a while, to see what we're missing. Or perhaps to reassure ourselves that we're not missing anything at all.

4

Board out of My Mind

CANANDAIGUA, NEW YORK

Every year, shortly after the shareholder's meeting, the Link held a retreat for the entire board of directors. In a waterfront inn on Canandaigua Lake, a sixteen-mile-long Finger Lake southeast of Rochester, we spent two days discussing the upcoming fiscal year. Mostly, it was an opportunity for the ten of us to listen to our leader rant and rave about the hundreds of things that were wrong with Tailburger and the two or three that were right.

Though a few of us, including me, could voice our honest opinion without eliciting an uncontrollable tirade by our CEO, the Link had assured himself of a predominantly yes-man environment by appointing his triplets Ned, Ted and Fred to the board. Ned, Ted and Fred, who looked, laughed, walked and talked alike, each had a thick thatch of dark black hair on their arms, legs, chest and head, where it was worn in a tightly ringletted perm. They were a husky bunch with slightly protruding paunches and the obnoxious habit of perpetually chewing gum. In all my years with the company, I'd never seen any of the brothers wear anything but golf attire. They came to all meetings in loud slacks, louder shirts and white spiked shoes.

Better qualified and more appropriately attired individuals filled out the remainder of the board's slate. Biff Dilworth, a wiry academic type partial to bifocals and three-piece suits, was president of Rochester State University. Chad Hemmingbone, a Brooks Brothers mannequin and fatuous blowhard if truth be told, was president of First Union, the area's largest bank, and could arrange personal loans for me when the need arose. Annette McNabnay, the city's first female mayor and our "token chick," as the Link referred to her, was always the smartest person in the room. Tim Truheart, the owner of three area carpet stores, wasn't good for much other than the occasional rug sample. The rest of the board was comprised of a rotating assortment of Kodak and Xerox executives who, because of the Link's short fuse, rarely lasted long enough for me to learn their names. The Link's patience was tested the most, however, by his own progeny.

"Ned, will you take off that damned visor? You look ridiculous. Ted, you and Fred, too. Just take the things off." The Link was displeased.

"Dad, there's a glare coming in off the lake. It's blinding," Ned whined.

"It is awful bright in here," Ted added as Fred nodded his head.

"Just take 'em off or I'll rip 'em off," the Link boomed.

"All right, all right. Don't have a coronary, Dad."

"Yeah, Dad. It's just a visor."

As soon as the visors came off, Ned, Ted and Fred put on sunglasses. Even the Link, who usually insisted on getting his way, gave up at this point and started the meeting. It began, like all others, with a troubleshooting exercise intended to protect the company from areas of potential exposure. Everyone was supposed to throw out issues for consideration, but, as usual, most of our time was spent trying to shoot down the Link's bad ideas. I'll give him this: he was a contrarian thinker. When everybody was screaming right, the Link yelled, "up."

"We need to arm our drive-thru people."

"What?" I asked in shock.

"There've been some holdups at our drive-thru windows. I want our people prepared."

"I think that's a great idea," Ned piped up.

"Me, too," added Ted.

"I have to agree. Hell of an idea, Dad," Fred chimed in.

I was certain it *wasn't* a great idea.

"Frank, we can't put weapons in the hands of the teenagers who man our pickup windows."

"Why the hell not? There's no problem in the world that can't be solved by an AK-47 automatic machine gun."

"Well, for one thing, you need to be eighteen years old for a gun permit, and most of our employees are still in high school."

The Link was not dissuaded easily.

"Fine. From now on, we're only hiring those lonely senior-citizen types, the kind in the McDonald's ads who spend every waking hour of their lives wishing they had a job swabbing out toilet bowls. And I want 'em all armed."

Biff Dilworth, the most refined member of the board, attempted to denounce the proposed new policy in his own way.

"Frank, as a man dedicated to the higher education of this country's young people for the past forty years, I fear that such a step will only contribute to the further demise of the thin line of civility currently separating man from beast. For the sake of humanity and the future of our kind as a people, I urge the reconsideration of this arming business."

The Link was clearly moved by such an impassioned plea. His soft side lurked just below the surface.

"You're right, Professor. Maybe I was a little hasty. I'll tell you what. We'll start with a military-strength pepper spray, and if that doesn't work, then we go to guns."

"Well, I don't know, Frank . . ."

"Look, I do know. This'll make us more money. I guarantee it. I just read a *Wall Street Journal* article about drive-thru times. For every ten seconds you shave off your average customer's visit from menu board to departure, the store makes an extra fifty thousand dollars per year. Do you know who has the fastest time from the menu board to departure? (Pause) Wendy's. One hundred fifty point three seconds. One hundred fifty point three fucking seconds. They've got high-tech timers and a greeting that takes less than one second. 'HowmayIhelpyou?' Less than one second. Do you know how long our average time is? Six hundred forty-three seconds. It's pathetic. Slowest time in the business. That's why we've got to arm our people. If the customer knows the shaky pre-Parkinson's fry guy living on a fixed income in a shithole studio apartment in Bakersfield is packing something, he's gonna think twice about returning a screwed-up order. Am I right? That right there will save us a few seconds."

"Maybe we should just shorten our greeting," I offered, hopeful to avoid arming everyone with pepper spray.

"That's good, Thorne. I don't know why we spend so much time with the friendly chitchat. From now on there'll be no more, 'Welcome to Tailburger, the burger of choice for the downtrodden, disabled and incarcerated. Whatever you decide to eat, don't forget to wash it all down with a Tailfrap.' Way too wordy. From now on out, we keep it simple. 'Order, asshole.' That's it. Plain and simple. We're the burger of abuse. It's time we started acting like it. People don't drive in for the fresh-faced, seventeen-year-old gal with the brace-filled smile anyway. They come by to see people like themselves—aging, regret-filled losers who are ready to be crapped on just like they've been crapped on for their entire lives. Now enough about that. Have we settled with Mother Teresa yet?"

Mother Teresa was the Link's nickname for Sister Ancilla Satter, a nun from Rochester's Sisters of the Sorrowful Mother convent. In a horrifying accident, Sister Ancilla's face had been burned by a blast of steaming hot microwaved air that escaped from the corner of one of our Fanny Packs, a sack of fried pork products which we marketed as ideal for those with an active lifestyle. According to eyewitnesses, after Sister Ancilla picked up her food at our window in the church's meals-on-wheels van, recognizable by the baby lamb painted on the side, she tried to peek in the pack to make sure her fried rib tips were accompanied by our secret sauce. Upon doing so, trapped heat rushed out, overwhelmed the sister and caused third-degree burns to her holy visage. Fortunately, her habit had protected her neck and part of her face.

"Her lawyers want more money," I informed the Link.

"Those cocksuckers. Fuck 'em! I say we blackmail her." The Link was livid now, his head the color of a ripe tomato. "What kind of dirt do we have on the old hag?"

The Link's belief in military intelligence, his extreme paranoia and his genuine concerns over the employability of his own children led him to initiate KGB-type activities within Tailburger. As the owners of three local spy shops called Who's Nailing Your Wife?, Ned, Ted and Fred profited greatly from this arrangement. So did the paterfamilias. While the boys got thousands of dollars selling nothing but surveillance equipment and paramilitary gear to Tailburger, the Link got information he could use against his enemies and allies.

Although Operation Tenderize was never officially discussed in board meetings or acknowledged to exist in the corporate minutes, its ongoing purpose was to gather incriminating bribe-worthy data—photographic, electronic or otherwise—about anyone or anything that got in Tailburger's way. It also allowed Ned, Ted and Fred to get rich and abuse their power without impediment.

Not surprisingly, with the use of a police radio, a few bugs and a well-placed wiretap, Ned, Ted and Fred's flunkies, reminiscent of Nixon's plumbers, had discovered the only available skinny on Sister Ancilla. She had given up Tailburger for Lent, a considerable sacrifice, given her fondness for the Fanny Pack. Coincidentally, her decision came at a time when the Sisters of the Sorrowful Mother convent, overweight and out of shape, had been ordered by the mother superior to slim down. Unfortunately, with the donation of a remote-controlled television and the advent of fat-free cookies, too many evenings were being spent watching reruns of Notre Dame football games and scarfing down SnackWell's. To combat this trend, the sisters had convened and committed themselves to diet and discipline in the name of God. Collectively, they served as one enormous support group and took a firm vow of caloric obedience that was not to be broken by anyone. In order to provide additional incentive, the mother superior had each nun solicit sponsors to pledge $10 per week to be donated to the Shriner's Hospital for Crippled Children, so long as the sponsored sister continued to meet specific weight-loss goals.

Thus when Sister Ancilla quietly drove the convent's lamb van up to the Tailburger window on that warm spring night, just days before the Easter Bunny would arrive, she was letting many people, both ordinary and supernatural, down. The source of her burns and her subsequent lawsuit, however, had somehow been kept a secret. How? She lied. Wanting to surprise the mother superior by contributing the settlement money to the Shriner's Fund in order to absolve her of her sins, Sister Ancilla said she had a cooking accident.

Whatever the cause of Sister Ancilla's burns, however, she remained an unsympathetic actor to the Link.

"I say we blow her in to the mother superior."

"Frank, this could be bad publicity for the company," Mayor McNabnay observed.

Annette McNabnay wore her honey-blond hair pulled back and dressed only in DKNY. She was well-spoken and intelligent, and her sophisticated good looks, distinguished by wonderful bone structure and fine features, lent a certain elegance to any gathering she graced. Picture Sharon Stone in *Basic Instinct,* but add underwear. Elected to Rochester's top office two years earlier, her honor possessed both a J.D. and an M.B.A. For her, putting up with the Link's shit was nothing more than savvy political posturing.

"Annette, in case you haven't noticed, the clergy isn't one of our big demographics. Do you think I care what that fat penguin Ancilla Satter has to say? Let's go to the papers and tell them what a phony she is and all about this Shriner's Hospital scam."

"Dad's right. I say we blow her in," said Ned.

"I agree. Blow her in," added Ted.

"Blow her," Fred followed. "The whole thing is a scam."

Annette didn't give up.

"Frank, with all due respect, I don't think we should blow Sister Ancilla in to the mother superior or the press. Ever since she came up with the idea for Palm Funday, she's been a very popular figure in the local community. Plus, the Shriner's Hospital weight-loss drive is not a scam. They're raising thousands of dollars to make these kids' lives a little more pleasant. Just because they don't fit into our demographic doesn't mean we want to alienate them. It's too big a risk."

Discomfort crept across the main sitting room of the Kerfoot Inn, where we had gathered for the afternoon's meeting. The wooden duck decoys and scaled schooner replicas that surrounded us were pretty to look at but held no answers. Biff Dilworth, our resident academic, and Chad Hemmingbone, our resident banker, sat silently while Tim Truheart, king of the carpet sample, stared out the window at *Bastard Boy,* the Link's sixty-five-foot cabin cruiser. Truheart had a good mind, but was unable to put it to use in our meetings. Through Operation Tenderize, the Link had obtained compromising photos of him with the seventeen-year-old French au pair Truheart's wife hired to look after their three kids. According to Ned, the pictures represented some of the "raunchiest shit" he'd ever seen, and rivaled anything in his silver-anniversary issue of *Swank.* In this version of the Mexican stand-off, Truheart supported all of the Link's positions, and the Link let him continue to collect $40,000 annually in director's fees. One bit of insurrection, and Truheart knew that a less than flattering picture of his tongue wrapped around someone other than his wife would find its way into the *Democrat & Chronicle*, Rochester's major daily.

Finally, the Link interrupted our solitude to ask me a question.

"How much are Sister Ancilla's lawyers asking for?"

"Nine hundred and sixty thousand dollars."

"You're shitting me, Sky! That's outrageous!"

"The money will go primarily to charity," I reminded him.

"My ass. Those bloodthirsty lawyers will be shoving their noses in the trough for at least a third."

"That's true, Frank, but there's no getting around it."

The Link gazed off into the distance and rubbed his hands together. In moments like this, I realized how sick and tired I was of waiting for this fat ball of pus to make decisions.

"Okay, fuck it. Settle with the sister, Sky. But here's what we're gonna do. We're gonna build a gym at the convent for the sisters to work off all that flab. There's nothing more disturbing than a fat nun. It really creeps me out."

Talk about the blimp calling the balloon overinflated. The Link paused for a minute before adding more.

"And, Thorne, get the gym named after me. I want some positive publicity out of this fiasco. You know the drill. Give the press the whole 'Tailburger has a heart' routine, and send some burgers to the crippled kids."

"Got it, Frank," I said as I jotted a note to myself. "Burgers for the cripples."

I agreed with my corpulent commander for no other reason than to get rid of the matter. I still had to break the bad news about the SERMON suit, an item that might push him over a dangerous anger ledge. Mostly dangerous to me. Biff Dilworth, however, couldn't leave well enough alone.

"Frank, have you thought about lowering the temperature of the Fanny Pack? I mean, isn't that how we got into this mess in the first place?"

"What do you think I am, Biff? Some kind of douche bag? Of course I've thought about that. Why don't you think about this? Our customers like their food good and goddamn hot, and that's how they're gonna get it."

Biff was showing unusual resolve.

"I'm all for hot, Frank. Gracious knows I enjoy a steaming beverage on occasion, but scalding the faces of our clientele seems a bit extreme."

The Link never reacted well to direct assaults on his opinion.

"Look, Dilworth, when I want any shit out of you, I'll squeeze your head, all right?"

"It was just a suggestion, Frank. By the by, your chosen riposte is a bit dated."

"Yeah, yeah, whatever," the Link responded dismissively. "What else do we need to discuss, Sky?"

As I prepared to answer, I noticed that Biff, Annette, Chad and the rest of the board had become dejected and disinterested, sitting with their heads down and their eyes averted.

"Well, there is a small annoyance involving our good friends from SERMON."

"What do those a-holes want now?"

News of the industry-wide suit was too much for the Link to take. He started whipping Triscuits at the board members, causing Ned, Ted, Fred and the rest to clear the room. After taking out a flask of shandy and downing what he referred to as his "medication," he asked the recording secretary to draft a proclamation of war against SERMON. Delivered in a rage, most of its provisions rambled on about the capture of Savannah and the resignation of Salmon P. Chase. I took cover under a conference table until he calmed down.

"C'mon out from under there, Thorne."

Strangely, the Link felt obliged to explain himself.

"I don't mean to get so agitated, Sky, but those jag-offs from McDonald's and Burger King have been trying to drive us out of business for years, and we've beat 'em back with nothin' but muskets and spit. So I'll be goddamned if I'm gonna sit by and watch SERMON destroy us now. You understand me, Thorne. I know you do. Hell, you're like a son to me."

This was how the Link concluded most meetings with me. By tacking on a few words of encouragement, he made sure I remained his number one Union soldier—an unquestioning loyalist. I, of course, dutifully listened, but I knew the sentiment was a chocolate Easter bunny—sweet and hollow.

"That's why it's so difficult to say what I have to say to you."

Wait a minute. The Link was adding something new.

"Thorne, if you don't get our market share up to five percent by the end of the fiscal year, I am going to be forced to make some changes."

"What do you mean by changes?"

"You'll have to leave. The stockholders will demand it."

"Frank, you know I don't have direct control over our market share figures."

"Thorne, when performance isn't there, heads have got to roll. We're all slaves to Wall Street."

"I understand that. But why should my head roll?"

"Visibility, Thorne. You are one visible motherfucker. I've been running your name up the flagpole for so many goddamned years, everybody knows you. And they like you. But if you don't hit the figures, you're gone."

"Frank, we've never had a market share higher than three and a half percent in the history of the company."

"You'll find a way to make it happen. I've got confidence in you, boy."

"I've got nineteen years with Tailburger. One more and I get my pension. If I don't make that, I walk away with nothing."

"I don't want to hear those negative thoughts. Just get out there and kill Confederates. You got me? (Pause) Oh, one last thing,

Thorne. How's the membership list look out at Crooked Creek? Any openings for an old guy like me?"

"I haven't heard of any," I replied, as if I'd lift one finger to help this fuck join a golf club.

"Well, let me know if you do. I'm itching to tee 'em up out there. You know that's always been a dream of mine."

I nodded, turned and walked out, ending our confrontation. Exchanges like this were difficult to take at my age. The Link had been a reasonably sane man when I went to work for him years before, but now he'd lost his way to the wheelhouse, and whatever respect I originally afforded him had diminished dramatically. Why the hell did I put up with his shit? I felt like a child in his presence, continually trying to please this oafish, hatemongering, manipulative maniac. Who was he to jeopardize my twenty-year record? All I could think about was getting out, but I couldn't. The company had to hit the 5 percent market figure or I was looking at the loss of any retirement plans I'd ever entertained, and the end of my insular Tahitian dream.

5

Hooray for Hollywood Scum

BACK IN LOS ANGELES

To bolster our impending Torture campaign, I returned to L.A. for a meeting with Ship Plankton, a hot young Hollywood director whose new movie, *Dongwood*, was due for a summer release. With "blockbuster" written all over it, and some of its scenes still not in the can, *Dongwood* was the perfect vehicle for a Tailburger product placement. If we could get Dirk Harrington, the film's star, to chow down a Tailpipe with cheese in front of thirty million people, sales would soar.

Although Ship insisted by telephone that no opportunity existed for this kind of crass commercialism in his movie, I begged him for five minutes of his time. When that didn't work, I reminded him of my closeness with Congressman Roxby and the pending National Endowment for the Arts funding bill that could go either way. With his leftward-leaning underbelly exposed, he agreed to a meeting within seconds.

Ship worked out of a bungalow on the back lot of Worldvision, a small production company he snared a development deal with after an ugly fallout with RCM, one of the industry's big players. The sordid details of his split, splashed all over the cover of *Vari-*

ety and the other trade papers, involved laughing gas, male prostitutes, gerbils and an expense account. I decided not to bring it up.

On a small brick patio, my prey, dressed in jeans and a black T-shirt, sat sipping a Coke. Lanky and in his late twenties, with a full head of hair, he rose to his feet and smiled as we shook hands.

"Good to see you, Ship." I greeted him like an old friend.

"Likewise, Sky. How's the burger biz?"

"Hey, we're in the entertainment biz, just like you."

"I guess so. May I offer you something to drink? A soda?"

"Sure. Anything diet."

Ship handed me a glass and struck an arty pose.

"So you want to talk about *Dongwood*?"

"I do. I'll be direct, Ship. We want to do a product tie-in with your *brilliant* new film."

"But you haven't seen my *brilliant* new film yet."

"I know. That's true. I admit it. But with you at the helm, it's bound to be that good."

The fact that I hadn't seen this brilliant new film didn't hold me back a bit. To Ship's credit, he ignored my transparent, and altogether pitiable, attempt at ass-kissing. When a man has to ask someone twenty years younger than him for anything, there's something askew in the world.

"Sky, you've got to understand. *Dongwood* is a drama. It isn't an action movie. It isn't a romantic comedy. It's the delicate story of a disgruntled carnival worker who wants a better life. In many ways, it defies categorization. I don't want to trivialize this picture with fast food. Can you appreciate that?"

"I do appreciate that, but I believe Tailburger has a place in your film. I mean, what carnival worker in the world doesn't eat a Tailpipe Deluxe now and again? Especially when he's feeling discouraged."

"Not discouraged, Sky. Disgruntled. There's a difference."

"Got it. Either way, he's hitting the drive-thru."

"Sky, I'm trying hard to be polite here, but let me explain things more clearly. The lead character in *Dongwood* is a born-again Christian and longtime vegetarian who subsists on nothing but leaves and berries. He quits his job assembling the Tilt-A-Whirl, wanders aimlessly, suffers a complete mental breakdown and eventually blows his own head clean off with a .357 magnum."

"It's perfect for us, Ship. It's a temptation story. Here he is, the model, upstanding vegetarian and he gets weak. He drives by a Tailburger billboard and suddenly finds himself craving a huge, fried hunk of meat. Or better yet, he develops a sinful addiction to the Tailfrap, our beef-flavored shake."

"Sky, the buzz is that Oscar may be watching this one. I know its sounds trite, but I can't risk compromising my artistic integrity."

Despite Plankton's growing reputation and success, the rights to his last three pictures were owned by RCM. Meanwhile, World-vision had suffered a recent series of box-office duds, including *Honey, I Had an Embolism* and *Son of Sharkboy III,* and was cash poor. Advantage Thorne.

"How does eight hundred thousand dollars sound?"

Ship put his drink down slowly and shook his head.

"For a single product-placement shot?"

"Of course not. We want four shots. We also want a licensing deal for clothing and toys—the usual stuff."

"Sky, unless you think the kiddies will want a manic-depressive suicide doll, I don't think my film lends itself to a toy line."

"Oh, I'm not talking about toys for kids. I'm talking about toys for our heavy users: dysfunctional adults and prison inmates. Our new campaign is all about self-torture, which is why your film ties in so nicely. We'll get four million doohickeys made cheap in the Far East, slap the word *Dongwood* across them and give them away with our special-edition *Dongwood* burger. They'll be little pieces of plastic crap."

"I'll want creative control over the crap, of course."

"No problem."

"Eight hundred grand, Sky?"

"Eight hundred."

"Well, I agree that it's important for an audience to see the full depravity of a man's soul. It makes him that much more appealing. I'll tell you what. Let me fiddle with the script a bit and see what can be done."

I had Plankton's ass on a platter and he knew it. I left the lot of Worldvision and drove to the Staples Center to check up on Jelloteous, our other big L.A. investment. Having returned to the lineup the week before, he was averaging forty-two points and fourteen blocks during games and three Laker girls afterward. The team was thirty-six and eight and talking about a possible championship run.

"Jelloteous, hello."

"Mr. Sky, hello. How are you?"

"Still breathing. And you?"

"I am cool."

"Glad to hear it. How's the ticker?"

Jelloteous thumped his chest with a closed fist.

"Berry good."

"And the video shoot with Blatherskite? How'd that go?"

"It was fun, but Blatherskite is crazy guys."

Blatherskite, an Orange County, California, outfit whose first album, *Stinky Finger,* had rocketed to number one, was known for its sophomoric antics. Although Jelloteous didn't mention it to me, I found out later that the band had set his gym bag on fire during the filming of the video. As a good-natured sort, Jelloteous took the stunt as well as could be expected, considering the fact that his passport and work visa were in the duffel. Fortunately the Belgian embassy straightened everything out and halted the deportment proceedings in plenty of time.

Assured that our investment was healthy, I returned to Rochester on a red-eye through Chicago, cautiously optimistic about the new campaign. It was revolutionary in a way. As far as I knew, the themes of personal abuse and self-torture had never been used to sell fast food. I felt a perverse pride overcoming me. *Why Just Abuse Your Body, When You Can Torture It?* might take its place in advertising history next to such legendary catchphrases as *Have It Your Way* and *Where's the Beef?* Admittedly, ours was a bit wordier, but execution would determine its fate as a shibboleth. This campaign needed to succeed unlike any other we'd done if I was to get our market share up to a full 5 percent and save my job. The stakes were so high for me personally, I preferred to focus on the plan.

The release of Blatherskite's "Torture Me" video would coincide with the start of the band's Torturing America's Ears Tour. There seemed to be an inordinate number of state fairs and tractor pulls on the summer schedule, but my advance people assured me these venues were breeding grounds for the pollen spores who bought our burgers.

At the same time, a blitz of thirty-second television spots, featuring interspersed shots of Jelloteous happily munching on Tailburgers and completing his "Felonious, Melodious" jam, would begin running on cable stations and the major networks in each of the top one hundred markets. A slew of Internet banners, billboard ads and radio spots, all of which were in development, would increase our penetration. And then, on top of it all, we'd add the *Dongwood* angle. Yes, wheeling my pre-owned, near luxury Eurosedan into my driveway, I felt I had a winner on my hands. It had to be.

Home. I still lived in the same four-bedroom Georgian colonial Jess and I bought two years before our split. Although I moved out when we separated, I returned after Trip Baden stole my wife and kids and forced them to live in his tacky mansion.

A blinking message machine greeted me in my drab, avocado kitchen. I placed my shoulder bag on the linoleum floor, hit the playback button and braced myself for the worst. Lately, nothing but bad news seemed to emerge from this contraption's speaker.

"Sky, it's Dick."

Dick Tinglehoff, also known as Dick Jinglehoff or Dick Jerkoff, depending upon the quality of his work, was Tailburger's main radio and television jingle writer. The rest of his time was spent as a junior high school music teacher at Hardale Country Day, a local prep school for the mildly affluent. He had composed many of our moderately successful, memory-jogging melodies in the past. Most, however, were instantly forgettable. For some masochistic reason, I had remained loyal despite his recent "Burgers All over the 'Hood" effort and the "Red Meat Rap" fiasco. Now, I was under pressure from the Link to fire Dick if he didn't come up big for us in the new campaign.

"Hey, I've got a hook that's da bomb on my hands! Listen up. Okay, here goes."

"Da bomb?" I repeated out loud.

Dick started hissing and alternatively chanting, "boom, boom, boom," trying his best to imitate an inner-city beat box. Then he began singing in his inimitable warble.

> *We don't bake 'em,*
> *We don't broil 'em*
> *We just grease and fry and oil 'em*
>
> *Here at Tailburger*
> *What you're eatin'*
> *Is a big old piece*
> *Of bloodred meatin'*
>
> *Every burger*
> *We just scorch 'er*
> *Every body*
> *We must torture!*

Despite repeated interventions by family and friends, including the vice principal at his school, Dick couldn't seem to shake his ghetto obsession. He confessed to me that it started in the '80s with someone called Run-DMC and had continued through the '90s with the groundbreaking work of a band called Niggaz with Attitude. Now, the walls of the music room at Hardale were covered with posters of somebody named Dr. Dre and a quilt with the words "Thug Life" in the middle, which Dick had stitched to get over the death of someone named Tupac Shakur. A hit with students, Dick was beginning to lose his popularity with parents.

"Imagine that coming out of a ghetto blaster in Compton. Let me know what you think when you get a minute, Sky. Call me."

Dick's enthusiasm was admirable, but once again he'd ignored my warnings that the food stamp demographic was only 2 percent of our total business. I opened the liquor cabinet and fixed myself a drink. My confidence in the campaign, like the double martini now in my hands, was shaken.

6

Family Matters
or So They Say

The next day, I decided to call my son, Ethan, twenty-two, one of the founders of a Silicon Valley start-up called Macrocock.com. Macrocock had something to do with computers, wakeboards and "living large," but I couldn't quite track it all. So far, it had nothing to do with turning a profit or, frankly, seeing *any* revenue. Ethan did, however, assure me of two things: (1) the business plan was "rad," and (2) the stock options would be worth "gazillions" when the IPO, which would be any week now, came. In the meantime, my job as a supportive parent was to keep sending my love and, until the second-round financing came through, a monthly check. I also held a small equity interest in the company.

"Hello."

"Ethan?"

"Yeah, this is Ethan. Who's this?"

Macrocock management evidently encouraged the playing of unlistenable music at ungodly decibel levels.

"Ethan, it's your father."

"Who?"

"Your dad. IT'S YOUR DAD!" I shouted.

"No need to raise your voice, Pop. I hear you. Let me turn down the tuneage."

Ethan returned to the telephone.

"There. That's better."

"What was that racket, Ethan?"

This was the closest I could come at the moment to showing an interest in my boy's musical taste.

"Oh, the music? It's this soca speed-metal band called Abundant Fuck. They rage, don't they?"

"Full on. No question about it," I replied, my sarcasm barely concealed.

"Dad, there's more to music than Kansas, Boston and Chicago. Trust me. Any band named after a place sucks."

He had a point with Manhattan Transfer and maybe the Bay City Rollers, but Chicago? Despite the hurtful criticism, I continued undeterred.

"Listen, I wanted to talk to you about . . ."

"Dad, can you hold a minute? I need to take a slash."

Without giving my response, I was put on hold by a child whose bladder was the size of an acorn. I couldn't remember the last time we'd had a telephone call without a bathroom break. A few minutes passed before he returned.

"Sorry 'bout that. All this Red Bull is sinking me. How are you doing?"

"Well, I'm fine, but I haven't heard from you. How's the Internet world?"

"Dad, it's incredible! We're so close to getting second-round financing, we need to develop our site. Then we're going to open the kimono."

"Open the kimono?"

"Reveal our idea."

"That's great. I was starting to wonder what was inside that kimono myself."

"I'm sure. It's insane out here. It's like we're shredding, but at the same time we're strappin'."

"Strappin'" was Ethanspeak for "I need more money."

"How much do you need?"

"Fifteen hundy would be huge."

"You guys aren't committing any felonies, right?"

"Dad, c'mon, this is me you're talking about. Everything's cool on the cube farm. We've had a bit of scope creep, but that's all right."

"What's scope creep?"

"The project's scope. It's just expanded a bit."

"Okay, I get it. Still living with Skull?" I asked, referring to Ethan's best friend.

"Oh, yeah. It's working out well. He programs code for us. He's a real propeller head."

Skull may have been a propeller head now, but in a prior life he was known as the guy at Ethan's high school who liked to drink bong water. It's important to know your kid's friends.

"Good. I just wanted to make sure you were alive. I hadn't heard from you in a few weeks."

"Sorry, Pop. I'm turning into a real bithead. Sometimes the world moves too fast for family contact."

"Well, slow it down once in a while and give me a call."

"I will. Look, I gotta go. Stay on the bleeding edge, all right?"

My son's vocabulary made him sound like the trailer for a movie nobody went to see.

"I'll try. Take care of yourself, okay? I'll talk to you soon."

"Bye, Dad."

"Good-bye, Ethan."

Like most things these days, my conversation with Ethan left me feeling vaguely unsatisfied. Maybe it was because I'd spent half the time on hold while he urinated, but I suspected there was more to it. It had taken me a long time, but I'd finally reached the point in my life where I was more concerned about my kids' dreams than my own. Perhaps it was because they stood a better chance of coming true, but whatever the reason, I was convinced that the inner happiness I so desperately sought was tied to their happiness. This had not always been the case. Having neglected Ethan's and my daughter Sophia's needs for too many years as I toiled for Tailburger, I was trying to make it up to them with more attentiveness. Problem was, they didn't have much time for me now.

Sophia was a junior at Cornell and seemed to be doing well, but I worried about her brother. I still felt guilty about the job I'd done helping to raise Ethan. He was a good kid, but a bit misdirected. When I divorced his mother, Ethan metamorphosed overnight from a happy young boy into a dour presence. Only now was he starting to flourish a bit. Without a college degree or any training, Ethan brought few skills to the table at Macrocock, but I didn't care. As long as he was excited, I would support him, even if that mostly meant sending money.

Raising a child who could support himself financially was important, but raising one who could support himself emotionally and spiritually was more important. I wasn't sure I'd succeeded on any of those fronts. I wanted Ethan to be independent and venture out on his own. On the other hand, I selfishly still wanted him to need me and to come to me with any big decisions he was facing. Mostly I wanted to prevent him from joining a cult. Somehow we had struck upon a hybrid of all this in our relationship. He came to me with most of his difficult dilemmas and a few I felt he could have wrestled with on his own. I wanted to be a good father, but a three-hour conference call about whether or not to sign up for basic cable *and* the movie channels seemed a bit much. I felt certain Ethan would find his way eventually. It just might take a little longer than I expected.

My reverie was interrupted by the Link, who came barreling into my office.

"Thorne, we've got a goddamn hydrogen bomb exploding in our faces. One of our asshole seniors working the window in

Amarillo hit a 'Nam vet in the face with his pepper spray. Last thing I want to do is go to war with a bunch of psycho Agent Orange types. Get on it."

To solve the Amarillo uprising, I began the process of calling across the country, first to our regional vice president in Dallas, then to the franchise owner of the affected store and finally to Zeb Nettles, our public relations guru, who would do whatever was required to keep our name out of the papers for pepper-spraying a war hero. In the middle of my efforts, the Link reentered my office and laid himself out on my couch. With his wife of thirty-five years, Wilhemina, gone, he often told me how lonely he'd gotten. Lately, the loneliness seemed to intensify. This proposition was hard for me to believe, considering the stable of prostitutes he kept busy. Put three shots of bourbon down his gullet and the Link would fuck a door handle if you put it in front of him. Nevertheless, he'd always insist, "Willy was my everything, Sky," whenever the topic came up. "Ned, Ted and Fred have their own families now. All I've got is the business." Sadly, I was starting to feel the same way.

"God, I miss her, Thorne."

"I know, Frank. I'm sure it's very hard."

"Hard isn't the word."

The Link was crying now, sobbing into the sleeve of his red sweatsuit. I comforted him the best I could until noon, when I gingerly excused myself and left him supine.

Wednesdays meant lunch with Cal Perkins, my best friend from childhood and a walking contradiction. By all outward appearances, this father of three was an upstanding member of the community. Dark-haired and trim, he served as a deacon at Pittsford's First Presbyterian Church, was a fixture at Little League games and ran a successful telemarketing business. Cal had married later than most of the guys in our circle of friends, a move that appeared Solomon-like in retrospect. While the rest of us were getting divorced or, at a minimum, bitter and disillusioned about love, he was still dating twenty-two-year-olds who were impressed by any man who ate with a fork. He finally chose Jenny, a beautiful and saccharine-sweet person whom he met, aptly, in the fresh produce section of the local Wegman's supermarket. They married (I was the best man), started a family—one boy and two girls—and settled comfortably into the American dream.

Cal had a secret, however, that even among those close to him, only I knew. The basis of his business success was an endless series of adult telephone and Internet sex services bringing in $4.99 to $29.99 a minute, day after day, night after night, as millions of men pleasured themselves and Cal got filthy rich. Oh sure, he had tried in the early days to sell other items via 1-800 numbers such as gift baskets, furniture and mattresses, but what really sold, when he looked at the various industries, was sex.

Cal got into the business early, and spent the first year reserving numbers like 1-800-BLOWJOB and 1-800-BIGTITS, to name a few. His cover was jellies and jams sold from 1-800-SPREDEM. The revenue from these breakfast spreads couldn't pay for his Direct TV, let alone make him wealthy, but the sex lines and sex products offered via mail-order catalog sold from day one. And they sold huge—especially the sex products. Multispeed, two-pronged vibrators, clit-pleasing tendril root rings, anal-probing Venus flytrap stimulators, flavored lubes, purple butterfly orgasmatron eggs, silicone masturbation sleeves. I don't know who used these things, but there were plenty of people buying them. Cal's family remained blissfully unaware of his dual identity, but from time to time, all the covering got to him. If he couldn't have confided in me, I think he would have gone crazy.

We always met at Pappy's Den of Kielbasa, an old rehabbed restaurant painted red and known, ironically, for its gut-busting pasta. The restaurant, previously called Smolenski's Den of Kielbasa, didn't even serve kielbasa anymore, but since the name brought in famished Poles in busloads from Buffalo, it stuck. Pappy, the proprietor and resident bookmaker, led us to our usual table by a big bay window. Pappy leaned in and talked to us under his breath.

"You two want action on the Barcelona game?"

"Barcelona?"

"World Football League. They play Frankfurt Thursday night. How about the over under? You want to play that?"

"Pappy, do you ever bet on these games yourself?" I asked, genuinely curious about the answer.

"No, no. Not anymore. I'm still paying off my Super Bowl bets on za Bills."

"My condolences."

"So what you say? How 'bout WNBA? Two dimes on New York Liberty? Rebecca Lobo? Utah Starzz?"

"Two thousand dollars? Not today, Pappy. I don't like the way the Starzz are playing. I'm more of a Detroit Shock fan. Maybe next Wednesday."

"Minnesota Lynx vairsis Miami Sol?"

Although I'd never actually placed a bet with Pappy, I always tried to appease him. He seemed to enjoy taking bets more than running a restaurant. Summer was a bit slow for him as well. He didn't take bets on baseball, and it was tough trying to push the teaser for a professional lacrosse game between the Rochester Rattlers and the Toronto Rock. Finally, he left me and Cal alone. There was no need to take our orders since we always had the same thing.

"You don't look well, Sky."

"It's good to see you, too."

"I don't mean to insult you. I just want to make sure you're all right."

"We're getting ready to launch this new campaign and I'm under a little pressure. We've also got these anti–red meat fanatics on our asses again. Same old shit. How about you? How are things?"

"Sky, the industry has never been better."

Whenever Cal talked about pornography he called it "the industry," mostly to make himself feel better, I think.

"We're growing like mad. I'm projecting a two hundred and fifty-eight percent increase in revenue this year. I can't get enough girls to work the phone lines. Our Internet revenue is soaring, and our sexual-products catalog is producing unlike ever before."

Cal shoved a piece of bread in his mouth and continued talking.

"And get this. We're in the process of building an actual ranch out in the Nevada desert. You'll be able to go out there and fuck anything you want for a hundred bucks. We're entering a golden age of adult entertainment. America has found its secret little outlet."

"I'm happy for you. And for America."

"Sky, it's time for Tailburger to take advantage of this trend."

"What do you mean?"

"You know what I mean. The industry has gone mainstream. It's getting more and more acceptable to be a part of it. Tailburger can be at the front end of it."

"I can't do that."

"Sure you can. Think of the product exposure. We start with some space on our Internet site and go from there."

At Cal's site, www.lustranch.com, a person could find something to satisfy any fetish. Guy on gal, guy on guy, guy on gecko. You name it, they had it. Although Tailburger catered to the fringe, there was a line I worried about crossing.

"Cal, as tempting as that sounds, I'm not in a position to make that happen."

"Of course you are. You're just afraid to pull the trigger."

"Maybe you're right, but I'm not convinced I *want* to pull the trigger. I mean, Tailburger is still an American institution with a reputation."

"As what? An also-ran in the burger business, selling awful, overfried hockey pucks to misfits and miscreants? You guys could be so much bigger. This could take you up to the majors, Sky."

"Possibly."

"No, not possibly. Definitely. I know I'm right on this one. I see the power of this thing every day. People can't get enough sex. They'd rather fuck than find money. This is your competitive advantage. You think McDonald's is going to touch the industry? Of course not. They can't. They've made their bed with the family-friendly vendors. Now they've got to sleep there."

"Yeah, along with ninety-two percent of the market. I really feel sorry for them."

Pappy arrived with two steaming plates of rigatoni. The fresh peas, prosciutto and light Parmesan sauce made it our favorite and got us to shut up for a few minutes. Cal didn't stop for long.

"Just think about it, Sky. That's all I'm saying."

"I will."

"If it's any consolation, you're not the only one with problems."

"Really? You mean your life's not all sunshine and virgins?"

Cal shook his head no.

"So, what's the matter?"

"You name it. I've got a video dominatrix with repetitive stress disorder, two self-love artists with carpal tunnel syndrome and our ISP keeps crashing."

"What's an ISP?"

"Internet service provider."

"My heart's bleeding for you."

"Lately, I keep having this nightmare that Jenny finds out what I do for a living."

"Eventually she's going to."

"Don't say that."

"Why don't you just tell her? Get it over with."

"I should. I know I should. I've just got to do it, right?"

"Yes. Tell her tonight."

"I'm going to. Tonight's the night. Tonight is it. No more delay. I'm going to pull her aside in the bedroom and say, 'Jen, I'm part of the adult services industry.' It won't be so bad."

"It won't be bad at all."

"This is as good a time as any, right?"

"Absolutely."

"I know."

"You're not going to do it, are you?"

"Not a chance. She'd kill me."

Out in the parking lot, it was difficult not to notice Cal's new car.

"How do you like it?"

"Is that the new Jag?"

"Yes it is. Gorgeous, don't you think?"

"It's okay," I replied halfheartedly, knowing it would piss him off.

"Okay? You're high. You love it."

"Must have sold a lot of jam to get that."

Cal smiled at me.

"You'd be amazed. It's the alternative spread today."

I had mixed feelings about Cal's success. I was happy for him, of course. He was making a ton of dough and hadn't become some raging asshole because of it. He also shared his financial success every chance he got and was the only friend I had who would call up with a spare ticket to the Super Bowl or Final Four. Still, years earlier, he offered me the chance to go into business with him and I said no. At the time, I considered a trip into the void of the porn industry dishonorable and beneath me. I was going to make my mark aboveboard in something legitimate and respectable. Then something unexpected happened. The gap between what he did and what I did narrowed, as sex became the primary sales vehicle in every industry including fast food, particularly for Tailburger. Now the difference between our career paths was as negligible as a bikini top. On or off? In hindsight, the choice seemed obvious.

7

Sunday's SERMON

Muffet Meaney, SERMON's executive director, was known in our business as the "Beef Bitch" for her self-righteous stand on everything involving steers and bovines. Because of the potential lawsuit Tailburger was facing, I was on my way back to Washington, D.C., to try to reason with this woman whom I'd met briefly two years before when we each testified before a Senate subcommittee about the effect of steroids on cattle. She believed they were getting too much, while I naturally held a more permissive view on the topic. To this day, whenever I get a scrawny piece of meat, I think of her.

After my customary fit of claustrophobia, I settled into my seat at the back of the plane (no first class for this executive) and started the Mott the Hoople CD residing in my Sony. "Thank God, they've remastered the classics," I thought as I slipped my headset on and settled in for the two-hour trip. I didn't know why Ethan couldn't appreciate the great music of the Nixon years. It was still speaking to people three decades later.

Baffled by the generation gap, I used the flight time to prepare for the next morning's meeting. Ned, Ted and Fred gave me the Operation Tenderize surveillance dossier to educate me about

Meaney's soft spots. She lived alone, spent most of her time work-ing for SERMON and indulged her taste for voyeurism by watch-ing *America's Most Wanted* and the *Antiques Roadshow*. She voted for Carter in '76 *and* '80, Mondale in '84, Dukakis in '88, wore an Admiral Stockdale T-shirt to a Perot rally in '92, failed to vote in '96 and volunteered for the 2000 ballot recount in Florida. She went to church on Sundays, after which she always stopped at a local TCBY for a plain vanilla, medium-size yogurt with Oreo topping. She also had a vibrator the size of West Virginia and, judging by her battery-buying habits, the necessary libido to use it frequently.

Soon I was in my bed at the Four Seasons, staring at the ceiling in the dark. Meaney was the devil, a complete crank who wouldn't know a fried calamari from a fried Tailburger if it lodged itself in her throat. I hated her kind, an extremist who saw one side of an argument and refused to be swayed by copious amounts of liquor or money. She was an environmental lobbyist until Octo-ber 1987, when her husband, Mark, keeled over at a Tailburger in Chevy Chase, Maryland. Doctors said it was his diet, but I think it was the stock market crash. He took a beating and his heart couldn't handle the strain. Meaney pointed out to the press that Mark was a member of our now defunct "Frequent Fryer" pro-gram and had consumed an estimated five thousand Tailburgers in his lifetime. What she called wrongful death in her lawsuit, we called a good customer.

Since that fateful day in Chevy Chase, she had agitated against us through her not-for-profit group SERMON, the type of radical leftist organization that supported UNICEF, Title IX and PBS. Flooding the airwaves with antimeat propaganda, she brought a religious fervor to the battle against beef. Every time I turned around, I saw her on *The News Hour with Jim Lehrer* barking about the use of pesticides on U.S. feed corn or the unsanitary conditions in American slaughterhouses. What a fraud. I bet her house was a mess.

To many people, she was a hero. To me, she was the epitome of the limousine liberal: a pro-choice, pro–gun control, anti–death penalty, social program–spending pinko with a Volvo station wagon and a house in Bethesda. I mean, didn't she know how to have any fun? The answer was pretty clear as I walked into the lobby of SERMON's headquarters on K Street. A large sign on the wall read, *Meat Is a Murderer.* "Very subtle," I decided. I gave my name to the receptionist and took a seat on a big, burgundy leather sofa. "What a bunch of hypocrites," I thought as I settled comfortably into its generous proportions and picked up a copy of *Eggplant Today*. With my guard down, I was confronted by the opposition.

"That's Pleather, Mr. Thorne."

I looked up from my magazine to see Muffet Meaney dressed smartly in a blue business suit and three-inch heels. I tried not to look at her dynamite legs and curvaceous pelvic region, but was unsuccessful and found my eyes lingering there a little too long. I still wasn't sure what she'd said to me and replied accordingly.

"What?"

"The couch you're sitting on. You probably think it's leather, but it's not. It's Pleather, a synthetic fabric."

"Very lifelike."

"Isn't it? Why don't you come with me to my office, where we'll have some privacy?"

For some reason, her use of the word "privacy" got me thinking the wrong kind of thoughts. As I followed her through a maze of cubicles, I couldn't help but wonder what it was about this woman that was giving me such an enormous woody. Maybe it was the heels or the way she spoke to me or the fact that I hadn't had sex in eight months. I didn't know. But whatever it was, it was powerful and it would be damn near impossible to be an effective advocate for Tailburger if I didn't get my longings under control quickly.

My enemy stared at me from behind a large, mahogany desk. What a boondoggle. The leaders of these nonprofits always had offices the size of aircraft carriers. Yet here they were sucking tax dollars out of the economy with their free land and their precious charitable and educational purposes. What a racket.

"Ms. Meaney."

"Call me Muffet."

"Okay. Then call me Sky."

"All right."

"Muffet, I'm not going to hedge. From what I understand, you are currently considering a class action lawsuit, in conjunction with the various state attorneys general, against Tailburger and our fellow competitors."

"We're not considering it, Sky. We're doing it. And don't ask me why, because you know damn well why."

"I *don't* know why. Please. Enlighten me."

I shifted uncomfortably in my seat and prepared for her verbal assault.

"Do you have any idea how many people die every year from heart attacks in this country?"

"I know it's a fair number. All those poor smokers."

"It's not just the smokers, Sky. It's the hardworking men and women who shovel one fried Tailburger after another down their throats until their cholesterol levels cause coronary meltdowns. Then the U.S. government and its citizens pay to nurse the survivors back to health through the various Medicare and Medicaid programs. It's time companies like Tailburger pay their fair share."

"Medicare and Medicaid are for the old and the destitute."

"Who do you think eats your burgers?"

"Can we come back from la la land for a second here? First of all, there is no scientific evidence that links beef to heart disease. Second, study after study shows that lean red meat is a nutritionally valuable part of any healthy diet."

"That's right. *Lean* red meat. Those studies don't say anything about deep-fried fatty pieces of cow carcass with five spoonfuls of mayonnaise on them. Do you have any idea how many grams of fat are in a Tailpipe Deluxe?"

"I honestly don't."

"Well, let me tell you. A hundred and twenty-four grams. And that's just the burger. Add a serving of your Enormofries and the total goes to nearly two hundred and forty-five grams of fat, most of it saturated. That's four days' worth of the recommended daily allowance for fat intake. And you want to sit there and tell me that your products are not causing heart disease?"

"What about our low-calorie option, the Halfpipe?"

"For your information, the Halfpipe is a deceptively named product. It's got ninety percent of the fat of the Tailpipe and seventy-five percent of the calories. Not what you'd call a heart-smart choice."

"Well, *hell,* we put a seaweed burger on the menu two years ago and I think we sold forty-three of them across the country. We're just giving people what they want. Is that a crime? I can't think of anything that doesn't cause ticker trouble. You can't hold us liable."

"Oh, yes we can. And we will."

Muffet Meaney was, in my son Ethan's vernacular, a hottie. About five feet four inches tall with a 36C chest, she had curves in all the right places and a face that reminded me of a young Marlo Thomas. Here I was trying to be a hard-ass negotiator and all I could think about was getting intimate with her. "Get a grip," I told myself as she rambled on about quadruple bypass surgery and artery blockages. There was sure as hell no problem with my blood flow. I was toast.

"What about settlement negotiations?" I asked.

"We'll listen to any serious settlement offer that's made."

"What kind of dollars are we talking?"

"The kind of dollars that Tailburger can't even come close to putting on the table. You're just a tadpole in this deal. We're going after the big fish. Once McDonald's and Burger King come to the table, we'll let you know what your share is going to be."

"So what you're saying is that all we can do right now is to sit on the sideline and wait."

"Basically."

"What if we wanted to cut our own deal and get out early?"

"You'd have to come up with something pretty attractive, but I'd be willing to listen."

Now I had met the real enemy and it wasn't Muffet—it was me. All of our arguing had created some bizarre sexual tension between us. Despite my natural frustration at the unenviable position I found Tailburger in, I couldn't help what came out of my mouth next.

"Would you also be willing to have dinner with me tonight?"

Muffet looked at me with some surprise and then smiled ever so slightly.

"I don't think that's a good idea."

"C'mon. You've got to eat."

"This would be strictly on a professional basis, right?"

"Well, not exactly."

Muffet smiled a bit more broadly.

"Sky, let me make sure of something before I agree to this. You don't think you can wine and dine this situation away?"

"Of course not."

Muffet hesitated and took a long look at me.

"I guess sharing a meal wouldn't be against the rules."

The potential repercussions of dating the opposition didn't occur to me right then. The moment she said yes, my imagination wandered until all I could picture was the two of us naked and alone on a bed of rose petals—a psychic remnant from watching *American Beauty* one too many times.

Later that night we met at Ristorante Piccolo, a tiny hideaway on 31st Street just off of M in Georgetown. The younger set surrounding us made me feel like a college boy who couldn't wait to get his date back to the dorm room. After a few drinks, her guard came down.

"Some days I wish I wasn't fighting against the beef industry."

"Why do you say that? You're pretty good at it."

"Mostly because of Mark. (Pause) If he hadn't died, I never would've gotten involved with SERMON. I guess I still miss him and work is a constant reminder he's gone."

"I know how you feel. I lost my wife back in '94."

"I didn't know that. I'm sorry."

"It's okay."

"Were you married long?"

"Ten years."

"That's how long I was with Mark. Didn't the house seem so empty?"

"Well, in my case, it was already empty."

"It was?"

"See she wasn't technically my wife at the time she died."

"No?"

"No. Not technically. (Pause) We were sort of divorced."

"I see."

"And she was sort of married to another guy."

"Sort of?"

"Yes. (Pause) To *Triperrr*. Isn't that an awful name?"

"I don't care for it."

"Me neither. I hate it. (Pause) Anyway, I still loved her. (Pause) A lot."

"It hurts, doesn't it?"

I nodded.

"I think about Mark every single day. Everyone said time would make it better, but it hasn't. In some ways, it's gotten worse. I find myself feeling lonely more often than I like to admit. (Pause) Do you think the pain ever just goes away for good?"

"No . . ."

Muffet was disappointed by the first part of my answer.

". . . but I think you'll be happy again."

"I hope so."

I'd misjudged Muffet Meaney. She wasn't the row of razor wire I'd observed from a distance. She was more like a flower—a sensitive, intelligent, thoughtful, caring, woman who only needed sunlight, some water and a spray or two of Miracle-Gro. She was vul-ner-a-ble, and just like me, she'd loved and lost.

Muffet and I made eyes at each other the rest of the night (except when I was outside smoking Commodores) and successfully forgot about our earlier meeting. Though the evening was devoid of rose petals, I knew that, upon kissing her good night, I had to see her again.

8

Long Live the King

BACK IN ROCHESTER

Two days after I returned to Rochester from D.C., my big brother, King, arrived unannounced. I found him on my front stoop with his head resting on a beat-to-shit backpack, the only piece of luggage in sight. A longtime fan of the Hawaiian shirt, he looked and smelled like he'd been on tour with Jimmy Buffett for the past three years. Although he was thin and tan, his angular face was badly weathered by the sun. This, however, didn't stop him from pointing out *my* physical failings.

"There's my baby brother. My word, you look awful."

King hugged me before I could voice my objection to the act.

"What are you doing here?" I asked, grimacing in the grip of my pungent sibling while trying not to sound too inhospitable.

"You invited me."

"I know, but your job with FARC seemed to be going so well, I guess I didn't expect to see you so soon. What happened with El Jefe?"

"I was working as his bodyguard and he sort of got shot on my watch, so I quit."

"You quit?"

"Fled might be a more accurate word."

"They chased you? Are you all right?"

"Of course. I'm fine."

"Did they try and kill you?"

"Only for a while. Right until they ran out of ammunition actually."

"My God, King. C'mon inside," I said, opening the front door.

To say my brother had personal issues was a bit of an understatement, like saying Michael Jordan was a decent basketball player. Still, as hard as I tried, I could never stay mad at him. There's something undeniably winning about a stark raving mad lunatic. I couldn't quite put my finger on it, but King clearly qualified.

"Can I stay with you for a while?"

"Of course you can. (Pause) Those maniacs aren't still chasing you, are they?"

"Highly unlikely."

"This is not going to endanger my life?"

"Doubtful. Hey, they never got Rushdie, did they?"

By drifting all over the world, both literally and figuratively, on various political crusades and, alternatively, on luxury cruise lines, King had picked up bits and pieces of various Western and Eastern philosophies which he had blended together to form his life view. This would have been more than acceptable had he not insisted on serving this indigestible smorgasbord to every person he encountered, including his own brother.

"Wow. I hate to say it, Sky, but the corporate life and all those Tailburgers with cheese have taken a huge toll on you."

King and I stood in the kitchen now, sizing each other up after several years of separation.

"You used to be the pretty one, but I'm afraid the mantle has been passed to your big bro."

King decided to inventory the refrigerator.

"Look at all these processed meats. Do you have any idea what the sodium content is in this stuff? Where are the fruits and veggies?"

"There's ketchup in there," I said defensively.

King's idea of healthy eating at this point in his life (subject to change at any time) was anything made of soy. His idea of healthy living (also subject to change at any time) was Qigong.

"After I left Carnival, I spent some time with the Falun Gong in Beijing and I'm telling you, those people have life figured out. Are you familiar with Qigong?"

"Chee koong? No."

"Well, it's this series of meditation exercises that channel your chi."

"My chee?"

"Your fundamental energy. See, Falun Gong blends the best parts of Taoism, Buddhism and Qigong together. It's like a spiritual juicer, but without all the cleanup. You've got to try it."

"My chee is just fine, thank you. And I have no interest in having my spirit juiced."

"Hear me out. See there's this orblike miniature of the universe located in your abdomen called the Falun. And these exercises bring positive energy to the Falun, which improves your health and morality."

"All that's going on in my abdomen, huh? Hard to believe there's room, considering that huge cheesesteak I had at lunch."

"I think this could work for you."

"I think you're out of your fucking mind."

"We've just got to harness the unseen natural forces in your body."

"King, you've just described a fart. Leave it to the Chinese to build a philosophy around gas."

"There are Qigong masters who can cure cancer with a jolt from their fingertips."

"You've obviously spent a few too many days baking on the Aloha deck."

"Will you at least try this?"

"No way. Why the hell should I try this?"

"To get in better shape. Physically and mentally. Do you plan on being alone the rest of your life?"

King's question triggered thoughts of Muffet Meaney, and immediately I reconsidered.

"If I try this, will it get you to shut up?"

"For a short time," King said, smiling.

"Just promise me I won't end up like one of those freaks you see in the park karate chopping invisible people."

"I promise."

The thought that I could improve my morality by doing a series of exercises on a regular basis was laughable and, worse, irrational, like a belief in an all-knowing God. Still it was tempting to accept the premise and quietly work toward the kind of soul cleansing that seemed so necessary and elusive to me on the off chance it was true. I agreed to start that afternoon.

"Okay. Now the first thing you have to understand is that there are eight vessels that store the chi in your body. These are called Qi Jing Ba Mai."

"All right. Eight vessels."

"Yes, but they've got a number of different names. Some call them the miraculous meridians. Some call them the homeostatic meridians. Some call them the eight psychic channels."

"Wait. Is Dionne Warwick involved with this stuff?"

"No. Dionne Warwick has nothing to do with this. Now listen to me. It's important that you understand this."

King was already getting frustrated with his student.

"You've got your governing vessel, also known as Du Mai, your conception vessel, also known as Ren Mai, your thrusting vessel . . ."

"I know where that one's located," I said, smiling.

King didn't find me amusing.

". . . also known as Chong Mai. Your girdle vessel, also known as Dai Mai. Your yin heel vessel, also known as Yin qiao Mai. Your . . ."

"Let me guess. Your *yang* heel vessel?"

"That's right."

"Martial arts always comes down to the yin and the yang. I remember that from those kung fu movies."

"Congratulations. Your years with David Carradine weren't wasted. So anyway, getting back to the point. There are the six vessels I've named as well the yin linking and yang linking vessels. That makes eight."

"Is there a point to all of this?"

"Yes. These vessels protect the various organs in your body by guarding against the evil chi."

"I thought chee was good."

"Usually it is. But there are also bad kinds of chi. The eight psychic channels guard against these intruders."

"King, this is ridiculously complicated. Can we just start?"

"All right. I'll teach you as we go along."

King went to his backpack and pulled out a piece of wood ten inches in length.

"We're going to start with what's called the sitting stage."

"What's the stick for?"

"This is not a stick," King said, carefully holding his prized possession. "This is my Taiji ruler. You're going to use it to meditate. Sit down on the floor."

I slowly lowered myself to the carpeting in my living room and waited for further instructions.

"Take the ruler and hold it in front of you."

"Okay. There it is," I said, doing as told.

"Now, focus on the center of the ruler. Empty your head of all thoughts."

"That won't take long."

"Focus! Breathe deeply and slowly."

My spine popped in two places as I attempted to fill my tobacco-racked lungs.

"Ooh, that hurts a bit."

"Shhh. Quiet the voice inside of you. Let the ruler absorb your negativity."

"I'm trying!"

King left me alone for the next two hours while I stared at that stupid ruler. Maybe reaching a state of calm was the idea, but I didn't approach that lofty goal in my first session. Instead, I felt the anger of a thousand years surging through my miraculous meridians. Every slight and snub I'd ever experienced in my life. Every rejection and failure. The very things I should have expunged, I had let lie dormant deep below the surface of my self, creating my own unending reservoir of evil chee. It sickened me to know it was inside my body, but it hardly surprised me. I'd been burying things there for a long time.

9

Hitch

DALLAS, TEXAS

To begin our battle against SERMON and its impending lawsuit, the Link sent me south to see Traylor Hitch, head of the aforementioned National Cattlemen's Meat Stampede, the largest organization of cattle farmers in the country. The Stampede was a powerful lobbying force and a longtime ally of Tailburger, and Hitch and the Link were old friends, sharing a deep love of military history, Matthew Brady photographs and NRA trivia.

Traylor Hitch was a farm boy from the hills of west Texas with a belt buckle the size of a waffle iron, cobra-skin boots, a bolo tie, a pickup truck with two gun racks and a license plate that read COONHNTR. Despite the vanity tag, Hitch wasn't an overt racist. He actually shot raccoons for sport and had won several awards for this disturbing skill.

Hitch's biggest accomplishment or brainchild, if you pardon the term, during his time at the Stampede was the erection of enormous billboards reading, *EAT MEAT*, all over America's interstates. For that alone, he'd been elected president for three successive ten-year terms. Other than that, there wasn't much to tell. Hitch hated vegetarians, *Dateline NBC* and women other than his mama, and was convinced that Ted Kennedy ran the

New York Times editorial page from an underground cabana on Martha's Vineyard.

Armed with my flight information, Hitch picked me up at DFW a half hour late. Having left his truck at home for the day, he wheeled his late-model turquoise Cadillac, its hood adorned with two steer horns, through Irving traffic and the sweltering heat on our way to his office in downtown Dallas.

"Damn good to see you, Sky. What's it been, son? Two or three years?"

"At least."

"Now wait, it's all comin' back to old Hitch. I think I remember. I do. I do remember. You came and spoke at the Cattlemen's convention in Austin. Remember that? We went out afterward and you tried to eat that hundred-and-six-ounce rib eye just so you could get your name on the wall at Tilley's Char-B-Q. What a hoot."

"Well, actually Hitch, if I remember it correctly, you threatened to get me fired if I didn't order *and* eat the entire thing."

"I guess that's right. You ended up gettin' sick all over the waitress. Pretty little thing. That was a real hoot I'll tell ya."

"I swallowed a bone, Hitch. I nearly died that night."

"I guess that's right. Still, you gotta admit it was fun."

Hitch fidgeted with his bolo tie before continuing.

"Anyhoo, let's talk about this God-blasted SERMON suit. That Muffet Meaney has been a burr in our collective buttocks for as long as I can remember."

"She's got the media all stirred up on this, Hitch. We need the Stampede to commit its resources to the cause."

"She's bluffin', Sky. She won't bring the suit. All hat, no cattle."

"I don't think so."

"What we need to do, Sky, is to buy up one of the major networks so we can stop the flow of lefty spew that's being upchucked all over America. Look at the anchormen, for the love of God. Peter Jennings? The guy's from Canada, a country that hasn't produced a decent piece of meat in its entire sorry history. Yet he's up there on the squawk box every night telling U.S. citizens what's wrong with our food safety. He needs to go back to Moosejaw. And Brokaw? You'd expect a bit of loyalty from a guy born in South Dakota, but noooooo. He has to maintain his precious journalistic integrity and report the news regardless of content. It makes you want to cry in your mama's lap."

"What about Dan Rather? He's from Texas."

"Don't get me started on Rather. We lost that boy to the lefties halfway through Iran Contra. Just another casualty as I see it."

Hitch ran the Stampede from the third floor of the Sixth Floor Museum building in downtown Dallas, the same brick structure from which Lee Harvey Oswald fired his fatal shots on November 22, 1963.

"Gives me a good feeling every time I come to work, Sky."

"I bet."

We settled into his office, where a desk the size of a Buick sat with six phones spread out across it. On the wall, assorted victims of Hitch's shotgun stared forlornly out into space. The furniture, well-worn and made of steer hide, sat quietly amidst several dying plants and a slew of black-and-white photographs showing Hitch with various luminaries including Newt Gingrich, Ralph Reed, George W. Bush and the San Diego Chicken. There was also a color picture of Hitch with the Swedish Bikini Team in front of his speedboat, *Little Miss Budweiser.*

The Stampede collected dues from cattlemen across the country and acted as a representative body, lobbying on their behalf and promoting all things related to the consumption of beef and beef by-products. It also used its funds to support the Corral Foundation, a research and development organization committed mainly to trumping up bogus scientific studies about the health benefits of red meat.

"Let me tell you what's on the grill, Sky. There's a study being done right now at the foundation that will prove, once and for all, that red meat, consumed in massive quantities, cures most forms of cancer."

"Hitch, who's going to believe that?"

"Everybody'll believe it. People'll believe anything that comes out in a study. You tell 'em it's good to wash their faces in butter and by God, there's a run on Land O Lakes the next day."

"But what if it turns out this red-meat cancer-cure theory isn't true?"

"Bite your tongue, son. Show me a study that says otherwise."

"Hitch, with all due respect, another study from the foundation is not going to stop this SERMON suit from going forward. We'll get positive press on it for a few days, maybe a shot on *Good Morning America,* and then it'll be forgotten like every other study ever done. We need to work together to find a long-term solution. This is serious business. We're talking about Tailburger's bottom line."

Hitch sensed the lessening of my patience.

"Now there's no need to get hostile with old Hitch here. I've got other ideas. You're no doubt familiar with my 'Eat Meat' billboards?"

I rolled my eyes.

"Of course. What American driver isn't?"

"Well, I've been working on a new campaign. All by myself. Sort of in secret. You want to hear it?"

"Sure," I replied without the slightest enthusiasm.

"Well, you know that 'Got Milk?' slogan?"

"Yes. I've seen it."

"I do a twist on it. Are you ready?"

"Fire away."

Hitch framed my face with his fingers.

"Picture the whole damn country plastered with billboards saying, 'Got Meat?'"

"That's it?"

"Yeah, that's it. It's perfect. What's wrong with it?"

"I don't know. Nothing, I guess. I'm just not sure the slogan translates as well with our product. Nobody ever reached for a strip steak after eating a chocolate brownie."

"I admit it needs a little work. But it's most of the way there. Between the new study and the new slogan we're gonna turn the tide, Sky. SERMON will be too afraid to fuck with us."

"That's not going to do it, Hitch. Together, we need to put pressure on the various attorneys general around the country to keep them from signing on to the lawsuit. Political pressure on them, as well as pressure on certain members of the House, is the only way to prevent a financial catastrophe."

"Sky, you know we don't have the financial resources we used to have. Membership is down, which means less money for us to take on these kinds of fights. I'll do what I can, but times are tough. Cattle farmers are going under left and right. Per capita consumption of beef is at an all-time low, and every time I turn around somebody new is taking a potshot at red meat. Hell, there was a study the other day that said it could make you impotent. Now that dog don't hunt. Just ask my six kids."

"Hitch, I know things are looking a bit bleak right now, but we need the Stampede's help. Frank is counting on you and so am I. Are you in this fight or not?"

Hitch stood up from his couch and walked slowly across the room to a window looking out on Dealey Plaza. He ran a hand through the few remaining strands of hair left on his head and let out an audible sigh.

"Ever feel like your best days are behind you, Sky?"

"Sometimes. Yes."

"You wouldn't recall it as well as I do, but there was a time when we called the shots. Back in the '70s, the beef industry was king. It was a glorious ride. Per capita consumption hit a hundred pounds one year. Goddamn we were flying high. My 'Eat Meat' slogan was electrifying highways. Jimmy Buffett came out with *Cheeseburger in Paradise*. American housewives were scarfing up every box of Hamburger Helper they could find. Meat equaled success. Do you remember?"

I nodded at Hitch and let him ramble on.

"It was simple. The ultimate status symbol was a steak on your table at night. Chicken was for border wetbacks who couldn't afford a decent meal. Tuna was something your kids ate at lunch. Hot dogs only came out at ball games. Pasta was for the Mafia. Turkey was for Thanksgiving. Duck for Christmas. But at certain times and places, all over this country, only American red meat would do. Family picnics, company outings, backyard barbecues. No questions asked. What happened, Sky?"

"I don't know. I guess we got fat."

"Fat and happy, Sky. Fat and happy. What's so awful about that?"

"Nothing."

"You're goddamn right. Absolutely nothing."

Hitch turned away from me and stared back out the window. The late-afternoon sun beat down on the streets of Dallas and cast a shadow across the faded wall of his office.

"My daddy gave me one piece of advice on his deathbed. (Pause) Do you know what it was?"

"Find a forgiving woman?"

"No. He said, 'Tell the truth, Traylor, and you'll always be happy. Just tell the truth.'"

"That's good advice. I bet you'd like to thank him."

"Hell, no. I'd like to kill him. That advice has been haunting me ever since the sick buzzard kicked off. Do you have any idea how hard it is to always tell the truth? That's the damn recipe for misery. Every time we roll out one of these bogus studies, I cringe, knowing the old man is staring down on me from the great beyond."

Hitch turned away from the window and looked directly at me.

"Hitch, you have *nothing* to feel bad about. Believe me, the Stampede hasn't cornered the market on shady science. Those gut-

tersnipes at SERMON put out false information about our industry every week. We have to band together and battle back. We've
got to restore beef to its rightful place as the king of meats!"

"Maybe you're right, son."

"Of course I'm right. This is our red scare. Don't go soft on me
now, Hitch."

The key to successful fishing is picking the right bait. I figured a
veiled reference to Communism would do the trick.

"Soft? Are you calling me soft? Goddamnit, there isn't a soft
bone in my body! Tell Frank he can count me and the Stampede in
on this fight!"

"Are you serious?"

"Would a mule skip a kickin' contest? I'm serious as a summer
drought."

"That's great."

Hitch, suddenly energized, slowly let a smile come across his
face.

"We're gonna whup some ass, son."

"There's no acceptable alternative."

"Whaddya say we go get a burger?"

"That would hit the spot."

Hitch slapped me on the back and out we went into the waiting
warmth and humidity.

"Do you know how many people the Dallas Po-lice shot last
year?"

"No."

"Forty-eight. That's down from seventy-five the year before.
And a hundred and twenty the year before that. (Pause) It's a
damn shame."

10

Soft Batch Burgers

TAILBURGER HEADQUARTERS

Jelloteous Junderstack's heart condition flared up during a game in Sacramento, and suddenly a major piece of Tailburger's impending Torture campaign was in jeopardy. No good news had ever come from the 2:00 A.M. airing of ESPN's *Sportscenter,* and this was no exception. I walked into headquarters, hat in hand. The Link didn't take bad news well.

"Belgians in body bags don't sell burgers, Thorne."

"I know that, Frank. I'm talking with Junderstack's doctor this afternoon to see how serious it is."

"I hated this Torture campaign from the start. I have half a mind to pull the plug right now."

"Frank, you can't do that. We've already invested a ton of time and money. Look, we'll work up a supplemental campaign to buy some time and scout a replacement player. If something happens to Jelloteous, we'll just reshoot the ads and the video, and push the Torture launch back a month."

"Did you put a death clause in that clod's contract? I don't want to pay one red cent to some freakish Eurostiff. If he's in a casket, he's seen his last dime."

"I'll have to check the wording, Frank. If I recall, Satan Man-chow sought some concessions in that area."

Translation: he took me to the cleaners.

"Well, what's this supplemental campaign you're talking about?"

"We're working on it right now."

"What's this 'we're' bullshit? What are *you* doing?"

I had done nothing at this point.

"I'm helping to fine-tune the campaign. It's not exactly fully developed."

"Aw shit, Thorne! Do we have something or not?"

"Yes. Yes we do."

"Good. Let me hear it."

I was afraid he was going to say that, but giving the Link what he wanted wasn't hard.

"Okay. Picture a group of high school girls."

"Got it. Are they in bikinis?"

"Exactly. Very scantily clad. In fact, nothing but thongs."

"Good. Skin sells burgers. Just make sure there aren't any fat ones. Use that agency that specializes in anorexics."

"Right. So anyway we've got these young girls in bikinis riding in a convoy of Jeeps. A red one. A blue one and a yellow one. All on their way to the beach."

"I can see it. Keep going."

"They pull onto the beach and they're all eating Tailburgers, and our new jingle is playing in the background."

"Sing it for me."

"Trust me, it's good."

"Sing it for me."

"Do you think that's necessary?"

"Sing the goddamn song or I'll kick your ass from here to Hat-tiesburg."

"Okay. It's got a real heavy bass bottom to it. Sort of a Sam and

Dave knockoff. Screaming organs, the whole deal. 'Gotta get some tail. Gotta get some tail. Gotta get some Tailburgers.'"

"Good. Go on."

"So the song's building when suddenly an armada of surfer stud boys, thirty or forty of them, come surfing in from the ocean."

"Are they built?"

"They're monsters. Real steroid abusers, straight from our heavy users profile. And when they see these girls with the Tailburgers, they come riding in on the waves to get some tail."

"I love it! It's perfect! Why do we even need Junderboob? Cut him loose."

"But, Frank, he's a central part of the Torture campaign. Plus, we do have a contract with him."

"What about the morals clause? You know he's been bangin' half the Laker girls. That ought to be enough to get us out."

"Satan insisted we remove the morals clause."

"That bastard."

The Link could have ended the Torture campaign right then and there, but he didn't. He knew it was my baby, that I would succeed or fail along with it, and that I had more to lose than he did. If my pet project didn't propel Tailburger's market share up to a full 5 percent of the fast-food industry, I was gone. And at some level, the Link didn't want to see that.

"I need to run one more thing by you."

"Uh-oh. What now?" I wondered as the Link shut the door to his office.

"Thorne, I know I've got you under a lot of pressure to improve sales."

"Nothing I can't handle," I said, wanting to project confidence.

"I'm sure. But I'd never leave you out there twisting in the wind."

"That sentiment is appreciated, Frank."

Was this going to be a genuinely kind gesture on the part of the

Link? Devoid of self-interest? Unprecedented. Maybe the man had a heart after all.

"So anyway, I've come up with a new way to light the sales mortar. Guaranteed. Just in case this whole Torture thing doesn't go so well."

"What is it?" I replied optimistically, hoping to hear something come out of his mouth that, for once, made sense.

"Do you know who Ralph Nader is?"

"Sure. From the Green party. The guy who ran for president."

"No. Not that guy. I'm talking about the consumer rights advocate."

"It's the same guy."

"No, it's not."

"I'm certain it is."

"It is?"

"Yes."

"Well, whatever. (Pause) Do you remember his book *Unsafe at Any Speed*? The one about the Corvair?"

The Link didn't give me a chance to respond.

"Actually, let me ask you another question. Do you like chocolate chip cookies?"

Where the Link was going with all of this was beyond me.

"Sure. Who doesn't?"

"And how do you like those cookies? Real gooey in the middle? Am I right?"

"I plead guilty."

"Do you know what makes 'em soft?"

"They're undercooked."

"Exactly. Which is just what I want to do with our burgers. From now on, they're going to be crunchy on the outside and one big mushball in the middle. We've got to get back to what makes a Tailburger so good."

"Frank, we're not talking about chocolate chip cookies here. We're talking about raw meat. The risk is different."

"No, it's not. Salmonella poisoning from the eggs in the cookie dough is every bit as big a danger as the E. coli bacteria. Maybe bigger."

Logical progressions were not the Link's thing, but he was on a roll.

"What about federal law? It says we have to cook every patty until the temperature inside hits a hundred and fifty-nine degrees Fahrenheit."

"That's where our friend Mr. Nader comes in. Do you know what he did? He found the smoking gun on the Corvair. There was this internal GM memorandum that said the cost of installing a three-dollar-and-fifty-cent part over the manufacturing lifetime of the automobile would be more expensive than paying for the deaths and subsequent lawsuits that resulted from the failure to install it. It was a business decision. Don't you understand? It's the same thing for us. Undercooking our burgers is a business decision. The increase in sales will more than cover any liability costs."

"Are you crazy? That was one of the biggest mistakes in the history of GM!" I protested, flabbergasted by my boss's stupidity. "It cost them millions in bad publicity alone."

"Yes, but here's the difference. We're not going to get caught. We've never lost a kid to E. coli, and we're never going to a lose a kid to E. coli. You know why . . . ?"

I slowly shook my head.

". . . I'll tell you why. Because the whole thing is a public scare campaign. I don't even believe E. coli exists."

Any previous notion I was dealing with a human being evaporated as the Link continued to talk.

"Don't you get it? Even in a worst-case scenario, the cost of a lawsuit or settlement will be less than the increase in sales. It's a business decision. Plain and simple. Pure economics."

"Why don't we get irradiated beef to protect ourselves? The USDA approved it last year."

"I know that, but have you ever tasted irradiated beef?"

"Yes. And I couldn't tell the difference."

"Well, I could. My hamburger tasted like a microwaved burrito. Plus I don't like the whole idea of running our meat under those gamma rays or whatever the hell they are. Some kid in Omaha will go radioactive on us and start glowing like the local power plant. Then we'll really have problems."

"Irradiation doesn't make the meat radioactive."

"I just don't think the process has been tested enough."

"They've been testing it for years. The Centers for Disease Control and Prevention fully endorses it."

"What do those fools know? You ever see the movie *Outbreak*? They couldn't control one monkey."

By the blank look on my face, the Link knew I wasn't on board with his idea.

"Now don't get squirrelly on me, Thorne. I'm trying to help you, but you need to help yourself by taking this news to the front."

Taking news to the front meant telling our managers and franchise owners to change standard operating procedure. Morally objectionable? Yes. Difficult to do? No. Not since the Link instituted his annual "Chain of Command" retreats. Held at a backwoods compound in Idaho next to what the Link referred to as Reverend Moon's Rolls-Royce dealership, these sessions qualified as low-grade brainwashing for all personnel and assured the Link that his orders would be followed.

"No more kowtowing to special interests anymore, Thorne. We're going to take some calculated risks and help save your job. Can't you see that?"

"Sure, I can see it, Frank."

All I could see was us, and in particular, me, ordering others to break the law. Of course, it wasn't worth raising the ethical implications with the Link because I knew it would be a nonstarter. The man felt no guilt when it came to business. "When you've got the will of the maker on your side," he once told me, "you throw out the rule book." This wasn't a direct quote from Honest Abe but, according to the Link, a modern interpretation. Religion was now used if expedient, and invoking the Lord's name had become an all-purpose salve for the wounds inflicted by our company's moral transgressions. Across the top of our corporate stationery it read, *GOD IS A TAILBURGER FANATIC.* I wasn't sure who had surveyed him, but what the hell; it certainly had panache.

I went home, poured myself an Ultra Slim-Fast and put on Van Morrison's *Back on Top,* the perfect panacea for my sorry condition, since every song was about a man in transition or at a crossroads or . . . well, whatever they were about, they were pretty damn introspective, which is just what I needed. Deep into the pathos of the fifth track was the last time I expected Annette McNabnay to call me.

"This is Sky."

"Sky, it's Annette."

"Annette?"

"Annette McNabnay, from the board."

"Annette, of course. How are you?"

Ordinarily Mayor Annette McNabnay, my fellow Tailburger director, would have referred to herself by her full name. And her tone of voice would have been cordial but businesslike, and very calm. For some unknown reason, she was nervous.

"Sky, I was wondering if you'd like to tour City Hall sometime?"

"Oh, Annette, that's awful nice of you to ask, but I did that way back in elementary school. I assume it hasn't changed too much."

"Well, probably not, but perhaps I could show you some things you've never seen before."

There was nothing overly coquettish or come-hither in her voice.

"I doubt it. We walked all over that place. I remember it like yesterday. My teacher, Mrs. Richardson, was . . ."

"Sky, I'm trying to ask you out in a subtle and clever way, but I'm failing miserably."

"Oh," I said. Now I felt like an idiot. I wasn't sure how to respond.

The thought of going on a date with Mayor McNabnay had significant appeal. For starters, I'd never gone out with a mayor. Walking around with her, I'd be the cobeneficiary of all the adulation she received, as well as lots of free stuff like frozen yogurts and lapel pins, two things you could never have enough of.

If this had been the old Sky, I would have accepted Annette's invitation immediately. Why not? I was a man. She was a mayor. You can't fight biology. But I couldn't say yes. I was smitten with Muffet. And for me, that was enough.

"Annette, I'm very flattered, but I'm sort of getting involved with someone right now, and I don't think it would be fair to her."

I was amazed by the words running off my tongue, but it had been years since I'd been physically attracted to someone the way I was with Muffet Meaney.

"I see. Well, that's all right. I understand. I thought it might be fun. Maybe another time."

"Yeah, sure. I mean, I'm sure it would be fun. I just . . . well . . . you understand."

"I do. I'll see you at the next meeting."

"Right. I'll see you then. I'm sorry, Annette."

"Good-bye, Sky."

I pressed the End button on my Motorola and momentarily questioned my refusal. Annette was a beautiful, accomplished woman who apparently saw something in me, and here I'd turned her away. Was I acting too hastily? I didn't know what, if anything, would happen with Muffet. In the back of my mind, I thought she might be the woman who would help me finally get over Jess, my beloved, but decidedly deceased, ex-wife, but I didn't know that for certain. Still, the thought of her made my knees weak, and that had to be a good sign. I'd grown tired of chasing a ghost. And so it was settled. No Annette.

11

East Meets West

With my unpredictable work schedule, King quickly became frustrated about my Qigong training and felt the need to speed my progress along by alternative means. When I got home from work the next day, I found a kitchen full of carob-flavored soy milk, tempeh hot dogs, tofu cereal and other unidentifiable soybean products.

"What the hell is all this crap?"

"This crap is part of the road to wellness," King informed me.

I opened the freezer and saw what appeared to be hamburger patties.

"Well, at least you had the good sense to get burgers."

"Those are soy burgers."

"I should've known. (Pause) How do they taste? And break it to me gently."

"Awful at first, but you'll grow to tolerate it."

"I won't grow to love it?"

"No. (Pause) Look what else I've got for you."

King moved toward the counter and pulled a small, plastic-wrapped box from a brown grocery bag.

"What's that?"

"It's Nicorette, that nicotine gum you see on TV. It'll help you quit smoking."

"What if I don't want to quit smoking?"

"Think about Sophia. Don't you want to dance at your own daughter's wedding?"

"I'd love to dance at her wedding. I just don't want to pay for it. Cigarettes may get me out of that obligation."

"All right, funny guy, just try it. If it doesn't work, we'll get you the patch. C'mon, it's minty and good," King teased while waving the box.

"Okay, I'll try it. But only because I heard the patch can kill you."

"True, if administered improperly. It's very, very rare. Kills mostly blind people who forget they've got a few stuck on already."

"I'll stick to the gum, thank you. What happened to Qigong? I thought that was going to cure me of everything."

"It will. But it takes a while to kick in."

"How long?"

"Well, at the rate you're going, it'll be two years before you feel your chi and five years before you believe it. In the meantime, we've got to get you some good old-fashioned pharmaceuticals."

"I don't need any damn medication. I'm fine. Can't we speed up my chee?"

"No. Not with your schedule. Your chi gets flabby if you don't work on it."

"Then it'll look like the rest of my body, all right? Give me a break."

"Sky, I've made a list of the dangerous health conditions we have to attack, but you've got to be willing to make changes. Are you willing?"

"No, I'm not willing. I know I'm not in Olympic shape, but fortunately I don't have a decathlon next week. Why should I make any changes?"

"Your hair's thinning pretty rapidly, isn't it?"

"Kind of. So what?"

"Then you need Follicor. It's a pill that suppresses your testosterone level and lets you keep the hair you've got."

"What about the side effects?"

"You may experience nausea, dry mouth, dizziness, hallucinations, the usual stuff. Oh, also, a small number of men experience erectile dysfunction. Pecker problems basically."

"So I'll have my hair, but no hard-on? What good does that do me? No thanks."

"The percentage of men who become impotent is like two. I'm sure you won't be part of that group. Plus, Follicor is also supposed to shrink your prostate."

"I don't have a prostate problem."

"Oh, no? How many times are you up at night to whiz? Four is my guess."

"Only three," I replied, resentful that he'd been even close to correct about something so personal.

"As I suspected, you've got a prostate problem. That gland's gettin' bigger and bigger, day by day. Pretty soon it'll be the size of a grapefruit."

"Go to hell!"

"You seem a bit moody to me as well."

"Do I? It's probably my grapefruit-sized prostate pressing on my bladder."

"The doctor can prescribe Xanax or maybe Prozac. That'll even you out. Maybe Zoloft."

"I don't need to be evened out. I like being odd."

"See. It may be worse than I thought."

"Are you done?"

"No. We've got to do something about that weight problem of yours. I'm thinking fen-phen tablets."

"Weren't those banned for causing aortic valve ruptures?"

"Yes, but I know a guy who can still get them. Sometimes

you've got to go the illegal route to get results. I learned that from El Jefe."

"Oh, great. And I suppose El Jefe was a real health nut."

"Not really. His diet consisted entirely of boar's feet and cocaine, but boy did he love to jog."

"Great. Very inspiring. Look, let's just do the chee koong training and forget about all these pills."

"Okay, but all this anger is very bad for your chi. It violates one of twenty-four rules of practice: never meditate when you have lost your temper or are too excited."

"Let's just get started."

"Not until you calm down."

"I'm calm. Let's go."

"No, you're not. Your mind is scattered. If you meditate now, it'll do more harm than good."

"I swear I'm calm."

"All right. We're still in the sitting stage. Slowly drop to the floor . . . oops wait a minute. Do you have to go to the bathroom?"

"No, why?"

"Because that's another one of the twenty-four rules."

"Going to the bathroom?"

"No. Practicing with a full bladder. Holding it in disturbs your concentration."

"My bladder is on E, all right?"

King handed me the Taiji ruler as we prepared to start.

"Good. Now we're going to start with some deep breaths. I want you to clear your mind of everything. Breathe in . . . and out . . . in . . . and out. Good. Focus on the middle of the ruler."

"What's this doing for me, again?"

"I told you before. You're inducing a state of meditation that will stimulate your blood and chi. You're tapping into the life force that flows around your body."

"You mean like urine?"

"No. I do not mean like urine. Now breathe in . . . and out . . . in . . . and out. You have to restore harmony and balance to your mind and body. Believe me, they're both out of whack."

"What will this help more? My yin or my yang?"

"It will help both equally. Now you have to concentrate in order to warm your Dan Tian."

"My Dan Tian?"

"Yes. The seat of your chi. Two inches below your navel, deep within your pelvis. Imagine a flow of energy, information, light and sound that enters through your head, passes down through your nose, out to your open palms and back into your Dan Tian."

"What is this thing? The bullet that killed Kennedy?"

"No more questions!"

King's patience was at the breaking point when the telephone rang and interrupted our session. Desperate to get out of his boring as all hell breathing exercises, I answered it before he could object. Good thing I did. On the other end of the line was Sophia, calling from Cornell.

"Hi, Daddy."

Sophia didn't call me Daddy when she wanted something. She called me Daddy when she wanted something expensive.

"Hey, babe, how's my little girl?" I asked cautiously, given her track record.

"Not so good."

There it went—the perfectly cast line with the big shiny hook.

"I don't like to hear that. What's the matter?"

"Well, I want to go to business school."

Finally, something I would be happy to pay for (if I had the money).

"That's terrific. I'm so proud of you."

The perfect game I was pitching got spoiled the moment Sophia announced that she wanted a boob job. My well-adjusted second-born child wasn't quite so crude, referring instead to a breast augmentation procedure. According to my daughter, her Delta Gamma sorority sisters had discovered a direct correlation between the size of their respective hooters and their grade point averages. With slots to business school growing more difficult to obtain, a sizable set could mean the difference between Wharton and Wayne State, or so the theory went. I tried to appeal to the latent feminist in Sophia by reminding her that this type of plastic surgery served only to reinforce the objectification of women in our society as sex objects, and that she should seriously consider taking a bold step against such exploitation. When that didn't work, I told her to get three estimates.

Fittingly, as I sat reeling from the blow of my daughter's request, the biggest boob of them all called.

"Sky, it's Trip Baden."

"Trip, what do you want?"

"I think you know why I'm calling. You're coming up on twenty years with Tailburger. And if you're going to take early retirement, I want my cut."

"I'm not taking retirement this year. And even if I was, you're not entitled to anything."

"Are you going to disrespect Jess by ignoring her wishes?"

"Her wishes? She didn't even have a will."

"She didn't need one. Her love for me said it all."

"Oh, spare me. She didn't love you. She loved me. She was just confused for a few years."

"You're the one who's confused."

"You know what? I'm going to work at least five more years, maybe ten, and you don't get a dime until my career ends. So get ready to wait for a long, long time."

Trip knew that the longer I worked, the bigger the benefit he'd receive, but he needed the money now. Still, the financial difference between twenty and twenty-five years vested was considerable, and the difference between twenty and thirty was enormous.

"My lawyer will force you into an advance settlement, Sky.

You're only kidding yourself if you think you can avoid me forever."

"Tell your pimp, excuse me, I mean lawyer, that I can do anything I damn well please!"

Trip said his shark would be circling me soon and to expect a phone call. The thought of losing half of what I'd worked for over the years made me queasy. With Sophia's tuition and Ethan's ongoing needs, not to mention the current cost of elective surgery, I was feeling a sharp financial pinch. My salary was pretty stagnant by now, and the stock options I'd collected over the years weren't worth much, if anything, since Tailburger stock had lagged for what seemed like forever. I didn't bother to tell Trip that my twenty-year retirement fund was itself in jeopardy. You don't put lighter fluid on a bonfire.

12

Ground Assault

Two weeks before the scheduled launch of the Torture campaign, the Link insisted I accompany him to the Sisters of the Sorrowful Mother convent for the groundbreaking of the Tailburger Health and Life Fitness Center. Deathly afraid of exercise equipment and fat nuns, the Link conspicuously hid behind a buffet table gorging himself on finger sandwiches while I prayed he could handle the physical exertion required to shovel one load of dirt.

Sister Ancilla was the first to find us. She and the Link were fast friends these days, having banded together to keep the sordid details of the Fanny Pack settlement from the papers and the Mother Superior. Now, both were basking in the glow of the good press that had attached itself to the fitness center event. The Link was particularly happy to see Katie Chang Gomez, Channel 7's weekend anchor, in attendance to cover the story. "The only thing blacker than her ass is her heart," the Link often complained about the African-American newswoman who had climbed her way up the station's ladder doing consumer health reports criticizing Tailburger's fatty food.

A collection of nuns, Tailburger employees and board members meandered around the convent grounds, slowly filing into the fifty rows of fold-out chairs. Burton Roxby, Rochester's beloved Congressman, and his wife, Yeti, were there, and from across the open courtyard, he waved at me. I diverted my stare and caught eyes with Annette McNabnay. It shouldn't have been uncomfortable, but it was. There's nothing worse than when rejectee encounters rejector.

Construction of the Frank T. Fanoflincoln Pavilion, the structure that would house the fitness center, would take four months to complete. Once finished, it would offer the sisters, and the public, weight training, aerobics, stairclimbers, treadmills, stationary bikes and the usual fitness flavor of the month, whether it was step classes, Pilates, Tae Bo or synchronized groin stretching. Though the Link would never participate in any of these activities, he would not miss his opportunity to address the crowd. Without putting down his two sandwiches or finishing what was in his mouth, he stepped behind the podium provided and began to speak with some impediment.

"Good afternoon, flellow flitness flanatics."

The Link held up a finger to indicate he was still chewing.

"Boy, those sandwiches are good. My compliments to the sisters."

Smiles and applause followed, particularly from Ned, Ted and Fred, who, resplendent in golf attire, sat attentively in the front row.

"The word that comes to mind right now is 'dream.' 'Cause that's what this is for me and my family: a dream come true. You see, at Tailburger, we're committed to serving high-quality all-American fare. And in doing so, we recognize that nothing, absolutely *nothing*, works up a hearty appetite better than vigorous exercise. Now maybe, and I emphasize the word 'maybe,' marijuana use does it better, but either way, vigorous exercise is right there with it. So when you're done working out here, I want you to run over to our nearest outlet, order up a big old Tailpipe with cheese and tell 'em Frank sent you."

Even when lying through his teeth about his views on exercise, the Link was at his most likable when making public appearances, and he knew it. The audience's enthusiastic cheers warmed him up like an opening act and gave him a dangerous amount of confidence.

"For years, we've heard about the diminishing number of young women who are entering the sisterhood. And with that vow of chastity, it's kind of hard to blame 'em if you ask me."

The Link paused for laughter that never came.

"I'm kidding about the vow, of course. But I'm serious about the fact that we don't have enough new nuns. What this means is that we've got to make sure the ones we do have last a long, long time. So the real question is how in Hades are we going to do that? Well, not to worry. I'll tell you what we're gonna do. We're gonna exercise 'em like racehorses, keep 'em on a strict training diet and use plenty of steroids. The lord's ladies may be getting a little long in the tooth, but we're gonna keep 'em in top condition so that the rest of us can make it up to that great fitness center in the sky."

The Link punctuated his comments by thrusting his fist into the air (for no apparent reason) as scattered applause bubbled up and Sister Ancilla took the microphone.

"Thank you, Frank, for those inspiring words. I know all the sisters, including myself, are counting the days until the stairclimbers and syringes arrive. Here at the convent, we are very proud of our new association with Tailburger, a relationship we're sure will continue long after the last of us has done our final lat pull."

Sister Ancilla's pronouncement brought the biggest smile to the Link's face that I'd ever seen. Though he was not a true Christian by anyone's definition, he desperately wanted the acknowledgment and blessing of the church so he wouldn't have to go to hell, just in case it existed.

With my boss in his best mood in months, I decided to use the ride back to headquarters as a litmus test.

"Did you read about Sara Lee's hot dog recall?"

"No. What happened?"

"Listeria. I guess it's been getting into the nooks and crannies of the assembly lines and infecting the meat. Can you believe that?"

"Yeah, but cooking kills it, right?"

"This meat was already cooked."

"Listeria. What a joke. When I was a kid we didn't have listeria. We had little pussies who couldn't eat a friggin' hot dog without crying to their mommies about a bellyache."

"Well, the USDA is coming out with a report, and Congress may make listeria testing mandatory as part of bill 214."

"You haven't killed that bill yet?"

"Not yet. I'm working on it."

"These people won't be happy until they destroy the meat industry."

"It's not just us. The cigarette makers have it even worse. Now I read that a group of private hospitals in New York have formed a consortium and are suing them for the unreimbursed expenses of treating smokers. Private hospitals. This is unprecedented."

"Un-American. That's what all this shit is. Un-American."

"The mood out there seems to be getting pretty hostile. I think we should seriously consider settling the SERMON suit."

"What? Have you gone crazy?"

"Frank, I think our best bet is to make a settlement offer and try to get out early. How long before all these groups come after us?"

"The hell with that, Thorne. The hell with that. The day we settle with those a-holes is the day the American way dies. Nothing but a bunch of bloodsuckers. That's what those people are. Trying to tear down the American businessman any chance they get. And who do they hurt? Who do they really hurt? Not you and me. No, sir. It's the average Joe Schleprock out there. The guy sitting at home in his double-wide with a Camaro up on blocks in the front yard. The guy who loves a good Tailburger."

The Link wiped his sweating brow with a Tailburger wrapper pulled from his pocket.

"You think McDonald's is going to pay some big settlement out of its own pockets? You think its executives are going to take a pay cut or let the stock get whacked when earnings disappear? The hell they will. They'll do just what tobacco did. Pass the cost on to the consumer. Plain and simple. Nothing but another goddamn wealth transfer. (Pause) And where are the political parties during all this? The Democrats and the Republicans? Both playing possum, just hoping to hold on to the most campaign contributions. It's pathetic, I'm telling you. Honest Abe must be rolling over in his grave."

I hadn't intended on waking the sleeping giant, but it was too late. Treading more lightly now would do me little good.

"So how do you want me to play this, Frank?"

"When are you scheduled to meet with that sorry excuse for a woman Meaney again?"

"Three weeks. Back down in D.C."

"Okay. That gives us some time to figure things out. This is going to be our Antietam, Thorne. The bloodiest battle you've ever seen."

It wasn't hard to see how my relationship with Muffet, if it escalated, could place both of us in the way of extreme harm. Just my good fortune, the first woman I desired for more than one night, in as long as I could remember, was hazardous to my health. I would have to cut things off with her before they really began. "This won't be so hard," I convinced myself driving over to Pappy's for lunch with Cal. She was off-limits. Forbidden fruit.

"You can pull it off," Cal insisted.

Cal's success at leading a duplicitous life until now made him believe that he, and those around him, were bulletproof.

"No way. If I get caught with her, it's career suicide."

"Of course it is. That's why you bring the Link in on it."

"What do you mean?"

"You tell him that you're going to get involved with Muffet Meaney as a way to soften her up for the settlement talks."

"Link says he won't settle."

"He says that now, but what are his options? He knows he's

eventually going to have to come to the table. Having you on the inside can only help Tailburger. He'll see that."

"You think this will work?"

"Of course it will. You tell him that you're taking one for the team. It's a perfect cover. You'll be like James Bond. Tailburger's secret agent. Double Oh Sky."

"You're sure?"

"Absolutely. She doesn't have to know a thing. The Link will buy it. And you get all the trimmings. It's perfect."

"You're good, Cal. Completely sneaky, but undeniably good."

"You have to be to survive in the industry."

"Don't get cocky, all right? I'll think about it."

Pappy came by and asked if we wanted any action on the Rochester Raging Rhinos, the city's A-League soccer team. We stuck with the rigatoni and sent him away disappointed.

"Let's talk about your campaign. When's the launch?"

"Two weeks."

"What's the buzz?"

"It's mixed. Whenever the NASDAQ starts bouncing up and down, conspicuous consumption suffers and we get hurt. Tailburger sales depend directly upon consumer confidence. Where that will be next week is anybody's guess."

"I wish you much luck, my friend."

"I appreciate it."

"Remember my offer remains open if you need the boost. I think you're missing a huge opportunity to get Tailburger integrated with the industry and my business."

"I know you do. Let's not talk about that. How's Jenny?"

"Oh Christ, don't ask."

"Why, what's wrong?"

"Nothing's wrong. She's great. It's just that it's getting harder to keep my chosen career a secret from her. Just last week she asked me if Emily's Girl Scout troop could come tour the jam plant out on Rush-Henrietta Road."

"So? What's wrong with that?"

"What's wrong is that we don't make jam there anymore. The whole space has been converted to private live performance booths that we broadcast over the Net."

"Live sex shows?"

"Exactly. You knew that."

"Do you get to watch?"

"If I want, but I'm pretty numb to the whole thing."

"Those girls don't get involved with making the jam, do they?"

"You're a riot. Of course not. We buy it from a company in California and stick our label on it. It's all done in a separate warehouse out in Livonia."

"So what's the big deal? You bring the troop by as part of a cultural exchange program. The Girl Scouts can spend the whole day learning about the exciting opportunities in the world of porn, and your actresses can try to earn a merit badge in the womanly arts."

"Hey, you wanna keep it down?" Cal asked, glancing around the restaurant.

"I have to admit, I love having lunch with anyone whose problems are as big as mine."

"I'm glad you're enjoying this."

"Cal, there's one sure way to successfully outfox your daughter's Girl Scout troop and your wife. Buy a shitload of cookies."

"When I'm done, there won't be one Thin Mint left in the city."

I lit a Commodore as a waitress took away my plate.

"You're still sucking down those coffin nails?"

"I know, I know. It's bad for my chee."

"Your chee?"

"Do you know about this chee koong stuff?"

"I may have read something about it. Isn't it one of those martial arts they practice in China?"

"Basically, yes. Anyway, King's got me started on it and I'm supposed to be making some kind of progress, you know, spiritually and morally, by breathing differently and meditating."

"And? Are you making progress?"

"I don't think so. I seem to be sliding backward."

"You're worrying way too much."

"Maybe."

"You'll feel better once the launch happens. It's going to be a success. Just wait."

"You're right. My chee will be fine."

"I have no doubt."

Talk about your chee-disturbing incidents, I got in my car just in time to catch a call from Trip's new lawyer and his Long Island accent.

"Sky, Herv Alverson heere. I represent Trip Baden."

"Herv or Herb? With a 'v' or a 'b'?"

"With a vee, as in victim."

"What do you want?"

"Trip wants his piece of yoor pension."

"He doesn't deserve that money."

"Shoor he does."

"Tell *Tripperrrr* he'll never see a dime of it."

"Sky, we can do this the hahrd way or we can do it the Herv way."

"The Herv way? Who do you think you are? Al fuckin' Pacino? Listen Herv, tell Trip that if he wants the money he'll have to drag my ass into court."

I slammed down the phone and sped up, control over the car's acceleration my only outlet for anger at the moment. I was dizzy and light-headed, my heart beating too fast for its own good. For a second, I thought I was having a stroke, but after calming down, I made the diagnosis of too much stress and not enough Nordic-Track. Unbowed, I wiped the perspiration from my face and drove on. I didn't have time to die. There were only two weeks until the launch.

13

In Deep

To my pleasant surprise, a message from Muffet was on my machine when I arrived home from work. It was somewhat shocking to hear that she wanted to come see me. I wasn't used to such an aggressive approach by a woman, but I didn't question it and quickly asked King to get lost. Muffet caught a cab from the airport and arrived at my house by 11:30 P.M.

When I opened the door it was awkward for a moment. Although she was dressed in blue jeans and a sexy lavender sweater set, I wasn't sure how things would go until seconds later when we were buck naked and balling on a piano bench. If she brought as much passion to her lovemaking as she did to her battle against beef, I feared my own hospitalization before the night was through.

Following my recent dry run in the area of female conquest, it felt good to have such satisfying sex. We moved from the piano bench to the staircase to a spot underneath the dining room table. At one point, I looked up and realized I was in a room I didn't even recognize. Further into the encounter, I started channeling the spirit of Barry White and referring to Muffet as "fuck bunny number one." She didn't seem to mind.

Afterward, we sat out on my sunporch and didn't say anything for a while. The cool night breeze felt good on my face and brought the smell of lilac in from the landscaped yard. Living off of a restricted-access road lent privacy to anything that occurred behind my house. A pool that had once been a second home to Ethan, Sophia and their friends mostly sat empty these days and made me a bit sad to stare at it. I lit a Commodore and sat back on a piece of all-weather furniture I'd owned for fifteen years.

"Would you like something to eat?"

Muffet was somewhat startled by my breach of silence.

"Sure. What were you thinking of?"

I proceeded without fear on the theory that we would have to cross this bridge eventually if this relationship was to go anywhere other than the boning hall of fame.

"I've got some steaks I could grill up."

Muffet smiled at me.

"Are you testing me?"

"Maybe."

"You want to see what kind of gal I am? See if I'll balk at your suggestion of steak?"

"Maybe I just feel like a steak."

"You know what? That actually sounds pretty good to me."

"Great."

I was happy that she wanted to eat steak. Mostly, I admit, because I wanted to eat steak, particularly the porterhouse I was hiding from my brother in the back of the freezer. Still, Muffet was willing to make an accommodation for this relationship and that had to count for something. Score one for my little fuck bunny. Eating our late meal together, I reflected on my five favorite hedonistic pleasures in life, listing each in descending order:

5. A good piss,
4. A great shit,

3. A satisfying sleep,
2. A balldraining orgasm, and
1. Watching a half-naked woman chew on a piece of blood-red meat.

Yes, I was in the right business. I could never let myself forget that. I loved meat and everything that went with it. Knives, grinders, wrapping supplies, sausage casings, stuffers, jerky shooters, and most of all, the killing floor. To celebrate my existence, I opened a bottle of wine and then another. Pretty soon, we were both drunk.

"You know what your problem is, Sky?" Muffet asked rhetorically.

"What?"

"You don't know how to have fun."

Muffet's grin gave her away, but I played along.

"You say this to a man who just qualified for the carnal olympics?"

"You need to loosen up."

"What did you have in mind?"

"Do you have a video camera?"

Muffet left the next morning on the first flight to D.C., but not before we had memorialized our attempt to exhaust the *Kama Sutra*. The phrase "lapse in judgment" popped into my mind a few times during the effort, but I ignored it at my own peril. Man's power of self-deception is unsurpassed in this world, particularly when it comes to the appearance of his own ass.

A telephone call from Sophia roused me from my dreamy slumber.

"Hello."

"Daddy, it's Soph."

"Hey, Sophia. How are you, pumpkin?"

"I'm okay."

The key to parenting is language interpretation. Sophia typically responded to the question "how are you?" by saying she was "great." Thus simple deduction told me her response of "okay" probably meant a life-altering crisis was imminent.

"You don't sound happy, babe. What's wrong?"

"Everything. I just found out I'm getting a B-plus in Professor Kellerman's course."

"Which one is that?"

"Sex and the Single Female. It's a total gut. Everybody gets an A-plus."

"Well, what happened?"

"My end-of-term project bombed. Tweeter and I made this home video for class, but when we got finished we realized the camera's battery had died halfway through."

"Who's Tweeter?"

"Oh, just some guy."

"Is he a student?"

"No, Daddy. The students are dorks. He's a townie."

So much for my dream of her marrying a guy who went to Choate.

"What was the video about?"

"Daddy, what do you think? The course is called Sex and the Single Female. Use your imagination."

"I'd rather not, if that's okay with you. Can we talk about something else?"

When I sent Sophia off to college I told her about the importance of getting a broad liberal arts education. Things, however, seemed to be getting a little too broad and a little too liberal. Still, it was difficult to come down too hard on her about the video given my prior night's activities.

"I got the estimates on the breast augmentation. I think saline is the way to go."

"Whoa, whoa. What's the cost?"

"The cheapest would be about thirty-eight hundred dollars, but there's a guy up in Syracuse who is supposed to be some kind of breast sculptor. He's a real artist."

"How much for the artist?"

"Sixty-eight hundred."

"Jesus Christ. Is this really necessary?"

"Daddy, I was hoping Sex and the Single Female would bring my grade point up, but now with the B-plus, I'm really going to need top-notch cosmetic surgery."

"It just seems a little extreme. Can't you do an extra-credit problem or something?"

"Oh, Daddy, be serious. It must have been fun going to school when there wasn't any pressure."

After approving her plan with the breast artist, I said good-bye to Sophia and decided to call Ethan to see how he was doing at Macrocock. Perhaps the second-round financing had come through and the IPO would be making him rich in a few days. I didn't anticipate such news or the pleasure of an encounter with his chatty roommate, Skull, who answered the phone like the respectful young man that he was.

"Yeah, what."

"Skull, is that you?"

"Yeah, whaddya want?"

"Skull, it's Mr. Thorne, Ethan's dad."

"Oh, hey."

"Is Ethan around?"

"Who?"

In a candid moment, Ethan had confessed to me Skull's continuing fondness for what he called "the chronic." Pot to you and me.

"I'm looking for Ethan. My son. Your roommate."

"I know who he is."

"That's great, Skull. Do you know *where* he is?"

"Nope."

"Well, can you tell him I called and ask him to call me?"

"Wait. He said he was going to the store."

"Just now? Did he go just now?"

"Oh you know what? That was about a week ago. Never mind."

"All right, Skull. You take care now."

"Bye, Mr. Thorne."

"Good-bye, Skull."

Although I was unable to find my son, the news wasn't all bad in my life. Jelloteous Junderstack's heart had stabilized, making the use of our replacement campaign unnecessary. The Link was disappointed, given the dramatic use of t & a, but it was just as well considering all the money we'd spent on the Blatherskite video. Even better, Ship Plankton had found four spots in *Dongwood* for Dirk Harrington to confront various Tailburger products, yet was still able to maintain the integrity of his film. The movie's release in two days would coincide with the introduction of our *Dongwood* Deluxe, available, of course, for a limited time at participating retailers. Order this sandwich and you'd receive an authentic carnival worker's head lice comb, courtesy of five thousand Beijing workers making fourteen cents a week. There was no denying it anymore. We were ready to launch.

14

Launch

EVERYWHERE

It came on a Friday, the biggest advertising onslaught in the history of Tailburger. Mercilessly repetitious by design, the campaign used every medium available to saturate the American marketplace with commercials touting the Torture ethic. Various catchphrases were employed in the effort, depending upon the target market and demographic. We liked to think we were offering something for everybody.

    For those who'd given up on attracting a mate:
        Why Just Abuse Your Body
        When You Can Torture It?

    For the chronically depressed:
        There's a Bit of the Grim Reaper in Every Bag

    For the criminally insane:
        Torture: Alive and Well Behind Our Prison Walls

    We went after the disenchanted, the disaffected, the dispirited and the dispossessed. We went after the self-mutilators, manic-depressives, agoraphobics, crackheads, scoop fiends and redneck trailer trash. We plastered buses, bridges, subway platforms, airport terminals, train stations, halfway houses, police stations and psychiatric hospitals. Tailmobiles (SUVs painted orange and purple) were driven through city streets with hood mounted speakers blaring, "Eat a Little More, You're a CarNiVore." By noon, it was impossible to turn on a radio, television or computer without hearing Phat Daddio, whose felony murder charges were still pending, singing Dick Tinglehoff's catchy jingle set to a hip-hop beat.

> *BOOM bat, I say boom boom BAT*
> *BOOM bat, I say boom boom BAT*
>
> *We don't bake 'em,*
> *We don't broil 'em*
> *We just grease and fry and oil 'em*
>
> *BOOM bat I say boom boom BAT*
> *TailBurGer will keep you PHAT*
>
> *Here at Tailburger*
> *What you're eatin'*
> *Is a big old piece*
> *Of bloodred meatin'*
>
> *BOOM bat I say boom boom BELLS*
> *Mama gotta butt like Orson WELLES*
>
> *Every burger*
> *We just scorch 'er*
> *Every body*
> *We must torture!*

From Sunset Boulevard to the New Jersey Turnpike, billboards announced the arrival of the *Dongwood* Deluxe and our carnival worker lice comb kit. Tailburger workers flooded the streets of New York, Boston, Chicago, L.A. and two dozen other metropolitan areas handing out free Torture T-shirts and complimentary burgers. Blatherskite opened their Tailburger-sponsored Torturing America's Ears Tour by playing their new hit song "Torture Me" via satellite from San Francisco to over ninety-six countries. Locally, Annette McNabnay, as mayor of Rochester, proclaimed it Tailburger Week and handed out free Tailpipes with cheese at a local female correctional facility. For a fringe player in the burger business, the collective energy was awesome and the initial response was better than expected. Traffic at Tailburger outlets across the U.S. increased nearly 10 percent as a result of the blitz. The Link called me with the overnight numbers, tracked continually by our fearless accountants, to offer his congratulations. We were off to a fantastic start.

That Saturday night I took Sophia to the Hollywood premiere of *Dongwood*. Sophia's cosmetic surgery had been successful and I wanted to celebrate her expanded womanhood with a real daddy-daughter evening. Of course, the new dress Sophia needed, one with reinforced underwire to hold up her colossal cleavage, ran $1,700 on Rodeo Drive. "What the hell," I thought while handing over my credit card. "It's not every day that your child gets a boob job. May as well live a little."

Once we were dressed in our finery, we drank a few martinis, all of them up with olives, in the cocktail lounge of the Beverly Hills Hotel and waited for our limousine to arrive. With my weekend dad parenting guilt ever-present, I desperately wanted to show Sophia the time of her life. Looking over at my baby, I realized she was all grown-up. Whatever value system I'd instilled in her would soon be tested in the real world. Naturally, the whole ride over she talked about the stars she hoped to see, only A-list types like Arnold and Maria, Tom and Rita, maybe Bruce and Demi if they'd gotten back together. Unfortunately *Dongwood* drew a strictly B-list crowd composed of such luminaries as Penn and

Teller, Siegfried and Roy and of course, the Captain and Tennille. Although Sophia wanted to show off her new breasts to a better breed of celebrity, I eased her pain with extra butter on the popcorn and a promise to introduce her to Ship Plankton.

Ship was resplendent in all black from his beret to his Jamaican walking stick. This was his night and he strutted into the Westwood Theatre with the confidence of a man who had just scaled the sheer face of a mountain. A small pack of paparazzi, a group whose personal hygiene was begging for some attention, snapped their shutters at him and anyone else they thought was exploitable. Suffice it to say, none of them took my photo, although a few did take shots of Sophia's rather remarkable chest. Ship waved at me from across the lobby while talking to reporters from *Entertainment Nightly* and *Accent Hollywood,* who clamored for his attention.

"Ship, Paul O'Reilly from *Entertainment Nightly.*"

"Hello, Paul."

"Can you believe all the excitement *Dongwood* is creating?"

"I really can't. It's just immensely rewarding to receive so much praise for a project that nobody believed in and that, frankly, nobody has seen yet."

"The buzz is tremendous. What do you think the reaction will be across the country?"

"People hear the words 'carnival worker' and 'head lice' and ordinarily shy away, but I think this is going to be the film that changes all that. The public is ready for a movie that disturbs them deeply by exposing the seedy underworld of the traveling sideshow."

"Ship, why the NC-17 rating? Is there a great deal of violence and gratuitous sex?"

"Paul, a carnival worker's life isn't all elephant ears and powdered sugar. Do you understand what I'm saying?"

"I don't, but I wish you the best of luck."

"Thank you."

Dirk Harrington, the star of *Dongwood* and the one responsible for eating Tailburgers on-screen, entered the theater with his fourth wife, Dannika. Reportedly, he beat her so badly before the Oscars, Valentino had to design a full body wrap at the last minute. Looking at her now, I couldn't see any bruises, although a makeup artist did hover quite closely. Harrington had done big box office before in his action feature *Pie Lard* and its sequel *Pie Lard II: On Thin Crust,* and we were counting on him to carry our campaign to new heights.

L.A. was seductive. Once you dipped your big toe into the warm water of its karmic hot tub, it was hard not to let yourself slip in and soak for a while. As ridiculous as it sounds, I couldn't deny the intoxicating mix of excitement and disgust I felt in Harrington's presence. Chiseled good looks, buxom babe on his arm (who wasn't his daughter), exquisitely tailored suit, muscular physique (and the inclination to use it on loved ones), three rehab stints and a witness gig in the Heidi Fleiss trial. Hey, we all have a few warts.

Paul O'Reilly pulled Dirk aside for some questioning.

"Dirk, you look refulgent tonight. May I ask you what you're wearing?"

"Armani. This is a preview of his fall line. You notice the collarless jacket? That's an Indian influence. It's chic, but not in a Gandhi way. The look this year is going to be ethnic influenced but not literally ethnic, do you understand?"

"I'm not sure."

"Look, I want to say something about the African ivory trade."

"Please, go ahead."

"It's wrong."

(Pause) "That's it?"

"Yes, that's it."

"Very good. You know, Dirk, I couldn't help but notice the choker around Dannika's neck."

"I never choked her."

"No, not you. The choker around her neck. I couldn't help but notice it appears to be made of ivory."

"It's fake."

"And the fur collar on her jacket?"

"It's fake."

"I see."

"Everything *on* Dannika and *about* Dannika is fake, from her ivory to her fur to her breasts. The only thing that is real is her love for me." Dirk laughed at his own joke.

"I bet," O'Brien responded. "Dannika, any comments for our audience?"

"She's not talking tonight," Dirk interjected. "She's just been in for a throat scraping."

Okay, so it was a mixed bag, but Dirk Harrington was a movie star. He didn't have to play by the rules, and rightfully so. He raised lots of money for the Democratic Party and paid tons of income and property taxes. He attended GLAAD functions and wore an AIDS ribbon—a veritable celluoid prince of Hollywood and its PC politics.

"Dad, isn't he amazing?"

"He's just a person, Soph. Remember that."

"Just a person. Do you know how many times he's slept at the White House?"

"Well, no. I haven't been keeping track."

"Seven times. And he's going back again next month for a state dinner honoring Ozzy Osbourne and Kid Rock."

"The president is obviously a fan of the arts, but let's keep film's contribution to society in perspective."

"Dad, Dirk is about more than just film. Where do you think the antifur fight would be without him? And the anticruelty movement? And the anti–animal testing militia? (Pause) Nowhere."

"Tell me. Is Dirk *for* anything?"

"Of course. He's pro-choice, pro–seventy-two-hour background check and pro–baby seal. But he is antiaging. When he dies, he plans to have himself cryogenically frozen so that he can come back when there's a cure for it."

"A cure for what?"

"For dying, of course."

"Sophia, dying is not a disease. It's a natural part of the life cycle. You know, dust to dust, ashes to ashes. Aren't you reading any Emerson in English class?"

"I'm not taking any English, Dad. You know that. Oh my God, here he comes. Hand me my inhaler."

Sophia's asthma had an annoying way of cropping up at big moments in her life. Still, it didn't stop her from trying to make eye contact with Dirk Harrington as he passed by. Dirk, on the other hand, was so transfixed by my daughter's breasts, his eyes never made it above her neck.

"He looked at me. Did you see that?" Sophia gasped.

By the end of the evening, I had Sophia convinced that I'd come around to her way of thinking. Yes, the world would be overrun by dogs if not for the truly monumental work of Bob Barker. Of course, we all owed a huge debt of gratitude to Goldie Hawn for her tireless efforts on behalf of circus elephants. And no, I found nothing amusing about Meryl Streep's battle against chemicals in apples. No question, Sally Struthers had struck a huge blow for the refugee children of the world as well as the repellent-spray industry as we now know it. Sometimes you have to appease your kids just to get on with your life.

When people came out of the theater talking about the costumes and the makeup, it was a sure sign the movie was a bomb. I'm no critic, but everyone knows an ending where the hero infests an entire sixth grade class with head lice, and then commits suicide, is box-office poison. The film, three and a half hours long, had an intermission where half the audience left, and a climactic scene where Dirk Harrington's character barfed up a Tailfrap, our beef-flavored shake, while riding the Tilt-A-Whirl. Not exactly the positive product placement we were looking for. Naturally, Ship Plankton, ubiquitous before, was nowhere to be seen now. And Dirk Harrington was in such a rush to leave, he didn't have time to sign autographs for a waiting crowd that included Sophia. Like the studio executives who mumbled expletives and grimaced as they climbed into their respective town cars, I entered the back of our limousine in a foul mood. If the numbers for *Dongwood's* first weekend turned out to be as bad as I expected, the first major problem with the new campaign was at hand.

15

Crash

Two days later, back at home, I received a call in the middle of the night.

"Hello?"

"Sky, it's Satan."

"Manchow?"

"You know another? I've got bad news."

"What is it?"

"Jello's dead."

I jerked up in bed.

"He's what?"

"He's dead. Collapsed after practice tonight."

"What happened? I just saw him. Was it his heart?"

"Nope. Peanut allergy. PayDay candy bar finished him off."

"I can't believe it. That's terrible."

"Yeah, it really is a shame. He had a hell of an endorsement future. We were even in talks with the PayDay people."

"I just can't believe it. I'm stunned."

"Well, believe this. As Jello's representative, I want to make sure that we get every cent he had coming."

"Yeah, sure, whatever. I don't think right now is the appropriate time to talk about that."

"I disagree. The moment these guys drop dead, everybody's memory starts getting real hazy. I'm here to tell you that kinda shit docsn't fly with Satan."

"Look, it'll all be taken care of. Why don't we talk after the funeral? I'll see you there, okay?"

"Actually, I won't be able to make that, but my assistant, Milan Stoshitz, will be there. I'll send him over to see you and set up a meeting."

"Okay, Satan. I'll keep an eye out for him. Good-bye."

I hung up the telephone and lay awake for the rest of the night. I couldn't believe Jelloteous was dead. What a cruel joke God had played on my Belgian buddy. The last time I'd seen him he looked so healthy, but then again, the same could be said of our Torture campaign.

My early morning surprise from Satan was followed by more bad news as the day progressed. The initial box-office numbers were in for *Dongwood,* and it was a disaster. Two and a half million dollars on an opening weekend with little competition didn't bode well for the film's long-term grosses. In fact, it almost assured it of a place among the least profitable films of the year. *Dongwood* would soon be out of theaters and Tailburger would be out of luck, left with millions of extra head lice combs.

With Plankton's movie dying and Jelloteous dead, the Torture campaign was losing any forward momentum that it had gained during its first few days. Then came the biggest blow yet—an overnight letter from SERMON arrived at headquarters addressed to the Link.

Muffet I. Meaney, Executive Director
S.E.R.M.O.N
Stop Eating Red Meat Now
1335 K Street N.W.
Washington, DC 20005

Mr. Frank A. Fanoflincoln, President
Tailburger, Inc.
Cheese Factory Road
Mendon, NY 14544

Dear Mr. Fanoflincoln:

You are a reprehensible pig. In total disregard for our country's chronic obesity problem, not to mention the millions of Americans who are dead or dying annually from heart failure, you have devised an advertising campaign that lauds the practice of self-abuse and personal torture. Shame on you!

As you read this, thousands of little boys and girls are blimping up and being unwittingly condemned to shop for the rest of their lives in stores that cater to the "husky" and "plus-sized." Thousands of adults are switching from Levi's relaxed-fit jeans to generic "I've decided to let myself go" lines. Hundreds of cardiologists are rushing out to their local Porsche dealerships in eager anticipation of the new business to come. I just hope you're happy, because we are most decidedly not.

We are calling for a nationwide boycott of all Tailburger outlets to protest what we believe is one of the most irresponsible marketing acts of all time. When my Mark, God rest his soul, left this unsavory planet over fifteen years ago, I vowed he would not die in vain. I urge you to pull all scheduled television ads, radio spots, print media and billboard coverage for this horrible campaign. Until you do, we will be speaking to the press and making your life miserable.

Without regard, Muffet Meaney

Subtlety was not Muffet's strong suit, and when the Link saw this letter, he barged into my office, threw it at me and proceeded to go berserk.

"Goddamnit, Thorne! Read this piece of shit!"

As I read the first line my stomach began to churn. Muffet had betrayed me. There was only one way out of this situation.

"Frank, I've got an idea."

"I've got one, too. Get on the horn to that cocksucker and tell her to call off her dogs!"

"Just listen to me for one minute."

The Link stopped ranting, but continued pacing back and forth in front of my desk.

"This better be good."

"I've got a good idea. It has to do with Muffet Meaney."

"Goddamn whore. I hope it involves a gun."

"What if I got involved with her?"

"What the hell are you talking about, Thorne?"

War talk was the only way to get through to the Link.

"I'm talking about infiltrating behind enemy lines."

"You mean espionage?"

"Exactly. I'm talking about personally improving Tailburger's position with SERMON by getting romantically involved with Ms. Meaney."

"Are you fucked in the head, Thorne? That's about the worst goddamn idea I've ever heard. What if it goes bad? Then we're worse off than before. Did you think about that?"

"No. I really didn't."

"The answer is no. Absolutely not. I forbid you from doing that. Just call that Jezebel and tell her to back off."

Things were not going as well as I'd hoped. The Link, whose sweaty, red face made him look like a burn-unit victim, stormed out of my office as quickly as he'd stormed in, leaving me alone with the letter and the unpleasant task at hand. I took a deep breath and proceeded to light up a Commodore. I was pissed. Muffet's stunt threatened to torpedo not only the Torture campaign but also my job, my pension and, for whatever it was worth, my identity. I hesitated to call her in such an agitated state, but what choice did I have? If the SERMON boycott went national before I got to her, our conversation would be pointless.

"Hello. You've reached SERMON. How may I direct your call?"

"Muffet Meaney, please."

"One moment."

How could Muffet treat me like this? For God's sake, we did it in every room of my house. Barry White himself had blessed our sexual union.

"Hello. Ms. Meaney's office."

"Yes, is Muffet there?"

"I'm sorry, she's in a meeting."

"Look. Tell her it's Sky Thorne."

"One minute, Mr. Thorne."

Why couldn't she call for a boycott of Wendy's or Fuddrucker's? They could afford it more easily than us. I had to keep my head on straight. I was letting my personal feelings interfere with business.

"Hello."

"Muffet, how could you?"

"How could I what?"

"Threaten us with a boycott."

"Sky, your campaign is the worst I've seen in fifteen years."

"But it's mine. You know, me, the guy you refer to in bed as the Atomic Fly."

"Sky, you're letting your personal feelings interfere with business."

"I am not. That's ridiculous. I just want fair treatment."

"Sky, I run an organization committed to the health of the American public. When I see something that I believe jeopardizes its health, I have no choice but to act. I hope you understand that."

"No, I don't understand. I'm the Atomic Fly. Doesn't that count for something?"

"Sky, I have to go. Call me tonight and we'll talk. Okay?"

I felt defeated. Muffet was ruthless.

"No. I need to talk to you now. Are you going to call off the boycott or not?"

"Not."

Muffet wasn't going to call off the boycott. That much was clear. I tried to spin it for the Link by telling him it would only enhance our outlaw image. Ever the pragmatist, the Link started crying at first, then shifted into Civil War mode and told me about the personal grooming habits of General Lee for an hour. Finally he said we'd assess the damage after the initial hit and form a battle plan. For once, the Link actually managed to make me feel better about something rather than worse.

I didn't have time to pout, since Jelloteous Junderstack's memorial service was on my immediate agenda. I caught an afternoon flight to LAX and checked in at the Beverly Wilshire. The Menendez and Simpson murder trials, seemingly significant blips on the California radar screen, hadn't changed L.A. one bit. The city found new sources of scandal to fill the void on a daily basis, and today was Jello's turn.

I reached my room, tipped the valet and closed the door, happy to be safe in my air-conditioned cocoon. I meant to call Muffet, but never did. I knew she wouldn't change her mind. I fell asleep watching TV and woke up at 3:00 A.M. in my clothes, not sure of where I was. I drifted back to sleep and reawoke by 7:00 A.M.

Perfect Southern California weather met me outside. I took a taxi to the Staples Center, where Jelloteous's casket was draped in purple and gold. All the big Laker fans were there: Jack Nicholson, Dyan Cannon, the guys from those "Whassupp?" ads. Even Ship Plankton, who was known as an enormous supporter of the Lakers' latest incarnation of Showtime, made an appearance. He was sobbing so uncontrollably, I felt obligated to comfort him.

"Ship, I'm really sorry."

Ship tried to pull himself together.

"I know, Sky. The whole thing is a travesty. I'm just devastated. Somebody's ripped my heart out. Can you feel my pain?"

Ship continued to cry.

"I can. I really feel it. I didn't know Jello well, but he seemed like a great guy."

Ship's thoughts were evidently elsewhere.

"I just can't believe it. The domestic box office for *Dongwood* should have been huge. Now my only hope is video and the foreign market."

I consoled Ship the best I could before I was accosted by Satan's assistant, Milan Stoshitz.

"Sky, Milan Stoshitz. We need to talk about Jello's contract."

"Hello, Milan. Have you met Ship Plankton?"

Without looking up, Ship extended a tear-drenched hand toward Milan, who shook it awkardly before letting go.

"Sky, I really want to talk to you about Jello's contract."

"C'mon. Can't it wait until after the service?"

"I guess so. Meet me under Magic's retired jersey when it's over."

"No problem."

The funeral was very moving in an L.A. kind of way. Jello's teammates talked about how tall he was and how he could fill up the lane "like a motherfucker." To what I'm sure was Stoshitz's delight, the captain of the team announced that Jello had been voted a full share of whatever play-off money was ultimately earned. Particularly touching was the owner's description of how Jello restructured his contract to help fit everyone under the salary cap. Numerous Laker girls, most with noticeable limps, wore black armbands to pay homage to their fallen hero. A dry eye couldn't be found during the Belgian national anthem.

Midway through the ditty, I started thinking about my own mortality. Despite my brother's efforts, I was still smoking, overweight and miles away from mastering my chee. What legacy would I leave if I died tomorrow? A failed marriage. A career promoting fried meat. A daughter with the biggest chest in the Ivies. A son with a high school education. And last but not least, a minority stake in a company called Macrocock.com. Yes, my slice of the American pie was pretty puny, and the happiness that I sought seemed farther away than ever.

Before Jello's service was over, I managed to slip out the back undetected by Stoshitz. I had no patience to deal with the asshole right then. I soon discovered the Tailburger boycott was under way and braced myself for the inevitably unpleasant repercussions. At the airport, the cover of the *USA Today* contained a blurb about SERMON and its plans. Just my luck, Muffet was scheduled to appear on *Larry King Live* that night. Somehow, I needed to get equal airtime or stand by and watch our Torture campaign go on life support.

16

Fighting Back

I went straight home from the airport, exhausted by my swing out to the left coast. Uncut grass and a pile of mail, composed entirely of bills, Pottery Barn catalogs and campaign donation requests from Burton Roxby, greeted me upon arrival. Didn't those mooks in his office ever quit? For therapy, I took some small pleasure in tearing up every piece of correspondence with his picture on it. A telephone message from Zeb Nettles, Tailburger's public relations director, reminded me to watch *Larry King* and assured me that efforts were ongoing to get me on the show in the next day or two. A note on the kitchen table from my brother informed me he was out at a poetry slam, whatever the hell that was, and would be home late. Coast clear, I went to the small wet bar in my study, poured myself four fingers of Dewar's and drank it neat.

There was no word yet on the impact of the boycott. It would take at least a day to see if store sales were down in any significant number. SERMON had been effective in the past at mobilizing large numbers of meat maniacs, but their success was limited to emotional issues such as food poisoning, where children died as the result of E. coli, salmonella or trichinosis. Here, Muffet would be simply advocating a health issue, and I was banking on the fact that most Americans would rather be fat and happy than thin and deprived. Traylor Hitch knew what he was talking about.

I moved slowly to the brown sofa sectional in my family room to watch Muffet on TV. Just a week before, this corduroy-covered monstrosity had been a place of passion for me. Now it was losing its status as fuck furniture and turning into a place of mourning. How could she sell me out? It still didn't make sense to the Atomic Fly.

I had a few minutes before the show to click my way around the cable clusterfuck of worthless television. Ah, pro wrestling. Thank God for World Wrestling Entertainment and its fans. Talk about your primary markets for Tailburger. They didn't get any better than that. Stadiums full of life's fringe players. People who thought a three-hundred-pound man spitting on them and belittling other three-hundred-pounders in mock anger while wearing chartreuse tights was the world's highest art form. It was a stockholder's dream and a cosmic joke on our founding fathers. Its sheer preposterousness was a testament to how low our cultural brow had sunk.

Then there was the Home Shopping Network, where people paid hundreds of dollars for allegedly rare pieces of hastily constructed crap that they didn't need and wouldn't want minutes after its arrival from the back of a UPS truck.

I lit a Commodore, flipped my fifty-inch flat screen to CNN and heard the familiar refrain of James Earl Jones. The blue-hued backdrop of *Larry King Live* was next and its comforting effect on my eyes was undeniable. Larry's owl-like appearance was unchanged with his slicked-back hair, thick tortoiseshell frames and generally natty attire. With a drop-dead gorgeous seventh wife and two new babies, Larry was the quintessentially greatest living proof our country had that women liked men with money and power regardless of their age or attractiveness. Muffet sat calmly across from him as the introductory music played. She looked better than good in a black sleeveless dress with a ruby red silk scarf around her neck and large diamond stud earrings. "Probably a gift from that dead husband of hers," I mumbled bitterly in my scotch-induced delirium.

"Good evening. I'm Larry King. My guest tonight is Muffet Meaney, executive director of the antibeef organization Stop Eating Red Meat Now, known more commonly by its acronym, SERMON. Good evening, Muffet. Nice to have you on the show."

"Thank you, Larry. It's good to be here."

She was kissing his ass already. Batter up. Here come the softballs.

"Muffet, your organization is the most vocal group in the country when it comes to beef. What's going on here? What's wrong with red meat?"

"It's a killer, Larry. Simple as that. Studies show that the fat and cholesterol contained in cooked red meat clogs your arteries until you die of coronary heart disease or stroke. And if that doesn't get you, one of the millions of bacteria crawling around on the meat will. Have you heard of the new strain of E. coli, Larry? It's twice as deadly."

She had to throw in the bit about the bacteria. That bitch.

"That's what they say. Doesn't sound too appetizing, Muffet."

"No, it's not, Larry. It's a serious health hazard to the public. And now there's evidence of a connection between food poisoning and IBS."

"What's IBS?"

"IBS stands for Irritable Bowel Syndrome, Larry. It's a condition discovered by British scientists who have found a connection between exposure to foodborne bacterias and a lifetime of painful irritation to the victim's large colon. Every time they use the bathroom, it just brings back memories of that one bad burger."

"My word, Muffet. A lifetime, huh? Sounds highly unpleasant."

"You bet it is, Larry."

"Now, you're calling for a boycott of Tailburger. Why this company? Why not one of the biggies?"

"Larry, as you may know, Tailburger has introduced a new ad campaign encouraging people to torture themselves."

"Interesting. Torture how?"

"By ingesting as much deep-fried food as their bodies can handle—literally gorging themselves on oversize portions of fat-addled meat and french fries. To make matters worse, they've doubled the size of their leading burger and added three extra dollops of Cajun mayonnaise. We find this total disregard for the health of consumers to be more egregious than anything we've seen in our nearly fifteen years of existence. It's outrageous and irresponsible, Larry."

"Powerful stuff. Let's take a call. Teaneck, New Jersey, you're on *Larry King*."

"Yeah, Larry, I wanted to ask Ms. Meaney if she thinks that Tailburger executives could be held criminally liable for the death of their company's customers?"

"Criminally liable, Muffet? What do you think?"

"Well, I'm not a lawyer, Larry, but that's something we're going to look into. These people know what their products do to the human body and they should be punished for it. I know I'd like to see them do jail time."

"Strong words from a strong lady."

"Jail time? Now you've gone too far," I shouted at the TV while Muffet continued.

"That said, Larry, I guess now is as good a time as any to announce that we will be filing a civil lawsuit, along with the various state attorneys general, against Tailburger and their bigger brethren, including McDonald's, to get them to pay for the health costs our country incurs as a result of their food."

"You heard it here first, folks. A civil suit is in the works. Thank you, caller."

"Thanks, Larry."

"Muffet, will this be as big as the tobacco litigation?"

"We think it will be bigger. Unfortunately, more people eat red meat than smoke, so it only follows that the health burden is greater."

"We're going to commercial, folks. Don't go away."

I called Zeb Nettles and got the number for the show. This one-sided diatribe had to be stopped immediately. After identifying who I was to the producers, I was told to stand by. I was drunk, desperate and angry now, not what you'd describe as an ideal caller.

"Okay, we're back and we're going to take another call now. Sky Thorne, chief operating officer for Tailburger, is joining us from Rochester, New York. Go ahead, Sky, you're on *Larry King*."

"Hello, Larry."

"Hello, Sky. How are you tonight?"

"I was doing just fine until your psycho guest started calling me a criminal."

"I don't think she called you a criminal. She just addressed the issue raised by the caller."

"Look, Larry. The bottom line is that Tailburger makes food that is loved by certain small segments of the American public. You can't go to a midget rodeo, Turkish bathhouse or parole board hearing in this country without seeing someone with a sack of Tailburgers. Those who love dwarf tossing and Crisco wrestling and distributing Amway. They all love Tailburger. And they should eat it as often as they like."

"What about the health risks, Sky?"

Before I could stop myself, it was out of my mouth.

"Larry, a new Corral Foundation study will show that eating large amounts of red meat can cure most forms of cancer. It's really America's wonder product."

"Sky says it's America's wonder product. How do you respond to that, Ms. Meaney?"

"Larry, Mr. Thorne is self-deluded. He and his cronies pay scientists to create these bogus studies every year to mislead the public about the health hazards of red meat. It's outrageous!"

"There are health risks in everything we do, Larry. Hell, it's dangerous to get involved with shrewish harpies who head health organizations. Just ask Ms. Meaney."

"Muffet, is there some history here between you two that I should know about?"

"The key word *is* history, Larry, because that's what Sky is to me."

"Powerful stuff. We'll be right back."

I must have passed out at some point during the show, because I woke up the next morning with the telephone still in my hand. I didn't remember what I'd said, but my hope that it was all a bad dream was dashed as soon as I replaced the handset on the receiver. An incessant ring forced me to pick it back up.

"Hello."

"Sky, what in the name of Ulysses S. Grant do you think you're doing?"

The Link was not happy, so I tried to play dumb. My head throbbed from overserving myself.

"What do you mean?"

The Link was enraged.

"Calling into that show dead drunk. Are you single-handedly trying to destroy my company? Last night was a public relations nightmare. Our stock dropped eight points this morning. The boycott is killing us, and I explicitly told you not to get involved with that woman. Goddamnit, Thorne, you better turn this situation around fast or you're gone. And I don't just mean from Tailburger. I'm talkin' about the whole industry. I'll blackball you so bad you won't be able to get a job flippin' dog burgers in Korea. Do you understand me? Do whatever it takes."

A tremendous surge of panic shot through my veins as the Link slammed the phone in my ear. I wasn't sure what to do now. Suddenly, Muffet was gone and everything else in my life was in serious jeopardy. I called Cal and asked him to meet me at Pappy's for breakfast immediately. The look on his face told me he'd seen *Larry King* the night before.

"Are you all right?"

"No."

"Sky, I'm worried about you. Do you have a booze problem?"

"Since when did four or five drinks a night make you an alcoholic?"

"Sky, you need to slow it down."

"What I need is a favor."

"Of course. Just name it."

Pappy came by and served us two espressos, then hovered above us until we each took a sip and gave our approval.

"The espresso's delicious, Pappy."

Pappy smiled like a proud father.

"I enjoyed you on *Larry King*, Sky." Pappy stared at me like I was a circus attraction.

"Thanks, Pappy. Hope I didn't scare anyone in your family."

"Not at all, Sky. Very entertaining show."

Pappy left, satisfied with his encounter with a semicelebrity.

"So what's the favor?"

"I want to put Tailburger into the industry."

"Are you sure?"

"Not really. It pretty much goes against every fiber in my body to do this."

"Will you stop the self-righteous, sanctimonious bullshit? You guys are already selling sex. You'd only be pushing it a little bit farther down the continuum. Hardly an enormous leap."

"It doesn't matter. I'm out of other options."

"Is it the boycott?"

"Not really. That'll hurt us a bit, but most of our demographic doesn't care too much about their personal health. We'll lose a few that way, but it's the whole Torture campaign. It's just stalling out on me. Junderstack's dead, *Dongwood*'s barely breathing and the lead singer of Blatherskite dove into a mosh pit and broke his neck two days ago in San Antonio. Their whole tour has been canceled. Pretty soon the SERMON suit will kick in and the company will be totally fucked."

"This is just bad luck. You've got to shake it off. There's always a new campaign right around the corner for you guys."

"You don't understand. This is it for me. If Tailburger doesn't reach a five percent market share by the end of the year, I'm out of a job and I lose my pension."

"Jesus, Sky. You can't control that."

"Try telling that to the Link."

"Once you get involved with me, you realize there's no going back. It's a permanent stain."

"Jeez, you make it sound so great."

"I just want to make sure you know what you're getting into."

I nodded at Cal and took another sip of espresso. I didn't really want to cross over into the unsavory business of pornography. When you've got to keep something a secret from the people you care about, it's a sure sign you shouldn't be doing it. This wasn't something I'd rush home to tell Ethan and Sophia, or even King, about, but what choice did I have? This was the one way left I could see to pull Tailburger out of its tailspin. The Link had given me my orders—do whatever it takes—and I would carry them out like a good Union soldier.

17

Plot

ALBANY, NEW YORK

Henry "Plot" Thickens, New York's attorney general, had his eye on the governor's office in Albany. Having made a name for himself with his tough stands on crime and consumer fraud, he was part of the conservatism, some said fascism, sweeping across the Empire State. The Republican incumbent, Mario Puma, was vulnerable, having failed to live up to his promises to cut taxes and televise state executions.

Originally a mentor to Thickens, Puma had isolated himself from even his closest allies by marrying an acknowledged transsexual named Joey. The installation of a hyperbaric oxygen chamber in the governor's mansion and the presence of Aerosmith at all official state dinners hadn't helped his cause either. Still, to win the gubernatorial election, Thickens would need an enormous war chest and a strong turnout at the upstate polls. I figured that Tailburger's money and Burton Roxby's endorsement, strategically placed together, would be the perfect cheese to trap our rat.

We met for drinks at Jack's, an old-style hangout for politicos located straight down the hill from the state capitol building. To walk inside was to be transported to another time. The waiters, all dressed in white tuxedo jackets with black accoutrements, frantically scurried about with trays overhead, delivering immense New York strip steaks to anxious customers. Billie Holiday's voice and a jazz accompaniment played unobtrusively in the background. Roxby (still holding up bill 214 in the Agriculture Committee, listeria provisions and all) and I took a table and waited for Thickens to arrive. The headwaiter, Andre, breezily arrived and took our orders: a Diet Coke for the wussball Congressman and a Long Island iced tea for yours truly.

"You've got to be careful about what you say, Sky."

"What do you mean?"

"What I mean is that there's a thin line between a legitimate political donation and a bribe."

"Well, you're the expert in bribery, that's for sure, but I'm not bribing him, Burt. I'm simply asking him to exclude Tailburger from the SERMON lawsuit."

"In exchange for what?"

"What do you think? How about a big sloppy blow job? I'll get down on my knees right here at this restaurant and give him the best head he's ever had in his life. Do you think that'll do the trick?"

I saw Thickens from afar, which wasn't difficult to do. A former football star at Penn State, he was six four, three hundred pounds and had a neck like a tree stump. Steroid use had destroyed both his hairline and his complexion. A knee injury had shortened his NFL career with Philadelphia and led him to law school, but it hadn't stopped his incessant talk about playing in "the League."

"Gentlemen."

Roxby stood up to shake hands with Thickens. I didn't have the energy.

"Hello, Plot. God, you look great," Roxby gushed.

"Nice to see you, Plot," was the best greeting I could muster.

"You two see the fog this morning?" Thickens asked.

"It was pretty thick."

"Damn straight. I'll tell ya, it reminded me of my days back in the League. Of course you guys remember the Fog Bowl in '88. We were playing the Bears up at Soldier in the first round of the play-offs. I'd just come off of I.R. and my knee was still killin' me."

For a brief moment, Andre saved us.

"Something to drink, sir?"

"I'd like a Seven and Seven."

Unfortunately, Thickens didn't miss a beat.

"So anyway, you can't see anything out there. I mean even the guy lining up against you is a little cloudy. Third quarter comes and I snap my fibula. You know how you hear the pop?"

Roxby and I shook our heads, but Thickens wasn't waiting for an answer.

"Well, I heard the pop. So I stick the bone back under the skin, take a few cortisone shots and get it taped up. A few minutes later, I'm sitting on the bench when Coach Ryan comes over to me. He says, 'Thickens, you're going back in the game and I want you to take out their quarterback.' So I ask him if I'm going back in at end or tackle, since I'd been alternating between the two, and he says, 'Neither, you're going in as our twelfth man.' 'Twelfth man?' I asked. 'Aren't we only allowed eleven?'"

By now, Roxby and I were done with our drinks and praying for Andre to come back.

"Then I'll never forget what he said to me. He said, 'Don't be an asshole, Thickens. They'll never see you in all this fog.' And they didn't. I smashed through the line, broken bone and all, and took McMahon's head off. We lost the game, but that was some of the most brilliant coaching I'd ever been around. (Pause) So anyway, what can I do for you gentlemen?"

"I want to talk to you about the SERMON suit."

"Sky, my office hasn't decided what our role will be in that suit. I've had a few preliminary meetings with Muffet Meaney, but nothing is definite."

"Oh, you've met with Muffet?" I asked nonchalantly.

"Do you know her, Sky?"

"I may have met her once or twice."

"Some number, eh?"

"She's attractive." My reply seemed suitably understated.

"Not only that. She's a real fuck monkey, too. I had the most wicked backache by the time I made it home from D.C."

I hid my extreme displeasure by biting down on a swizzle stick and reminding myself that I needed this guy. Then Roxby, for no reason other than to hear his own voice, decided to get into the mix.

"Look, Plot. It's no secret that you're planning to run for governor next year. Now Tailburger is one of the best corporate constituents in my district, and I'm very interested in seeing them thrive. They employ a lot of people, and they pay a lot of taxes. That said, I'm also very interested in seeing a pro-business Republican governor, preferably one with a dickless wife, take office. I think you can be that governor, and I'd like to tell the three million voters in western New York how I feel."

Roxby's words made me feel a little bit better about Muffet, but not much.

"Burt, I would of course welcome your support in any future campaign I may or may not undertake. I would welcome it openly. But this SERMON suit is something that involves the health of the citizens of New York, and as attorney general, my first obligation is to them."

My tone was direct as I jumped back into the fray.

"Let me tell you what I want, Plot. Help me broker a side settlement before the suit starts, or even better, use your influence with Muffet Meaney to get us excluded entirely."

"Sky, if you think I can promise you either of those things, you're crazy."

"I don't want to insult you, Plot, or worse, end up tossing some gangbanger's salad in Attica state prison, but Tailburger would be most appreciative of any efforts you could make on our behalf."

"As would I," Roxby chimed in.

"I understand, and I promise I will try. I know it's a competitive time in the fast-food industry and these lawsuits can be damned expensive. Let's just keep talking. Keep the lines of communication open. You know, it reminds me of being back in the League. Seems every week I was getting hit with a palimony suit or attending a child support hearing or getting slapped with a restraining order. You name it, I saw it. Shit, I spent more time in the local courthouse than in the film room. It really got me interested in the legal profession."

"I'd love to hear more, Plot, but I have to get back to Rochester. My daughter, Sophia, is coming home for the weekend from college."

Roxby followed my lead with his own lie.

"I've got to go, too. Big date with my wife tonight. Have to keep those home fires burning."

"Okay, gents. Then we'll be talking."

"You got it, Plot. Thanks for your time."

"Thanks, Plot."

Roxby and I left, pretty well convinced that Thickens could be manipulated. It would mostly take money, but if it saved Tailburger from the SERMON suit, it would be worth every penny.

18

Simmering

The mood at corporate headquarters was less somber than I anticipated. I said hello to Sheila, our receptionist, and made my way
to the executive conference room for our monthly board meeting.
Ned, Ted and Fred, dressed in bright green pants, multicolored
shirts, white golf shoes and visors, had arrived early, as usual, in
order to monopolize the doughnut tray.

"Hey, guys," I muttered upon entering.

"Hey, Sky," came back at me in triplicate.

"That was some stunt you pulled on Larry King," Ned offered,
his mouth full of glazed dough.

"Absolutely," agreed Ted as he licked chocolate off his fingers.

"What's going on with you and that chick?" Fred subtly asked
while fingering a cruller.

"I'd rather not talk about it. Just a bad night all around," I
responded, hoping to deflect their interest. "What did you shoot
this morning, Ned?"

"Sky, get this. I'm a hundred fifty, maybe a hundred seventy-
five yards from the hole on the sixteenth at Shady Bush. I pull out
a six-iron, stroke her smooth and put that puppy three inches
from the cup. Prettiest thing you ever saw."

"He shot a one-forty," Ted blurted.

"Shut up, Ted. It was a one-thirty. We weren't playing water penalties, remember?"

"Would sure like to join out at Crooked Creek, Sky. Heck of a club," Ted agitated for a reaction.

"I know, Ted. I'd love to help you out there. The waiting list is just brutal. I'll let you know when your name pops up."

Biff Dilworth, wearing his trademark three-piece suit, sat with his legs crossed near the head of the table, reading the *Wall Street Journal*. He didn't engage in small talk prior to the start of our meetings, mostly because he hated the rest of us. Chad Hemmingbone felt similarly and usually arrived a few minutes late in order to avoid the inevitably mundane conversations one is subjected to at such gatherings. In contrast, Annette McNabnay, apparently over my earlier snub, smiled at me upon her arrival and asked how I was doing. As we chatted and waited for stragglers, the Link took great pride in introducing Sister Ancilla as our newest board member. Though her business acumen could be compared to that of a goat, she would add "moral insurance," in the words of the Link.

"What kind of ball do you play, Sister?"

"Ball?" she replied, clearly confused by Ned's question.

"Yeah, you know, golf ball. What kind of golf ball do you use?"

"I'm afraid I don't play the game."

Ted, being a complete turd, took offense to her characterization of his favorite activity.

"Hey, Sister, it's a sport, okay? Not a game. Pinball. Now that's a game."

"I meant no offense."

"None taken, Sister. None taken. Just watch what you say."

Ned wanted to get back to his point despite the sister's evident lack of interest.

"Anyway, Sister, the new Titleists are amazing. Great touch

around the greens and long as Christmas Eve off the tee. So if you're in the market, give 'em some thought."

"I'll do that."

Fred, despite knowing that I thought he was retarded, attempted to engage me in conversation, much to his credit.

"Taking any vacation this summer, Sky?"

"I don't think so, Fred. Too much going on with the new campaign to get away right now. What about you?"

"Yeah. I'm taking the whole crew over to the British Isles to play the legendary courses. St. Andrews, Balmoral, Carnoustie, all of them. We'll get in fifty-four holes a day."

"Bet the kids'll love that."

"You know, they're only six and four, but I think it's going to be a good experience for them, and Marcia, well, she can't wait. I told her the RV I'm renting has a stove *and* an oven. Can you believe it?"

"No. It sounds wonderful."

"She's really excited."

Once our entire assemblage had gathered, we proceeded as usual. After the minutes were approved, we formally voted Sister Ancilla onto the board and began the various committee reports. When the time arrived for marketing, I took the lead as committee chairman and recounted some of the initial problems we'd been having with the Torture campaign. Soon, the topic turned to a new giveaway scheme in light of the carnival worker comb set surplus. The Link got us started.

"How about a knife giveaway? Kids love knives."

"I don't think that's a good idea, Frank," Chad Hemmingbone conjectured.

"Sure it is. What child doesn't enjoy a good game of mumblety-peg?"

"That seems a bit violent to me," Sister Ancilla said. "How about handing out copies of the Bible?"

The Link, who was not used to having his ideas dismissed so summarily, reasserted himself immediately.

"Sister, the name of the company is Tailburger, not Jesus Burger."

Biff Dilworth, who was always pushing the educational angle, suggested we distribute great books. His idea was, of course, shot down by the Link.

"Biff, you old coot, will you please join us in the new millennium? Kids don't want to read. Hell, half of them don't know how to read. Books are not going to bring them by our stores."

"Don't we have a responsibility to our youth market to help them better themselves?" Biff persisted. "Sister, don't you agree?"

"I do. I think books are a wonderful idea."

The skillful use of Sister Ancilla to leverage an idea against the Link was something our fat führer had not anticipated and certainly didn't like. His anger spilled out as he spoke.

"Are you two done? We're not running the book-of-the-month club here. We're running a fast-food company. Whatever we give away has to appeal to our current customers, seventy-eight percent of whom, according to our research, are illiterate. So we're not gonna sell more burgers by giving away Moby Fucking Dick, Tom Fucking Sawyer or the Invisible Fucking Man. Are you tracking?"

"I think I'm tracking, Frank, but your foul language is entirely unnecessary," Sister Ancilla responded, a bit bewildered by the Link's profanity.

"Sister, I apologize. I'm just passionate about our product, and I want to see it sell."

"God forgives you, my child."

Suddenly the board meeting was turning into a confessional. What was next? Wafers and grape juice?

"Thank you, Sister. Now let's hear some better ideas."

"What about a nice titanium driver?" Fred asked.

"Now that's a good idea," Ned added.

"Hell of a good idea," Ted followed.

"Are you three brain-dead?" the Link asked.

Chad Hemmingbone saw the limitations of the proposed offer.

"Don't those go for three hundred dollars a pop?"

"Well, some of your Big Berthas do, but we could give away knockoffs," Fred answered.

"Our patrons would be more likely to use them on each other's windshields than on a golf course," Annette McNabnay observed.

"Road rage could be a problem with a club giveaway," Dilworth concurred.

Ted Truheart, still afraid the Link would release the pictures of him with his French au pair, said nothing.

"What about domestic violence?" Hemmingbone inquired.

"What about it?" I wondered aloud.

"Well, we have a high number of wife beaters among our clientele. I'm concerned we might be held liable for any clubbings."

The Link was fed up.

"Oh, for Christ's sake. Can we come back from the brink of insanity here, please? We're not giving away titanium drivers. Okay?"

Fred wasn't quite ready to let go.

"How about putters?"

"That could work," Ned opined.

"That could definitely work," Ted completed the triumvirate of stupidity.

The Link shook his head and turned his attention to me.

"Sky, what do you think? You're the one who got us into this mess. How're ya gonna get us out?"

I figured I could dance around the issue for a short time.

"Frank, I can report to the board that I'm in touch with an outside consultant, Cal Perkins, who is an expert in marketing and is going to work with me on some new ideas. I'll have more to say next time but I'm excited about the possibilities."

"Good, Sky. I'm glad to hear that, but you better move your ass quickly before this whole company is bankrupt!"

The meeting adjourned after a blood vessel popped in the Link's neck and he needed to seek medical attention. Ned's suggestion that we give away electric golf carts was more than his father could take. In all my years at Tailburger, the board had never made it through an entire meeting's agenda, and today was no exception.

I saw Annette in the parking lot as the other cars cleared and sensed an opportunity. I felt a bit awkward approaching her, but I was determined to move on from Muffet, and asking Annette out seemed like the best way to do it.

"Hey, Annette, could you hold up?" I picked up my pace until I stood next to her.

"Sky, I don't mean to be rude, but I'm off to another meeting, believe it or not."

"Sure, sure. I understand. This'll just take a minute."

Having turned her down once, I was now met with suspicion. The slight prick to her person that accompanied my rejection had healed, and there was no interest in reopening the wound, however tiny.

"Listen, I'd like to take you out sometime."

She sighed. "Sky, I don't know. I mean, didn't you say you were getting involved with someone? What about that?"

If I'd been totally honest, I would have told Annette that I still had feelings for Muffet, and that somewhere deep in the lower recesses of my heart, I hoped we could be together again.

"That? That's all over now."

"Well . . ."

"I promise to get you home before curfew."

Annette's face lit up. For a moment, I had won her vague affections back.

"I guess so."

"That's a yes?"

"Yes. Give me a call."

"Great."

I stood and watched as Annette drove away. The sputtering exhaust from her car provided the soundtrack to a movie moment in my life. As she disappeared out of sight, it struck me that she was somehow important in whatever cosmic plan existed for me. With any luck, she'd help me forget all about the loss of Jess and the pain in my gut caused by Ms. Meaney, and would put me on the path to happiness. In many ways, I was at her mercy.

19

Breach

To ensure complete privacy for our discussions, Cal agreed to meet me at my house. Although I was still uncertain about entering the world of pornography, I knew it was my only option. To calm my raw nerves, I lit a Commodore and put on Mozart's *Turkish Rondo*. With my wretched career nearing its tragic conclusion, I figured I'd better start appreciating some of the finer things. Cal came through my front door with his typical exuberance. He was in top shape, the result of regular running, and looked about fifteen years younger than me. It was true what they said. Money did make you more attractive.

"You make me sick, Cal. Do you know that?"

"What do you mean?"

"Never mind. You wouldn't understand," I said, taking another drag on my butt.

"I've got some great ideas for Tailburger, Sky."

"Good, come on in to the kitchen. I've got some beer."

"It's ten A.M."

"Don't worry. It's light beer."

Cal had a laptop with him that he flipped on and used to pull up his Lust Ranch site.

"We get six million hits a month on this sucker, and that number is growing."

I looked at the comely female form on the screen and found my prurient interests piquing. To Cal, the same set of huge knockers registered as dollar signs. "What a shame," I thought, rubbing my schwantz against the nearest table leg.

"What I propose as a first step is to place a large ad banner on the wallpaper. That way, every time a horny, and hopefully hungry, male logs on, he will see the Tailburger logo and the catchphrase 'Torture Yourself.' You like that?"

"That's good. I like it."

"Alone, it'll give you a one percent bump. Your consumers and ours mesh perfectly."

"I don't know if I should feel flattered or insulted by that remark."

"C'mon, Sky, don't tell me that surprises you."

"It doesn't. I'm just fucking around. What else do you have?"

"Today's your lucky day. Construction on our actual Lust Ranch in Nevada is almost finished. Why doesn't Tailburger sponsor some kind of contest to win a free trip out there along with a year's supply of food? We'll promote it exclusively through the site."

"Cal, that's good. We can call it the 'Nail Some Tail Sweepstakes.' "

"Perfect. And the great thing is that you'll hit one of your big target markets. Disgruntled teens."

"Isn't the site restricted?"

"Yes, but the kids find ways to get in. And let's just say we don't work too hard to stop them."

"I don't want to know anything about that end of the business. Just keep it legal."

"Don't worry about that. It's all covered."

"Christ, it really sounds promising, Cal. But how am I going to keep this quiet from my own organization?"

"We'll run it through our marketing group. I'll make sure the details are kept secret and you pay us under a consulting arrangement. It's no problem. Plus, if someone at Tailburger wants to blow your cover, they'll have to admit they've been trolling for porn on the Web. Do you think anybody would do that?"

"Well, I'm sure half the board trolls for porn, but they're mostly cowards and I don't think any of them would say anything. I'll take my chances. I've got to get our market share up."

"Then it's settled. We start on Monday. I'm sure my people will have some other ideas as well."

"Do you think this is going to work?"

"Sky, I'm telling you, we'll get a Tailburger in the mouth of every sick, twisted pervert out there."

"That's all I want."

"I know it is."

Cal and I clinked our bottles of Bud Light together and drank. We had come a long way from our days in Mrs. Larrabee's second grade class. "She'd be proud of us now," I thought, "a couple of smut kings all grown-up." Maybe we could put on a wing at Thornell Road Elementary School in her honor: the Harriet Larrabee Center for Budding Pornographers.

Although Cal was my best friend by far, I couldn't help but feel like I was making a deal with the devil. Mozart's music seemed too elegant a witness to our sordid business, so I suggested we move outside to the brick patio behind my house. In the arms of my Adirondack chairs we shot the shit about old times, sleeping out for tickets to the Stones, senior prom, Bills games and bachelor parties. By the time we finished, I'd made some kind of peace with myself. Better the devil you know than the one you don't.

After Cal left, Ethan called to catch up on my news. All had been so quiet on the Macrocock front, I feared he had forgotten me, his banker. Those concerns were quickly put to rest.

"Dad, how's it going? It's Ethan. Your son."

Ethan clearly wanted to stress the familial connection.

"My son? Ah yes, I seem to remember such a creature."

"Sorry I've been so tough to reach. Skull told me you called a few times. We've just been shredding."

"Did you get your second round of financing?"

"Not yet. But we met with Eddie Wu, you know the guy who started Wahoo. He's got the bones to do it if he's willing. The dude was so cool. Came driving up in a new Testarossa. He's worth like eight billion, and he's only twenty-three."

"Yeah, but is he happy?"

"C'mon, Dad." Ethan laughed at my apparently amusing inquiry.

"Well, I'm glad to hear things are going well."

"Hey, I saw the Torture campaign for Tailburger. Did you put that together?"

"I played a part."

"Kudos, Popala. That Blatherskite video is da domb. You're a Martian genius."

"And that's good?"

"Definitely."

"Thanks, Ethan, but to be honest the campaign's not going so well."

"Hakuna Matada, mi poppa. Don't let it stomp on your buzz."

"I'll try not to. Listen, how are the finances?"

"Well, I wanted to talk to you about that. I've been working like twenty-four-seven, so I was planning on heading down to Palm Beach with my posse. I could use some extra cash."

"Palm Beach with your posse? For how long, Puff Daddy?"

"Just a few days. Everybody from Macrocock is going. This one dude's stepfather has a place where we can crash."

"Maybe Eddie Wu will pay for you guys."

"I wish. We'd be stylin' if that was the case."

"I'll send you a few hundred, but that's it."

"Dad, you're all-time. Thanks a lot. I'll talk to you later."

"Good-bye, Ethan."

To be called "all-time" was the ultimate compliment in Ethan-speak. It put me in a pantheon of greats ranging from Jim Carrey to Austin Powers to the lead singer for Abundant Fuck, and it was certainly enough to keep me sending money, however ill-advised that course of action was. There are a million ways to tell somebody you love them in this world, but nothing is as effective, or as welcomed by a child, as a check in the mail.

20

The Standing Stage

"Truthfulness. Benevolence. Forbearance. These are the things you should be focusing on."

King had not given up on my Qigong training or me.

"Even a chi as wayward as yours can be channeled."

"I don't feel well, King."

I really didn't. And not just physically. The strain of the last few months was undoubtedly taking its toll on my body, which ached in ways that were difficult to describe, but there was also something wrong with my head, maybe even my soul or my spirit, or that part of me that flowed around and made me feel bad or good. Dare I say, my chee.

"Perhaps your yang heel vessel is blocked."

"I don't know what's plugged up, but something's not right."

"Well, that's why we're doing this—to get you unblocked—to allow you to reach a state of inner harmony. Now I need you to focus. We're going to start the standing stage today. Are you ready?"

"Sure."

I didn't tell King, but I was breaking another of the twenty-four rules of Qigong training by failing to regulate my mind. Although

I was supposed to be avoiding miscellaneous thoughts and "cutting them off at their origins," I was having a hard time reconciling my chosen descent into the world of pornography with this meditation process and my life. It didn't sound like such a big deal at the time, but now, having done it, I questioned my moral rooting. And it made dealing with concepts like truthfulness and forbearance, and the pursuit of inner harmony, more difficult, if not impossible.

"In the standing stage, you learn to take the energy that you've built up during the sitting stage—your chi reservoir—and move with it."

"Move with it?"

"Channel it from your Dan Tian to your five ancestral organs: the brain and spinal cord, the liver and gall bladder, the bone marrow, the penis and the blood system."

"That's more than five."

"Some go together in pairs."

"Oh. Well, what kind of chee comes from my penis?"

"That would be your essence chi, but it doesn't come *from* your penis; it flows *to* your penis."

"I really don't feel like doing this right now."

"Don't doubt your training and become lazy."

"Let me guess. That's another of the twenty-four rules."

"Yes, it is. Do you have any idea what a privilege it is to be able to freely practice Qigong? If we were in China right now, you'd have an electric cattle prod poking at your genitalia."

"I bet that gets the essence chee flowing."

"Can we focus? Now as we begin meditating today, I want you to reaffirm the values of morality espoused by the Falun Gong: doing good works, speaking honestly, believing in extraterrestrial life . . ."

"You mean like aliens?"

"Breathe. In and out. Warm your Dan Tian. Imagine fire in your belly. A flowing river of vital energy."

"Got it."

"Okay, we're ready for some backbends. These are going to energize your yang. Place your hands on your hips and . . . starting slowly . . . lean backward. Can you feel that?"

"I feel something."

"Good. The mind and the body are acting as one."

After finishing my session with King, we sat outside with a couple of Frescas and let our Dan Tians cool down.

"Have you ever thought about a more conventional existence, King?"

"Oh, sure, I've thought about it. In fact, lately I've been thinking about getting my Ph.D."

"Your Ph.D.? You need a college degree before you can get that."

"Not for the school I'm looking at."

"What school is that?"

"E-Tech University. It's all Web-based. You hunker down in your bedroom and six weeks later, you walk out with your degree."

"Six weeks? What kind of degree can you get in six weeks?"

"Any degree you want really. Ph.D., J.D., M.D. I was thinking of becoming a surgeon."

"In six weeks?"

"Well, no. Not just six weeks. There's a residency period afterward, which is another four weeks. But I'm more inclined to go the Ph.D. route."

"In what?"

"Paranormal activities. (Pause) Poltergeists, specters, apparitions, the whole *Ghostbusters* thing."

"You want to be a ghostbuster?"

"I think so."

My conversation with King confirmed everything I already suspected. I wasn't cut out to roam the world the way he did. Thus I arrived at work resigned to riding an American wave of perversion into retirement and my pension. Six months and two market share percentage points away from finishing my twentieth year at Tailburger, I couldn't let anything, including my chee or my ghost-busting brother, get in the way.

My pension. Its importance to me had grown disproportionately large. There were good reasons, though. I saw it as part of my salvation. Sure, I'd have to give a big chunk of it to Trip Baden, but what remained would be enough for me to quit work and to do some of things I'd always wanted, like learning my neighbor's names and fixing up the 1963 Austin Healy that currently sat in pieces in my basement. The pension money would also give me time. Time to spend with my kids, time to pursue a relationship with someone (possibly Annette), maybe even time to find and channel my chee. Time to get well in my own way. Life, I'd learned, was just one big accumulation of wounds. Now I needed time to heal.

The more I thought about things, the more I wondered why I felt the need to morally chastise myself. I'd never been any kind of saint, and today's porn wasn't the dirty business I'd witnessed in the days before the Internet. I recounted the positive attributes of Cal's site in my mind:

1. It was a victimless endeavor. Nobody would be shedding any blood here. Just lots of love.
2. These women got paid for their performances. They were artists, and it was important to support the arts.
3. Both disease and the population were reduced. You can't catch herpes off your hard drive, and perhaps more important, cybersex meant less actual sex and fewer babies, saving our precious natural resources.
4. Lustranch.com provided a wonderful service for millions of chronic masturbators, sex addicts and the truly ugly.

My free-association session ended when the Link called me into his office with news about the SERMON suit.

"We've been served," the Link said grimly as he pointed to a copy of the filed complaint on his desk. He was calm, all things considered.

"When?" I asked, incredulous we'd been sued.

"This morning. Just now. Some kid with a pierced eyebrow and a Marilyn Manson tattoo caught up with me in the parking lot."

"Is the New York attorney general a named plaintiff?"

"Does a Tailpipe with cheese make you shit blood? What do you think?"

"Goddamnit! Thickens caved. He said he'd help us out."

"Well, he lied. What a novel friggin' concept—a public servant who's a complete goddamn liar."

"You know he's sleeping with Muffet Meaney."

"How do you know that?"

"He said so when we met in Albany."

"So you're telling me we're getting sued so this guy can keep getting laid?"

"It looks that way. I still don't understand it. If Thickens expects to run for governor and win, he's going to need our money, and even more, he's going to need Roxby. Burt's the only guy who can deliver the upstate vote for him."

"Call Roxby and tell him what this prick did."

I pulled out my cellular and dialed Roxby's private line. He had graced me with the number after a particularly large Tailburger donation to his last campaign.

"Hello."

Roxby sounded nervous.

"Burt, it's Sky Thorne."

"Sky, all I want you to know is that I'm innocent. Completely and totally innocent."

"What are you talking about?"

Roxby quickly became hysterical.

"I was set up. Governor Puma's people heard I was backing Plot Thickens. You have to believe me."

I appeased him for no particular reason.

"I believe you, Burt. Whatever you say."

All of a sudden a voice I didn't recognize came on the line.

"Representative Roxby will not be making any further comments to the media about his case. Good-bye."

Completely perplexed, I flipped my phone shut and looked at the Link.

"What's wrong, Thorne?"

"Something happened to Roxby. Turn on the television."

The perpetual tedium of CNN's *Headline News* usually anesthetized me. A continuous wave of interchangeable faces with fake names repeated the same stories over and over again at an octave below normal until the reported events were nothing more than background noise. Voices modulated little whether a cute cat had been rescued from a Memphis tree or Boris Yeltsin had been rescued from a Moscow nightclub. So I was somewhat surprised by the tone of urgency coming from the Atlanta news desk.

"To repeat our top story, Congressman Burton Roxby has been arrested on charges of statutory rape for his alleged involvement with the family's baby-sitter. He has also been charged with possession of cocaine and contributing to the delinquency of a minor. The arraignment has just been held and preliminary reports indicate that Mr. Roxby has pleaded not guilty to the charges. When reached for comment, the president, who served in the House with Mr. Roxby, said that, if the charges were true, he was deeply saddened and, frankly, shocked that Representative Roxby didn't have the decency or common sense to wait until the baby-sitter turned eighteen. We now go to a live press conference being held in Rochester, New York, with Representative Roxby's lawyer, M.C. Shufelbarger."

I snuffed out my smoke and sat up to watch our horny little House member. Out in front of the state courthouse, halfway up the marble stairs that led to its entrance, stood a gaggle of at least fifty reporters huddled around Roxby and his attorney. Shufelbarger was an old criminal law hack whose jowly face nearly eclipsed his bow tie. He'd represented every piece of human bilge that had washed up on Lake Ontario's shore. As expected, Roxby stood to the side and indicated by his body language that he would not be speaking. Shufelbarger stepped up to a microphone resting on a makeshift podium.

"Before I answer any questions, I want to read a statement."

The balding lawyer pulled a pair of glasses from the left breast pocket of his suit jacket and placed them on the tip of his bulbous nose, rife with broken blood vessels. He put a single piece of paper on the lectern and began.

"Representative Roxby is completely innocent of all charges leveled against him here today. Although he is quite fond of the young woman in question, and believes she is an excellent baby-sitter, he did at no time have any sexual or improper contact with her or encourage her to use drugs. We are confident that a jury of his peers will acquit him and put to rest these outrageous allegations that have no basis in fact and are extremely hurtful to the entire Roxby family. Burton Roxby is a tireless public servant who puts himself on the line for the American people every single day, and this is just one of the many risks such a man is exposed to in his line of work. Justice will prevail. I'll take a few questions now."

"How old is the girl?" a reporter from Buffalo's Channel 5 asked.

"Twelve."

"How *was* she, Roxby?" a cry came from the back.

Shufelbarger was miffed.

"People, please. Keep your questions appropriate and direct them at me."

"Isn't it true that Mr. Roxby was found alone with the girl up in a tree fort?"

"That is correct. Representative Roxby was helping the young woman with a school science project on leaves."

"Why were his pants off?"

"People, I'm telling you. One more inappropriate question and this press conference is over. And by the way, they were not off. He merely loosened them for purposes of comfort and they fell down. Representative Roxby's recent low-carb diet is the real culprit here."

"How much toot did they do before fucking?"

"That's it. This press conference is over."

Roxby was led away by his attorney to a waiting car. My best hope for brokering a deal with SERMON was off to presumably post bail and plan for a life after politics and possible time in state prison. He would be useless to Plot Thickens in the governor's race now, making the attorney general's actions somewhat more understandable. Still, Plot had been a real shitbag to immediately abandon Tailburger, and if he thought he could quietly slip away without hearing from me, he was sorely mistaken.

"Frank, I'll call Plot right away."

"This means war," the Link threatened as he began to ramble on. "I'll put the bayonet up to their throats myself if I have to. We've got to pack the gunpowder tight and keep it dry, Thorne. Meaney and Thickens are fucking with the wrong burger brigade. We'll get these fuckers to Appomattox yet, I swear. Now where in the hell is my flask?"

I retreated to my office to telephone Plot. His secretary answered and, to my surprise, put me through. Like the consummate politician, Plot answered the phone as if I were an old friend calling for a favor.

"Sky Thorne. What can I do for you?"

"What can you do for me? How about stop being a two-faced asshole?"

"Sky, that's totally inappropriate. Is this about the lawsuit?"

"What do you think, blockhead?"

"I think you're rude. What do you expect me to do? Roxby's

useless to me now. He got caught. As we used to say in the League, fifteen yards for illegal use of the hands."

"Will you shut up with that? Nobody cares about the fucking League! I want you to withdraw from the suit. There's a quid pro quo in effect here. We'll support your campaign big-time if you get out now. We had a deal."

"We didn't have any deal. Anyway, I can't, Sky. Chicken Hut and Pizza King have both thrown their support behind me in the past week. I'm going to have plenty of money. I don't need Tailburger. Look, the political winds are blowing against beef. Back in the League, this is what we called fourth down. Time to punt, Sky."

"I'm going to punt my foot into your ass. Can you grasp that?"

"Sky, I think that's fifteen yards for unnecessary roughness."

"Stop making those stupid football analogies. Nobody wants to hear them. You know, I hope you and Meaney both rot in hell. I really do. And by the way, I'm voting for Puma!"

I pounded the telephone back into its cradle and just like that, Tailburger was doomed to endure a long legal battle. The odds of changing anybody's mind about the inclusion of my employer in the SERMON lawsuit were not good, and the implications for me were worse. Lawsuits cost money, lots of money, and were absolute poison for earnings. They also caused bad publicity, which was murder for market share. I could see my pension sailing off into the sea toward Tahiti on a boat I had not boarded.

21

Threats

Within two weeks of its start, Tailburger's involvement with Cal Perkins began to pay dividends. According to his Lust Ranch experts, among contests combining food and legalized prostitution, our Nail Some Tail Sweepstakes was drawing entries at a record pace. Sales were up at every store in the Tailburger chain, and with that came more money to spend on advertising.

With the SERMON boycott still in effect and the announcement of the class action lawsuit, all indicators should have been down, but they weren't. This meant I could keep pushing the Torture campaign, claim credit for the company's turnaround and watch our stock price and market share rise. It was the perfect plan. The Link, however, had other ideas about where credit was due.

"Did you see this month's numbers, Thorne?"

"Yes, I did. Pretty impressive, huh? I knew the Torture campaign would just take a little while to kick in."

"No offense, Thorne, but I really don't think it's the campaign that's producing these results."

Did he know something about the Nail Some Tail Sweepstakes? Suddenly, I was feeling very nervous.

"You don't?"

"Hell, no. Let's not kid each other. It's the soft batch burgers we've been serving up. The undercooking on the inside. That's what's bringing them into the stores in droves."

So relieved was I to hear his conclusion, I had no motive to contradict him.

"That's probably playing a big part, Frank."

"Damn right it is. Now we go after Muffet Meaney. And we go after her hard, Thorne. I'm talking Stonewall Jackson hard. I take it you're out of the saddle."

"Yeah. The *Larry King* appearance sort of ended things."

"That's too bad. I've asked Ned, Ted and Fred to arrange for some high-level surveillance work under Operation Tenderize. We're going to tap her phones and put a tracer on her car. We need something we can nail her with. Something so embarrassing she'll beg us to back off. I'd love to get some raunchy footage of her with Plot Thickens. We could sink both of them at the same time. You still think they're doin' it?"

"I think so," I answered painfully.

The Link leaned back and lit a cigar, pulled from his desk drawer. His pursed his lips and inhaled before blowing a billowing cloud of smoke out in my general direction and reflecting on the quality of the tobacco.

"Smooth as a prom queen's thighs, Thorne. Just not as dangerous. (Pause) Hey, how are things looking out at Crooked Creek? My name has to be coming up on the membership waiting list, eh?"

"I'll have to check again, Frank. You know I'd love to get you in there," I lied.

"You do that."

Through the haze of the Link's cigar smoke, I suddenly saw something clearly. Why hadn't it occurred to me before? How could I have been so stupid? I was already in possession of the only thing necessary to destroy Muffet Meaney: the videotape of us having sex at my house. I simply forgot I had it.

The delicate balance of undercooked burgers, the Torture campaign and Cal, mysteriously causing our increased sales, wouldn't last forever. To ensure myself of lasting growth in Tailburger market share, I needed to remove the SERMON lawsuit as a threat to the financial condition of the company. The videotape was the key. All of my incentives were aligned. I could assure myself of a rising market share and receipt of my beloved pension while exacting a bit of sweet revenge against a woman who had not only attacked me on national television, but had also slept with half the adult population. So why wasn't I immediately offering up the tape to the Link? Easy. I didn't trust him with my insurance policy. I needed to think this whole thing through first. After all, there was another person on that tape, and its contents could prove quite embarrassing to someone other than Ms. Meaney.

"You know what's a fuckin' shame, Thorne?"

"What, Frank?"

"You can't even get a medium-rare hamburger in this country anymore. Goddamn government has everybody scared out of their goddamn minds about this goddamn E. coli shit."

"It is a shame."

"We're showin 'em though, aren't we? Our undercooked insides have people flocking to Tailburger like vultures to a corpse."

"It is remarkable."

"I remember working in my uncle's butcher shop when I was six years old. We used to eat gobs of ground beef by the handful as an afternoon snack. Raw right out of the fridge. Never got sick once."

"That's amazing."

"We did lose my brother from a mysterious digestive illness around the same time, but I'm certain it had nothing to do with the meat. Anyway, the point is that this country is going right the hell downhill because of too much regulatory interference. Christ, you can't scratch your ass these days without a permit. Slowly but surely all the pleasures of life are being taken away. Can't drink.

Can't smoke. Can't pay women less than men. Can't discriminate because of race or religion. Can't carry a concealed weapon to the grocery store. I mean, really, what's left worth living for?"

"Times have changed, Frank. Look at my life. I encourage Sophia to join the Young Republicans at Cornell. So what does she do? She moves out of her dorm room and into a VW bus with a guy named Tweeter. The world's slipping away on us."

"You're right. The whole thing is just slipping away. Religion. That's all that's left. That's why I'm embracing Sister Ancilla and building the gym for the convent. Those nuns are the only women you can trust."

The Link became increasingly agitated as he spoke.

"The only women who won't run around on you, won't ring up huge credit card bills, won't call you in the middle of the night, reverse the charges and then tell you they're leaving you for the fencing coach at an all-girls junior college in Missouri. IT JUST ISN'T FAIR!"

Silence passed between us for a few seconds.

"You all right?"

"Oh yeah, I'm fine. Did I tell you that the Tailburger Health and Life Fitness Center is nearing completion?"

"No. That's great."

"Sister Ancilla wants me to speak at the ribbon cutting. I'd like you to be there."

"I'll be there. That'll be a proud moment for you, Frank."

"Maybe my proudest."

The mild poignancy of the moment made the Link anxious to change the topic.

"Hey, have you seen the Stampede's 'Got Meat?' ads?"

"Yes, I have."

"Strong work by Hitch, don't you think?"

"Very inventive. No question about it."

"I think he's up for a Clio award this year."

"No kidding?"

I returned to my office, determined to make the most of my videotape with Muffet. A piece of evidence so potent had to be used at the proper time or it could backfire on me. I decided to call Muffet at SERMON and try to broker a deal. With both feet up on my desk, I bargained from a position of strength.

"What do you want, Sky?"

"Hello to you, too. Guess what I'm holding in my hands right now."

"Oh, I don't know. Your penis?"

"I'm afraid not, although you would've been right an hour ago. (Pause) No, I've got something that, believe it or not, is even more powerful."

"Sky, peashooters are for children. When are you going to grow up?"

"Never, if I can help it. Muffet, have you ever dreamed of being a movie star?"

"Can't say that I have. Look, what do you want? You're wasting my time."

"Do you remember our little rendezvous up in Rochester? The one we so boldly committed to celluloid?"

Silence could be heard on the other end of the line.

"Muffet, are you there?"

Still silence.

"You know, I can think of only one other instance where you've been unable to speak, and I think that's on the tape."

Muffet's icy response finally came.

"Sky, if you ever release that tape, I promise I'll make your life miserable."

"Well, I think it's a little premature to talk about marriage, but I'm flattered that you feel so strongly."

"You go public with that video and you'll look just as bad, if not worse, than me. And you can kiss your career good-bye. Nobody'll touch you after that."

"As long as I've got you, I think I can make it."

Muffet didn't seem to appreciate my sarcastic charms.

"Muffet, all you need to do is pull Tailburger out of the SER-MON suit. We'll even settle for a small sum."

"You'll be hearing from my lawyers," she threatened before violently hanging up.

With my work done for the day, I drove home to get ready for love. For the first time in my life, a woman would be picking me up for a date. I didn't really mind when Annette said she'd drive, although my antenna would be up for other signs of emasculation. When I suggested dinner, she said she had tickets to a show and told me to be ready at 7:00 P.M. Yes, ma'am.

Her choice of transportation, a black Volvo sedan, was just about what I expected: something sleek but solid, a bit practical and not too flashy—as much car as a public servant could get away with without being subjected to scorn.

"So where are we going?" I asked, getting into the passenger side.

"The Blue Cross Arena."

Rochester's Blue Cross Arena, formerly called the War Memorial, was the city's closest facsimile to a major venue for concerts and sports, and did lure a Tom Petty or a Janet Jackson on occasion. It also saw its share of high school wrestling championships and BMX bike rallies.

"Great. Are you going to tell me who or what is playing there?"

"No. It's a surprise," Annette said playfully.

"I see. Well, at least give me a hint."

"No."

"C'mon. Give me something."

"Okay," she relented. "Here's your hint." She grinned. "We're going to see something you've never seen before."

"A monster truck rally?"

"No."

"A cockfight?"

"No, Sky."

"An all-lesbian circus?"

"Close."

"I'm getting warm."

"Just wait, all right? You're out of guesses."

The underground parking garage was full of families and a scattering of people dressed like greasers and bobby-soxers, many of whom recognized Annette from television and called out to her.

"Madame Mayor," shouted one man, a dead ringer for Sha Na Na's Bowser. "How ya doin' tonight? Keep up the good work," he encouraged her without waiting for a reply to his original question. As we encountered our fellow Rochestarians, mothers pointed Annette out to their daughters and everyone nodded and acknowledged her one way or another. Inside the arena, a makeshift marquee gave away my date's surprise in large red letters.

NOW APPEARING: GREASE ON ICE

"Are you ready to rock and roll, Sky?" Annette coyly inquired.

Despite her position of enormous responsibility and authority, Annette had retained all of her femininity. She'd grown up in Chicago, gone to a local private school and spent most of her childhood playing the cello. After college she earned a fellowship to the prestigious Eastman School of Music, which brought her to Rochester. After two years of playing with the Rochester Philharmonic Orchestra, she got involved with local politics and rode to power on her promise of downtown economic development. Today she was a player in the community but remained largely unimpressed with herself and her accomplishments. I couldn't say the same about most people I met.

Although I was in good company, I wasn't sure how I felt about this whole *Grease* thing. If my recollection served me, the story hit on some pretty tender boy-meets-girl themes, ones that I probably wasn't ready to face. Sure enough, as the evening wore on, I felt the two of us morphing into Sandy and Danny. The good girl and the bad boy. The prim and proper schoolgirl and the untamed biker. Okay, so the analogy wasn't dead-on, but when Sandy and Danny kissed under the boardwalk, I took Annette's hand. When they broke it off at the end of the summer, I headed out to the nearest beverage bar and got us a couple of sixty-four-ounce Scuz Colas. By the time "You're the One That I Want" kicked in and the ice chips on the rink were flying up, we were dancing wildly on a concrete aisle. Annette's white blouse, now partially untucked from her knee-length skirt, gave me a glimpse at her more than ample breasts. I knew there was a reason why these ice shows were so popular.

I liked Annette from the first time we met, and by the end of our first date, I liked her even more. I had to be cautious, though. She was still a fantasy, a woman who would never ask me to spend a whole day at an outlet mall or an evening watching a movie on the Lifetime channel. And until proven otherwise, she was still someone who would love me in spite of my obvious peccadilloes, something only Jess had done up to this point in my life and something that I desperately missed.

The date ended with one good, long, warm kiss at the door. I didn't ask her to come in because I knew the answer would be no. The mayor couldn't afford to be seen coming out of a strange man's home in the wee hours of the morning, particularly mine.

22

Politically Impotent

LOS ANGELES, YET AGAIN

Once the class action lawsuit was filed, the battle in the press began in earnest. Our PR guru, Zeb Nettles, now under tremendous pressure from the Link to produce positive spin for Tailburger, advised me that ABC, having seen the fireworks between me and Muffet Meaney on *Larry King Live,* hoped to have us face off again on *Real Time,* the late-night talk show with Bill Maher. With no recent school slayings or prominent white supremacists in the news, there was time apparently for a debate about beef.

This was a perfect opportunity for me. Finally, I'd have a chance to let Muffet publicly know what I thought of her and her lawsuit, and to let the hardworking customers of Tailburger know that our food was safe and good for them. Of course, I'd also have to conceal the fact we were purposefully undercooking our meat in order to increase sales.

Unfortunately, Maher, a stand-up comedian turned television host, wasn't what you'd call a sympathetic ear. He met everyone with a certain distrust and every issue with cynicism, which made me nervous and meant I'd need to be on top of my game.

After arriving at the studio, a beautiful production assistant, Gabby, escorted me to a makeup chair and then the green room.

Scheduled to appear with Morgan Fairchild and Arianna Huffington, I was surprised to find myself alone with Muffet. I opened a bottle of Evian and took a seat on the red velvet couch directly across from her. She pretended to study her day planner for a minute or two and then looked up at me.

"I see your plane didn't crash."

"I missed you, too."

"I want that tape, Sky."

"I'm sure you do, but you'll just have to wait 'til Christmas. Have you been a good girl?"

"Asshole!"

"Flattery will get you everywhere."

Although Muffet grew pissier by the moment, I was really starting to have fun now. I couldn't wait to get out onstage, maybe chat up Ms. Fairchild, break a few hearts. Ten minutes before showtime, however, Gabby poked her headsetted face into the green room.

"Did you two hear about the change in guests?"

Muffet and I shook our heads in unison.

"Bill usually likes to get a few celebrities into the mix, but Morgan Fairchild and Arianna Huffington canceled so we've flown in replacements."

My mind raced. Who would be in the chair next to me? Robert Klein? Sister Souljah? Roshumba? George Will?

"Sky, do you know Traylor Hitch?"

Before I could answer, over the transom came Hitch, the blinding glare from his belt buckle unmistakable.

"Sky, you old sum bitch. How the hell are ya?"

"Hitch, what a surprise."

I tried to shake Hitch's hand but he insisted on some kind of Texas bear hug.

"Hey, Sky, I see you're not missin' a meal. No sir."

Hitch then noticed Muffet.

"Whoa Nellie. Did I just enter an igloo or is that my imagination?"

"Hitch, you know Muffet Meaney, of course."

"Well, sure I do. How doo, little lady?"

Hitch extended a hand.

"No, thank you," Muffet replied, recoiling from the offer.

"Suit yourself, missy," Hitch responded, hardly missing a beat. "So, pardner, looks like we're gonna be TV stars."

"Looks that way."

Hitch moved over to the refreshments and helped himself. A moment later, much to my chagrin, Bill Maher's remaining mystery guest entered the green room. Dilda Wiggins, president of Citizens for Cleaner Colons, was a broom-toting activist who'd spent most of her career advocating a radical feminist agenda, including *The Vagina Monologues* and women's soccer.

Prior to her stint at the Triple C, Dilda was at Justice for the Jailed, a well-known private agency, where she tried to tell anyone who'd listen that executing the insane was a bad idea. Most recently, before being kicked out for her ardent male castration stance, Dilda had been the executive director of W.A.R., the Womyn Are Right organization; a group committed to gender-neutral language, the Indigo Girls and the comedy stylings of Paula Poundstone.

Upon entering the room, each of the original inhabitants, including Hitch, managed a muffled hello. Even Muffet, who for purposes of the impending debate was Dilda's ally, seemed frightened by this bald woman wearing a muumuu and mukluks. Fortunately, Gabby saved us all from ongoing discomfort by ushering us out of this hatespace and into the backstage area, where we waited for a few minutes while Maher did a short routine.

Soon we were introduced one at a time until I found myself under hot lights in a comfortable chair before a live studio audience. Our host started us off.

"Okay, there's been a lot in the news lately about beef. Is it good for you? Is it dangerous? I think it's a lot to do about very little."

"Getting meat from cows is the equivalent of rape," Dilda announced, her first words landing with a thud.

"Now c'mon, Dilda, isn't that a bit extreme?" Maher asked.

"The woman's detached, Mr. Maher. Detached, I tell ya," Hitch said.

"Am I? We drug them, mate them forcibly and then slaughter them."

"Hey, if you know a better way to get a girl in this country, by all means speak up," Maher quipped.

"That is not funny, Bill. We rape these cows of their lives."

"Muffet, what do you think of that argument?" Maher asked as he turned the attention of the audience her way.

"Well, it is a very strong statement and I cannot speak for all the members of SERMON, but my own opinion is that Dilda is essentially correct."

"You can't be serious," I blurted out in disbelief. "We're not raping cows. You're missing the whole point. What about all the people we feed? Beef is a source of great nutritive value and, more importantly, joy. How about the great American cookout? You can't hold a cookout without beef."

"Dad'gum right," Hitch added. "Who in the name of Sam Hill wants a turkey burger on Independence Day? Maybe some commie out in California, but not a red-blooded American."

Muffet did not bow.

"Bill, I'm more concerned about the organophosphates."

"Organophosphates?"

"Yes, the pesticides used to help grow corn which is then used for feeding livestock. Bill, have you heard of methyl parathion?"

"No, I haven't. Is he the U.N. representative from Greece?"

"Not exactly, Bill. Commonly called PenncapM, this stuff has been shown to cause brain damage in children."

Hitch adjusted his belt buckle with both hands and leaned up in his seat.

"Mr. Maher, may I say something? May I say something?"

"Sure, Hitch. Call me Bill."

"Bill, she's got to get the facts straight. First of all, it wasn't brain damage, it was nervous system damage."

"Isn't that the same thing?"

"Well, I don't know, but brain damage sounds a lot worse. Anyway, my point is that we haven't used PenncapM for years, not since the EPA banned it."

The debate was clearly not going our way, so I redirected it.

"Bill, we've got to get back to the real issue here, which is that American beef is a safe, nutritious, delicious food that should be a staple of every citizen's diet."

"That's true, if they want to come down with mad cow disease," Dilda piped up.

"Dilda, that's nonsense! If you ask me, the only mad cow around here is you."

"Temper, temper, Mr. Thorne. See Bill, that's the attitude of the fast-food industry. Instead of discussing the issues, they just attack people personally."

"Great," I thought to myself. "Now Maher will want to talk about mad cow disease."

"Let's talk about mad cow disease for a minute because that's been in the news lately, too. For three years the European Union banned British beef, and just recently the American Red Cross has said that anyone who has spent six months or more in England since 1980 may not give blood. Pretty scary stuff. Just what is this mad cow disease?"

"It's a boil on an ant's ass, Bill," Hitch artfully explained.

"Besides AIDS, I'd say it's the biggest public health problem facing the world as we start the new millennium," Dilda countered.

"That's just not true," I said. "There hasn't been one reported case of BSE in the United States."

"BSE?"

Maher asked me the question, but Muffet rudely interrupted and answered.

"That's Mr. Thorne's, and the beef industry's, preferred description of Bovine Spongiform Encephalopathy."

"My God, it sounds like something you'd get if you left your tampon in too long," Maher joked.

"It's nothing to laugh about, Bill, I assure you. Have you ever seen the way these cows stagger and drool as their brain tissue is destroyed?"

"I've seen the footage. It's like St. Patrick's Day in Chicago. Seriously, it looks awful."

"It is awful, Bill, and I fear the American cattle supply is next."

"Bill, the reason they've had problems in Britain is because of the way they feed their cattle. The animal feed that caused BSE was made from ground-up animal remains. We don't do that here in the U.S.," I informed him.

Maher nodded, but somehow the unappetizing image of ground-up animal remains hung in the air. Muffet, of course, had to go for my Achilles' heel.

"Bill, it's common knowledge that companies like Tailburger don't cook their meat to the recommended government temperature, exposing children and the elderly to disease and possible death."

Now I stood perilously close to the edge of moral turpitude. If Maher asked me about our cooking policies at Tailburger, I'd be forced to tell a direct lie on national television, something I didn't want to do.

"So Sky, what *is* Tailburger's policy on cooking its meat?"

In response to this question, I did what every self-hating, God-fearing and, quite frankly, desperate man would do. I went on the attack.

"Bill, the real question here is why can't these women and their extremist, anti-American, militant, pro–radical feminist agenda groups peacefully coexist with the beef industry? We harbor no ill will toward them, yet they seem so agitated by every move we make."

"Ladies. A response?"

Muffet took the lead.

"Bill, Sky Thorne, and others like him in the beef industry, represent a real threat to the children of America."

"How would y'all know?" Hitch asked. "Last I checked, neither of you had any."

I started assessing the public relations damage before the show had ended. I don't know if it was me or the fact that Hitch wasn't accustomed to the talk show format or what, but I felt like these women kicked our asses up and down the studio. "How many people actually watch this show?" I wondered.

Afterward, Hitch assured me that we'd gotten "our licks in," and Muffet threatened to destroy me if I didn't return the videotape of us having sex to her within a week. All in all, it was a pretty rough day. Dilda did trip on her muumuu on the way offstage, however, so it wasn't a total loss.

23

Reaping

Calls from my kids came in waves: tidal waves. I wouldn't hear from them for a few weeks and then all of a sudden they'd both ring me up on the same day, usually with problems that required immediate attention. The best I could hope for was that the predicaments of the moment didn't require enormous financial outlays on my part. Upon my return from the taping of *Real Time,* however, I didn't get that lucky.

"Daddy, it's me."

I could tell by Sophia's muted tone of voice that she was upset.

"Hi, babe. What's wrong? You sound a little down."

"I don't know."

Sophia was stalling, a sure sign that she wanted me to coax the crisis out of her.

"Hey, this is your dad. You can tell me. What is it?"

"Well . . ."

"Out with it, Soph."

"Daddy, I need laser surgery."

My heart sank. I had read that doctors used lasers to get at precancerous lesions in the uterus and various other female private parts. "My poor baby," I thought. I needed to be strong for her.

"Sweetie, listen to me. I don't want you to be afraid. I will be with you through this every step of the way. We're going to get you healthy. There's nothing to be frightened about."

"I'm not frightened."

"You're not?"

"No. Of course not. I mean, we're only talking about my teeth."

"Your teeth? You mean you don't have a vaginal lesion?"

"No, Daddy. That's disgusting. Is that what you thought?"

"Well, to be honest, yes."

"The laser is for whitening my teeth."

"You don't need that. I spent four thousand dollars on your braces. You have beautiful teeth."

"No, I don't. They're dingy and gross. They're corn yellow."

"They're not corn yellow. They're a natural pearl. That's the color they're supposed to be."

"I don't like them. They're maize-colored. I'll never get a job looking like this."

"I thought you wanted to go to business school. Isn't that why I bought you new breasts?"

"I thought I'd work for a while."

As with the boob job, I tried to appeal to the feministic leanings of my daughter by stressing that people should like her for who she is, and that those who placed value on the superficial were generally not worth knowing. I told her that in today's world, it was only the strong that held on to the principles of inner beauty that ultimately dictated true happiness. When that didn't work, I told her to get three estimates.

Sophia's brother did not disappoint me by failing to call shortly thereafter. His problem was of a different sort, but certainly no less dire or costly. Evidently the fever of day trading had gripped my son. Unfortunately, the requisite skills to be successful at it had not. Not only had he lost the last fifteen hundred dollars I'd sent him, he'd also managed to go deeper into the hole by getting a cash advance on a credit card he'd received in the mail.

"How much are you in for, Ethan?"

"About twelve K."

"Twelve thousand dollars? Ethan, what the hell were you thinking?"

"Well, I got in on some shares of this hot IPO at seven dollars. Right after the opening, it shot up to a hundred eighty-five a share. It was all-time. Then the shares just took a dive and closed up at about three-fifty. Next I knew the SEC got involved and delisted the company. It was a huge bummer."

"Goddamnit, Ethan! What's the annual interest rate on your credit card?"

"I think it's twenty-eight percent."

"Holy shit."

"Dad, don't worry. Not all of the debt's on the card. I borrowed some of the money from Skull. So we can pay him back without interest."

"We? *We* can pay him back? No, no, no. This is all you. Jesus, son. I don't understand. What are you doing out there?"

"Dad, I'm sorry. I just saw a chance to make a success out of something, and I wanted to give it a shot. I wanted to make you proud of me."

And there it was. The lowest blow a child could hit a parent with: the old "I wanted to make you proud" paradox. What can a parent say in response to that other than, "I'm already proud of you"? And how mad can you get when your child justifies his behavior as an effort to please you? The conversation was effectively over.

"Ethan, I'm already proud of you."

"No, you're not. I'm a total disappointment."

"That's not true. I'm very proud of you. I just want you to exercise better judgment. And no more playing the market with other people's money, mine or Skull's. Do you understand me?"

"I do. Dad, I'm sorry I let you down."

"It's all right. Tell Skull you'll pay him back as soon as possible. I'll figure something out on this end, all right?"

"You're the best, Dad. Thanks."

"Okay. I'll call you this week."

Although Ethan had seen fit to call me the best, I felt like the worst after hanging up with him. I tried to remember if I'd been as scattershot in my decision making at his age. These are things you tend to conveniently forget as time passes, convincing yourself more and more that you had always made good choices befitting a mature person. But who was I fooling? It wasn't until my marriage had broken up that I found myself looking beyond the next paycheck and planning anything in my life. Everything prior to that had just sort of happened to me and I willingly let it. The acorn hadn't fallen far from the oak.

By the time I got off the telephone with Sophia and Ethan, it was almost 10:00 P.M. and I was hungry. Despite my renewed effort at dieting, including semistrict adherence to soybean-based foods (save the occasional Tailpipe with cheese), my paunch seemed to be getting paunchier. Like every aging American male, I was learning that suit pants could only be taken out so many times before your tailor cried, *"No más."* "What to eat, what to eat, what to eat," I asked aloud while basking in the glow of the refrigerator's light. My Qigong training was supposed to reduce my stress, which, according to King, produced extra cortisol, a hormone that was causing me to retain more abdominal fat. "Not to worry," King assured me. Pretty soon I'd be able to channel my chee toward my gut and eradicate the blubber around my midsection. Until then, it was soy milk and cereal.

I sat down with my bowl of Special K at the kitchen table. I noticed it was raining and watched the first droplets bead up on the sliding glass door that led out to my patio. Mesmerized for a few seconds, I was quickly brought to by frantic pounding on the front door. A little scared and a lot startled, I moved slowly through the foyer and peered out one of the small windows to the side of the entryway. To my relief, it was Cal.

"What are you doing here? Come in out of the rain," I told him as I opened the door far enough for him to fit through.

"Thanks, Sky."

Cal was shivering as he came across the threshold and began working his way out of his coat. Unflappable to a fault, he unnerved me with the crestfallen look on his face. When he wiped the rainwater off his brow, I could tell he'd been crying by the redness of his eyes.

"Cal, what's wrong?"

"It's Kyle. He's in the hospital."

Kyle was Cal's nine-year-old son, a cute, towheaded rugrat who called me Uncle Sky.

"My God. What happened?"

Cal was distressed and began ranting.

"His birthday was last Saturday so we had a *Star Wars* party for him. I dressed up as Darth Vader and all the neighborhood kids came over. I had the cape. The helmet. The light saber. Everything was going great. We did all the usual shit—games, candy, party favors. You know the deal. Then I went to cook some burgers for him and his friends, but I couldn't get the grill going. I was out of propane or something. So I ran out to Tailburger and picked up a bunch of those *Dongwood* burgers and Tailfraps. One week later, half the kids are doubled over and throwing up."

"Oh, no, Cal. What did the doctor say?"

"He's running some tests. He thinks it may be one of these bacterias—E. coli or something."

"Is Kyle going to be okay?"

"He's in the ICU. The doctor says it's fity-fifty at this point. Jenny's hysterical. They had to give her some sedatives—the kind they use on elephants."

"Oh my God, Cal. I feel horrible."

"It's not your fault, Sky. You can't control something like this."

Whatever color was left in my face drained away. My biggest nightmare was coming true. The decision to undercook our burgers was going to kill someone—my best friend's son and his *Star Wars* party buddies.

"Cal, I've got to tell you something."

"Wait, that's not all. I've got something else to tell you."

"No, Cal. This is really important."

"Listen to me, Sky."

"What?"

"I can't run your campaign anymore."

"That's no problem. Don't even think about that right now. I totally understand."

This made perfect sense to me. Who'd want to spend one minute helping to promote a company that had poisoned their child? I understood. Tailburger was a despicable enterprise and I was its main proponent.

"No, you don't understand. Today was the worst day of my life."

Cal slumped down on the front hall staircase and rested his head in his hands. He started crying again.

"I'm getting out. I've got to get out."

"Out of what?"

I wasn't sure what Cal meant, but I sure knew how he felt. I'd spent most of my life trying to get out of things. Marriage. Debt. Awkward relationships. Working for Tailburger. Going to church. Potluck dinners. Parent-teacher conferences. And that's just for starters. For all I knew, Cal's list could've been just as long as mine or longer. Men are funny like that. Most times, we won't tell even our best friends that we're feeling disillusioned, depressed or even suicidal. We'd rather let them find us dead at the bottom of a ravine with a note in the front pocket of our favorite jeans. It's less trouble like that.

"Are you and Jenny having problems?"

"No," Cal replied through a muffled sob.

"Are you in debt?"

"No."

"You want to get out of Rochester?"

"No. The industry. I've got to get out of the industry."

The answer seemed a bit anticlimactic to me.

"Oh," I replied, pausing for a moment. "Why?"

"Because of Christine."

Christine was Cal's fifteen-year-old daughter, a blond stunner who'd been blossoming faster than a hothouse flower.

"She's not in the hospital, too, is she?"

Cal blew his nose on the sleeve of his dark blue shirt.

"No, no. Nothing like that. This is a different problem. I'm a bad father."

"That's bullshit and you know it. You're a great father."

"Just listen to me. Two weeks ago I'm coming out of services with Jenny and the kids when Reverend Showalter stops us. You know how he is with his post-church chitchat."

I hadn't been to church in such a long time, I drew a blank on Reverend Showalter.

"Is he new?"

"No. Been there about five years. Anyway, he asks Christine what she's doing for the summer, and she pipes up and says she's going to drama camp. Now, there's no way in hell I'm letting her go to one of those fruity, out-in-the-woods, act-like-a-cantaloupe camps, so I say, 'She's getting a job.'

"At the time, I think I'm being a good dad by teaching her the whole value of a dollar thing. Evidently she didn't think so. Two minutes later, she bursts into tears in the car and then storms out of the house when we get home. When she finally returns she's calm and I think everything has blown over. Turns out I was totally wrong. Today, my regional supervisor tells me that my own daughter has applied for one of our sex phone positions—the ones we post in the classifieds. I'm devastated."

"Shit, Cal."

"Shit is right. It's so goddamn depressing."

"Did she get the job?"

"Will you shut up?"

"I thought you had to be eighteen to be a phone sex girl."

"You do. She said she was eighteen in the application."

"So she's a tramp and a liar."

Cal gave me a look that let me know I should stop.

"Sorry. I'm just trying to lighten the mood."

My joking was the equivalent of laughter at a funeral—an involuntary reaction to extreme discomfort and upset. The guilt that I may have hurt Kyle because of my own personal weakness and inability to stand up for what I thought was right was overwhelming. Although I empathized with Cal's Christine problem, and was trying to be a good friend, my mind was miles away—focused on Kyle and what I may have done.

"It's all right. I just feel like I've got to talk to her about this, and yet I don't want her to know that I'm involved in such a sleazy business."

"You don't have to tell her."

"Then how would I know she'd done this?"

"I see your point."

"You try and keep your kids away from this crap, but it just sucks them in. It's pervasive."

"You said it yourself. Porn has gone mainstream. Every year it loses a little more of its stigma."

"I still don't want my daughter involved. I can't contribute to the demise of my own children anymore."

"You're not seriously considering quitting?"

"I am. I'm going to do it, as soon as I'm able. I'm selling my stake in the business."

"Cal, slow down. You'll never replicate the money you're making in any other business."

"I know that. It's going to be much harder financially, but some things are more important. Plus, I should be able to sell it for a pretty good buck."

"Are you sure?"

"I think so. I just don't feel good anymore about being in this business."

Cal departed at midnight, unaware of Tailburger's corporate policy of undercooking its meat. I should have told him, but I didn't, and now I felt awful. Some coward I was. I'd started my life with the desire to have the fortitude of David Copperfield, and I'd ended up with the weakness of Pip. I had seven hours before work to worry about my next move in this ongoing and feeble attempt to save my own ass. Somehow, it didn't seem like enough time.

The terrible thing about having a friend in moral crisis is that it forces you to examine your own morals. I'd been blithely lying, scheming and manipulating my way across the world landscape, blindly following orders and being what I'd generously describe as an all-around asshole. The question now: what was I going to do about it? Cal had inadvertently thrown me into my own ethical dilemma, and my carefully rolled ball of yarn was rapidly unraveling.

For years, I'd convinced myself, or maybe pretended, that our products didn't cause heart disease, E. coli, cancer or obesity, laying all the blame at the feet of cigarettes, inactivity and fresh vegetables. But now, I was directly responsible for the illness and possible death of little children, including my best friend's son, and I couldn't deny the truth any longer. I was some kind of sicko. Even if the kids survived, I was furthering society's decay by promoting prostitution on the www.lustranch.com swamp of Internet sex and pornography.

Who did I think was entering our Nail Some Tail Sweepstakes from their computers? At the time we started, I told myself it was a group of consenting adults over the age of eighteen, but in my heart of hearts, I knew better. I was contributing to the delinquency of minors who I was certain logged on to the Lust Ranch site with alarming frequency. Who were these kids? Probably ones not so different from Ethan or Sophia, just a bit younger.

The darkest thoughts crossed my mind about those exposed. They were the children of broken homes who went unsupervised for hours at a time. Kids who sure as hell weren't doing their homework. Kids who were bored and indifferent to anything being taught at school. They were interested in hoarding weapons and making bombs, and had easy access to both the materials and the know-how. They wore trench coats to class (when they went), and saw glory in defacing themselves with swastikas while resurrecting the ghost of Adolf Hitler and his intolerant band of hatemongers. They were the disaffected youth of today. Numbed by the incessant and unprincipled grab for gold they observed their parents take part in, they perceived themselves to be worthless objects of neglect. People could eat shit and die. Apathy. One vision of America: for sale.

"Pull back from the edge, Sky," I warned myself. I was drinking now, voluntarily making vivid the many thoughts that crossed my mind. I was scattered and vacillating. Maybe this whole thing was just about burgers and some skin. Nothing to get too hung up about. Hamburgers and pretty girls—the same things that had been making this country great since the advent of rock and roll. A convertible Corvette. A big-titted blonde with her hair in a ponytail. A cold can of Budweiser. That's what we stood for. That's what Tailburger and America were all about. Who cared if the blonde's shirt was off and she was blasted out of her mind and she was riding the biggest anal vibrator you'd ever seen? Surely those facts alone couldn't distort the American dream and everything else we'd woven so tightly into its fabric. We'd been marketed a new bill of rights. Making gobs of money. Skiing at Telluride. Driving a Range Rover. Owning a chocolate lab. Retiring comfortably at forty. Buying a second home. Watching our stock portfolios triple every year. Sending our kids to Ivy League colleges. Traveling to Fiji. These were the God-given rights of every U.S. citizen. It was marketing. That's all. Plain and simple marketing. No more, but no goddamn less. And the newest right, one that flouted the natural order and ranked high among the all-time sales jobs, was our right to cheat death. Plastic surgery, vitamins, skin creams. The frayed end pieces of the American dream were showing, and there was little to believe in or to do anymore except worship at the altar of youth that we had created. Once our culture of convention was ridiculed to death and then banished to obscurity, we forced ourselves to live within a paradigm of inevitable self-hatred. If youth was equated with all that is good, the opposite was true, and our long march toward old age was little more than a Bataan death march toward all that is bad.

I was drunk and delirious now, a lit Commodore resting between my forefinger and thumb. Life *was* one big accumulation of wounds, and if I'd been able to irradiate myself like the meat in the supermarket, I would have. To suffer one calamitous radioactive blast of gamma rays in order to clean away the hate and the fear and the pain I felt would have been worth every health hazard posed. Bad enough I couldn't protect my children from this worldview, but worse, I was partially responsible for it. I knew they were going to find out about Internet porn and cock rings and cocaine-inspired orgies, and that one more sex site hadn't tipped the scale in favor of moral chaos. It was simply another choice like everything else in life, and either you had the skills to cope with the freedom to choose or you didn't. And if you didn't, God save you, because the slope has never had more silicone on it. But I also knew that the false idols of money and fame and power and youth thrived because of the perceived void of worthier things to believe in, a perception cemented by massive advertising and the promotion of everything Tailburger stood for.

Who did I think I was fooling? Were my kids more obsessed with the celebrity culture than they should have been? Probably. No, definitely. Did they idolize the musicians and film stars and athletes for their money and lifestyle above all else? The answer was yes. Did they put up posters of AIDS researchers or Nobel prize–winning poets? Of course not. What did they think of their political leaders? That they were a big joke? Yes. That they were untrustworthy?

Unbelievable? Unworthy? Yes, to all of the above. The politicians didn't make enough money to be respected. They were hacks knocking out 145 K. There were Division II basketball coaches making better bucks than that. The only images put forward were those of intolerant, gun-toting Republicans and tax-happy, abortion-crazed Democrats. What about the new president? All they heard for months was that he was a moron. Then suddenly, after nine-eleven, he was brilliant. And the old one? For as long as they could remember he was portrayed as little more than a colossal joke. Labels. Marketing. Packaging. What was true? Who knew? A womanizing lech with an inability to articulate what he stood for in any consistent manner. That's how they knew him. A liar and a cheat who swayed like a limp dick in the political winds. A man who kissed up to constituencies when it was expedient, acted indignant when it would help in the polls and catered to the Hollywood community whose love and approval he so desperately sought. He epitomized the philosophy that public deeds forgive private acts. To my kids, he was the ultimate hypocrite. If they'd known what their old man had been up to, however, they might have felt differently.

I'd contributed to the toxic environment as much as anybody, and my desire to do the right things in my life didn't make up for all the times I hadn't. It was the marketing process. The right burger. The right clothes. The right car. Quicker. Faster. Richer. More surface. Less substance. Videos. Sound bites. Super Bowl ads. Video games. Sex. Sex. Sex. A swirling, sweeping, twisted mass of commercialization polluting everything that it touched, including our children— including my children. We'd sold something to them, but what was it? An American utopia or a gilded prison? Everything was justifiable to make the dollars—to live the very lifestyle we touted. We were so much unhappier as a nation because of the direction we'd gone in. So much unhappiness. "A consumer culture that consumed itself" is how our epitaph would read one day. I pulled the covers over my head in shame. My only other emotion: guilt. There was a mean-spiritedness to it all—a self-hating mean-spiritedness.

24

Treading

The Link called the monthly Tailburger board meeting to order with a Frisbee-sized cookie in one hand and a can of Scuz Cola in the other.

"Mmmm, that's good. Now we've got a, mmmmm, ooh that's a good cookie, full schedule so we need to get started. A small piece of, mmmm that's a good cookie, good news—SERMON's boycott has lost all of its steam. SLLRRRPPPP!"

The Link brushed cookie crumbs from his hands and wiped a drop of Scuz from his chin.

"Picketing has come to an end for the most part, and even better, the police accidentally shot three vegetarian protesters outside one of our stores in St. Louis. So we're making progress. Now, Sister Ancilla has an announcement she'd like to make. Sister, are you ready?"

"Yes, I am, Frank."

Sister Ancilla scanned the long conference table from under her habit as if searching for a friendly face. Most of her burns from the Fanny Pack incident had healed by now and she was looking more or less like her old self. She wasn't ready for runway modeling, but she'd regained the wholesome appearance one expects from a nun, or your average backup singer in a *Sound of Music* tribute band.

"As you all know, Tailburger has been a very good friend to the Sisters of the Sorrowful Mother over the past year. Through your generosity, and in particular, the generosity of Mr. Fanoflincoln, who I thank very, very much, Tailburger's Health and Life Fitness Center has been built on our convent campus and is ready to open. In celebration of this, I would like to invite all of you to the grand opening of the fitness center and the glorious Fanoflincoln Pavilion, one month from this coming Saturday, where we will honor your company and your wonderful chairman."

The Link led the forced applause that followed.

"I expect all of you to be there," he ordered before taking a long swig of Scuz.

After largely ignoring community service for the better part of thirty years, the Link was suddenly on a caring bender.

"If any of you have good ideas to make Tailburger a better corporate citizen, I want you to let me know."

A father should know when and when *not* to encourage his sons.

"We should have a memorial golf tournament," Ned blurted out.

"That would be HUGE!" Ted agreed, as he reached over to give his brother a high five.

"Enormo," came Fred amidst his own effort to high-five Ned, nearly losing his visor in the process.

The Link was mortified.

"Stop shifting in your seat, Fred. There will be no high-fiving at the board meetings! Do you understand?"

"A memorial golf tournament? Who died?" Chad Hemming-bone inquired.

"Well, nobody yet. But as soon as someone does, we could tee off," Ned replied.

"We could be ready to go right when they drop," Ted concurred.

"Or it could be a fund-raiser for unwed mothers," Fred opined.

"That's not a bad idea, Fred."

The brothers soon lost everyone around them by talking amongst themselves.

"I'm thinking we hold it at Knurly Bush."

"I don't know. The back nine at Knurly is just brutal."

"You know, you're right. It may be a charity event, but I still want to shoot a respectable score."

"What about Locust Valley?"

"Now that's a place I hadn't thought of. Have you seen their new locker room?"

"The lockers are gorgeous! All beechwood. Just unbelievable."

The Link had heard enough.

"Will the three of you shut up? PLEASE!"

"Sorry, Dad."

"Yeah, sorry, Dad."

"Sorry, everybody."

The Link took control of the meeting again.

"I've got a new cost-cutting measure I want to discuss with the board. As you know, we are living in uncertain times here at Tailburger, what with the SERMON lawsuit and the up-and-down sales we've been experiencing. Although revenues have increased in the last few weeks, we must be prepared for some serious belt tightening."

Phrases like "belt tightening" are frightening when spoken by a man with a sixty-six-inch waist.

"I've got one word for you. I want you to listen to it and then think about it."

The Link's long history of asinine ideas was so legendary among board members, we actually looked forward to them as comic relief. Laughter turned to fear only when, and if, he attempted to implement one of them. At this point, however, everybody's ears were happily attuned.

"Baboon!"

Silence hung heavily in the air as we stared at the Link and then each other.

"Did you say, baboon?" Annette asked.

"Yes, baboon."

"As in baboon meat?" I asked, hoping to be wrong. "Are you serious?"

"Of course I'm serious. We can import it from South Africa and it's a third cheaper than U.S. Grade A."

"What grade is the baboon meat?" Annette asked.

"I have no idea. I think it's more of a pass-fail system over there."

Annette looked at me and rolled her eyes.

Instead of dismissing the Link's ideas immediately, the board had learned to systematically punch holes in them and let them sink under their own weight.

"Would we be telling people what they were eating?" Sister Ancilla wondered aloud.

"Sure. We could call it our Primate Burger or maybe do a combo platter with ribs, you know Bab on a Slab, something like that."

"Frank, what about the taste?" I still couldn't believe he wanted to do this.

"Have you ever had baboon?"

"I haven't been so fortunate," I responded.

"It's pretty damn good."

"Let me guess. It tastes like chicken."

"Hell, no! It tastes like buffalo meat, only gamier. We'd have to doll it up with tons of mayo and maybe a barbecue sauce, but it could work."

"And who would be our suppliers?"

"I told you. South African baboon farmers. There's a town called Warmbaths where they're raised."

Biff Dilworth, our resident academic, adjusted his bow tie, signifying he was about to speak.

"Frank, I hate to be a wet blanket on the baboon front, but there is an ethical issue."

The Link was nonplussed.

"What fuckin' ethical issue?"

"Primates, such as the baboon and the chimpanzee, are the closest species to Homo sapiens. We share ninety-eight percent of our genes with these animals. They are sentient and intellectually sophisticated creatures."

"Hey, Professor, you wanna put it in English for the rest of us?"

"All right, Frank. Monkeys and men are similar creatures. It follows therefore that eating monkeys is similar to eating each other and thus morally reprehensible."

"That's the biggest load of bullshit I've ever heard."

Biff could mount only an intellectual defense to such a direct attack.

"Well, I happen to know a senior research fellow at St. Catherine's College, Oxford, who would disagree with you wholeheartedly."

"Whoop dee freakin' doo, Biff."

"I just don't believe we should extend the number of species we eat. The whole thing is a bad idea, and that's all I have to say," Biff huffed, crossing his arms across his vest.

"What do you think, Thorne?"

"Frank, I'm inclined to agree with Biff for a more practical reason. Our customers are used to beef, and I think the idea of eating baboon may gross them out and cost us market share. It sure as hell grosses me out."

Annette nodded her head along with Biff, Chad and the rest of the board.

"All right. I can see you're going to fight me on this one. We'll table the decision for the next meeting. In the meantime, Sky, I want you to do some focus groups and taste tests. I don't want Tailburger to be last on the baboon bandwagon when it rolls across this country."

When any of the Link's ideas were dismissed, nobody on the board gloated. We knew there'd be another along to take the prior one's place momentarily. The Link would mutter "shitheads" loudly enough for the rest of us to hear and then get back to the business at hand, otherwise unmoved.

"We've got to do something on the BSE front," the Link said, using our company's preferred reference to Bovine Spongiform Encephalopathy or mad cow disease. "Now I hate to say it to you again, Thorne, but we got killed on Bill Maher's show. I don't know what you and Hitch were doing out there, but you looked like a couple of doofuses. People probably think they can catch this crap now."

The Link had told me every day since the airing that I'd "stunk up the joint," during my television appearance, but he wanted the satisfaction of telling me in front of the board. Once he had done so, he got the faraway look in his eyes that we collectively dreaded, the one that signified his launch into the land of Lincoln.

"So Thorne, I ask you and the whole board, 'Can we do better? The dogmas of the quiet past are inadequate to the stormy present . . .'"

Halfway through the Link's recitation of the Railsplitter's words, the rest of the board members, except me, joined in to form a chorus.

". . . The occasion is piled high with difficulty, and we must rise to the occasion . . ."

I didn't say a word, afraid the anger inside of me would erupt. I was furious at the Link for ordering me to change the cooking policy—for threatening my job and financial security if our market share didn't reach 5 percent—for literally driving me to the point of pornographic desperation that I'd now reached. But I was angrier at myself for the weakness of my character—for my lack of backbone when it came to making unethical decisions—for my failure to do what I knew was the right thing on so many occasions. I suffered while the others just kept talking.

". . . As our case is new, so we must think anew, and act anew!"

"You're damn right we do," the Link exulted as they finished in unison. "Hey, I've got an idea," he continued.

The board groaned.

"What about putting a Mad Cow Burger on the menu? We'll cook it extra rare. I'm talkin' over and off—smother it with bleu cheese and put it on moldy bread. Add a catchy slogan, 'Go Crazy Like the Cow,' and I see big sales."

"I see big lawsuits," I said. "You have no idea what a mistake that would be, given the current regulatory climate, Frank."

I wanted to come out with it right there and tell everybody present that our stupid burgers had put eight kids in the hospital, but I held back. Embarrassing the Link that way would serve no purpose.

"Damn lawyers have wrecked everything. Lincoln's the only decent one who ever lived."

"Maybe here's where we do our golf fund-raiser," Ned said, to no one's surprise. "It can benefit all the little boys and girls suffering from mad cow here in Rochester."

"Good thinking, big brother," Ted added, adjusting his visor to cut the glare from the boardroom's artificial lighting.

"That would be great," Fred chirped enthusiastically. "Can I sponsor the closest to the pin, Ned? I'd really like to do that for the kids."

"Hey, hey, closest to the pinhead," the Link angrily called to his youngest son. "There's just one problem, numbnuts. There aren't any kids suffering from mad cow disease here. It's only in England. We're just fighting the perception of danger."

"Oh," Fred replied despondently, his enthusiasm momentarily jettisoned. "Well, then let's do a golf fund-raiser to fight that."

"To fight the perception of danger? What are you, stupid?" Chad Hemmingbone, who had lost his patience, asked.

"Watch it, Hemmingbone!" the Link warned.

"All I'm saying is that we could do a best-ball tournament. That's all I'm saying," Fred, now clearly on the defensive, futilely tried to explain.

Annette, the most intelligent member of the board, announced that she had a mayoral commitment, mercifully expediting the end of our meeting. She smiled at me as she left, blissfully unaware of the pain I was enduring. The room gradually emptied until I was alone with the Link.

"Frank, we need to talk."

"What is it, Thorne? And keep in mind I've got battlefield practice tonight. We're reenacting Sherman's burning of Atlanta."

"Look, it's about our cooking policy. Some kids, friends of mine actually, got sick last weekend from eating Tailburgers. They think it may be E. coli."

"Are they sure?"

"Well, no. Not yet. The doctors are running tests and the families have agreed to wait for the results before going to the press. But we're sitting on a time bomb."

"Jesus H double Popsicle sticks. How in the hell did this happen, Thorne?"

"It's got to be our policy of undercooking the meat."

"What policy?"

"The one you authorized. Remember? You wanted the insides soft?"

"I never authorized that policy."

"What?"

"I said I never authorized that policy."

"You did, too! You demanded that I roll it out. You made me 'take it to the front.' All against my better judgment!"

"Funny. I just don't remember that."

"I don't believe this shit."

The Link smiled mischievously at me.

"Just calm down, Thorne. Calm your Confederate ass down. I'm only yankin' your chain. I know I called for that policy. And I'd do it again in a minute if I had the chance. Have you seen our sales lately? Shootin' through the goddamn roof. Remember Ralph Nader? Patron saint of Tailburger?"

I tried to compose myself, but it was difficult.

"Sky, here's what I want you to do. You say you know these people?"

I nodded. "Well, sort of. My best friend's son is one of the kids who's sick."

"Good. Here's what I want you to do. First, go talk to your friend. Tell him to get a handle on all the other parents. Then mention a possible settlement. But whatever you do, don't admit anything. Do you understand me? If this thing turns out to be E. coli, we'll pay up, but we've got to keep it out of the papers."

I drove straight to Annette's house after work. She met me with open and unquestioning arms, the kind of limbs I couldn't get enough of, now that I'd found them. For weeks, she'd been my sole source of comfort. Simple and straightforward. Loving and honest. Regrettably, all the things that I wanted my relationship with Annette to be would have to wait. I should have told her everything that was going on in my life and at Tailburger, but I couldn't. I was a liability to her, although she had no idea how true that was. Even in the warmth of her embrace, I was a false actor, selfishly hiding my darkest secrets and greatest needs. I was obsessed with only one thing: Tailburger market share, which had almost reached 5 percent. If I could just hold on a little longer, I'd be home free and on my way to insular Tahiti.

25

Tailfire

Burton Roxby, out on bail and awaiting trial, came to see me at Tailburger headquarters the next morning. Suspended indefinitely from Congress, he appeared at my doorway dressed neatly in jeans and a flannel shirt, a mode of attire I'd never seen him in, given his religious adherence to dark gray suits. He looked thinner and shorter to me, a meek presence devoid of the nerdish bravado he once projected. I motioned for him to take a seat and then watched cautiously as he did so.

"Sky, I need your help."

Roxby continuously fidgeted with his hands, oblivious of how guilty it made him look.

"Burt, I don't know what I can do for you."

"Look at me, Sky," Roxby pleaded, pointing at his feet. "They're making me wear an ankle bracelet to monitor my whereabouts. They've taken away my dignity."

"You did that to yourself."

"That's not true. I was set up. That little girl was an instrument of the devil."

"C'mon, Burt. Save your story for the jury."

"Look, my trial is coming up. I'd like you to be a character witness."

"Did you know that bill 214 passed through the Agriculture Committee and into law because of your little stunt?"

"I heard. And I'm sorry."

"Do you have any idea how much money that will cost us?"

"I'm sorry."

"That's not all. Plot Thickens added New York as a plaintiff in the SERMON suit against Tailburger. Now that he doesn't need your help in the governor's race, we're getting screwed."

"I can still help you."

"I doubt it."

"I'm innocent, Sky. I swear. You gotta believe me."

"I don't believe you! Not for a minute."

"Sky, Thickens is an empty suit. He just follows the polls. Once I'm cleared, we can work together against SERMON. I'll pull every string I can to make sure you and Tailburger are taken care of, but first I need you to vouch for my character."

"I can't do that."

"Sure you can. Help me and help yourself at the same time."

There it was again, another opportunity to compromise my character for worldly gain—something I'd become quite proficient at since my first transgression. Roxby figured I had my price, just like every man he'd met in Washington, D.C., and all along the rubber chicken circuit of pork barrel politics.

"I can't," I repeated.

Roxby looked mildly surprised that I didn't immediately crumble. He knew I needed to extricate Tailburger from the SERMON suit, but he'd overestimated my desperation. Ever the consummate politician, he simply switched tactics. The manipulative player I remembered was suddenly back and sitting in my office.

"All right, Sky. I'm going to level with you because I like you and I respect you. However, I must warn you that what I'm about to say may be shocking. (Pause) I'm a sex addict."

"What?"

"I'm a sex addict. I can't control my urges. It's a disease and I'm getting help."

"Will you spare me the monumental bullshit, Burt?"

"Men have needs that can't always be met at home. Look at our former president. I'm not alone."

Roxby actually was alone. Yeti, his understanding wife, filed for divorce following his arrest and then proceeded to lock him out of their house. Though this was the one positive result of the entire treehouse incident for him, it didn't help when Channel 2 broadcast footage of him pounding on a back door demanding to be let in or else.

"You don't understand, Sky. I've found the good book."

"Which book is that? *Chicken Soup for the Child Molester's Soul?*"

"The St. James Bible, of course. I've cast out my demons and stepped into the kingdom of God."

"You're shameless, Burt. Stop embarrassing yourself."

"I'm not embarrassed to walk with the Lord."

"Are you done?"

"Will you be a character witness for me or not?"

"No! You're a piece of dung! Now get out of my office."

Roxby's motives were so transparent I was ashamed to have kissed his useless ass for so many years.

"Sky, Princeton wants to take away my honorary degree if I'm convicted."

"They gave you an honorary degree?"

"Yeah, a few years back. It was for my child-advocacy work."

"Ironic, don't you think?"

"Be a character witness."

"No! Get out of here!"

"Sky, I still know people at the FDA. Remember, I worked there for seven years." Roxby's tone was slightly threatening.

"Sure, I remember. So what?"

"So don't be surprised if I make a few phone calls and you find your precious beef being regulated like a drug."

"What the hell are you talking about? They couldn't even get cigarettes under their control."

"Beef has a hypnotic effect. It's as addictive as nicotine or sex. And that information, in the hands of highly paid lobbyist lawyers, is all I'd need to drag you down."

"Get the hell out of my office."

"I didn't want it to come to this, Sky."

"Get out!"

"Arms can reach out beyond prison walls."

"Are you threatening to have me killed?"

"What do you think?"

"I think you're an infinitesimal piece of snail shit and I want you out of my office!"

The Roxby bridge was irretrievably burned, a prospect that would have terrified me just weeks before. Something surged through my veins. I didn't know if it was my Du Mai or my Chong Mai or maybe my yang heel vessel. But regardless of the tributary being used, what was coursing through my miraculous meridians didn't feel like my chee. It just felt like anger and guilt, emotions I struggled to subdue, given the occasion at hand. Today was the dedication for the Tailburger Health and Life Fitness Center and the Fanoflincoln Pavilion.

The Link picked me up at headquarters in his new Continental. He wore a purple sweatsuit, a bold choice considering he now looked like Fruit of the Loom's grape with a thyroid condition. Those who don't exercise want to look like they do, but the Link's crushed velour ensemble wasn't fooling anyone. To make matters worse, his excitement about the ceremony had made him delusional. He actually asked me how his hair looked. To place that in context, not only was the Link a member of the Hair Club for Men, he was a victim. Still, glancing at the snarled rat's nest he called his mane, I smiled dutifully and said, "Never better."

"How do you like my sweats, Thorne? Pretty sporty, eh?"

"Sharp, Frank. Perfect for the event."

"I thought so. I may have to take one of those newfangled machines for a ride. What do they call 'em?"

"Stationary bikes?"

"Yeah, that's it. Jesus, what'll they think of next? Moving stairs?"

It was a safe bet that this was the Link's first visit to a gym of any kind. After talking about his irrational fear of fat nuns for the entire ride over, we toured the facility for half an hour with Sister Ancilla and the mother superior, a woman with a stern and forbidding demeanor. It was an impressive space, with long rows of gleaming equipment and open workout areas with mirrored walls. A snack bar, serving only Tailburgers, Tailfraps and other meat-flavored products, sat in the middle, apparently a cruel hoax on those people actually trying to lose weight. Although burning two hundred calories on a stairclimber was a waste of time if you immediately ate our new twelve-hundred-calorie Mad Cow Burger, 5 percent of all profits would go to the crippled children at the Shriner's Hospital. The Link tried to negotiate this figure down to 3 percent, but the nuns held firm.

The name Fanoflincoln and the Tailburger logo were visible everywhere throughout the facility. The Link wasn't one to ask for a small, tasteful plaque. He wanted his money's worth and, more importantly, he wanted something around for posterity's sake. This blatant piece of self-promotion got me thinking about my own death. Not in an unusually morbid way, although I suppose there's no other way to contemplate your own demise. Just seeing how happy the Link was, I couldn't help but think how nice it would be to have my name on something other than my tombstone. I didn't have the money to donate a building anywhere, but there had to be something. Maybe I could give a local college like Nazareth a library carrel or a desk or a rare book that some freshman would pull from the shelves in fifty years and ask, "Who the hell is Sky Thorne?" A very good question.

Sister Ancilla showed us the karate dojo on the second floor, the Link's one architectural demand. The mother superior's refusal to call him Sensei for the rest of the day sent him into a temporary funk that he didn't break out of until he saw the buffet tables being set up. "Can we eat now?" the Link asked like an impatient child.

"Let's wait until after the ribbon cutting," the mother superior replied tersely.

Outside, on the front yard of the convent, workers scurried to place the podium on the makeshift stage and line up the last few collapsible chairs. Minutes later, people from all over Rochester began filing into the narrow rows, and we found our respective seats up on the dais. The Link nervously played with the zipper on his purple top while studying the notes for his speech. Public displays of generosity were something new for the Link. Notoriously tightfisted in the past, and a fallen Catholic to boot, he planned to get back into the community's and the church's good graces with this single donative act.

"Make sure the crippled kids are up front," the Link told me, looking up from the crumpled paper in his hands. "I want the media to get a good look at the little monkeys. Especially that Katie Chang Gomez from Channel 7. She's always been out to get me. Maybe this'll shut her up."

I left the stage and attempted to orchestrate the intended seating pattern of handicapped children and church types in the first several reserved rows. This wasn't easy. The Rochester area diocese had dozens of representatives present, including Bishop Clark, who would deliver the benediction. Dressed in full regalia, he naturally proceeded to the stage and took his place next to the Link, while the priests and the Shriner kids milled about in a state of confusion, unsure of where to sit. With the situation spiraling out of control, it became a free-for-all as the clergy and the lame fought for the open spots in a game of musical chairs gone bad. I did my best to get everyone settled and to relocate those squeezed out of a slot. About the same time, a sea of fezzed Shriners drifted in aimlessly and shuffled slowly into the growing throng.

To the Link's delight, Katie Chang Gomez, as well as a whole slew of media personalities, was in attendance to report the gym's opening. Channel 4's Soledad Murphy. Channel 2's Rock Bledsoe. Even Channel 9's action weatherman, Stormy Winters, was there, evidently ready to report on the death toll in case a tornado blew through. Although this amounted to a major happening in Rochester, you would have thought it was a hostage crisis by the number of news vans parked out front.

Ned, Ted and Fred, just off the back nine at Tinkle Creek, ambled in and took seats. Dressed in matching argyle tam-o'-shanters and knickers, they looked like a trio of oversize lawn jockeys as they argued loudly about who had the most triple bogeys and failed to notice Annette, who quietly slid into their row and sat down. She smiled broadly at me and, for a moment, my world narrowed to her lovely face and nothing else. Ted Truheart and his wife arrived, along with their new au pair, a former Turkish prison guard named Sekhmet. Chad Hemming-bone, Biff Dilworth and the rest of the Tailburger board followed.

By the time Bishop Clark was introduced by the mother supe-rior, the lawn of the convent was a great American melting pot of golfers, reporters, Shriners, Catholics and the physically challenged. Shutters clicked continually and film rolled as every second of this moderately momentous occasion was recorded.

"Today is a gift from God," the bishop started. "A great, glori-ous gift from God."

"Don't forget my little gift, Bishop," the Link whispered aloud, overly concerned that credit for the day was being misplaced.

"Fear not, my son," the bishop reassured the Link before continuing. "I want to welcome everybody to this wonderful day. This wonderful, wonderful day."

Admittedly, I was contending with a few problems in my life, but it was hard to argue with Bishop Clark's assessment as he presided over the dedication ceremony. The sun shone brightly from a clear blue sky, and the trees swayed gently from a light summer breeze that made the temperature perfect. Yes, everything was ideal for a brief, shining moment, right until I heard a faint sound in the distance.

What started as a murmur was soon a muddled rumbling, though the bishop, whose hearing had perhaps diminished in his older years, continued undeterred.

"So we say thank-you to God for blessing us with this day."

The crowd applauded the bishop's words, momentarily obscuring the growing din.

"Frank Fanoflincoln deserves our heartfelt thanks as well . . ."

More applause.

". . . for it was his generosity and the generosity of Tailburger that made this beautiful structure possible."

The Link beamed as the bishop's words washed over him like baptismal water. But by now, the faint sound from far away had become clearly audible and the audience members craned their heads to see what was causing the ruckus.

And then it was upon us—an obstreperous mob of angry protesters at the gates of the convent.

"WHAT DO WE WANT?"
They shouted in a chorus 200 strong.
"NO MORE PORN!"
The reply came in a refrain even louder.
"WHEN DO WE WANT IT?"
"NOW!"

The protest leader appeared to be a leftover radical from the 1960s who hadn't been told the movement was over. Although a number of the priests nervously got up and left quickly, apparently fearful their extracurricular activities with altar boys had been discovered, my heart sank when I saw the words printed on endless picket signs.

Tailburger and Porn Is No Happy Meal!
Tailburger and Prostitution = Deadly Combo Platter
Kids on Computers Don't Need Porn

My little scheme to improve market share had been found out.

"WHAT DO WE WANT?"
"NO MORE PORN!"
"WHEN DO WE WANT IT?"
"NOW!"

The bishop stood frozen at the podium as the marchers made their way down the center aisle and approached the stage.

"Good Lord. This is most unusual. I urge everyone to stay calm."

"WHAT DO WE WANT?"
"NO MORE PORN!"
"WHEN DO WE WANT IT?"
"NOW!"

The Link immediately blamed me for the mishap, this time rightfully so.

"What the hell is this, Thorne? What are they talking about?"

"I don't know, Frank," I lied unconvincingly.

Chaos ruled the afternoon now as the media found itself in a feeding frenzy of religion, pornography and the handicapped. Sister Ancilla pulled out her rosary beads and began praying while placards and chanting continued to fill the air.

"WHAT DO WE WANT?"
"NO MORE PORN!"
"WHEN DO WE WANT IT?"
"NOW!"

Katie Chang Gomez, having picked up on the possibility of Tailburger's involvement with computer porn, turned her questions to the kids from the Shriner's Hospital gathered in front.

"Do you kids know anything about Tailburger and its possible involvement in these sex-related computer sites?"

"Sure," a hunched over boy with a large back brace responded. "They're sponsoring the Nail Some Tail Sweepstakes."

"Nail some tail?" Chang Gomez asked, her brow furrowed in ludicrously serious journalistic fashion.

"That's right," came another debilitated boy. "First prize is a trip to the Lust Ranch out in Nevada for a free date with a hooker."

"And you all entered this?" Chang Gomez directed the question at the large group who'd been bused out for the dedication.

Nods all around sent a pack of reporters, now in on the story, up onto the stage, rushing to interview the Link.

"Mr. Fanoflincoln, what do you know about Tailburger's involvement in the pornography business?"

"Get those damn things out of my face," the Link answered, swatting his fat hand at the microphones. "We're not in the pornography business. We never have been. This is all trumped up by our enemies. Tell 'em, Thorne."

"Well, Frank . . . You see it's all . . ."

My momentary hesitation and the look on my face told the Link everything he had to know.

"Thorne! You're FIRED! Do you HEAR me? FIRED!!!"

I couldn't bring myself to look at Annette. I walked off the stage dejectedly and, after declining further comment to a pack of agitated reporters, fought through the dispersing mob to my car. The game I'd been playing was a losing one. I had known from the beginning that I was going to get caught. It was only a question of when. Now I had the answer—three weeks before qualifying for my Tailburger pension. I'd blown it. By embarrassing the Link on the biggest day of his life, I would receive no clemency from him. He might even take deranged pleasure in denying me what I'd earned over a lifetime. It was over.

26

Reeling

According to her ex-roommate Natalie, Sophia was at an AA meeting with Tweeter when I called to break the bad news. Even if I received a severance package, which was unlikely given the circumstances, tuition for her next semester at Cornell was going to be a challenge. And she could forget about the collagen injections. Her lips would have to remain thin and birdlike for the near future.

I now dared to utter the three words every college student fears the most: part-time job. Tweeter's van, my daughter's adopted home, didn't have a telephone, so I asked Natalie to have Sophia call me the next time she rolled into Ithaca. I rarely burdened my children with personal problems, but my new financial condition compelled me to warn them of the impending need for their gainful employment. Ethan wasn't home, but his message, recorded with the poetic assistance of Skull, encouraged me to "grab life by the *cojones*," all in all good advice when you've just been downsized. I told my son to call me when he got in.

King came home and found me in my funk.

"Do you want to meditate?"

"No. I *don't* want to meditate."

"It'll make you feel better."

"King, I just lost my job, my pension, my reputation and, in all likelihood, my girlfriend."

"At least you've got your chi reservoir."

"My chee reservoir is all tapped out. Do you understand?"

"You can't meditate when you're angry. That's one of the twenty-four rules."

"I don't care about the twenty-four fucking rules! I told you. I don't want to meditate! Will you just leave me alone?"

"If you think I don't understand, you're wrong. I've been right where you are."

"When have you *ever* been right where I am? You don't even know what the work world is like."

"That's not true. When I walked away from Norwegian Cruise Lines, I left with nothing but a sunburn and a bad case of genital herpes. You don't think that was painful? I've been there."

"King, I appreciate your empathy. I really do. But right now, I'd just like to be left alone."

"Okay, okay. But I won't let your evil chi consume you. Tomorrow we meditate."

A few dirty martinis. A few Commodores. A pair of comfortable pajamas. The remote control. Soon I didn't feel so bad about this firing stuff. Truth be told, it was liberating. I couldn't decide whether or not to quit my crap-ass job. Now the decision had been made for me. The pension problem was a bit of a bitch, but maybe I could finagle something. Or I could sue. How would my story play to a jury? Pretty damn well. Three weeks short of my retirement and the cold corporate hand cuts me off. I might get even more money this way. Being fired was a blessing. I was convinced. And drunk.

Local news did a job on me, the Link and Tailburger. When you're described as the linchpin between the church and a porn ring aimed at crippled minors, it's hard to call it a good day politically. Katie Chang Gomez, exercising her usual editorial restraint, called it the most galactically disturbing story she'd ever covered. Latest reports had the Fanoflincoln Pavilion being burned down to remove the impurity of the event from convent grounds. Suddenly my jury case wasn't looking as good.

My thoughts turned to Cal's son Kyle and the other kids in the hospital as a result of our undercooked meat. When the doorbell rang, I feared I'd find Cal standing on my front stoop, a loyal friend looking for comfort over the tragic news of a child's death. But it wasn't Cal. It was Annette, still dressed in the suit she wore to the dedication. I opened the door, dreading what she might have to say.

"Annette. What are you doing here?"

"I'm not welcome?"

"I didn't think you'd want to see me."

"Fanoflincoln is in the hospital."

"He is? What happened?"

"Stroke. Right after you left the convent, he keeled over on the bishop. It took three or four Shriner kids to get him off."

"My God. That's terrible."

"May I come in?"

"Of course."

I walked Annette to the kitchen and offered her a seat.

"I can't believe the Link had a stroke. Everybody's gonna say it was my fault for shocking him."

"Oh, I don't know," Annette said skeptically. "I think the extra four hundred pounds he carries around is a suspect as well."

"Would you like something to drink?"

"Sure."

I brought a bottle of wine and two glasses to the table.

"I'm sorry about your job."

"You heard?"

"Everybody at the ceremony heard."

"There's a reasonable explanation for all of this, I swear. I had to get our market share up or lose my job. You were at the board meetings. You know how the Link pushed people. He just pushed me and pushed me."

"Sky, I won't lie to you. I'm angry as hell that you weren't up-front with me and that you didn't tell me what you were involved in."

"I know. I know. I'm sorry. I should've told you. At least then you could have distanced yourself from me and prevented any political damage."

"Sky, I'm not just talking about things from a political standpoint. I'm talking from a personal one. I trusted you. This is about honesty."

"I'm sorry."

"You let me down. And it hurts."

I hung my head in boyish shame, prepared to receive the punishment I so richly deserved: losing Annette.

"Look. (Pause) I know what kind of pressure you were under. Fanoflincoln is a jerk. I just want you to know that I'm resigning from the board."

"What?"

"I've given it a lot of thought. He just bullies everyone. It's not worth it to me anymore."

"Annette, you don't have to do that for me."

"I know that. I'm not doing it for you. I'm doing it for me."

"It sounds like you've made up your mind."

"I have. I've also made up my mind about something else."

"Here it comes," I thought. "El dumperoo."

"I want us to be together."

I wasn't sure I'd heard her right.

"You do?"

"Yes. But, Sky, I have to know if there's anything else you haven't told me. I do have an election coming up, and I won't be able to withstand a second bombshell. People will be associating me with you from here on out. So I've got to know. Is there anything else out there? Anything sordid or embarrassing?"

"No. Of course not. I mean, what else could there be?"

"You're certain?"

"Yes. Absolutely."

Annette walked over to me and wrapped her arms around my back.

"I missed you."

"Me too."

I kissed Annette softly on the lips.

"Stay over?"

"No. I've got to go. I have a meeting in the morning, and I'm exhausted. I just came by to make sure you were all right."

"You're incredible, Annette."

Annette and I embraced at the door and said good-bye. Ethan reached me an hour later, just as I was falling asleep.

"Dad, what's wrong? Your voice sounded funny on your message."

"Ethan, listen. I lost my job."

"Noooo. That is *brutal,* Dad. What happened?"

"Well, that's the other part of the news. See, you may hear some things in the press about Tailburger and an Internet contest we were running."

"You mean the Nail Some Tail Sweepstakes?"

"Yes. You knew about that?"

"Of course. When are they announcing the winner? I'm hoping to score that Lust Ranch trip."

"Look, I don't want you to score anything. That contest was a bad idea."

"Let me guess. You were the guy behind it?"

"I'm ashamed to say it, but yes."

"Awwwriiight, Pop! That's all-time. I can't believe you were the guy behind that gig. I can't wait to tell my buds."

"*Don't* tell your buds! Don't tell anyone!"

"Why not?"

"Let's just say it's not something I'm proud of."

"So why'd you get in trouble for it?"

"It's a long story. Let's just say some people weren't happy about it."

"I'll tell you, Dad, they did you a favor by ankling your ass."

Time for some of my son's legendary career counseling.

"Why do you say that?"

"Isn't it obvious? You're in the death zone."

"What do you mean, the death zone?"

"You don't know?"

"No, I don't know. What are you talking about?"

"Well, you're over forty-five years old, which means you could drop any day. The studies show it. Very few men die before forty-five, but after that life turns into a crapshoot. You could bite it today."

"I'm not going to bite it today, all right?"

"No need to go postal. I'm just saying. I thought you knew."

Maybe my son was on to something. Why not listen to him? I sure hadn't found many answers to life's questions on my own.

"So this death zone I'm in, how does it relate to my firing?"

"Dad, I've learned a few things out here. One is that everybody retires by forty-five. Nobody wants to be hanging around the office sitting on the cube farm, hunched over all day, just watching their body and brain deteriorate. You make your money and you get out while you still have time to enjoy it. It's all about being young. Doing the things you want to do in life. Use work. Don't let it use you. Travel. Paint. Collect wine."

"Collect wine? What the hell do you know about collecting wine?"

"Nothing yet, but I'm not retired."

"Ethan, it's not as simple as you make it sound."

"All I'm saying is, what's the use of piling up all this dough just to die? Hell, if you're still working at the age of fifty in Silicon Valley, people feel sorry for you. It's like, 'What happened, dude?' We're all just company cattle. When you try to invest yourself in a corporation, you waste your time. You won't be there long enough for it to pay off. And there's no loyalty anymore, Dad. Companies don't care about their people. It's all about the Benjamins. The dead presidents."

"The Benjamins?"

"The money. Hundred-dollar bills. Ben Franklins."

"Oh."

"Don't you see? You put your *fuck you* money together and then you bolt."

How had the world changed so much on my watch? When I left school, work was a noble pursuit. A lifetime spent behind a desk was the price you paid for a better life for your wife and your children. Sure, it sucked, but you put in the time and at the end of the road you reaped the reward: a pension and some security, perhaps a place in Florida. What you did was who you were and your source of respect. Being a certain age mattered. Gray hair was equated with wisdom, not doddering incompetency. And if you were bold enough to be an entrepreneur, you never imagined a company could be built and sold in six months. It took years, and then, if you were lucky, you might be able to cash out a bit early.

Now nobody cared. Working any longer than you absolutely had to was for suckers. And the age by which you had to get out was getting younger. Pretty soon it would be, "Poor bastard, thirty years old and still grinding it out for the man." Wearing a suit? That was the sure sign that you were a capitalist tool or, worse, irrelevant in the new economy. The mercantile ethic said to make your pile and get out. But what if you didn't have a pile? Get out anyway and take your chances? That might have meant something to a twenty-two-year-old like Ethan, but to me, it didn't mean anything. The shift in the paradigm had been too radical and too swift for me. With my current car's alignment, I wouldn't be able to make the turn at the corner.

"Dad, trust me. You're lucky they fired you. You just don't see it yet."

"I can't send you any more money, Ethan."

I thought that the stark reality of being cut off would cause Ethan to bolt up in his seat and reconsider his newly found philosophies. I was dead wrong.

"That's okay. We're going public. The IPO is next week."

"It is?"

"Yes. This is it. Strap in and get ready for the ride. Six months from now, if all goes well, we'll be sipping piña coladas and getting rolfed on a daily basis. Macrocock rules!"

"Ethan, that's great!"

"We'll see what happens, but it looks pretty good."

"What will you do for money until the lockup period is over?"

"I'll deal, Dad. Don't worry."

The way Ethan took my news gave me reason for pause. All this time, I thought I'd be letting him down if I didn't support him financially. Turns out, I had it backward.

"Listen, don't tell your sister anything until I speak with her, okay?"

"Sure, Dad. Whatever you want."

Remarkably, my kids were growing more agreeable as they got older; a very pleasant compensation of age. I said good night to Ethan and shut off the light on my nightstand. A new day would be dawning tomorrow, and with it would arrive my last chance to make amends for the things I'd done and to turn my boat toward insular Tahiti. I climbed out of bed and dropped to my knees. Prayer and patriotism are the last two refuges of a scoundrel, but I needed shelter and I didn't own a flag.

Confessor

4:38 A.M.

Campylobacter. Salmonella. Shigella. Cryptosporidium. Escherichia coli 0157:H7. Ghastly sounding one and all, these were the five most common forms of food poisoning, according to the Centers for Disease Control and Prevention. I figured it was time to become better educated about the subject if it was going to destroy my life. The pamphlet that I read from S.T.O.P., the acronym for the organization Safe Tables Our Priority, said that 76 million people per year got sick with a foodborne illness and scared the hell out of me when it came to E. coli and what it might be doing to Cal's son and his friends.

This stuff was awful. Forget your basic food poisoning. The list of possible conditions it induced read like a medical manual of horrors. Hemolytic Uremic Syndrome. Thrombotic Thrombocytopoenic Pupura. Blood disorders. Kidney malfunction. Neurological dysfunction. And the possible treatments didn't sound any better. Dialysis. Plasma Pheresis. Bone marrow biopsies. Splenectomies. Chemotherapy. My God, what had I done?

Cal agreed to meet me at Pappy's for breakfast at 7:30 A.M. The hangdog expression he wore was unlike any I'd ever seen. It was obvious he'd come straight from the hospital.

"How's Kyle?"

"It's touch and go. I've been there all night."

"Jesus. I'm so sorry, Cal."

"I feel helpless. The doctors say we just have to hope for the best. Some of the other kids are being released today."

"That's great."

"Yeah, I guess so. To be honest, I'm having a hard time being happy for anybody else right now. I'm too busy feeling sorry for myself."

Cal slouched down in our banquette and reached for a handful of sugar packets. He tore them open one at a time and poured the white crystals down his throat with 50 percent accuracy.

"That's understandable. I'd feel the same way. (Pause) Look, I have something to tell you."

I was ready to tell Cal about the undercooking. I owed it to him as a friend. And if I wanted to start turning my own sorry existence around, it seemed like a good first step.

"I already heard about your job."

"Oh, you did?"

"Yes. Didn't everybody? I'm sorry you got canned."

"Thanks. That's all right. But actually, that's not what I need to talk to you about."

"Is it the police investigation? 'Cause I already know all about that, too."

"The what?"

"The police investigation of us."

"Us?"

"Yes. You and me for Tailburger's Internet sweepstakes."

"What are you talking about?"

"After the press broke the story about the Nail Some Tail Sweepstakes at the convent dedication, they started poking their fucking noses around my business. . . ."

"What?"

". . . One thing led to another and now they're saying we both knew that minors were entering the contest. The whole thing is a fucking mess."

"What the hell happened, Cal?"

"Well, some new child protection law requires Internet sites to obtain permission from parents to take data from children under eighteen, and we didn't get it all the time."

"How often did you get it?"

"To be honest, never."

"Why not?"

"Well, for starters, we're a porn site. We're not supposed to allow underage kids to log on or to take any information from them. We had a parental warning posted, but our intake function was a rubber stamp. The kids caught on pretty quickly that we weren't being too careful about checking their ages when they entered the sweepstakes. Word spread and we ended up collecting lots of data from minors. We got a little sloppy."

"So what are we talking here? A slap on the wrist? Maybe a misdemeanor?"

"Actually, it's a felony because of the prostitution prize. The contest drew a lot of twelve-year-olds."

"Jesus Christ, Cal. This can't happen. Why the fuck didn't you close off the Web site to minors? Period."

"You wanted to sell more burgers. You said, 'Cal, raise my market share.' How the hell do you think that happens? By magic wand?"

"I told you to keep it legal."

"You told me to increase your market share. You knew we were tapping into the teen market."

Cal was right. I'd buried my head in the sand when it came to the decision about minors. The fact was, I didn't want to know the truth so long as he produced results for me. And now, I had the audacity to get mad at *him*. My slide into hell had to stop.

"You're right. I knew. (Pause) I knew something else, too."

"What's that?"

"Cal, it's about Kyle. I fucked up."

"What are you talking about?"

"I fucked up royally, Cal. Kyle's sickness—it's my fault."

"Sky, I told you. I don't blame you just because you work for Tailburger. It's not your fault."

"No. *Listen* to me. The Link told me he wanted Tailburger to start undercooking its burgers—the insides—to make them soft. He told me to put the policy in place. The Link gave the order, but I carried it out. I did it."

"Why would you do that?"

"Because I needed to keep my job—long enough to get my pension. I know it's pathetic, but I never thought it would affect anyone. I'm truly sorry, Cal."

"You're sorry? You're a complete asshole. Are you telling me my son is lying in a fucking hospital, near death, because of some goddamn corporate policy you didn't have the balls to squash?"

I nodded.

"I'm sorry, Cal."

"Why didn't you tell me what was going on? Do you think I would have kept buying burgers from you guys? Are you fucking kidding me?"

"I'm sorry, Cal. I want to make it up to you any way I can."

"You *can't* make this up to me!"

"I'm sorry. I am so sorry."

"That's not good enough, Sky. If Kyle dies, it's on your head. Do you hear me? And another thing. We're not friends anymore. Fuck you!"

Cal picked up and left me alone in the booth. He had been my best friend for as long as I could remember. And now, he was gone.

28

Caught

When I returned home that evening, my worst fears were realized. A police squad car sat in my driveway, and a wall of a man, dressed in blue, stood at my door. For a split second I thought about going on the lam—making a run for it like Butch and Sundance. "No," I told myself. "That'll only make you look guilty. And you're not guilty. You're just a man who used adult entertainment for purposes of marketing. That's all. Stick to the story."

"May I help you, officer?" I was out of the car now, walking slowly up the driveway. The officer turned around and met me halfway down the blacktop.

"Are you Schuyler Thorne?"

"Yes, I am. What seems to be the matter?"

"Mr. Thorne, I need you to come downtown with me."

"What for?"

"We just want to ask you a few questions."

"About what?"

"A matter we're investigating. It involves a guy named Cal Perkins. Do you know him?"

My inner voice went into overdrive. *Act like you have no idea what he's talking about. Play it cool.*

"Never heard of him."

What are you doing? You're lying to a cop. Are you crazy?

"I see. Well, I still need you to come with me."

"What are you after him for?"

"I'm really not at liberty to say anything more. I need you to come with me to the station."

Whatever you do, don't act guilty. He'll smell it on you like English Leather.

By now I was standing face-to-face with Officer Krupke. Actually, it was more like face-to-chest. Still, I wasn't going to let this guy intimidate me.

"Aren't you going to read me my rights?"

"I'm not arresting you. I'm just taking you in for questioning."

"Oh. All right."

"Are you ready to go or do you need a minute?"

"I want to call a lawyer."

I'd seen *NYPD Blue* and knew these interrogations could get pretty rough. I called M.C. Shufelbarger from my cell phone on the ride downtown and told him to meet me at the fifth precinct. When it came right down to it, I liked the way he had handled the whole Roxby matter. Dignified. Restrained. Discreet. Roxby's trial, set to begin in a few weeks, would only sharpen the razor blade of my chosen counsel. No question about it. When you were in trouble with the long, hairy arm of the law, Shufelbarger was your man.

Police headquarters smelled like a hamster cage. After filling out some forms, I was led into a windowless room and told to wait. Thirty minutes and four cups of bad coffee later, a squat man in a pale blue short-sleeved dress shirt and standard-issue police pants entered. A second man, silver-haired and dressed in street clothes, followed closely behind. Last was Shufelbarger, his bow tie askew as usual, who shut the door behind him and threw his enormous leather satchel on the metal table in the middle of the room. I shook hands with my attorney as the short cop started a small tape recorder and began.

"For the record, please state your full name."

"Hold on a minute," Shufelbarger interrupted. He opened his bag and slowly began pulling out assorted materials. Two minutes later he was still going strong.

"What are you doing?" I asked him under my breath.

"Trust me," he replied.

When Shufelbarger finally finished, a mountain of extraneous legal matter including hornbooks, pens, stationery, Wite-Out, legal pads and a ruler sat between us and them. Since none of this stuff could have anything to do with my case, I surmised it was all for effect.

"Okay, now I'm ready," Shufelbarger informed my interrogators.

The officer in charge, slightly perturbed, continued.

"For the record, please state your full name."

"You don't have to answer that, Sky," Shufelbarger blurted out.

"Yes, he does. I'm only asking him his name," the officer insisted.

"If you're going to badger my client, this interview will end right here."

The two cops looked at Shufelbarger like he was nuts, but I admit I enjoyed the overzealousness.

"It's all right, M.C.," I assured him.

"Okay, but it's your ass," he protested.

"Schuyler Witherbee Thorne."

"Mr. Thorne, do you know why we brought you down here tonight?"

"No. Not exactly."

"Don't play games with us, Thorne," the plainclothes officer threatened.

The good cop–bad cop routine had begun.

"Don't talk to my client like that. He's innocent until proven guilty."

"Good point, M.C.," I encouraged my counselor.

"Mr. Thorne, we're investigating Cal Perkins. Do you know him?'

"You don't have to answer that, Sky."

"M.C.! Let me just answer the questions!"

"Okay, but it's your ass," Shufelbarger repeated.

"Yes, I know him. He's my best friend."

"I see," said the diminutive detective in a knowing way. "And how long have the two of you been in the porn game?"

"I am *not* in the porn game."

"My client has rights! And one of them is to be free from accusations of being a pornographer." Shufelbarger was standing now, shaking his finger at the accusing officer. This guy was good.

"Did you or did you not play a role in the Nail Some Tail Sweepstakes?"

"Don't answer that, Sky."

"That's a complicated question," I admitted.

"Yes or no. Did you have anything to do with that contest?"

"Don't answer that, Sky. Admit nothing."

This time Shufelbarger's instruction made sense. I was suddenly feeling vulnerable to word twisting and coercion.

"Admit it," shouted the taller of the two. "You masterminded a prostitution contest aimed at children. You and your sick-bastard friend, Cal Perkins. Admit it."

"That's not true! I had no idea young children would see the site."

"So you *knew* about the contest?"

"Well, yes, I mean, no. I mean, I didn't know what was happening with the kids." My stammering unnerved Shufelbarger.

"Shut up, Sky. That's it. This interview is over. I'm not going to sit here and let my client get railroaded by a couple of rent-a-cops."

"Rent-a-cops?! Fuck you, Shufelbarger!" the stout cop barked.

"No. Fuck you!" Shufelbarger shot back.

"M.C., I'm not sure all of this animosity is necessary." I was concerned about pissing off the police.

"They're trying to screw you, Sky, and you don't even know it."

Shufelbarger began furiously packing his pile of notepads, pens and papers—all of them covered with yellow stickies—back into his briefcase. He had clearly offended the detectives, but what could they do about it?

"We're going to have to detain your client. We've got more questions."

"What the hell are you talking about, you Miranda-less leeches? You can't detain him and you know it."

"We can if we arrest him."

"You wouldn't dare, you shitheaps."

"Oh, yeah. You want to test us?"

Shufelbarger's face was flushed now, and I couldn't help but feel like things were trending quickly against my best interests.

"Hey, M.C., why don't we live to fight another day? I think the officers are just trying to do their jobs."

"Is denying you your constitutional rights part of their job? I don't think so!"

"That's it. Mr. Thorne is under arrest."

"On what charge?" I demanded.

"Contributing to the delinquency of a minor. Disorderly conduct. Take your pick."

"That's horseshit," Shufelbarger cried out, pounding his fist on the table.

As I was led out of the room in handcuffs, Shufelbarger assured me he'd arrange for bail.

"I'll get you out, Sky."

"You better. You're the one who got me in," I called back, pissed he had been so belligerent with my freedom at stake. Adding insult to injury, since the arraignment couldn't take place until morning (something about the judge being at his summer cottage), I had to stay the night in a Monroe County jail cell with a suspected serial rapist named Fingers Tremble, who spent most of the evening masturbating and asking me what I thought about the special effects in *Star Wars: Episode One*. My one phone call, to Annette, was strained, to say the least.

"You're where?"

"In jail. Just temporarily though."

"What happened?"

"Well, they're accusing me of corrupting minors with the prostitution sweepstakes we were running."

"Sky, how could you let this happen?"

"Annette, I didn't mean to. I had no idea things would turn out this way." Excuses were flying fast now, like bat shit at a barn dance. "The situation was beyond my control."

"Yes, but getting involved with Cal in the first place wasn't."

"This wasn't all my fault."

"It doesn't matter, Sky."

"So what are you saying?"

"Sky, I can't continue on in this relationship anymore. It's too much. I'll get eaten alive in the papers if I'm part of this story. You know that."

"I know."

"Sky, I'm sorry. I love you. I just can't be with you anymore."

"I understand."

And then Annette hung up on me. This was turning out to be one hell of a night. Once the news of my arrest hit the police blotter and newswire, the media saw blood in the water. Katie Chang Gomez stood in the front row of the press corps gathered for a midmorning press conference arranged by Shufelbarger. On the marble steps of the state courthouse, following my arraignment, Shufelbarger approached me and whispered in my ear.

"You ever work in a soup kitchen or a shelter?"

I pulled back from him and spoke aloud.

"I don't remember. Maybe one time. Why?"

"No reason."

Shufelbarger went back to shuffling his papers, pulling various items in and out of his satchel until he was ready to speak. He acknowledged the growing mass of reporters with a nod and began.

"Good morning, ladies and gentlemen. I'd like to read a statement to you."

Shufelbarger cleared his tar-stained throat.

"Schuyler Thorne is totally innocent of the charges leveled against him. There is absolutely no truth to any of the allegations, and he is confident that he will be vindicated completely in this matter. Sky is one of Rochester, New York's, most upstanding citizens. As the chief operating officer, excuse me, former chief operating officer, of Tailburger Incorporated, Sky has been responsible for creating hundreds of jobs in our community, and for the donation of thousands of dollars to local causes that improve our daily lives and the lives of those around us. He's spent countless hours in soup kitchens all over this city, and in social work circles, he's known as 'Mr. Homeless Shelter,' because that's where you'll find him most holidays, handing out turkeys, ladling gravy and whatnot. Now Mr. Thorne will not be speaking today, but I'm willing to take a few questions. Ms. Chang Gomez, please go ahead."

"Mr. Shufelbarger, did your client know that minors were entering the Nail Some Tail Sweepstakes?"

"Absolutely not. He had no idea."

"So what was the primary purpose of the contest?"

"To sell more burgers. Plain and simple."

I was encouraged by the first few questions and answers. We were getting the facts out—our side of the story. Everything that was true and good about me was coming to light.

"Next question. Yes, you, in the front row."

"Is Mr. Thorne a pimp?"

"People, please! Keep the questions appropriate or this news conference will be over before you can spell Britney Spears. Next question. Yes, you."

"When is Tailburger announcing the winner of the sweepstakes?"

"Mr. Thorne is no longer an employee of Tailburger and has no access to that information. Next question."

"If you win the trip to Vegas, do you get to pick the hooker you sleep with? Or do they just give you some leftover skank?"

"That's it, people! This press conference is over!"

Shufelbarger led me by the arm to a waiting car.

"Those hookworms don't know when to quit," Shufelbarger fumed as the driver whisked us toward M.C.'s office for a debriefing. I was furious about the pimp question and nearly as mad at Shufelbarger.

"Hey, what was all that homeless shelter bullshit? You were lying."

"I was not, Sky. That's called lawyering. There's a big difference. It's my responsibility to paint an accurate picture of you for the public to see. And you are obviously a very civic-minded person. That's all I was saying. Was there some hyperbole involved? Perhaps. But that just comes from my heart. I don't see the harm."

"Well, why don't you take it down a notch next time? Stick a little closer to the facts. All right?"

"Okay, but it's your ass."

"*Stop* saying that!"

Okay, okay. Calm down."

Shufelbarger and I rode together in silence for a minute. While my thoughts drifted to Annette and the fact that I'd lost her— probably for good—he pulled out a Johnny Cash cassette from a drawer under the liquor decanters. "This is what you need to listen to, Sky. A little *Boy Named Sue*'ll cure ya."

When it came to my failed relationship, I didn't have anybody to blame but myself. That was the truth, and I'd have to accept it.

Although I'd seek pity from everyone around me, I didn't expect to receive it.

"So when *are* they announcing the winner of the sweepstakes, Sky?" Shufelbarger casually inquired.

"Why do you care?"

"No reason. Just curious. It seems to have generated a tremendous amount of interest. Me, myself, I hadn't heard of it."

"Right."

"*Do* you get to pick the hooker? Or *is* it some skank?"

"How would I know?"

"Just asking."

"I don't believe you. You're pond scum."

"Easy, Sky. I'm not the pornographer here."

"I am *not* a pornographer!" I shouted at Shufelbarger.

"Don't pop your top!"

"M.C., I want to go home. Driver, head for Mendon."

"That's fine, Sky. I have to meet with Burton Roxby this afternoon anyway. This'll give me a chance to prepare for that. We can meet tomorrow."

"Fine."

Sometimes when you're away from home, even for a day a two, you see the true physical condition of your house when you return. You could go years without noticing the chipped paint or the faded shutters, the weeds in the driveway or the rusted mailbox. And then, having been gone, you pull up with fresh eyes and you realize the whole place needs a lot of work. So much work, you're not sure where to begin. You stop for a minute and wonder how your house ever got so dilapidated. When did you start letting it go? How did this happen? You won't be able to remember. And it's frightening because repairing the damage will take certain resources and you must assess whether or not you've got them. The patience. The time. The money. The desire. Maybe you do, but maybe you don't. And maybe you're all alone. And if you *don't* have the resources and you *are* all alone, you face a difficult decision. Will you let your house fade even further, personally holing up inside the deteriorating structure? Or will you sell it and quietly move far away, forgotten by all but a few?

My house needed a lot of work.

29

Tenderloin

King was out when I returned. It was just as well. I didn't really want him making a big fuss over my first prison homecoming. At this rate, there'd be others anyway. Then again, where the hell was he? Didn't he know I'd been in jail?

I stood still for a moment in the front hallway and listened for the normal noises I'd missed: the ticking of the clock on the living room mantel, the clanging of the water heater from the basement, the crunching of soy nuts by King as he espoused the virtues of tantric sex. I was alone and lonely, a most unfortunate condition. Usually I was one or the other, but not both. The combination was a killer.

The telephone rang, and I let the machine pick up.

"Sky, it's Trip Baden calling. I don't know what kind of a mid-life meltdown you're going through, but you better get your shit together. If you think I'm gong to let some scuzzy, low-life flesh peddler like you prevent me from getting what's legally mine, you're woefully mistaken. Your career is officially over at Tail-burger and I want my half of your pension. You have one week to call my lawyer, Herv Alverson, and begin the paperwork. Otherwise, I'll see you in court. Good-bye!"

I went to the refrigerator, twisted open a Molson and sat down in my dreary kitchen. This symbolized freedom to me, however pathetic it sounds, and so I sat, feeling sorry for myself. But hey, I felt entitled to a bit of self-pity, having lost so much (add girlfriend, self-respect, watch—Fingers Tremble duped me on a Jar Jar Binks trivia question—dignity and possibly liberty to my aforementioned list of job, pension and reputation). Hard to say which loss was the worst, although Annette was most on my mind. "At least I have my health," I consoled myself, swilling down the last sip of beer and choking back the cough of a man with early-stage emphysema.

I was paralyzed. Couldn't call Annette. She didn't want to hear from me. Couldn't call Cal. He hated me. Couldn't go to work. I didn't have a job. Couldn't call my kids. I prayed they would miss this part of their father's demise. Couldn't watch television. I was too afraid to face the character assassination that was undoubtedly taking place on the local news. I grabbed a pile of mail from the counter and started sorting through it. Cable bill. Electric bill. Request for a donation from Roxby's legal defense fund. Columbia Compact Disc Club offer (mental note: check for Bread Anthology CD). Publisher's Clearinghouse packet. Crooked Creek club dues. Another Publisher's Clearinghouse packet addressed to someone named Ski Torne. Credit card offer. Gas bill. Cornell tuition bill (mental note: remind Sophia you weren't kidding about her getting a part-time job). Another credit card offer. J. Crew catalog. Late notice from mortgage company. Victoria's Secret catalog (whoever sent me this—you're cruel). Telephone bill. The end. (Pause). My conclusion. Looking to the mail for comfort was like looking to Liz Taylor for marital advice.

Moving toward the hot shower I so badly needed, I heard a rumbling outside. Sure enough, out the front window I saw a lime green van, covered with rust and bumper stickers, sitting in my driveway. I couldn't see what the bumper stickers said but instinct told me the collection included "Practice Random Acts of Kindness," "Think Globally, Act Locally" and "Jesus Is My Copilot," not to mention every other annoying saying ever foisted on the American car-driving public.

Just when I thought no further ill fate could possibly befall me, I was proved wrong by a gangly punk with a bad goatee and two earrings who spryly hopped down from the driver's side of the van, and a strange woman in dreadlocks who did the same from the passenger's side. Hand in hand, the two of them, both clad in sandals, sunglasses and knitted, tricolored, Rastafarian lids, strolled toward my house. They only looked moderately dangerous so I opened the front door to greet them.

"May I help you?"

"How could you, Daddy?" the female asked.

"Yeah, how could you, man?" her companion followed. It was Sophia and my biggest nightmare: Tweeter, the non-Choate townie.

After all the times I'd supported my daughter through lost loves, unfair teachers, catty girlfriends and cosmetic surgery, I thought that she would be the first to support me in my hour of greatest need. Her dear old dad was fighting for his personal and professional life, and what he really needed was a hug. But did I get that? Of course not. Instead, I stood in the foyer of my own home getting verbally attacked by her and a guy wearing an Insane Clown Posse concert jersey. Too stunned to react, I threw up my arms and shrugged while my persecutors sauntered in from the front stoop.

"Daddy, this is Tweeter," Sophia called out as she headed for the bathroom. "I've gotta pee so bad."

Suddenly I was left alone with David Soul.

"So, Tweeter, is your name short for something?" I asked, extending my nicotine-stained hand to shake his.

"Nope. Just Tweeter," he responded, returning my traditional gesture of greeting halfheartedly. "My folks named me after a speaker, I think. It was either going to be Woofer or Tweeter."

"I see. I think you got the better end of that bargain."

"I like to think so."

The thought of this cretin having sex with my daughter made my brain go numb. I had avoided imagining it before, but now with him standing in front of me I couldn't, so I allowed myself to go into some kind of protective parental shock.

Sophia returned from the bathroom still steaming.

"Daddy, Ethan told me what you did, and I think it's awful. How could you support the exploitation of women with that prostitution contest?"

"It was just marketing, Sophia. Prostitution is legal in Nevada. Those women are professionals."

"That doesn't make it right. Men have been making sex objects out of women since the beginning of time, and this only adds to the problem."

"Sophia, I'm not saying it's an ideal situation. But it is legal, and I was under extraordinary pressure at work. You're going to have to forgive me, or at the very least, try to understand."

"I don't understand, Daddy. Is it true that crippled little kids were entering the contest? That really bothers me."

"That part of the story has been blown way out of proportion. They weren't all crippled, and I had no idea that was happening anyway. Think of the illegal entrants as horny high schoolers. You remember that time of your life Soph, don't you?"

"*I* sure do," Tweeter piped up.

"Shut up, Tweeter," Sophia snapped. "Daddy, this sets the cause of females back about twenty years. My fem lit professor says we're getting physically, spiritually and emotionally raped by the white man in power. That's you, Daddy! You're part of the problem."

"All right, Soph, that's enough. This hasn't been the best day of your father's life. I just got out of jail, and I need some peace and quiet. Do you understand?"

I'd really had it with my daughter at this point, and I knew if she pushed me any further I'd probably say something I regretted.

"Daddy, we can't just drop this."

"Okay, fine! Tell me then, what does your fem lit professor say about your breast implants? Are they part of the problem?"

"No. There's a difference."

"Those aren't real?" Tweeter interjected, a surprised look on his face as he pointed to Sophia's chest.

"No, they're not real. God, Tweeter, don't be stupid," Sophia barked.

"What difference?" I persisted.

"The difference is that with my augmentation procedure, I exploited myself. It was an act of self-empowerment. I had a choice."

"I can't believe those aren't real," Tweeter observed, scratching his scraggly beard.

"Shut up, Tweeter!" Sophia shouted.

"These women in Nevada have a choice, too," I protested. "They don't have to have sex for money."

"You just don't get it, Daddy," Sophia said, telling me in her customary way that the conversation was over as far as she was concerned. Life's a funny thing. Just twenty-four hours before I'd been in prison debating the merits of *The Shawshank Redemption* with a serial rapist named Fingers Tremble, and now here I was arguing about the merits of legalized prostitution with my daughter and a guy most likely conceived during Lynyrd Skynyrd's second encore at the Gator Bowl in 1976.

"Sophia, don't be mad at me."

Silence.

"Well, are you staying for a bit?"

"We're just passing through, Sky," Tweeter informed me.

Sky? Did this kid just call me Sky?

"Call me Colonel, Tweeter." Although I'd never served a day in my life in the service, I wanted Tweeter to fear me.

"Got it."

Sophia looked at Tweeter as if she was waiting for him to say something.

"Daddy, the reason we're here is because Tweeter has something to say to you."

Tweeter looked back at Sophia and audibly gulped.

"Go ahead, Tweeter," Sophia urged.

"Well, Colonel Thorne . . ."

"You don't have to call him Colonel."

"Yes, he does."

"Well, sir . . . uh Colonel, uh Mr. Thorne, I wanted to talk to you about me and Sophia."

Tweeter placed his index finger under the loose-fitting neckline of his jersey and began to shift his weight from side to side. This couldn't be what I feared it was. It just couldn't.

"What about you and Sophia?" I countered nervously.

"Well, you see . . . we've been living in my van . . . that green one outside."

"I saw it. So what?" My heart sank under the weight of his words.

"Well, we'd like to get married. And I wanted to ask your permission."

Sophia moved over to Tweeter, placed her arm around his back and gave him a kiss on the cheek. I would need to handle this gently, delicately and with finesse.

"You know you seem like a nice guy, Tweeter. But I've got to tell you something. There's NO WAY in FUCKING HELL you two are getting married!"

"I just thought that maybe . . ."

"MAYBE NOTHING!"

"Oh, Daddy, how could you be so mean?" Sophia broke into tears after my outburst. "Tweeter and I are in love. Can't you see that?"

"It'll pass, Soph, I promise you. And all you'll be left with is a rusted-out van covered by a 'Honk If You're Horny' bumper sticker. I can't let you make that mistake."

"I *hate* you, Daddy! I hate you! We *are* going to get married, whether you like it or not. C'mon, Tweeter. We're leaving. (Pause) I bet Trip would understand."

Sophia knew that remark would hurt me.

"Sorry, Colonel," Tweeter said as he shuffled out and shut the door behind them.

I watched Sophia and Tweeter climb back into the van and added my daughter's name to the growing list of things and people that I'd apparently lost. This was just one of her phases though. I was certain about that. Twenty or thirty years from now, everything would be back to normal.

30

Indecent Exposure

Soy nuts. Organic polenta. Ready-to-drink, nondairy, blended chai tea and spice soy beverage, Tofutti vanilla snacks. These monstrosities were my brother's idea of problem solving.

"You've just been in jail. You need to focus on your nutrition."

"I don't want *anything* with soy in it. It tastes like crap. What I need is a cigarette."

I desperately searched my kitchen drawer for a pack of Commodores.

"Sky, you're not in the clink anymore. You can't trade your soul for a carton of smokes. You need to heal your spirit. Why don't we meditate together? We'll warm up your Dan Tian and try to channel your chi."

"Forget my chee. I've got a better idea. Let's go to the Sweet."

The Country Sweet, a late-night spot we'd frequented since we were teenagers, was the only place I thought I could clear my mind. The restaurant's Monroe Avenue location in downtown Rochester was ideal if you wanted to hit three head shops and four adult theaters without leaving a two-block area. The Sweet, as the faux-oak paneled establishment was belovedly known, drew a dangerous collection of hustlers, dealers and derelicts . . . and those were just the people who worked behind the counter. Sticky floors and the smell of wet naps welcomed you to a joint where the food was scary and the bathroom, a place you entered with no guarantee you'd be leaving, was scarier. For old time's sake, we ordered the 200-piece party pack, a delicious but visually disgusting load of the best chicken wings known to man, woman or beast. This was comfort food to me, not simply because it tasted so good, but because for years this had been the place I'd come for continuity. In a world where everything changed, the Sweet was the one thing that didn't. Eating there was a well-worn ritual with three inviolable rules:

1. You only ordered the hot sauce on your wings. Never mild. This rule was not without irony. Ordering mild sauce was a sign of weakness as a man, yet if you ordered the hot, crying was perfectly acceptable as long as you endured the lip-scorching pepper flakes scattered across the surface of the oversize pieces of burning sweet poultry.

2. There was no talking while you ate. All worries could wait until your plate was cleared.

3. Water was the only allowable beverage and you never drank it until you were done with all your wings. Too many had made the rookie mistake of sipping in between bites and lived (barely) to regret it.

Adherence to the Sweet rules temporarily brought order out of chaos for me. Once King and I finished gorging ourselves, we got down to the business at hand. First I came clean about the under-cooking policy and how I'd endangered Cal's son, Kyle, and his little friends. Next I told him how I would atone for my sins if Cal gave me the chance. Finally, we spoke of the root of all evil.

"I need your advice." It killed me to say that to King, but I was out of advisers.

"My advice? This is a first."

"I've got a plan to get my pension, and I want to run it by you."

"Your pension? Is that what you're most worried about?"

"Well, no. Of course not. Are you implying that Kyle's health isn't foremost on my mind? Why would you do that?"

"I wasn't implying anything."

"I know this is difficult for you to understand, but pretty soon, my finances are going to look like Willie Nelson's. And without enough money, I'm going to be screwed. I could lose the house. Sophia's tuition is due. I've got a stack of bills piling up. Without money, I won't be of use to anybody."

"So get a job."

"After everything that's been in the papers? Who do you think is going to hire me right now?"

"I know I wouldn't."

"Shut up."

"So what's the plan?"

"Well, it sort of involves bribery."

"Sort of? Sky, may I remind you of what we've been working on the last few months? Truthfulness. Benevolence. Forbearance. Not bribery. Not moral trickery."

"I know that, but things are a bit complicated right now. I'm facing relationship purgatory and financial catastrophe, not to mention jail time and potential lawsuits from Cal, Tailburger and Trip Baden. Isn't there a temporary exception from virtue when you're flat broke and busted in every way?"

"No. There's not."

"Well, hear me out. Maybe you'll change your mind."

I leaned in toward King and spoke to him under my breath.

"I have a videotape of Muffet Meaney and me having sex."

"Bullshit!"

"I mean it."

"You taped your sex with her?"

"Keep it down. We did it together. Actually, it was her idea."

"Oh, man. You've got to let me see this tape."

"You've got to be kidding. I don't want you watching me."

"First of all, I won't be watching you. That I can assure you of. Second, you said she was hot. I want to judge for myself. C'mon, you've got to let me see it."

"No. What about your own benevolence and forbearance?"

"Forget that. I want to see the tape. What are you going to do with it?"

"Simple. I tell the Link what I've got. He uses the tape to get Tailburger dropped from the SERMON suit by threatening Muffet. Share value goes back up. I get my pension back."

"It's a perfect plan."

"Not exactly."

"Why not?"

"Because my ass is all over the tape. I release it and I'm a joke."

"Or a hero, depending on who you ask. Plus, no offense, but your reputation is for shit now anyway."

"True, but I don't want Annette to find out about it."

"That is a problem."

"And I don't want my kids to find out about it. They already think I'm some kind of porno king. If they see this tape and find out what I've been doing, it'll probably scar them forever."

"Hey, Sky, I've got it. Maybe you're not recognizable on the tape. Unless your house was professionally lit, I bet the picture is dark and shady. Have you watched it?"

"Not yet."

"That's what you've got to do."

"Maybe tonight."

"Let's do it now."

"You really want to see this thing?"

We returned back home, where my desire to show my brother that I'd bedded a beautiful woman got the best of me. That was the only reason I was letting King watch, 'cause God knows I wasn't ready for an appearance on ESPN's *Body Shapers*. Halfway into a bottle of Dewar's, I took one more tug before popping in the videocassette. This was one time I regretted my decision to buy a big-screen TV.

"You got any popcorn?" King teased.

"One crack from you about my size, my performance or the infinite whiteness of my ass and your viewing privileges will be immediately revoked."

"Got it, fleshmaster."

A few seconds later, the tape began to roll. First came Muffet mugging for the camera as I set it up on a tripod in my bedroom. She looked great, dressed in a pair of dark blue satin panties and a matching lacy bra, sitting up on the mattress on her knees.

"How do you like these, Sky?" Muffet asked as she undid the front clasp of her Maidenform and revealed her delicious melons. Large, silver dollar–sized areolas with thick, half-inch-long nipples brought memories and my blood flow back.

"My God! She's smoking!" King exclaimed.

"Shut up! I know! This is painful to watch."

"Why?" King asked, a bit perplexed.

"Because I know I'll never taste those beautiful breasts again."

"Good point. Hey, but at least you've got this video. Jesus, just look at her."

Muffet giggled as I came out from behind the camera, bared my ivory butt and joined her on the bed. We were both so hot already that initial foreplay was abandoned in favor of soft, slow screwing. Soon the pace and intensity changed.

"Ooooh, fuck me, Sky. Fuck me, please. Fuck me hard with that big cock."

"Good Lord, she's amazing," King said excitedly.

"You like that, Muffet, don't you? You like that big, hard cock?"

"I do. You know I do. Am I your little slut? Am I your little whore?"

"Yes! You're my dirty little slut!"

Without taking his eyes off the TV, King shuffled over to the wet bar, poured himself a shot of tequila and downed it.

"Ahhhh," he exhaled as he smacked the shot glass back on the counter. "Holy Christ!"

"I forgot how good it was."

"You forgot *this?*" King shouted. "Nobody could forget this."

"I must have blocked it out of my mind for self-preservation."

"Sure. Sort of like a wounded animal gnawing off his foot in the wild. That makes sense."

Muffet rolled over on her stomach and demanded the love that is forbidden, as well as illegal in a number of states.

"Fuck my little button, Atomic Fly!"

After the action had gone on for quite some time, King, who now had the bottle of tequila in his hands and was several shots further along toward its bottom, looked over at me and just shook his head.

"Atomic Fly? You are one sick motherfucker!"

"I think we've both seen enough. I'm shutting it off."

"Noooo. It's just getting good."

Despite King's protestations, I walked to the VCR and stopped the tape.

"That was amazing, Sky. I must say I have newfound respect for you and your big, hard cock."

"Shut up, King."

"All right, all right."

"Well, one thing's clear. I can't release the tape. My name's all over it."

"Tailburger won't have to actually release it. They'll just need to threaten to release it."

"What if Muffet calls their bluff? I'll have no control."

"She won't."

"I don't know. She's unpredictable. And if they release it, I'll never get Annette back. That's for sure."

"I don't know. After a performance like this, you may be in higher demand than you think."

"I doubt it."

"Shit. You know who you're like?"

"Who?"

"Jack Lemmon in *Save the Tiger.*"

"Never saw it."

"You never saw *Save the Tiger?* Lemmon won the Oscar for it in 1973, for Chrissakes. How could you have missed it?"

"I just did. Who cares? What's the connection?"

"Lemmon plays this garment manufacturer who's got all these problems. His business is on the skids. His marriage has hit the rocks. And his mind is starting to leave him."

"I'll regret asking this, but why?"

"Well, it's like he's tried to play by the rules his whole life; you know, believed in honesty and integrity and honor, and it's just not working anymore. So he's losing faith in the system and in his fellow man, and at the same time he starts getting faced with all these moral dilemmas, like being faithful to his wife and setting clients up with hookers and whether or not to burn down one of his buildings to get the insurance money to get out of debt."

"God, this is depressing. Was his daughter engaged to a speaker component?"

"Just listen. So after a while he gets real bitter that playing by the rules isn't working and he starts making all these moral compromises. He sleeps around. He lies. He cheats. And eventually he decides to burn down the building."

"Tell me there's a happy ending here somewhere."

"Just listen. I'm not finished. He goes to give this speech at some kind of garment convention and he starts having hallucinations of the soldiers that he served with in World War II, and he realizes how he's dishonored their memory and compromised the very values that they fought for. It destroys him as a man."

"Jesus, I was low, and now I'm lower. What is the point of all this, King?"

"The point is that you can't let what's happening destroy you."

"It's not going to destroy me. It won't. I'm predicting deep wounds, but no destruction."

"Qigong can be your salvation."

"Qigong and soybeans, right?"

"Right. I'm telling you."

"I'm taking that under advisement, I promise."

"Have you read the book *Bowling Alone?*"

"No. Is it the sequel to *Save the Tiger?*"

"Not quite. It's about the breakdown of the social fabric in America. This guy took a look at who people were bowling with, and it turns out that league bowling numbers are way off. Most people are just doing it with their families, but not with other workers or neighbors like they used to."

"So the answers lie in league bowling?"

"No, but it does give you reason to pause. I mean, look at you and me. When was the last time we even went bowling, let alone league bowling?"

"But you're still sticking with Qigong and soybeans?"

"I think for now."

"I'm going to bed, King."

"Good night. (Pause) Sky," King called out to me as I trudged upward.

"Yes. What is it?"

"Do you ever miss Mom and Dad?"

I turned around and took a seat on the landing halfway up the stairs.

"All the time."

"Me, too. (Pause) Dad was very proud of you."

"He was proud of you, too."

"No, he wasn't, Sky. It's okay. I can accept it. I didn't do much to earn his respect."

"He loved you."

"I know he did. (Pause) He had to. "

For all my brother's self-assured philosophizing and proselytizing, he looked lost as I left him sitting in my study. Perhaps I wasn't the only one who'd spent a lifetime looking for answers. Perhaps I wasn't the only one traveling toward a nearing horizon without a glimpse of his own insular Tahiti. Perhaps I wasn't the only one who needed to look into league bowling.

31

Dealing

Two days after my arrest, New York's attorney general, Plot Thickens, held a news conference in Albany to announce the launch of a statewide investigation into the marketing of Internet pornography to children. Thickens, now poised to challenge Governor Puma in the fall gubernatorial race, saw a crusade against porn as the perfect vehicle to win over the public.

"You know, back in the League, we had a name for this kind of behavior: illegal procedure. I want to send out a message to all you sickos launching pornographic Web sites. If you make your filth accessible to children, I'm coming after your ass like a steroid-crazed linebacker on a blindside blitz. To paraphrase the brave men who served this country in Vietnam, 'We're gonna shoot first and aim later.'"

Thickens, who'd staggered through some fourth-rate law school in Alabama, was dumber than a doorjamb. And in spite of his Academy Award–worthy vehemence, the reporters present weren't convinced of his claims.

"Mr. Thickens, isn't it true that you're grandstanding on this issue in an attempt to kick start your candidacy for governor?"

"That's absolute nonsense. This has nothing to do with politics and everything to do with protecting kids. Believe me, the issue of dirty pictures is near and dear to my heart."

"Mr. Thickens, did you read dirty magazines growing up?"

"Uh . . . well, I may have thumbed through one or two in my day."

"Isn't it true you've subscribed to *Jugs Illustrated* since 1972?"

"That's a total fabrication. For your information, I didn't subscribe until '74, and anyway, that's different. The point is, I believe in family values."

I'm sure Plot's handlers told him to stay on message, but it was difficult for a flawed man to do so once the press smelled fear.

"Mr. Thickens, how many illegitimate children do you have?"

"Three, wait . . . four, and I prefer the phrase 'out-of-wedlock' to describe my five wonderful kids."

"Is it four or five?"

"Did I say five?" Plot looked nervously over at his press secretary. "Let me get back to you with an exact number."

"So would you let these four or five out-of-wedlock kids read *Jugs?*"

"That magazine, for your information, got me through some of my darkest days as a youth. It's a vestige of my past, like my Converse high-tops or my Trans Am. These things keep me grounded."

"Are you comparing footwear with female genitalia?"

"Look, my generation didn't have the virtual-reality sex products that are so wonderful, uh . . . I mean so corrosive today. *Jugs* is a small indulgence on my part, but I'm an adult."

"So magazines are okay, but Web sites are off-limits?"

"Yes. I mean, no. Hey, you're twisting my words."

An hour later, the Centers for Disease Control in Atlanta released a statement saying that food contamination caused five thousand deaths annually in the United States. It was bad news for Tailburger, which made it a perfect time for me to pay my former boss a visit.

According to his secretary, the Link was admitted at St. Mary's Hospital on Genesee Street, a rough part of Rochester where hookers and the homeless more than outnumbered the nuns. What I saw upon entering his private room was heartwarming in its own strange way. Ned, Ted and Fred, still dressed in matching striped knickers and tam-o'-shanters from their morning round, sat next to their father's bed holding a vigil of sorts. Flat on his back, the Link was hooked up to some kind of respirator, his eyes closed. Soon, I was spied.

"What are you doing here?" Ned asked angrily.

"I came to see your father."

"Why don't you go away? You nearly killed him," Ted said, pointing his finger at me.

"I never imagined this would happen. (Pause) How's he doing?"

"Like you care," Ted scoffed.

"Why did you get Tailburger involved with the porn industry?" Fred inquired, forgetting he'd spent half his life writing letters to *Penthouse*.

"I was trying to increase market share. That's all. It was just marketing."

"Just marketing?" Ned's question dripped with disbelief.

"I need to speak to your father."

"Well, that's going to be difficult, since he's in a coma."

"Do you expect him back soon?"

Blank stares.

"That was a joke."

"It wasn't funny," Ned responded. "I want you out of here. Right now."

Ned, the oldest of the Link's sons, had been appointed by the board as the interim president and CEO of Tailburger. My only hope was that power had corrupted him.

"I've got an offer for you."

"What could you possibly offer us?"

"A way out of the SERMON suit."

"I don't believe you. (Pause) How?"

"Let's just say I've got a very useful videotape."

"Of who?"

"Muffet Meaney."

"So what? We've got tons of surveillance tape on her. Have you forgotten what we do for a living?"

"You don't have any tapes of her having sex."

"You don't have that."

"I do."

"With who?"

"Does it matter?"

"Is it graphic?"

"Very."

"What do you want for it?"

"Just my pension. That's all."

"What else are you offering?"

"Isn't that enough?"

"I don't think so."

"What else do you want?"

Ned, Ted and Fred asked for a minute to confer with each other behind the hospital curtain rigged up around their father's bed. The curtain closed. A minute passed and the curtain swung open.

"Crooked Creek."

"You want to become members at Crooked Creek? All three of you?"

Ned, Ted and Fred nodded, grinning all the while.

Crooked Creek remained the white whale of golf club memberships for the Fanoflincoln clan. Long shut out by their new-money status, their father's table manners and the mythical waiting list (the flames of which I'd fanned over the years like a Boy Scout at a bonfire), they hungrily eyed their opportunity to bargain their way into the elite of Rochester's links.

"Done. I want a letter reinstating my pension and a lump-sum distribution check by Monday. Then you'll get your tape."

"Not so fast, Sky. Not so fast. We hold the upper hand here, not you. You get our memberships at Crooked Creek authorized and show us the tape, and then we'll give you the pension money."

I didn't bother to tell the brothers that my membership at Crooked Creek had been placed on indefinite suspension pending the resolution of my "legal difficulties." Although Tad Hamilton, club president, assured me of the board's deep-rooted belief in my innocence and offered me full use of all facilities between the hours of 2:00 A.M. and 3:00 A.M. in his letter, I knew my questionable status would make it difficult, but hopefully not impossible, to sponsor a new member or three. I would simply have to get other people to do the sponsoring. With admission to Crooked Creek a murky process at best, however, I left the hospital far from terra firma.

Before I departed, I took a long look at the heaving carcass spread out on the bedsheets before me. Pale, bloated and breathing by the aid of electric device, he held no great affection in my heart and that was a sad truth. I'd spent twenty years working for someone whom I didn't respect and didn't particularly like. "Why?" was the question that came to mind. Why?

32

Going Public

Macrocock.com opened at $8.50 on the day of its initial public offering. Soon it skyrocketed on hot CNBC buzz and busy trading, finishing the day at $56 and a quarter on the NASDAQ. Although the company had no revenues, no earnings, inexperienced management and a business plan with the word "spam" liberally sprinkled throughout, the Money Honey liked it, and so into the stratosphere went the price, along with my parental pride.

"Ethan, it's Dad. I saw the IPO!"

"Hey, Dad. Isn't this amazing?"

"Yes."

"I've got two million five on paper right now. Skull's got a mil."

It really stuck in my craw that Skull (a guy I found passed out on my lawn more times than I care to remember) had more than me, but I chose to focus on my blood relation.

"You're doing great!"

I wasn't doing so badly myself. With ten thousand shares from my initial investment, I was up more than half a million, thanks to my son's company, whatever it was they did.

"So are you ready to open the kimono for me?"

"Well, Dad, it's really complicated. I don't know if you'd understand. We're an infomediary site."

"In-fo-mediary? What the hell's that?"

"We're a portal for vendors of cutting-edge electronic products. We capture customers' information and then protect them from unwanted home invasion and spam."

"Spam, huh? Are we talking about the sodium-rich luncheon meat I enjoyed as a boy?"

"No, we're talking about electronic junk mail."

"I see. I still have no clue what you guys do."

"Dad, this is going to make you rich. That's all you need to know."

Ethan and I didn't dare speak about the six-month lockup period that loomed over our giddy heads. For either of us to truly get rich, Macrocock's share value had to sustain itself for the next half year, when we would be legally entitled to sell our stock under the securities laws. Would it hold on? Could it hold on? So obvious was the subtext, we ignored it completely. So our gains could disappear in a day—so what? There was no good reason to mention the lockup. Why cast a pall on the parade?

For Ethan, a successful sale after the lockup would mean he'd fulfilled the destiny of every member of his generation—to make his money young and to get out unscathed, left to dabble at his leisure in the things that truly interested him. He could start a nonprofit, collect rare wine coolers, Do the Dew—whatever the hell turned him on. I wanted that for him. If the stock tanked, he could simply start again.

For me, it was a bit more complicated. If the stock went from $56 TO $100 and stayed there, I might not need my Tailburger pension. The possibilities were endless and intoxicating. Maybe I wouldn't have to turn over the tape of Muffet and me or do any other self-degrading act for my own financial survival. Maybe I could buy my way out of my legal trouble like a well-connected investment banker or C-grade celebrity. Maybe the stock would go to $200 and I'd become a beloved local philanthropist who threw dimes at the kids on Halloween and obsessed over airborne pathogens.

Then again, to wait for the lockup to expire and rely on the stock was a big risk on my part. What if the price leveled off to $20? At ten thousand shares, $200,000 wouldn't buy much of a retirement. Even at $56 a share, I wouldn't have the *fuck you* money necessary to walk away from the world on my own terms. Worse, by the end of six months, the SERMON suit might proceed to the point where Tailburger's involvement would be intractable, making my video bargaining chip worthless. Who was I kidding? Regardless of how much money I made on Macrocock.com, I needed my pension. Trip Baden and his attorney, along with two dozen other creditors, would all have their hands out for a piece of my newfound fortune. I was fucked. I couldn't take a chance on the stock alone.

For as long as I could remember, one thought traversed the shallow circuitry of my mind: as soon as I was done serving my time at Tailburger, I would fill up my life with all the things I was dying to do. I would clutter every hour of every day with important pursuits, giving greater meaning to my existence, drawing the admiration and envy of others—living well as a form of revenge. But the closer I drew to the end of my corporate career, the less I longed for any of that. If I'd learned anything from King it was that clutter was fear (something he told me during a late-night rap session on feng shui). I needed to shed clutter and simply wanted the financial freedom to do as I pleased, a later-in-time version of the liberty I envisioned for my son and a faded facsimile of what Ethan felt entitled to. What did I want? The option to do nothing for hours on end or to cut the grass if so moved. The luxury of such a choice was still just a dream—big and beyond my reach.

I called Cal, as I'd done for days now, expecting to hear his machine pick up. None of the kids from the food poisoning incident, including Kyle, had died, but their story was in the press now, and the Tailburger franchise owner who sold the infested fare was blaming me publicly. He said I'd given the order to undercook the meat and told him he'd lose his store if he didn't follow orders. Although that defense didn't work for the Nazi war criminals, it was working here, and now everybody was piling on my back. Even the store's assistant manager, Randall P. McMurphy, made a point of holding his own news conference to commend Tailburger for my firing and to condemn me not only as a purveyor of the skin trade, but as a life-threatening danger to children everywhere. My reputation as a prime candidate for castration was secure. Now I existed only as some kind of horrible Hannibal Lecter figure whose phone calls went unanswered and unreturned. Another victim of caller ID. Until I caught a break.

"Hello."

"Jenny, it's Sky."

I hadn't spoken to Cal's wife in weeks, a streak she wished to extend.

"Sky, I really have no desire to speak with you right now or ever again. Please stop calling."

"Wait, wait. Let me explain a few things, please. How's Kyle?"

"Barely alive, thanks to you. I'm going to go now, Sky."

"Jenny, listen to me. That wasn't my idea. It was the Link. I swear it was the Link. He gave the order to undercook the burgers."

"Sky, I really don't care who gave the order. I've got a very sick little boy because of you and Tailburger. I don't know what role you played in all of this, but whatever it was, shame on you."

"I can't tell you how sorry I am. I made a mistake. I would never do anything to intentionally hurt Kyle. You have to believe me."

"Sky, I'm not sure what to believe anymore. After twenty years of marriage, I have to find out on the news that my husband and his best friend are porno kings."

"We're not porno kings."

"How could you two keep this from me all these years? What

am I going to find out next, that you two are a couple of angel dust dealers? Drugs and porn go hand in hand, don't they?"

"We're not angel dust dealers. I promise you."

"Or maybe it's Ecstasy. Isn't that what the kids are using these days? Who knows? Certainly not me. I'm just the stupid, stay-at-home, sit-in-the-dark wife who finds out last about everything."

"Jenny, we're not Ecstasy dealers. (Pause). Don't you see? Cal just wanted to protect you."

"Well, he's done a lousy job."

Jenny's gripes were legitimate, no question about it. But her tone of voice and the overall direction of the conversation put fresh paint on the fence for me as to why I wasn't married anymore. I was bad at reasoning with women. I didn't lie very well and my ear was pure tin when it came to picking up the subtleties of female inflection that cued a man to reflexively say things like, "I was wrong," "Awwww" and, most importantly, "I was wrong." Did I mention the phrase, "I was wrong"?

"Cal loves you. He was afraid of what you'd think."

"What I'd think? How about what I'd feel when the truth came out. Did he ever think about *that?*"

"He worried about it constantly."

"Well, he'll have plenty of time to worry about it on his own."

"You didn't kick him out, did you?"

"Oh, yes I did. He's staying at Woodcliff."

Woodcliff Lodge was a modern, hunting-themed, hilltop hotel surrounded by golf courses and condominium developments. Located on one of the highest points in Monroe County, Woodcliff, with its brick and glass facade, overlooked much of Rochester and was one of the few places where you could physically place yourself above the fray. It was an obvious choice for Cal's accommodations during his marital crisis.

I found my friend in the hotel's gym on an industrial-sized treadmill, sweating like a man who was fighting his age—and losing. Cal saw me enter, but pretended that he didn't. As I walked closer, he focused more intently on the television set hanging from the far wall.

"Are you going to ignore me forever?"

"If that's how long it takes for you to leave."

Cal refused to make eye contact with me.

"Cal, I'm here as your friend."

"Is that what you're calling yourself these days?"

"I'd like to show you that the title still fits."

Cal finally looked over at me and then away, but didn't say a word.

"I talked to Jenny. She told me that Kyle's going to be okay."

"Lucky for you."

"I'm glad, Cal. I want to apologize to you again."

"What else did she say?"

"She's very angry. She feels like you betrayed her. Like we betrayed her."

"I think it may be over."

"I don't believe that for a minute. She still loves you very much."

"When she kicked me out, she said our whole relationship was based on a lie."

"Oh, c'mon. Show me a good one that isn't."

"She said she didn't want the kids living with a porno king."

"Why does she keep using that phrase? It's so offensive."

"I know. I'm no porno king. My market share is maybe three percent. That's far from king-size. (Pause) I can't live without her, Sky."

"You'll get her back. I'll help you."

If I'd killed Kyle with my boneheaded burger policy error, I think it would have been difficult to patch up my friendship with Cal. Not impossible, mind you (men don't take these things as hard as women), but definitely difficult. Kyle lived, however, giving Cal and me the chance to resume a friendship we'd begun 40 years before. And I've got to tell you, it felt pretty damn good.

First we resolved to help each other get our women back. Cal stood a better chance to succeed on this account than I did. He was, after all, married to the object of his affection and the father of her children. I, on the other hand, was merely a political liability to my amour, not to mention a social pariah, equally unwelcome at private parties and public gatherings, from Denny's to the discount mall. Nonetheless, we agreed that this mutual objective could be accomplished with copious amounts of groveling and profuse gift giving. Begging and baubles alone, however, wouldn't be enough.

In order to win back the hearts of those we'd hurt (some might say irretrievably devastated), we needed to stay jail-free, which brought us face-to-face with our next hurdle: how to handle our small legal matter involving the Nail Some Tail Sweepstakes. Divide and conquer. That would be the strategy of the prosecutor—to turn Cal and me against each other until we ratted out our own best friend. Plea bargain. That would be our strategy. We'd have to give the prosecutor something he wanted in exchange for a deal—but what? After I noodled over this with Cal for most of the evening, he sent me home to get some rest.

For some reason, Cal's willingness to forgive me for what I'd done to Kyle spurred a strong desire in me to make amends with Sophia. I hadn't heard from her since our blowout over Tweeter, and I was anxious to be back on speaking terms with my daughter. My drive home from Woodcliff was thus full of reflection on my role as a parent, and, in particular, one exchange with Sophia that stuck out. The day before she left for college, she asked me why I'd never taken her to Disneyland. I didn't have a good answer for her. It was simply something I'd never gotten around to doing with her and her brother, nor considered crucial to their personal development. I pointed out that we'd been to Pedro's South of the Border and Wall Drug, the biggest pharmacy in the state of South Dakota, but to no avail. To her, those were merely missed opportunities to go to Disney World, EPCOT, Busch Gardens, Six Flags over Georgia and, most importantly, Disney*land*. I could tell that she was genuinely disappointed despite the years that had passed. And so it was the nature of parenthood, and of most relationships I concluded, for others to remember what you didn't do instead of what you did—to remember your screwups, errors, omissions and mistakes, leaving you with an overall feeling of underappreciation, something I wished upon no one. This was human nature. And this was why, as a parent and as a person, it made any moment of true appreciation, one unimpeachable exchange with your own child where you knew you'd come through for her and she was trying to thank you for that, the most gratifying experience on Earth I've ever had and one that, more and more, I sought out.

I reached Sophia on a cell phone I'd given her for Christmas.

"Soph, it's Dad."

"Daddy, what are you doing? It's so late. . . ."

"I know it's late, but I need to talk to you."

"What for?"

"I need to tell you something. I need to tell you that I'm sorry about what happened at the house with Tweeter."

"It's all right, Daddy. . . ."

"No, it's not all right. Listen to me. I'm sorry about what happened and I want you to know that I support your decisions and I trust your judgment, and if being with Tweeter is what's going to make you happy, then I will be behind you the whole way. (Pause) What I'm saying, Soph, is that if *you* love Tweeter, *I* love Tweeter. End of discussion."

Sophia was silent for a moment.

"Daddy, Tweeter and I broke up a week ago. We're just friends now."

"Sweet, merciful Jesus!"

Sophia went on to explain that she and Tweeter were really very different people with very different goals. To sum it up, she didn't want to live in a van for the rest of her life, and he did. When Sophia informed him of her decision, Tweeter decried the irony that a vehicle designed to bring people closer together had actually ripped them apart. Sales of used Vanogens (circa 1982) would surely plummet.

33

Lying Low

The next morning I found King at the breakfast table with a strange assortment of food laid out in front of him.

"Good morning. (Pause) What's all that?"

"That, for your information, is day one of the Ornish Plan."

"What happened to your soy?"

"I haven't abandoned it. I just thought I'd try something different for a while."

"What the hell's the Ornish Plan?"

"It's a diet where the only animal products you're allowed to eat are nonfat milk, yogurt and egg whites."

"Sounds disgusting," I said, reaching to the back of the pantry for my secret stash of Frosted Flakes.

"It fights heart disease."

"You don't have heart disease."

"I know. I want to keep it that way."

"So now you have to subsist on egg whites and yogurt?"

"No. Lunch includes hummus, tabbouleh and pita bread. And for dinner, you get to eat black-bean burritos and orange-jicama salad with pickled onions."

"Jesus, you need to get laid."

"If that happy contingency occurs, this diet will give me the proper energy to perform at my peak."

"Let me ask you something. All this focusing on your diet and your chee—is that making you happy?"

King paused for a moment before answering.

"To be honest, not really."

"So why not try something else?"

"Like what?"

"How about a job and a girlfriend? Those might be better places to put your energy."

"Sky, you know I've never sought that kind of outside validation."

"Well, maybe you should! You might like it. You might learn something about yourself that all the books, diets and programs in the world combined couldn't teach you in a million years."

"Fortunately for you, I'm onto something that helps me deal with unpleasant exchanges such as this."

"What's that?"

"*The Four Agreements: A Practical Guide to Personal Freedom* by Don Miguel Ruiz. It's based on ancient Mexican Toltec wisdom. I'm just reading about the second agreement: Don't take anything personally, something that is proving difficult at this very moment."

For years, I had condemned King for his searching ways—his rampant job- and philosophy-hopping, his inability to settle down and take on responsibility. But now, the anger I directed at him was as much aimed at myself for my own futile search. The frustrations that boiled over were uncalled for, and I took solace only in the fact I recognized it.

"King, I'm sorry. I'm just a little edgy right now about the upcoming trial and everything. Please understand."

"You've got to read Don Miguel's book. I think the four agreements could really help you out. Toltec wisdom is a powerful thing."

"I promise I'll pick up a copy."

I wasn't sure what had happened to King's commitment to the Falun Gong and the practice of Qigong, but I didn't ask. Despite my outburst, it was getting easier for me to accept my brother for who he was and the way he chose to live his life. I saw this ability to accept as a good thing—an important step away from my inclination to judge others, particularly those closest to me. In hindsight, chiding King for lack of direction, including his lack of a girlfriend and job, was laughable, given my own current predicament. Marx. Gibb. Ringling. Wright. Righteous. Everly. Osmond. Smothers. Carradine. Kennedy. Blues. Karamozov. Among great brothers, we were taking our place.

True to her word, Annette resigned from the Tailburger board of directors. Unfortunately, I had to read about it in the paper, having lost all contact with her. She was yet another person who wouldn't return my calls. She also didn't respond to my Hallmark cards or acknowledge the flowers I sent each week. I needed a legitimate reason to approach her at City Hall, and the Fanoflincoln brothers' candidacies at Crooked Creek seemed as good as any. Annette, as mayor, was an honorary member of the club and the only person I could think of who would be a powerful enough sponsor to make the previously inconceivable possible. Ned, Ted and Fred weren't particularly well-liked in the community, given the fact the equipment from their three Who's Nailing Your Wife? spy shops had broken up more marriages than Anne Heche and Billy Bob Thornton combined. Annette was also the only person who would protect the identity of the true sponsor, namely me, who couldn't show his face at the club (other than from 2:00 to 3:00 A.M.).

Asking for help is supposed to be a step forward in life. This time, however, it felt like a step backward. What a weak, down-on-my-knees position to show myself in—so desperate for my pension that I'd grease the admission process at a local golf club for three goons. She'd think I was pathetic and sad at best, odious and unlovable at worst. And then there was the video, the part of the bargain I wouldn't be able to tell her about out of shame and fear of permanently damaging my chances to be with her. I thought about the scenario unfolding in front of me for a minute and decided not to move in the wrong direction. This was the dawning of a new Sky. Focused. Honorable. Clear of mind. Determined. A cowardly ascent up the marble steps at City Hall was the only kind I could make if I wasn't prepared to tell Annette the whole truth.

Past the metal detector lay the elevator bank and my fate. Somewhere on the third floor, Annette was making decisions about important things: budgets and bus passes, stadiums and sales taxes. I wasn't even on her agenda. Doubt flooded my mind. This was a bad idea. She might refuse to see me. I'd be lucky to get past reception. So many thoughts rendered pointless the moment I stepped off the elevator and nearly ran over the mayor.

"Oh my gosh, Annette. I'm sorry. You're not hurt, are you?"

"Sky, what are you doing here?"

I'd been getting that question a lot lately.

"I wanted to talk to you. You won't return my phone calls."

"Maybe you should take the hint."

"Can I just talk to you for a minute? It won't take long, I promise."

Annette ushered me through the labyrinth of office space that led to her corner suite with its view of the Genesee River and Kodak's headquarters. She closed the door and offered me a seat on her floral-patterned couch.

"I really wish you hadn't shown up here, Sky. I'm insanely busy, and I thought I made it clear I didn't want to see you."

"Annette, please don't make this more awkward for me than it already is. I need to ask you a favor."

"You want a favor from me? Are you joking?"

Suddenly it was here—my opportunity to tell Annette the entire truth about the pension and the video and my desire for financial freedom and my search for insular Tahiti. This was my chance to tell her how I truly felt about her and our relationship and the importance of honesty between two mature adults.

"Annette, I'm dying."

"What?"

"Doctor says I don't have long."

"Sky, that's terrible. What's wrong with you?"

I figured I'd better go with something serious.

"Rectal cancer."

Annette moved from behind her desk to a spot on the couch next to me and put her arms around my shoulders.

"My God. I don't know what to say."

"You don't need to say anything. Early death runs in my family. My Uncle Blakelock died at forty-three."

"That's so young."

"I know, I know. But hey, take away the unemployment, bedsores and heavy gambling losses, and his was a pretty sweet ride. I can't complain either."

"You're too young, Sky."

"It's just my time."

My intentions on the way into this meeting were good. You have to believe me. I wanted to do the right thing, but women will only forgive so much, and the video was not going to go over well. Call it male intuition.

"You said you needed a favor. Just name it."

"You're too kind. You see . . . well, this will seem like a strange request, but the Link is hooked up to a respirator and I feel a bit guilty about it."

"Sky, you have nothing to feel guilty about."

"Perhaps not. It's just . . . I guess we all feel a need to set things right before we go, and I'd like to do something nice for him."

"After he fired you?"

"I'm a Christian, Annette. I suppose you never really saw that side of me, but that's who I am at heart."

"You're remarkable, Sky. How can I help?"

"Well, as you may know, the Link's fondest wish was to become a member out at Crooked Creek."

"I heard him mention it at the Tailburger board meetings a few times."

"Yes, well, it appears it's too late for him, but it's not too late for his sons. I want you to sponsor them."

"Ned, Ted and Fred? I don't know, Sky. They're pretty awful people."

"Annette, consider this the request of two dying men. I'd sponsor them myself but I'm persona non grata at Crooked Creek. They all think I'm some kind of smut baron."

"All right, Sky. I'll do it. They keep these things confidential, don't they?"

"Strictly. Nobody other than the members of the admissions committee will know you're the sponsor."

"Okay."

"Thank you, Annette."

"I'm glad to help under the circumstances."

"May I ask you for one more thing?"

"Name it."

"I'd like to spend whatever time I have left with you."

"I don't know how I can say no to that request, Sky. This must be a very frightening time for you."

"It's more terrifying than you can imagine."

"We'll have to be discreet."

"Of course."

Somewhere over the course of my visit with Annette, I acquired a limp (after all, I was suffering from rectal cancer), which I displayed fully on my way out of her office.

"Do you need any help?"

"No, I'll be all right. The chemo's got me weak."

"You're so brave, Sky. I'll call you tonight."

Cal would be proud I'd wooed back my lady love without a single trinket. Lies were wonderful devices that way. Like hidden land mines, however, they forever threatened to blow you up if you weren't careful. Why hadn't I simply told her the truth? Liar's remorse hit me the moment I left City Hall.

34

Bribery

Burton Roxby's statutory rape trial, now under way and being televised on *Courting Rochester*, a local version of *Court TV*, dominated the local news, temporarily taking the heat off Cal and me. Most of the Kennedy clan came to Roxby's defense, publicly citing the evil, yet understandable, temptations of baby-sitters everywhere with their Catholic schoolgirl uniforms and damn Christina Aguilera albums. Roxby, looking anxious and afraid, silently sat next to M.C. Shufelbarger at counsel's table, nervously rubbing his hands together.

Shufelbarger's primary strategy was to prove that vaginal penetration never occurred. Up against irrefutable DNA evidence and ripped underwear, however, Shufelbarger offered the girl's use of a Miracle Bra and unchecked consumption of Zima as proof positive she "wanted it." In his words, "This was a brazen hussy who lured Congressman Roxby up to her tree fort on the false premise of a school science project." He admitted the fact that she was twelve, looked eleven and was wearing Garanimals at the time of the attack, cut against his client's case, ultimately conceding that the girl's intent was irrelevant under a statutory law prohibiting sex with minors.

After putting on a string of character witnesses, mostly senile elementary school teachers whose chalkboards he used to wash, Roxby threw himself on the mercy of the court, citing his honorary degree from Princeton, his willingness to withhold taxes for domestic help and his refusal to rent out his Congressional parking place despite the prevalence of this practice by his fellow representatives at the end of each session. All of this was to no avail, as Judge Stander, known in sexual crime circles as the banging judge, sentenced Roxby to fifteen years in the state penitentiary. The freshly convicted felon wailed as marshals walked him from the courtroom in leg shackles.

I would've enjoyed the spectacle more if I wasn't facing a similar, though slightly less dire, legal test myself. As I made my way over to Woodcliff for my nightly brainstorming session with Cal, I wondered if I'd be able to avoid such abject humiliation. We were officially charged with contributing to the delinquency of minors and violating some new federal statutes related to the Internet, none of which seemed jail-worthy to me. The prosecutor, a local Indian named Hiawatha "Humpy" Wheeler, had other ideas. Hunchbacked since birth, Humpy was determined to straighten us out, and if he had his way, we'd fry like the genetically engineered potatoes now listed on the Tailburger menu. The prospect of it all made me ill as I knocked on Cal's hotel room door.

"C'mon in. We're celebrating!"

Cal stood at the doorway with an enormous smile and a bottle of champagne.

"Why? What the hell happened?"

"Guess who won the Nail Some Tail Sweepstakes? Guess."

"I don't know. Andy Rooney?"

"No."

"Morley Safer?"

"No. Close, but no. Give up?"

"Yes, I give up. No wait . . . Leslie Stahl?"

"Nope. Plot Thickens."

"Get out of here."

"I mean it. My Web master told me an hour ago. I tried to call you."

"We're talking about Attorney General Plot Thickens?"

"Is there another? Biggest perv in public service. You said it yourself."

"That hypocrite. That total hypocrite."

"According to our computer records, he entered the contest a hundred and eighty-three times."

"So much for his crusade against porn. I can't believe it. How stupid can you get?"

"Hey, don't forget it can happen to anyone." Cal smiled at me.

"All right. We made our share of mistakes, but now our luck has changed. I can't wait to see Thickens's face when we threaten to expose him."

"Well, now wait a minute."

Cal put his champagne down on the mahogany nightstand.

"Do you think threatening the attorney general is a good idea?"

"Of course it is. What else did you have in mind? I want to see this guy squirm."

"I don't know. I figured we could gently encourage Thickens to intervene on our behalf with Humpy Wheeler and Judge Stander, but I didn't really want to *threaten* him."

"Cal, you can call it a threat or gentle encouragement or whatever you want, but at the end of the day, it's a bribe."

"No, that's no good. I don't like the word 'bribe.' It's sounds so negative."

"Then don't think of it as a bribe. Think of it as a tip."

"I like that. 'Tip' has a good wholesome tone to it."

For a guy whose whole career had been in adult entertainment, Cal sure cared a lot about wholesomeness.

"You know another thing, Sky. Thickens might try to double-cross us."

"He might, but I think you've seen too many movies."

"No, no, no. Remember *Wall Street,* when Charlie Sheen and Michael Douglas met out in Central Park? And Sheen was wired?"

"I remember."

"So what's our protection from something like that? If Thickens gets us on tape trying to bribe, er . . . I mean tip him, we're screwed."

"Just let me handle it, okay? I'll set up the meeting with Thickens and your name won't even be mentioned."

"You'd do that?"

After everything I'd put Cal through over the last few weeks with Kyle, I figured I owed him the favor of brokering this deal. With one phone call, Thickens could get us one-year probation terms for our alleged crimes against the young and curious. He could also get Tailburger dropped from the SERMON suit being brought by his office and Muffet Meaney. This would give me the necessary leverage with Ned, Ted and Fred to get my pension back without having to share the videotape.

"Of course I'd do that. It'll give me a chance to talk to him about our little legal entanglement as well as the SERMON suit."

"What do you mean?"

"The SERMON suit. The lawsuit being brought against Tailburger by Thickens's office and Muffet Meaney?"

"What does that have to do with this?"

"I want to use this piece of information about the sweepstakes to get the suit dropped and get my pension back."

"Sky, we've got to use this information to stay out of prison, remember?"

"Of course. That's what I'm going to do. But if I can get Thickens to drop Tailburger from the state's class action, I can get my pension reinstated by the Fanoflincoln brothers."

"I don't want you to use it for that."

"Why not? What's the difference?"

"Because this is more important. We've got our families to think about. My marriage is on the line here. Now is not the time to be worrying about money."

"Maybe not for someone who has plenty of it. But I'm worrying like crazy. If you didn't know it, Cal, I'm going broke."

"What about your stock in Ethan's company?"

"I can't sell that yet."

With our argument growing more heated, I decided to lay off. I had been fortunate to earn Cal's friendship back, and I couldn't afford to lose it again. After agreeing not to broach the subject of the SERMON suit with Thickens, I reluctantly told Cal about the videotape of Muffet and my standing offer to Ned, Ted and Fred of its contents in exchange for my pension. After laughing his ass off, Cal agreed to take the videotape to work and have my voice edited out and my appearance obscured. And so it was agreed. Plot wouldn't pull Tailburger out of its pending lawsuit. Muffet would.

I left Woodcliff and drove home, my head full of pleasant possibilities. Things were starting to roll my way. My best friend was back. My girl was back (albeit under the false pretenses of rectal cancer). Tweeter was gone (along with his van). Macrocock.com was showing me love (I picked that phrase up from Ethan). And soon I'd have my pension without any of the embarrassment that often attends a nude video of yourself. Even Trip's lawyer, Herv Alverson, had been quiet lately (despite the fact I never called him after being threatened).

I drove past Eastview Mall on Route 96 and saw a sign for its upcoming boat show, Toys for Titans, a title certain to improve attendance from the prior year's Cruisers for Boozers.

I'd always wanted a boat. Not some dinky Sailfish or thirty-foot Catalina, but an ocean-bound cabin cruiser I could take around the world and live on like Chevy Chase in *Foul Play* (I know it was a houseboat, but you get the idea). It was a fantasy, of course, and until my financial condition stabilized, it would remain just that and nothing more. Reality, though, awaited me in my driveway, where I found the front door of my house wide open.

I saw no one on the property as I stepped out of my car and looked into the moonlit darkness. Cautiously, I crept along the slate path that led to the main entrance until I could peer into the foyer from behind a large evergreen bush. There on the floor, flat on his back, was King. I rushed to my brother's aid.

"King, what happened?" I cried out, running toward him.

King had been beaten and was bleeding from the stomach. I tore off his Santana concert jersey and found a large stab wound just below his belly button.

"Oh my God, King. Who did this to you?"

I put pressure on the gash and took a momentary look around. The house was trashed, the contents of every closet, cabinet and drawer dumped haphazardly by the perpetrators. Little, however, appeared to be gone. King, for his part, was conscious but a bit dazed.

"King, are you all right?"

King groaned while writhing back and forth.

"King, are you all right?"

"I-I-I'm okay."

"Who did this to you?"

"Two guys," King replied weakly. "Two big guys."

"What'd they do?"

"They barged in the door. They wanted some videotape."

"What?"

"They kept asking me, 'Where's the videotape? Where's the videotape?'"

"Oh, no."

I jumped up from King's side and raced to my bedroom. Sure enough, my camcorder and all of my videotapes, including the one of Muffet and me, were gone from my closet.

"That bitch! I can't believe this. She stole the tape. She and her fucking goons stole my tape."

I ran back downstairs and returned to King.

"King, you've got to tell me exactly what happened."

King grimaced in apparent pain.

"Okay. I'll try. Well, let's see . . . I had just juiced some carrots and was getting ready to read *A Practical Guide to Personal Freedom* by Don Miguel Ruiz. Did I mention that book to you?"

"Yes," I said in exasperation. "King, I need you to get to the point."

"Take me to the hospital, Sky."

"I can't do that."

"Why not?"

"Because if I take you to the hospital, the police will have to get involved, and I'm already in enough trouble with the police. I can't run the risk they'll find the guys who did this to you and confiscate the videotape. I'll never get it back, and I need it."

"But, Sky, I've been stabbed." King forced the words out.

"I know that, and I'm going to take care of you. I've got some Neosporin upstairs."

"I don't need Neosporin. I need a doctor."

"King, you're going to be fine."

"I've lost a lot of blood."

"You've got plenty left. Now stop talking and save your strength."

I called Cal and told him to come over as quickly as possible. He had been premed for a semester at SUNY Potsdam and could dress a wound like a son of a bitch.

"Holy shit. What happened to your house, Sky?" Cal asked as he came through the door.

"The goon squad from SERMON. They stole the videotape of Muffet."

"That's bullshit! That's breaking and entering."

"I know it is. But so what? I can't go to the police about a missing porno tape."

Cal knelt down next to King.

"Let me get a look here."

"I got stabbed in the stomach, Cal."

"So the bloody towel isn't just for show?"

King shook his head as Cal examined the cut and went to work.

"Sky, do you have any Neosporin?"

"It's upstairs. I'll get it."

"I don't need Neosporin. I need to go to the hospital," King persisted.

"You're going to be fine, King."

I returned from upstairs with the miracle cure for all cuts while Cal tried to place the crime.

"Sky, this is attempted murder. The police will be interested in that."

"No, it's not. They didn't want to kill King. They just wanted to scare him."

"It worked," King whimpered from the floor.

"Cal, with everything that's going on right now, I don't want to get the police involved."

It was my fault that King had been stabbed. When you play a high-stakes game of bribery with someone as devious as Muffet Meaney, you put your loved ones at risk. The guilt alone should have driven me to take King to the hospital. For all I knew, he could be near death. He was bleeding like a motherfucker all over the carpet and moaning like a man passing a kidney stone. This was my only brother. My flesh and blood. But I didn't take him to the hospital. And I didn't call the police. I had to think.

35

Sales Job

Macrocock.com was up to $73.50 three weeks after its IPO. Ethan assured me that, in between runs on his new Hyperlite 142 Project Honeycomb wakeboarding plank (I'm told the swallow-tail shape allows you to catch something called big air), he was working hard to maintain the stock's momentum. This was a pretty cavalier attitude considering his father's *fuck you* money was riding on the outcome. We were in this together though, and, having come this far on blind faith and a closed kimono, I figured I may as well go the rest of the way with him.

Annette and I were closer than ever, thanks to my rectal cancer. She marveled at my upbeat attitude and took me to a wig shop in anticipation of my hair loss. When it didn't come, despite regular radiation treatments at a local bar called Hoot'n Nanny's, she marveled at that, too. Better yet, thanks to my beloved's position of influence, the Crooked Creek candidacies of Ned, Ted and Fred Fanoflincoln were moving forward. Now the only obstacle to getting my pension back was my lack of the Muffet Meaney video-tape. After attending to King for a few days, I called my tormentor at SERMON.

"You know your henchmen almost killed my brother."

"What are you talking about?"

"You know exactly what I'm talking about."

"I'm a very busy woman, Sky, so if you have anything worthwhile to say, I suggest you spit it out."

"Now there's something you've never done."

"You know what your problem is?"

"I don't know how to have fun?"

"No. You're a bad loser. And you're also a lousy lay."

"Well, why don't we let others be the judge of that? I've got plenty of copies of that tape you stole from me, and pretty soon your ass will be spread across screens from Westwood to Washington, D.C."

"You're bluffing."

"Oh, am I? You wish I was bluffing."

There was only one problem with my puffery: I was bluffing. I never bothered to make a copy of the tape because I never imagined that Muffet would actually send someone into my home to steal it.

"Sky, I think we've said everything there is to say."

"No, we haven't."

"What else is there?"

I paused for a moment.

"You're a bitch on eighteen wheels."

I was left with limited options. I could try to steal the videotape back, but, considering my upcoming court date and lack of heavy weaponry or a Humvee, it probably wasn't a realistic possibility. The tape could be anywhere. Alternatively, I could find a new source of leverage over the Fanoflincoln brothers to get my pension back. This made infinitely more sense, but what more did I have to offer? Nothing. Even the impending Crooked Creek club memberships had required me to contract terminal cancer. At this rate, I'd be dead before I received my first retirement check. Out of desperation, I enlisted Cal to pay a visit to my old boss and his idiot children at the hospital. Cal wanted to get his wife, Jenny, back, and I had a plan.

The Link was still comatose at St. Mary's, and his sons, between rounds of golf, Crooked Creek membership mixers and trips to the driving range, were maintaining a constant bedside vigil. When we entered, however, the peaceful scene I anticipated was under assault from a heated debate.

"Fred, you are so full of shit!" Ned's voice was raised.

"All I'm saying is I heard it on the Discovery Channel."

"Lincoln was *not* gay. He had four kids, for God's sake," Ted followed.

"I can't believe you'd say that within earshot of Dad. Shame on you."

"They found these letters to his lover, though," Fred persisted. "They say he was flaming."

"Shut up! Just shut up! He was not flaming. You're talking about the Old Railsplitter. The Great Emancipator. The man our whole family is named after. I don't want to ever hear you say that again."

"All right, but I think he was splitting more than just rails."

"Shut up, I said!"

As soon as they saw my face, the brothers clammed up out of apparent embarrassment. Relations, though not friendly, were more civil between the Fanoflincolns and me since we'd struck our deal. To their credit, after blood work revealed the Link's cholesterol level was 880 and his body fat percentage was 98, they grudgingly backed off their position that I was the only party responsible for their father's demise. I didn't gloat over the admission, however, hoping that on some level, my approach would improve my bargaining position.

"Sky Thorne. What brings you here?" Ted inquired upon spying me.

"Well, I was in the neighborhood and thought I'd say hello."

"Did you bring the videotape you've been promising?"

"Not yet. It's being edited."

"Edited for what?" Ned asked.

"Edited to eliminate my white ass. You don't want to see that, do you?"

"Hell, no," roared Ted.

"How are the Crooked Creek cocktail parties going?"

"Okay, I guess," Ted replied. "Why do we have to go to so many?"

"It's just standard procedure. You're required to meet a certain number of members."

"Well, it's a pain in the ass," Ned opined. "And I don't like the people I'm meeting."

"Neither do I," Fred added.

"Then you'll fit right in. Most of the people there hate each other anyway. It's part of the place's charm."

"So if you didn't bring the videotape, what are you doing here?"

Ted didn't like to make small talk.

"Believe it or not, I'm here about a business proposition."

"What do you mean?" Ted asked, a confused look on his face.

"Let me introduce you to Cal Perkins."

Cal stepped forward from the sterile hallway where he'd been lurking and waved nonchalantly at the brothers.

"Hello."

"Who's this mope?" Fred asked with scorn, putting me on the defensive immediately.

"This mope, for your information . . ."

"Wait a minute. Is this the guy who did PR work for us?" Ted suddenly recognized Cal's name.

"Wait, is this the porno guy? What's he doing here?" Ned was displeased. "You've got some nerve showing up here."

"Now, hold on a second, Ned. Cal's here with an offer you can't refuse."

"Oh, yeah. Just watch us," Fred spewed.

Cal, infinitely more skillful and savvy than he appeared, knew to tread gingerly as he made his pitch.

"First of all, I'm very sorry for your father's condition. I'm really hoping he pulls through."

"Yeah, yeah. Right. Now out with it. What's this offer we can't refuse?"

"Okay. I'll get to it. How would you gentlemen like to own a business with a 3,000 percent profit margin?"

"What? The porno business?" Ted scoffed.

"Not quite. The adult entertainment business. Video, Internet, telephone, mail order, retail and wholesale. Chat lines. Love lotions. Vibrators. I could go on and on. If you don't know, it's one of the fastest growing businesses in the world."

"You must be joking. Do you really think we'd willingly enter the very industry that nearly killed our father and shamed Tailburger?" Fred thought he spoke for the whole family, but was wrong.

"Fred, will you please put a sock in it? (Pause) Cal, if this business is so profitable, why are you selling it?"

Just as I expected, Ted was interested.

"Personal reasons. Some of them related to unwanted publicity. Let's just say I'm ready to get out."

"Ted, this is the guy who was responsible for the Nail Some Tail contest." Fred was indignant.

"I know that, but just give him a chance. Cal, what's the business worth?"

"I'd say about fifteen million."

"And what are you asking for it?"

"Eight."

"That's all?"

"That's all. (Pause) Plus Sky's pension. Payable immediately."

Ned, Ted and Fred looked at each other, suddenly suspicious of our entire visit.

"Why are you asking for the pension? We've already struck a deal for that." Ted looked at me. "What's going on here, Sky?"

Cal stepped in.

"Sky's not asking for it. I am. My reasons are my own. I want to make sure my friend here gets his retirement money no matter what."

"Whoa, whoa, whoa. What are you saying here? Are you saying there's a problem with our club memberships going through? Sky, is there a problem with our club memberships at Crooked Creek?"

Just as I'd hoped, the brothers' pathetic need to belong to a stupid golf club threw them off the scent of the missing videotape.

"Guys, as far as I know, there's no problem. Your candidacies are on track. But I can't guarantee anything. Somebody could blackball any one of you and you'd be done."

"That's bullshit. You never talked about blackballs before. You said we'd be members."

"And you will be. (Pause) So long as you don't get balled."

"Who's going to ball us?" Ted asked nervously.

"Nobody in his right mind. That I can say for sure," I answered with confidence. "But, then again, you just never know."

The brothers seemed staggered by the mere possibility of exclusion, having come this far in the process.

"Sky, you titfucker, you're changing the deal." Ted was animated now.

"I am not. This isn't my deal. It's Cal's deal."

"Then Cal is the titfucker, and you both can go to hell. The only deal is the first one. Club memberships and the videotape in exchange for the pension. That's it. Now get the hell out of here."

"Just think about buying my business, Ted. A better offer will never come around again. Do you have any idea what it costs to get a million cock rings made in Malaysia? Pennies, I'm telling you. Talk about markup."

"I said get the hell out of here," Ted barked as he pushed us out the door of his father's room.

Cal and I left, justifiably worried (particularly me) that our calculated risk had backfired. Cal asked me if I'd expected the backlash and, of course, I covered and said yes. Secretly, though, I wondered if I'd misjudged the Fanoflincoln brothers, the same anthropoid apes I'd been observing in boardroom captivity for years. Was it possible their lingering deathwatch changed them as human beings for the better? Perhaps it had. They say that can happen to the worst of men. But to the Fanoflincolns—men whose redeeming qualities were so well masked you'd need Rick Baker and an industrial-size vat of Noxzema to try to find them? It was hard for me to believe. If true, the result for me was disastrous. Without the videotape to bribe Muffet Meaney into pulling Tailburger out of the SERMON suit, I was entirely reliant on Plot "Back in the League" Thickens to do the deed. Only one problem: I'd promised Cal I wouldn't use the information about our perverted attorney general and his victory in the Nail Some Tail Sweepstakes to do anything other than help us escape prosecution in our pending criminal suit. "Just secure a short probation term for each of us," Cal insisted. "The most important thing to me is my marriage." His words left little room for equivocation.

And so I was stuck. Placed in the unenviable position of lying to my best friend or, alternatively, losing my last opportunity to capture my pension. What Cal didn't know wouldn't hurt him, I tried to convince myself. On the other hand, if the whole thing cratered, I might have his broken marriage on my conscience for the rest of my life. I had something to lose here, too. A jail term of any length could end the last remaining hope either of us had for female companionship for a very long time. We'd be dating men named Bubba and trading cigarettes for protection. What a way to spend our golden years. It wasn't, however, just about our love lives. The bottom line: I didn't want to break my promise to Cal. Whatever progress I'd made as a person had been largely obliterated by my lies to Annette and others, and now I risked snuffing out my self-worth and the last scintilla of my integrity by breaching the unbreachable and putting Cal and his marriage in jeopardy by my actions. Why did my desires and basic needs continually put me at odds with the truth? There was no time to answer this question. Albany awaited.

36

Plea Bargain

ALBANY, NEW YORK

Plot Thickens was a moth who wanted to be a butterfly, or, to be precise, New York's next governor, but the immutable laws of nature dictated he would always be a pest and never part of the Papilionidae. I reminded myself of this as I walked into Valentine's, a nondescript watering hole packed with people who calendar ten-cent-wing night and leave their government jobs at 4:15 P.M. every day. As a state employee and a bit of a boozehound, the attorney general would be found under the bar's black spray-painted ceiling, somewhere in the vicinity of the big-screen TV located in back (this information courtesy of the attorneys in his office still working well after 5:00 P.M. when I called). Sure enough, as I made my way through the crowd, I saw his unmistakably thick neck and heard his vexing laugh issuing forth from a booth loaded with legal interns whose collective love for Thickens was probably second in quantity only to his own. It bothered me to interrupt what I'm sure was a fascinating lesson on the finer points of civil procedure, but I forced myself onward.

"Hey, Thickens, shouldn't you be home with your wife?"

To put Plot back on his heels, I asked about his new bride, a legislative aide and former lap dancer, according to published reports. The directness of my question and a large handful of Cajun-flavored CornNuts caused him to choke and then begin coughing. With his eyes watering up from the continual hacking, he looked at me like he'd seen a ghost or, more accurately, a guy he'd screwed over and then promptly forgotten about.

"What the hell are *you* doing here?"

Plot's tone was hostile at first, but, cognizant of his subordinates, he regained his composure and proceeded to politick me as he had countless others. He couldn't quite remember my name, but that didn't stop him.

"Why don't you join us for a drink?"

"All right. I think I will."

Plot's mental Rolodex (picture a torturously slow-moving device) was working overtime to pinpoint our last encounter. Oh, yeah. Now he was starting to get it. I was the guy from Tailburger. But what else? Uh-oh. I was the guy he said he'd help with the SERMON suit until Burton Roxby and Tailburger's campaign dollars became expendable. The whites of his eyes widened the moment it all registered.

"This is such a surprise, Sky."

Plot was now painfully aware of my identity.

"Aren't you going to introduce me to your friends, Plot?"

"Well, sure. Uh . . . these are some of the law students who are working for me this summer in the office. This is Caroline. And that's Rebecca."

Thickens pointed toward two attractive, stylishly dressed females—Kate Spade bags hugged to their hips.

"Nice to meet you," I said, returning the nods and smiles of acknowledgment that greeted me.

"And that's . . . that's . . . I'm sorry. What's your name again?" Plot asked the ugliest of the bunch.

"Heather."

"That's right. That's right. Heather. I dated a Heather when I was back in the League. She was a Buffalo Jill, you know, one of their pom-pom gals. Real nice. I think she was from Lackawanna, which is where Ron Jaworski's from, you know, the Polish Rifle? Took the Eagles to the Big Dance in '81?"

Although Thickens's story was met with blank stares by the entire group, my nerve-inducing presence made him prattle on more brainlessly by the second.

"Anyway, nice gal. (Pause) Huge taters. (Pause) No offense to anybody here, but boy, could she fill out a singlet, if you know what I mean. Looked great in horns, too. I'm really digging myself a hole, aren't I? Hoo boy. We need another round."

While Plot signaled for a waiter, his group of interns remained silent, politely sipping their Seabreezes and waiting for the awkward conversation gap to be filled.

"I need to speak with you alone, Plot."

"Okay. I think I can arrange for that. Girls, would you mind giving us a few minutes? (Pause) Make sure you come back," Plot added desperately.

With the law students gone from our booth, Plot embarked on still more small talk.

"What's your poison, pal?"

"Plot, I know about the Tailburger contest."

"What are you talking about?"

"The Nail Some Tail Internet contest? Ring any bells?"

Thickens finally flagged down one of the servers.

"What are you drinking? How 'bout Pete's Wicked Ale? Nothing better with wings. Waiter, can I get two more Pete's here and two plates of wings?"

"I'm really not hungry, Plot."

"I insist. It's on me. Hey, what's the money for if you can't share it with friends? That's what I always say."

"Very generous of you, but I'm here to talk about the Tailburger contest."

"I'm afraid I don't know what you're talking about."

"You don't?"

"Nope. Never heard of it."

"I see. (Pause) Well, that's too bad, considering you won the grand prize."

Plot's face, hardly poker to this point, lit up.

"I did? I won?" he asked excitedly. "You're kidding me. The trip to the Lust Ranch?"

"Yup."

"With my choice of hookers for a weekend?"

"Uh-huh."

"And free use of a Tailmobile for a year?"

"It's a four-wheel-drive SUV. Orange and purple. All yours."

"I can't believe it."

"You bagged the big burrito."

"Hot damn . . . !"

Plot's undoing was his uncontrollable need to talk strategy.

". . . You know, I figured if I just entered enough times . . . oops."

The attorney general knew he was caught.

"All right, what the hell do you want?"

Plot Thickens wasn't a bright man, but he was savvy enough to know public disclosure of his involvement with Tailburger's contest would cost him the upcoming election against Governor Puma. Plot's crusade against porn was the cornerstone of his campaign, and despite revelations about the incumbent's transsexual wife, Joey, Plot saw things from the voters' perspective—better the sick, twisted pervert you know than the one you don't.

"I want you to talk to Humpy Wheeler."

"Humpy Wheeler? Is he on your ass? That crazy injun tried to prosecute me for child support. (Pause) Twice. There's nothing I can do for you there."

"Listen to me. Cal Perkins . . ."

"Who's that?"

"He owns the Lust Ranch."

"Good man."

"Listen! He also ran the Tailburger contest promotion. (Pause) He and I have been indicted on a couple of charges. They're minor felonies, but they carry time, and Wheeler wants blood."

"Sky, I told you. Wheeler hates me. And even if he didn't, I don't know what I'd be able to do. Crazy fuckin' humpbacked injun," Plot added disparagingly.

"Don't screw around here, Plot. People always want something they can't have. An Achilles' heel. Your job is to find out Wheeler's weakness, his fondest unmet desire, and then cut a deal to fulfill it. Cal and I will take short probation terms, but that's it."

"And in return?"

"Your contest victory will disappear under a pile of paperwork, soon to be shredded and lost forever."

Thickens leaned back in the booth and pondered the proposed exchange.

"Can I still go on the trip to the ranch?"

"I think that can be arranged."

Thickens thought about the situation for another fifteen seconds.

"Okay. You've got a deal."

Plot reached his hand across the table to shake on our agreement. I began to do the same out of habit, but stopped short of his grip.

"There's one more thing."

Plot pulled his hand back.

"What do you mean? What else is there?"

I fell silent for a moment, engulfed by the cacophony of smoky conversation. My body and soul wanted to leave the topic of the SERMON suit alone. My heart. My head. My sense of right and wrong. My word. My loyalty to Cal. Only the money troll wanted to come out and cross the bridge. And admittedly, my surging self-preservation mechanism, the part of a person that allows him to turn cannibal on a deserted island, had been tripped. Sure, the risk of raising the SERMON suit ran high, and if the conversation boomeranged on me, I would place myself and others in jeopardy, legal and otherwise. But the Fanoflincoln brothers had been clear about the deal. The video and the Crooked Creek membership in exchange for my retirement money. Without the video, I needed something big, like Tailburger's exclusion from the impending legal class action, to secure my pension.

"Sky, I said what else is there?" Thickens repeated his question. (Pause). "Sky, are you listening to me? (Pause) Sky?"

* * * * *

I made the long drive west along Route 90 listening to news radio. An E. coli outbreak at a Sizzler in Wauwatosa, Wisconsin, had caused the owners to voluntarily shut the place down. Somehow the bacteria leapt from the meat to the melon, and now fruit lovers were dropping like fruit flies and regretting their decision to belly up to the enticing Sizzler salad bar. Though I'd once been numb to reports of foodborne illness, my experience with Cal's son forever altered my attitude and reaction to such stories. Now I empathized and genuinely commiserated with the people affected. In sympathy, I even assessed the energy necessary to get involved somehow in fighting for food safety. And although I knew I was an unlikely activist, I was glad to be free from my association with Tailburger. Well . . . almost free.

37

Passages

BACK HOME

In my absence, rain plastered a smattering of leaves and grass on my driveway. My garage door opener revealed a surprisingly spry King, who should've been convalescing upstairs, but for some unknown reason was preparing to play handyman. Dressed in a pair of old denim overalls and a painter's cap, he looked like a poor man's Bob Vila as he mixed a can of Dutch Boy blue with his Taiji ruler.

"What the hell are you doing?" I asked as I climbed out of my car.

"I'm going to paint your house for you."

"You're supposed to be in bed. You were stabbed ten days ago. Remember that?"

"How about showing some gratitude? Your place could use a coat or two, if you haven't noticed. How do you like the color?"

"I don't mean to be an ingrate. I really don't. It's just that I'm familiar with your historical reliability as a provider of services."

"What's that supposed to mean?"

"It means I don't want a half-painted house when you head out to Aruba on a Princess cruise ship in two weeks."

My criticism struck a determined nerve.

"I'm not going anywhere. I want to paint the fucking house."

"I'm not sure which of your two pronouncements is more troubling to me. Probably the first, but it's close."

"Step out here for a minute, wise guy."

King, who had healed quite nicely despite a lack of professional care, took me by the arm and led me out of the garage.

"Turn around."

I did as instructed and stared up at my dilapidated dwelling. I'd never seen it look so bad.

"Now, Sky. (Pause) Look at this place and tell me it doesn't need work."

He was right, of course. It was falling apart, the victim of neglect for too long. The sad part—it was still hard for me to say yes to an offer of help, particularly one from him.

"The place looks fine."

"What are you talking about? Are we looking at the same house?"

"I think it's okay."

"Trust me. It is *not* okay. The wood's rotting out. The shutters are faded. The trim is cracked and chipped. You can't let it go another winter."

"Look, I don't want you to paint it, okay? I just want you to leave it alone."

"Let me paint it."

"No! It can last another winter. Maybe two."

"You're an asshole. You know that? A real asshole."

King stormed back into the house and I followed, dragging my briefcase and body over the domestic threshold yet one more time. I wanted to tell King about Albany, but he'd scarcely care now, not that I'd blame him, given my loutish behavior. I owed him an apology, but somehow couldn't find the energy to deliver it. Instead, I consoled myself with the list of telephone messages he'd taken for me while I was away. Cal. Annette. M.C. Shufelbarger. Ethan. It was close to 5:00 P.M., and I wanted a drink before I did anything.

The early edition of the local news would be coming on and I indulged the thought of one half hour's mindless viewing. I plopped down on my brown sectional, lit a Commodore and channel-surfed until my nemesis, Katie Gomez Chang, was staring me straight in the face. Before I could turn away, she spoke.

"Tonight's top story is the tragic death of one of our community's biggest, and I do mean biggest, business leaders. Frank Fanoflincoln, founder of the Tailburger restaurant chain, is dead tonight at seventy-four. According to a St. Mary's Hospital spokesperson, Mr. Fanoflincoln died an hour ago after watching a DVD of the film *Glory*, starring Matthew Broderick and Denzel Washington, one of his all-time favorite movies, and eating a large bowl of diet lime Jell-O, his first meal after awakening from a coma. Although his life ended in a humiliating miasma of pornography, atheism and the handicapped, he meant many things to many people in the greater Rochester area. Later in the broadcast, we'll look at the life of this hometown hamburger king, Civil War enthusiast and enormously fat man."

I sat stunned, a glass of bourbon glued to one hand, a burning cigarette in the other. You never know how you genuinely feel about someone until they're dead. And now I knew how I felt about the Link. Somehow, some way, despite everything he'd put me through, despite the countless times he'd forced me to compromise myself, he'd gotten to me. I cared about that fat fuck. I cared about him a lot. You would've thought I'd be dancing on his grave, but I wasn't. Instead, I was in tears. The sobbing started quietly and then crescendoed, leveling off to a loud, rhythmic heaving. King heard me and came downstairs to the study.

"What's wrong?"

"Itsa Link," I blubbered.

"What?"

"Tha Link."

"Jesus. What did that asshole do to you now?"

"He . . . he . . . he . . ."

"Out with it. What'd he do?"

"He . . . he . . ." My sobbing made speaking impossible.

"I'll kill that guy. I swear. You know me, Sky. I'm not a violent man, but I will kill that guy or I'll get someone else to kill him. El Jefe is one phone call away. Now, c'mon. Get yourself together and just tell me what he did."

"He . . . he . . . he . . . died."

Suddenly my composure returned.

"He died?"

I nodded at my brother while catching my breath.

"Oh. (Pause) Well, good. Then I can cross his murder off my list. (Pause) But wait, now I'm confused. Why in the hell are you so upset? Isn't this the guy who's made your life miserable for the last twenty years?"

"Yes."

"Then I don't get it."

"I don't either."

King came over and sat next to me, placed his arm around my back and cradled my head against his shoulder. For a few minutes we sat together, one aging man holding another, both expecting the embrace to feel awkward at any moment. But it never did.

"Sky, do you need anything? How 'bout a run to the Sweet? That'll make you feel better."

"No, not tonight. I think I'd rather be here. Thanks for the offer though. (Pause) Maybe tomorrow."

"Are you sure?"

"Yeah, I'm sure." I nodded.

King stood up and reflexively crossed his arms.

"No problem. (Pause) I'll tell you what. I'm going to leave you alone for a bit, but I'll be upstairs if you change your mind."

"Fair enough." I managed a smile for King before he turned to leave.

"King."

He paused at the doorway and looked back at me.

"About . . . you know, earlier, in the garage?"

"You're sorry?"

"I am."

"It's okay . . . I'm a shitty painter anyway."

King's exit left me alone with my original unanswered question and an opportunity to examine my mourning a bit closer. Why *was* I so upset? As a child, I'd once pretended my parents had died and allowed myself to feel imagined emotions, acting out a version of grief I wouldn't experience for real until many years later. It was then I'd learned, in the most painful way, that the profundity of loss for someone you truly care about is deeper than anything you could ever imagine or wish upon an enemy. This was a different kind of grief though, entirely distinct from what I'd felt for my mother, father or Jess. So what was it?

I concluded that my feelings were as much about my own mortality as they were about the Link's. From somewhere within, I felt a deep sense of loss because a piece of my own personal history, for better or worse, was gone. And with it, a large passage of my life. My theory was an evolving one. If surviving longer than the Link meant winning, I cried the way a victor cries for a vanquished foe. The way Frazier would cry if Ali died. My greatest opponent—gone. But if surviving longer simply meant surviving and nothing more, I cried the way you do when someone significant in your life, whether cruel or kind, lives no longer. The way a son cries for a sometimes abusive father. The way Cratchit would cry if Scrooge died. The person you love and hate at the same time— off with the angels.

The telephone rang and, out of habit, I picked it up.

"Hello."

"Sky, it's M.C. Shufelbarger."

"M.C., this is a bad time. Can I call you later?"

"Sure, Sky, but I've got good news."

Plot couldn't have cut a deal with Humpy Wheeler this quickly. Or could he? Either way, it was an inappropriate time to discuss the matter. It would have to wait.

"I don't want to talk about my case right now, M.C."

"I'm not calling about your case."

"You're not?"

"No."

"Humpy Wheeler didn't call you?"

"No. Why would he?"

"No reason," I said, suddenly a bit defensive. "It's just that you said you had good news."

"I do. Frank Fanoflincoln died. Isn't that great?"

"Hey, I know he wasn't a saint, but how about a little respect for the dead?"

"Respect? I've got more than that. I've got his last will and testament. You'll have to forgive my enthusiasm. I get a little excited whenever one of my estates matures."

"Did you draft the Link's will?"

"Yes, I did. But even better, I'm the executor of the estate."

"I thought the rules of ethics prohibited the lawyer who drew the will from also serving as the executor. Something about a conflict of interest."

"Sky, Sky, Sky. The ethics guys try to take all the fun, and worse, all the fees, out of practicing law. None of that conflicts bullshit is important. What's important here is that, if memory serves, you are the intended beneficiary of a sizable bequest."

I swallowed.

"I am?"

"Yes. I'm going to be reading the will tomorrow morning at my office. Why don't you come over around ten A.M.?"

"Okay," I answered, a bit stunned by the news. "I'll stop by."

After the call ended, I wandered around the house in disbelief for some time. Why would the Link leave me anything after what happened at the convent? Then the obvious hit me. Of course.

He'd never had the chance to change his will. He'd been in a coma. But still, before that, before I helped put him in a coma, he'd thought enough of me to leave me something. Suddenly, whatever warm words he'd ever shared with me in life took on added significance in death. I could no longer disregard them as manipulative gestures, like I had when he was living. The Link cared about me. He cared a lot. This shouldn't have been important to me, but it was.

I called Cal to tell him about the trip.

"How'd everything go?"

"I think it went well."

"Were you tailed?"

"No, I wasn't tailed. Who would be tailing me?"

"I don't know. This whole thing has me jumpy."

"Well, there's nothing to be jumpy about. It's all over."

"So Thickens is going to talk to Humpy Wheeler?"

"He said he would."

"God, that's great."

"Just make sure the contest evidence is secure."

"I will. (Pause) Did the SERMON suit come up?"

I hesitated.

"No, it didn't. I'll have to find another way to get my pension."

"You're a good friend."

"Thanks. (Pause) Listen, I need to call Annette. I'll catch up with you tomorrow."

"Okay. Talk to you tomorrow."

I purposely avoided telling Cal about the Link's will. In a strange way I felt guilty about inheriting anything from someone I'd disparaged so frequently in front of my best friend. I called Annette to clear my conscience, a difficult thing to do, considering my rectal cancer charade. It was academic anyway, since she wasn't around, forced out for the evening by some political fund-raiser, no doubt.

Ethan was also out when I tried him, but Skull advised me

Macrocock.com's share price was off $20 from its peak and that management had been forced to make eighteen layoffs recently. Fortunately, my son was not among them, but his roommate painted a bleaker picture of the fledgling start-up's finances than I'd ever heard before. All staff were now subjected to Mussolini-like motivational speeches from their appointed leader, some twenty-seven-year-old named Bilbo with a nipple piercing. When Skull joked that soon he'd be back to passing out on my lawn for a living, I knew not to rely too heavily on Ethan's enterprise for my fiscal future. From what M.C. said, however, it didn't sound like I'd need to. The irony that the source of my money problems might prove to be their solution was impossible to ignore. Exhausted, I went to bed, humbled by the Link's death and my own life.

38

Bequest

THE LAW OFFICES OF M.C. SHUFELBARGER

The brown shag carpeting and orange vinyl furniture in M.C. Shufelbarger's office were as rude as Randi, the receptionist.

"Whaddya want?" The question sprang from her red-lipsticked mouth, along with a loud snap of gum.

"Uh . . . yes, I'm here to see M.C."

"'Bout what?" Without looking up at me, Randi busily lined up a toenail to trim from the foot propped up on her desk.

"About the Fanoflincoln will."

"And who are *you?*"

"I'm Sky Thorne. I'm a client."

"Nah. I don't think so. I know all of M.C.'s clients."

"Believe me, I'm a client. I've been in here more times than I care to think about the past three months. I'm sure you recognize me."

"Nah. You don't look familiar."

"Will you at least look up at me before you say that?"

Visibly perturbed, Randi craned her neck upward and took a long look at my frowning face.

"Wait."

"Recognize me now?"

"Yeah, I do. You're the guy who got all those crippled kids hooked on porn. Shame on you."

"I didn't get anyone hooked on porn. It was an advertising campaign that . . ."

"They're all in back," she said, cutting me off midsentence and signaling for me to take leave of her.

Sullied by the exchange, I put my head down and traveled further into the bowels of M.C.'s brown carpetdom, guided only by the voices of the Fanoflincoln brothers—men clearly still in the grip of their grieving.

"I'm telling you right now, he's number one in scoring average, number one in driving distance, *and* number one in greens in regulation, but only number *two* in sand save percentage."

"Ted, you don't know shit," Ned declared. "He's number two in scoring average, two in driving distance, one in greens in regulation and number eight in sand save percentage."

"Yeah, but what about his driving accuracy and scrambling rank?" Fred asked, not wanting to be left out of the conversation. "He's nowhere in those categories. Goddamn Duffy Waldorf blows his doors in scrambling."

"Will you shut up, Fred?"

"All I'm saying is that Tiger's got a long way to go before he's number one in my book."

"As if he cares."

"You don't think he cares what the fans think?"

"He sure as hell doesn't care what *you* think."

My entrance to the room brought the great golf debate to a close. The brothers, dressed identically in black shirts, knickers, tam-o'-shanters and spiked shoes, were shocked to see me. I spoke to break the silence.

"Guys, I'm very sorry about your father. (Pause) I knew him for a long time and well, (Pause) he was really something."

Dead air returned until Ned filled it.

"Sky, why are you here?"

"Well, uh, M.C. told me to come down. Didn't he mention anything to you?"

"Oh, I get it," Ned said, a lightbulb going off above his head. "You're here to talk about your upcoming trial."

"Ordinarily yes, but not today. I, uh . . ."

"He's here for the reading of your father's will," M.C. blurted out, entering the room with an armful of files and a Slim Jim dangling from his mouth.

"What?" the brothers exclaimed in disbelieving unison.

"He's in the will. I told you that."

"No, you didn't. This has got to be a mistake," Fred insisted.

"There's no way our father put Sky in his will."

"That's right. There's no way!"

"Now don't get your undies in a wad," M.C. warned. "Just sit down and let's get started."

"This is *total* B.S.," Ned fumed.

Ned, Ted and Fred took seats, crammed three across on an orange vinyl couch, while I remained standing near the door and befriended a dead potted plant.

"Take a seat, Sky."

"I'd rather stand, M.C."

"Suit yourself."

M.C. shuffled the papers in front of him like a deck of cards until he located what he was looking for. Organized files were not his strong suit.

"Okay, this is it. I've found the will. Are you ready?"

Palpable tension, the product of fear and anticipation, could be felt as M.C. held up the document from across the room and began to read.

"'I, Frank Fanoflincoln, being of sound body and mind, hereby bequeath all right, title and interest in my worldly possessions as follows: To the Monroe County Chapter of the Ulysses S. Grant

Society, I leave my guns, my collection of Matthew Brady photographs and all of my rayon sweatsuits for use as ponchos in future battle reenactments.' "

"He gave them the guns?" Ted asked in disbelief. "I wanted those," he whined.

"Shut up, Ted," Ned demanded.

" 'To the Queer Nation, in honor of my hero, Abraham Lincoln, I leave three hundred thousand dollars for the establishment of a scholarship fund in his name.' "

"No waayyy!" Ned shouted in agony.

"I *told* you Lincoln was gay!" Fred jumped up from the couch and pointed his finger at his brothers. "I told you! But you wouldn't listen!"

"I don't believe it." Ned was defiant.

"Neither do I. Where does it say that in the will, M.C.? I want to see that," Ted demanded.

The three Fanoflincoln brothers stormed toward M.C. and surrounded him at his desk, daring the executor to point out the provision.

"Son of a bitch! It's right there. I see it," Ted conceded.

"Three hundred grand. Right down the shooter," said Ned.

"More like *up* the shooter."

"I told you Lincoln was gay, but you wouldn't listen to me."

"We're named after a gay guy. This is *total* B.S.!"

"Boys, you have to get back on the couch so we can continue," M.C. implored them.

Ned, Ted and Fred, collectively stunned, slowly stumbled back to their respective seats of orange vinyl while M.C. continued.

"Let's see what else we have here. (Pause) Well, well, well. Sky, let me be the first to congratulate you. It looks like your ship has finally come in."

An audible chorus of gasps came from Ned, Ted and Fred as they contemplated the impossible: the loss of their inheritance.

"I mean it has *literally* come in."

"What did he leave me?" I asked excitedly, financial independence mere moments away.

"Settle down now. Let me read the will."

Shufelbarger ran his finger down the yellowed document until he found the desired passage.

" 'To Sky Thorne, in gratitude for keeping my spirits and my company afloat more times than I care to remember, I leave my beloved boat *Bastard Boy* and . . .' "

M.C. paused.

"Hold on a moment. I seem to have lost my place."

There was still a chance. Anything could follow the word "and." Cash, stock, jewelry. I could still be taken out of servitude. I could still walk away from all of this with a pile of *fuck you* money.

"Okay, here we go," M.C. continued. "It says, 'I leave my beloved boat *Bastard Boy* and my collection of adult films that I keep down below in the main cabin.' "

"He got the boat *and* the films? Didn't he leave *anything* for us?" Ned wondered bitterly.

"Yes, he did. He left this video," M.C. shot back, holding aloft a black cassette.

M.C. stood and opened a cabinet behind him housing a large television and VCR. As he popped in the tape, my mind drifted off to what could have been. Still, I had the boat, something I could sell for a fair amount. I had no right to be the slightest bit disappointed.

"Hello, boys, this is your father speaking."

The Link's fat face lit up the television screen. He was dressed in a purple sweatsuit (his favorite) and appeared to be eating strips of bacon.

"Just finishing breakfast here and thought I'd make this tape. I'm not getting any younger and I want to talk to you, father to son."

The Link paused to wipe grease from his mouth with a paper towel.

"First of all, you get the old homestead. It would have killed me to sell Gristle-Vale while I was living, but now that I'm gone, I want you to get rid of it. I'd die twice knowing my family was there having fun without me. I'm sure you understand. (Pause) Sell it and split the proceeds one-third each. Actually, on second thought, Ned and Ted, you take forty percent each and give Fred twenty. He needs to shape up a bit."

"Aw shit," Fred moaned dejectedly.

"Neddie, (Pause) Teddie, (Pause) Freddie (Pause). These are troubled times we're (Pause), I guess I should say you're living in today." The Link's face turned visibly more somber.

"You've got all these crazy activists from PETA and Greenpeace and the Junior League. You've got those Jackie Chan movies and that stupid *Survivor* show. You've got people spellin' 'woman' with a 'y' and that guy from *Inside the Actor's Studio* with his asinine French questionnaire. There's this whole lattice, I don't know what else to call it, covering the country like a sheet of cellophane on top of a casserole, and you can't get out from under it."

The Link ate another piece of bacon, swallowing it quickly.

"See, I never told you the whole truth about the American dream. In America, we love to build people up. We build 'em up and up and up. Higher than they ever thought they'd go and higher than they ever *wanted* to go. Why? (Pause) So we can tear 'em down. Bill Clinton. Clarence Thomas. O.J. Simpson. Newt Gingrich. Pee Wee Herman. Successful men America tore down. Everybody's a target. Everybody who's willing to stick their nose up above the pack and say, 'Hey, I've got something special to offer—something nobody else has got.' Now there are folks who think they can get out from under the cellophane—master-of-the-universe types like Larry Ellison and Bill Gates and that little red-haired chick on the Pepsi commericals—but they can't for one simple reason. America's out there waiting. Just waiting for the slightest screwup, the smallest crack, that one piece of information that'll begin the process of destruction. And if it doesn't exist, America will manufacture it, make it up out of thin air. Used to be you had to be a big star for this to happen. You had to be president or heavyweight champion or Frank Sinatra. America wouldn't waste its time with Congressmen or talk show hosts or those kids from *Diff'rent Strokes*. But now it doesn't matter. We'll rip down any*one* who's built up any*thing*, including me, your old man."

The Link shook his head, conveying his disappointment.

"Take a look around. They're coming after Tailburger and they're coming after her hard. The animal rights cabal, the food safety freaks, the fitness fanatics, SERMON. And *that's* just for starters. Sadly, the list goes on and on and on. (Pause) So I'm doing what an officer does for his infantrymen. I'm leaving you all my shares in Tailburger, a fifty-one percent interest in the company, on one condition: that you get out of the business right now and dump the stock—when it still has some value. Ten-dollar shares of Tailburger won't be worth ten cents in two years. Mark my words. (Pause) This is an order. If you don't sell the securities within two weeks of my death, the shares go to Joey Puma's campaign fund. I don't care if his wife *does* have a beard, I don't want to see Thickens in the governor's mansion."

The Link stopped talking and looked wistfully into the camera.

"Boys, you know I love you. More than I ever said when I was alive. (Pause) And I'm damn proud of you. (Pause) Remember that."

M.C.'s office was silent with the exception of the sniffles emanating from the Fanoflincoln brothers. They had the approval every child seeks, and I had a buyer for Cal's business.

The Link finished with his favorite words.

"So for the final time, I ask you, as the great Abraham Lincoln once asked Congress, 'Can we do better? The dogmas of the quiet past are inadequate to the stormy present. The occasion is piled high with difficulty, and we must rise to the occasion. As our case is new, so we must think anew, and act anew!' (Pause) Good-bye."

39

Life Preserver Thrown

ANNETTE'S KITCHEN

"Let's go on a trip."

"Sky, that's a *great* idea. We can go to Vermont for a weekend. Just get away from it all. Just you and me."

"Actually, I was thinking of someplace a little more exotic."

"How about Burlington? You never know what you'll see there."

"I don't think you understand. I want to go to Tahiti."

"Tahiti? For a weekend?"

"Annette, I'm not talking about a weekend. I want to go away for a while."

"You mean a week?"

"Longer."

"*Not* a month?"

"Longer."

"But your health. You need to be here for treatment."

"I'm feeling fine."

"What about your trial? It's starting in three weeks."

"There isn't going to be a trial."

"There isn't?"

"Well, I'm not sure, but I don't think so."

"Sky, what's going on?"

"It's hard to explain. See, I just came from the reading of the Link's will and (Pause) well, it made me realize some things. (Pause) Annette, I owe you an apology."

"Why? We've had a few ups and downs, but you don't owe me an apology."

"Yes, I do. I've been walking around this past year feeling sorry for myself. I've been blaming others and making excuses for why I wasn't living the life I wanted."

"We *all* do that sometimes."

"Maybe, but I did something worse. I put myself in a position where I felt I had to lie to the people I care about in order to protect my own self-interests. (Pause) I can't do that anymore. It's not right. When you sacrifice the truth just to keep something, you don't have anything worth keeping in the first place."

"I want to understand, Sky. I really do. But I'm not sure what you're saying."

"What I'm saying is, I lied to you."

"About what?"

"That's not important."

"I'd like to be the judge of that."

"You're missing the point. Don't you see? Today I realized that every bad thing that's happened to me lately, and during my life, was the result of a poor decision I made long before. I should've left Tailburger years ago, but I didn't have the courage, and it's cost me in so many ways."

"But you were just trying to get a pension. That's why you stayed. There's nothing wrong with that."

"Yes, there is. I traded myself for the promise of those payments. The moment they were placed in jeopardy, I started saying and doing anything to protect them, but the promise was hollow. Whatever money I was supposed to receive couldn't come close to covering the damage I did to my own spirit. Waiting wasn't worth it. (Pause) I know all of this sounds confusing, but I'm seeing things clearly for the first time ever. I never had the guts to make tough choices, but I think I do now."

"Sky, please slow down."

"I can't. I've wasted too much time already. I'm going to sell my house and car and take the Link's boat to the South Pacific."

"His boat?"

"He left it to me. (Pause) I want to make a fresh start with you. Go away with me to Tahiti."

Annette looked touched and heartbroken at the same time.

"Sky, I can't go away with you."

"What do you mean? We can live in Papeete."

"I'm the mayor, Sky. I've got responsibilities. I've got a campaign coming up."

"Forget about those things. Don't you get it? You're living under a big sheet of cellophane. You can't win."

"Cellophane? What are you talking about?"

"There's this big sheet of cellophane covering us and (Pause) look, forget about the cellophane. I'm just telling you we need to get away from here."

Annette considered my words for a moment and then changed the topic.

"What did you lie to me about?"

"It doesn't matter."

"It matters to me."

"Fine. I'll tell you. You want to know?"

"Yes, I want to know."

"All right. Fine. I don't have cancer. There. I've said it."

"What?"

"I don't have cancer anymore."

"You're cured?"

"Sort of. Technically, I never actually had it in the first place."

"Technically? You sick son of a bitch! How could you manipulate me like that?"

"Annette, I'm sorry. I had to do it to get close to you again."

"All those appointments I took you to at the hospital. I can't believe it. They were all lies."

"That's not true. One doctor said there's a mole on my forehead he thinks may be malignant."

"Oh, c'mon. Why did you have to lie to me?"

"You wouldn't have given me a chance otherwise."

"That's not true."

"Now you're the one lying."

"Don't try and turn this around, Sky. You can forget about me going anywhere with you. Get out of my house!"

"Wait. Let's talk about this."

"There's nothing to talk about. You're a liar and I don't want to see you anymore."

"Annette . . ."

"Get out!"

"But . . ."

"Get out!"

"I'm trying to be a better man."

"Get out!"

After banging on the door for an hour, I left and drove to the Rochester Yacht Club, where the Link docked *Bastard Boy* for the season. My enthusiasm about inspecting my inheritance was now admittedly tempered by my confrontation with Annette. I hadn't even considered the possibility that she wouldn't go with me to Tahiti. Truth be told, I hadn't considered much at all. I was operating entirely on instinct now, like a dog being led by his strongest sense. I could smell what I wanted and needed, and I felt confident my nose would lead me to the right place. And although my sniffer had led me temporarily to an unpleasant place on the female front, there were no secrets between Annette and me for the first time. The fact that our relationship was beyond dead from her standpoint was something I viewed as a mere hiccup to be cured— just like my cancer.

I parked my car and entered RYC's white clapboard clubhouse, walked past a picture of the current commodore and made my way upstairs. From the outdoor deck, I surveyed the slips until I saw my magnificent new boat, gleaming in the afternoon sun and looming large over the other crafts. Suddenly excited as a child on Christmas morning, I barreled back down to the club's first floor, ran outside and rushed toward *Bastard Boy*. From what I could see, she was in pretty good shape. Big, luxurious and outfitted with every navigational device imaginable, she welcomed her new owner with a beer from below and a comfortable seat behind the wheel. Pretending to steer toward my destiny, I couldn't wait any longer to find out if I'd be meeting it anytime soon. I took out my Motorola and called Plot.

"Thickens here."

"Plot, it's Sky."

"Sky, you won't believe what Wheeler wants."

"What?"

"A goddamn casino license. I just got off the horn with him."

"So what's the problem?"

"Turns out he's not an Indian. He just looks like an Indian."

"So what is he?"

"He's Lebanese."

"Well, how much of an Indian do you have to be to get a license?"

"One-sixteenth of your blood must be traceable to a recognized tribe."

"Jesus Christ, isn't he a little bit Indian?"

"His son goes to Florida State. He says he was made an honorary Seminole during parents' weekend last fall."

"Can you use that?"

"I don't think so."

"What's the problem?"

"They're a Florida tribe, for starters."

"They're still recognized, right?"

"Sure. But they've never set foot in western New York."

"Then we say he was banished."

"That's not the point. He doesn't have the blood. Plus, it's politics. According to my guy in the state gaming division, we've got full-blooded Senecas still waiting for their licenses. To give one to a Lebanese guy named Humpy would create a huge uproar."

"I don't understand. If he's not an Indian, why the hell does he go around dressed in tribal gear and carrying that wampum pouch?"

"He says he gets cheap gas and cigarettes on the local reservations."

"Shit. Look Plot, I don't care what you do, but we've got to get this guy his casino license. Don't forget, your contest victory could become public in a big hurry."

Here I was again, doing everything I despised. Lying. Threatening. Scheming. Covering my own ass. I said I wanted to be a better man. I said I valued truthfulness, benevolence and forbearance, but as soon as I considered the possibility of pulling the plug on my latest lapse of honor, I thought of Cal and used him as a worthy excuse to continue. This sordid matter went way beyond Sky Thorne. My best friend was counting on me to keep him out of jail and I couldn't let him down. If he didn't get probation, his marriage could be over. So the way I looked at it, I didn't have a choice. Like a black flag, one more pack of lies would fly from the mast of *Bastard Boy*.

"I'll talk to gaming again."

"Good."

Night fell on Lake Ontario and I decided to sleep on board. The gentle rocking from the waves turned the main cabin into a cradle as I curled up under a blue cotton blanket. Alone in the dark, I found myself thinking only of my parents. Were they watching all this from above? I hoped not.

40

Skiing Powder

THREE DAYS LATER, 8:00 A.M.

I picked up Cal at Woodcliff Lodge, where he was still staying, thanks to his wife's stubborn streak. Jenny's insistence that he sell his business or stay away turned our scheduled 8:30 A.M. meeting with the Fanoflincoln brothers into Cal's Super Bowl. With his family life down by six, late in the fourth quarter, he needed to score. Up to this point, he'd had no success finding a buyer for his porn empire, and Ned, Ted and Fred looked like his last chance.

"I'm nervous, Sky."

"Don't be. This is your day."

If this was Cal's Super Bowl, it was my Poulan Weedeater Bowl. I had a lot on the line, but somehow the stakes, mostly my pension and pride, seemed lower.

"You think they'll buy?"

"They have to sell their stock. Where else will they park all that cash?"

I wanted Cal to believe the Fanoflincolns needed him more than he needed them, even if it wasn't true. I didn't know who the brothers' financial adviser was, but I doubted he was pushing X-rated videos and flavored lubricants over long-term treasury notes. Still, the Link's sons were greedy if nothing else, and this was an industry with unlimited potential, given America's horny history and future.

"Hey, how about an Egg McMuffin?" I offered my friend his favorite option as we drove toward a row of fast-food establishments on Monroe Avenue.

"You know what I could really go for?"

"What?"

"Rump-Cut Croissant."

"No way. You're still willing to eat at Tailburger? I've sworn off the stuff."

"Would you mind? I love the McMuffin, but ever since they added the extra pork, the Rump-Cut's been my favorite."

I cringed.

"All right. I guess driving through won't kill me. (Pause) Can't say the same about the food."

Pulling up to the speaker, we received a simultaneously tinny and profane greeting from somebody's grandmother.

"Order, asshole."

"Okay," Cal started. "Give me a Rump-Cut with cheese. And to drink, let's see . . ."

"Get the Tailfrap—best beef-flavored shake on the market."

"Isn't it the only beef-flavored shake on the market?"

"Don't sass me, sonny. I'm armed up here."

Sure enough, when we arrived at the window, our elderly server had an automatic weapon slung over her shoulder. The Link's legacy in the flesh.

"Have a good day."

"Easy for her to say," I thought as we drove off. Her fate wasn't in the hands of a hunchbacked Lebanese Indian named Humpy and three dimwits armed with nine-irons.

"Have you heard back from Plot?" Cal asked, stuffing his Rump-Cut into his mouth.

"Not yet. I'll know this afternoon if the casino license went through."

"Got it." Cal's response was terse. No matter how well our morning meeting went, it amounted to only half the equation, and we both knew it.

No longer comfortable roaming Tailburger headquarters, the Fanoflincolns suggested Powder Mill Park, a glorified patch of grass with a few trees and a fish hatchery, for our gathering. A narrow winding road took us into the heart of the park, where the brothers were lounging on a picnic bench.

"How's that boat?" Ned shouted in displeasure as we walked toward him.

Evidently I hadn't been forgiven yet for his father's floating gift.

"I'm taking good care of her. (Pause) She's beautiful."

My remarks were ignored.

"Did you bring the valuation?"

Cal placed his briefcase on the table, opened it and handed over Ernst & Young's busywork to Ned, who eagerly began perusing the figures.

"Are you still asking eight mil?" Fred inquired, too impatient to wait for his brother to finish.

"A little more, now that I've seen the estimate."

"How much more?"

"Let me finish reading, Fred!" Ned barked angrily.

"Sky's pension is still part of the deal," Cal announced.

"No, it's not," Ted said defiantly. "It never was."

"Cal, you don't need to put that into the mix here," I implored my friend.

"I want to. (Pause) I want you to get paid what you're owed."

Ned was done reading now and looked up at Cal and me with disdain. He knew instinctively that Cal was desperate to sell and he planned to take full advantage of his bargaining position just to humiliate me.

"We have our own deal with Sky, and he hasn't met all of its terms yet. Where's the video?"

"You don't need the video anymore."

"So?"

Ned was being a prick. He only wanted the video in the first place to try to stop Muffet Meaney and the SERMON suit. Now that the suit would be irrelevant to him as a soon-to-be ex-shareholder of Tailburger, he was just playing head games.

"You're selling your shares."

"So?"

"So the suit hasn't affected the share price yet. And it won't for a few more months. You're going to get out unscathed."

"That doesn't matter. We had a deal."

"Hold on a second," I said, excusing myself and walking to the trunk of my car. Once there, I opened it and pull out a wrinkled lump of cloth I'd been carrying around on the off chance I ever performed my own oil change.

"Recognize this?" I asked, holding it aloft and letting it fall out to its full length.

"How could you keep that in your trunk?" Fred asked in disbelief.

"Because it doesn't mean anything to me. But I know it means something to you. (Pause) All of you."

The official Crooked Creek Golf Club blazer, a horrible gold garment, had caused every member, myself included, to be confused with a Century 21 agent at least once in his life. After that experience, anyone who wore it had my condolences and pity.

"I didn't want it to come to this, but I swear I'll blackball you."

"You wouldn't dare."

"Not if you buy Cal's company."

"And give Sky his pension," Cal added.

"So that's what it comes to, eh Sky? After all our father did for you, you're blackmailing us."

"Oh shut up, Ned. Stop being an asshole. Do you want to be a member out at Crooked Creek or not?"

Ned, Ted and Fred looked at each other, then back at me, and started nodding. A deal had been struck. Within a few hours, Cal came to terms with the brothers for his business and the two of us retreated to the Country Sweet to refuel. In our favorite establishment, we observed our own code of conduct, devouring each and every chicken wing in complete silence until the last bone had been plucked clean.

"God, that was good."

"Always is."

"Do the wings look bigger to you?"

"You say that every time we're down here."

"Well, they look bigger to me. What do you want me to say?"

My cell phone rang and our lighthearted conversation came to a sudden halt. This was the call we'd been waiting for: the one from Plot Thickens.

"Hello. (Pause) Hey, Plot. (Pause) He did? (Pause) He does? (Pause) I knew it would be close. (Pause) Okay, I'll talk to you later."

I closed my Motorola while Cal, nearly prostrated himself trying to get my attention.

"What'd he say? What'd he say?" Cal asked in rapid succession.

I handed Cal the contraption in my hand.

"Call Jenny and tell her you're coming home. (Pause) For good."

I broke into a big grin and stood to meet Cal, where we embraced, sticky fingers and all, thrilled to have escaped the prison system.

"We got probation," he said in a relieved tone. "We got probation," Cal repeated, making sure it was real.

"Just probation," I confirmed, relieved myself that the plea bargain had worked.

"I can't believe it. (Pause) Sky, take me to Woodcliff. I want to get my stuff and go see the kids."

Together we drove out 490 East from the city. A Springsteen tune, "No Surrender," played in the background on CMF (courtesy of Brother Wease), sounding wholly appropriate given what we'd survived. The wind whipped through the car on a day that just didn't seem right for air-conditioning. Out in the elements, I turned my thoughts to what was coming next in my life.

"Cal, I need to tell you something."

"What?" he shouted over the roar of traffic.

"I'm leaving Rochester."

"You're what?"

"I'm leaving Rochester."

Cal looked at me while reaching for the button to put his window up. I did the same to conduct our conversation in quieter surroundings.

"You can't do that."

"I've thought about this a lot."

"Why would you do that?"

"It's a change I need."

"You don't need a change. You need a break."

"I know. And I can't get it here."

Cal thought about my reason for leaving for a moment before commenting further.

"What if I said I didn't want you to go? Would that make a difference?"

I shook my head.

"Is anybody going with you?"

"I don't know."

"(Pause) Well, *if* you went somewhere, and notice I'm saying *if,* where would you go?"

"There's no if. I'm leaving this week for Tahiti."

"Tahiti? To live?"

I nodded.

"That's crazy. You'll hate it down there."

"This seems out of the blue, I'm sure. But I really believe I'm going to find something there I can't find here."

"Oh, don't get flaky on me and tell me you need to *find* yourself."

"That's not what I'm looking for."

"So what *are* you looking for?"

I drove on in silence, letting Cal's question hang in the air.

"Peace of mind. (Pause) That's all I'm looking for."

By now we'd reached Cal's driveway and he was torn, anxious to run inside and share his good news, yet loyal to a fault as a friend.

"I want you to be happy, Sky. As your friend, I've never wished anything else for you."

"I'm going to be happy. (Pause) That's what this is about."

"We'll talk more later, all right?"

Cal and I shook hands and he climbed out of my car. I'd known him since the second grade and I loved him dearly, although I'd never told him, not even one time. He looked back at me briefly as he walked to the door and gave me a thumbs-up, which is the way I intended to picture him until the next time we met. Seconds later, he disappeared behind his front door and away I went. I missed him already.

41

Charred

48 HOURS LATER

The plan was grand. Cruise through the St. Lawrence Seaway to the Atlantic, jettison down the coast to Florida, stream into the Gulf and then head for the Panama Canal. From there, it was through the locks, out into the Pacific and onward to the island of Tahiti. Fourteen hundred miles southeast of Hawaii.

King would be my first mate. He had loads of cruise ship experience, and if worse came to worst, I figured he could mix us a couple of dynamite margaritas. After we'd loaded up at the local Wegman's supermarket, provisions were plenty, but so were doubts down at the dock.

"This is going to be some trip."

"You're sure you want to do this?"

"I put the house on the market, didn't I? I'm ready to go."

My words lacked confidence, and my brother's tuneful ear picked up on it.

"We don't have to do this, Sky."

"I do."

And that was the rub of it. As often as I'd told myself and others that I *wanted* to do this, the truth was I *had* to do it. I had to force myself to take a step forward that wouldn't, and couldn't, be taken back so easily. I had to take myself out of my comfort zone in a complete and final fashion.

"Okay," King acknowledged my serious reply. (Pause) "Do you want to call Annette one more time?"

Annette wasn't coming with me. Hours of pleading and apologizing hadn't dented her armor, and with each passing minute, a change of heart became less likely.

"I don't know. Why would her answer be any different this time?"

"Don't worry. This isn't your last chance to patch things up. We'll be pulling into ports all the way down the East Coast. She can fly in and meet us."

King was being a good brother by trying to make me feel better, but we both knew this was the end for Annette and me. Voicing the reasons for our demise felt pointless and far too self-indulgent. So I didn't. Instead I silently acknowledged that I'd lied to her one too many times and let her down in too painful a way. Her absence was nothing but the direct result of my hurtful acts, and holding that mirror up to myself yet again had no appeal. I needed to move on.

"Let's go, King."

As soon as King got the ropes, I began slowly motoring the boat backward out of the late Link's slip. I looked to the shore as I shifted the throttle forward and felt the heft of the boat moving through the cold water of Lake Ontario. I was making a getaway, but it was far from clean. There was a trail of deeds churning in the wake of *Bastard Boy* that threatened to follow me all the way to Tahiti. Still, I'd avoided jail and wrangled my pension from Tailburger's grip (Trip Baden got 15 percent of it under our settlement agreement, and Shufelbarger got 10 percent), so I should've counted myself lucky.

"Did you call Ethan yet?"

"I talked to him last night."

"Is he all right?"

"I think so."

Macrocock.com was kaput now, leaving Ethan without a job. Over the phone, he tearfully bemoaned the loss of his *fuck you* money, but I assured him that, at twenty-two, he had at least eight years to make it all back and exit the working world a success in the eyes of his peers. Unfortunately, all of his shares (not to mention mine and Skull's) were worthless now that whiz-kid financier Eddie Wu had pulled out of the only company hit with more lawsuits than Napster. I asked Ethan to come with me on the trip, but he said he'd met a girl at a Palo Alto piercing parlor and wanted to see where it was going. Although I was disappointed he couldn't come, it was hard to take offense at my son's search for happiness when I was starting one of my own.

A late summer weather system moved in above us as we made our way eastward toward the Atlantic. Under gathering clouds a light rain began to fall, and King went down below to get us two windbreakers.

"You want a beer while I'm down here?" he shouted up.

"Sure," I answered halfheartedly, my head full of thoughts about the events that led me to leave my hometown. I pushed the boat's throttle further forward. The faster I got away from Rochester, the sooner my regrets would wither—like rotted limbs falling off a living tree. At least that was my theory. In practice, I found an entirely different truth.

"I never told you this, but I lied to Cal."

"About what?"

King stood with me now, each of us drinking a green-bottled beer on deck.

"About raising the issue of the SERMON suit with Plot Thickens when I went to Albany. (Pause) I told Cal I wouldn't do it, because there was too big a risk involved."

"What risk?"

"That if we asked Plot to help keep us out of jail *and* take Tailburger out of the SERMON suit, he might not do either and we'd end up with prison sentences instead of probation."

"Jesus, why'd you do it?"

"I was selfish. I wanted my pension and I needed the suit lifted to get it. (Pause) But it sickens me now to think about how I jeopardized my friend's freedom and his family's future. It sickens me."

"You made a mistake. (Pause) It all worked out in the end."

"It wasn't a mistake. It was a decision. (Pause) There's a difference."

The rain grew heavier as the engine roared on.

"This shit is really starting to come down now. Maybe we should think about taking her ashore for the night," King said.

"Do you know why Annette isn't here?" So much for moving on and avoiding self-indulgence.

"I assume it's because you did something stupid."

"I did something cruel."

"That's too bad, because stupid's definitely more forgivable. What the hell did you do?"

I hesitated to tell my brother because I was ashamed.

"I told her I had rectal cancer so that she'd start seeing me again."

"You didn't."

"I did."

"How'd she find out you were lying?"

"I told her."

"Well, then you did something cruel *and* stupid."

"I had to tell her. Or at least I thought I did. (Pause) Anyway, it seemed right at the time. What do you think?"

"It's just like the pension. You did what you felt you had to."

"But it was wrong."

"Maybe it was."

"Do you believe a man can change?"

"Of course I do. That's what I was trying to teach you with

Qigong and our training sessions until *you* quit. You always should be striving toward personal improvement."

"But aren't there limits? Earthly limits. A man's wants. His needs. His survival. The things that prevent him from forbearance and truthfulness and all that other stuff."

"No. The only limits are the ones you place on yourself."

"But aren't some limits placed on you by others?"

"It's possible, but we've all got the capacity to change for the better. The virtues we've talked about *are* obtainable here on Earth."

"In a perfect form?"

"I think so."

"How do you know that?"

King wiped the pouring rain from his face as he thought about my question.

"I guess I don't."

"Of course you don't. You've never met a perfect person and neither have I. We're all sinners who need to be forgiven by somebody."

The rain was coming in sheets now, and King's frustration level had peaked.

"Will you spare me? Look, I don't have an answer for all these questions and I don't want to sit through Bible class. I'm going down below. Turn this thing for shore and let's get in for the night."

King climbed into the cabin, leaving me alone with the weather and the wheel. His advice was sound, but for some reason, I just kept going—farther and farther into the darkness and inclement conditions until the sky was totally black. I'd like to tell you that in the pitch of night I was able to forgive myself for the things I'd done to my friends, my family and my own soul in the time that led up to my departure for the islands. But I wasn't. I'd like to tell you that Annette and I reunited and eventually got married, but then I'd be lying, and that's an activity I've long since given up. I'd like to tell you that on Earth, I found the peace of mind I sought, but that never came to pass.

The end arrived in a single strike of lightning followed by what must have been an incredible boom of thunder, although I can't say I heard it. In one miraculous act of God, I went out the way I should have—charred on the outside, tender on the inside. Finally aboard the boat to my own insular Tahiti. I drifted for a while. But then I was found. Chastened by the human condition and ready to move higher.

Acknowledgments

I wish to give special thanks to Marty Asher, Bob Diforio, Marc Engel, Steve Fitzpatrick, Price Kerfoot, Eric Martinez, Alex Menendez and Russell Perreault for their invaluable advice, feedback and friendship during this process. I also want to recognize the contributions of Marianne Bohr, Peg Booth, Kristen Carr, Larry Fox, Kelly Frost, Barry Kerrigan, Jen Linck and everyone at Vintage and to express my appreciation.

JENNIFER GOVERNMENT
by Max Barry

In Max Barry's twisted, hilarious vision of the future, the world is run by giant corporations, taxes are illegal, employees take the last names of the companies they work for, and the Police and the NRA are publicly traded security firms. It's a free-market paradise! But life starts to go awry for Hack Nike when he signs a contract to shoot teenagers to build up street cred for Nike's new line of $2,500 sneakers. Soon Hack finds himself pursued by Jennifer Government, a tough-talking agent who is the consumer watchdog from hell.

Fiction/1-4000-3092-7

KRAZY KAT
by Jay Cantor

Krazy Kat is Jay Cantor's inspired reimagining of George Herriman's classic comic strip, a postmodern masterpiece as profound as it is funny. Having just witnessed a 1945 test for the atomic bomb, Krazy Kat is depressed, and to the exasperation of her costar, Ignatz Mouse, she refuses to work. To coax her back to work so that they can regain the limelight, Ignatz subjects Krazy to his own brand of psychotherapy, orchestrates her kidnapping, and tries to seduce her with promises of stardom from a Hollywood producer.

Fiction/0-375-71382-4

M31: A FAMILY ROMANCE
by Stephen Wright

Husband and wife Dash and Dot—possibly descendants of aliens from the M31 galaxy—are the world's most in-demand lecturers on the UFO circuit. They live in a decommissioned church in the middle of America, with a radar dish on its steeple and a spacecraft in its sanctuary. When a couple of UFO groupies show up looking for the extraterrestrial duo, they find instead a nuclear family—or rather, a family gone nuclear—whose comically discomfiting world resembles our own as much as it does another world altogether.

Fiction/0-375-71294-1

Available at your local bookstore, or call toll-free to order:
1-800-793-2665 (credit cards only).